The Remnant Blade

WARHAMMER
40,000

THE REMNANT BLADE

MIKE VINCENT

BLACK LIBRARY

A BLACK LIBRARY PUBLICATION

First published in 2025.
This edition published in Great Britain in 2026 by
Black Library, Games Workshop Ltd., Willow Road,
Nottingham, NG7 2WS, UK.

Represented by: Games Workshop Limited – Irish branch,
Unit 3, Lower Liffey Street, Dublin 1,
D01 K199, Ireland.

10 9 8 7 6 5 4 3 2 1

Produced by Games Workshop in Nottingham.
Cover illustration by Christopher Cant.

A CIP record for this book is available from the British Library.

ISBN 13: 978-1-83609-379-4

See Black Library on the internet at

blacklibrary.com

Find out more about Games Workshop
and the worlds of Warhammer at

warhammer.com

Printed and bound in the UK.

For Mandy, of course.

For more than a hundred centuries the Emperor
has sat immobile on the Golden Throne of Earth.
He is the Master of Mankind. By the might of his
inexhaustible armies a million worlds stand
against the dark.

Yet, he is a rotting carcass, the Carrion Lord of
the Imperium held in life by marvels from the
Dark Age of Technology and the thousand souls
sacrificed each day so his may continue to burn.

To be a man in such times is to be one amongst
untold billions. It is to live in the cruelest and
most bloody regime imaginable. It is to suffer an
eternity of carnage and slaughter. It is to have cries
of anguish and sorrow drowned by the thirsting
laughter of dark gods.

This is a dark and terrible era where you will find
little comfort or hope. Forget the power of technology
and science. Forget the promise of progress and
advancement. Forget any notion of common
humanity or compassion.

There is no peace amongst the stars, for in the grim
darkness of the far future, there is only war.

DRAMATIS PERSONAE

NIGHT LORDS WARBAND THE BLADES OF ATROCITY

Dalchian Rassaq	The Skin-Taker, Lord of the Blades of Atrocity
Zorean	Second-in-command
Krutaan	Former claw leader
Qi Umshar	Surgeon-Apothecary
Ang Heltris	Legionary
Dagardis	Legionary
Saryuz	Legionary
Zhikarga	Legionary
Vellet	Legionary
Keth Naa	Legionary
Gamarth	Legionary
Olokro	Legionary

THE ABYSSAL KINDRED

Leil Jathok	Sorcerer lord, scion of the Red Cyclops
Gyren Naritsa	Warpsmith, keeper of the *Ikhtheos*
Endagur	Exalted champion
Nallath	Aspiring champion
Larakh	Warrior
Vurdomal	Master of Possessions

THE CRIMSON SLAUGHTER

Thelissicus	The Gorelord, Supreme Commander of the Alliance
Durveist	Exalted champion
Glausius	Executioner

PROLOGUE

The datasaint and her escort had been four days in the blue-green desert. The Mere Cuprum stretched hundreds of miles in all directions, its verdigris undulations glowing with ethereal splendour with each twin sunset. The caravan described a winding passage through the dunes: half a dozen electro-priests; two dragoon-walker outriders; a killclade of Sicarian Ruststalkers. It was formidable protection, though the datasaint showed little gratitude. At the heart of the caravan, she hovered seven feet off the ground, a bulbous oblong of curling pipes and bronze casework fifteen feet long and eight feet wide. Her biological component bathed in amniotic stasis deep within the structure. Only a round hatch, clenched tightly shut by ornate torque-clamps, betrayed the place of her liquid interment.

Tech-priest Manipulus Rur-Arplex-9-4 did not begrudge the escort duty. Quite the reverse. Rur-Arplex had all but pleaded to accompany the datasaint to her blessed alcove in the relative safety of the Bore. To him, the honour of the escort duty went a small way to mitigate the shame of its necessity.

The Archenemy had come to Uzurmandius. Chaos had come to *his* forge world, and with them its followers had brought ruin and calamity. Rur-Arplex shuddered with hatred, and the broad axe chem-welded to his thoracic arms crackled with power in emotional sympathy. With an effort, he calmed himself. Many of his order had remained to defend the forge temples, and still others had collated interdiction cadres and struck back at the vile Heretic Astartes who had attacked with such force. Few had deigned to lower themselves to an escort duty, and some had offered him violence for choosing such a charge. There were datastacks, they said. Mem-cores and precious relics, irreparable should they be damaged, irreplaceable if lost. Protect those, they had demanded. But Rur-Arplex was a pious soul, and so he had chosen to oversee the datasaint's exhumation and her safe conveyance.

Not a flyer could be spared from the defence, and even if one could, a lone craft would be too-tempting prey for the slavering heretics. No, the datasaint would travel overland. Not off-world. Never that. She had been born on Uzurmandius, and by holy writ was the world's historiatrix. The knower of its stories. The collector of details irrelevant either to Mars' great audits or its many tithes.

Rur-Arplex had had a biological mother. His vat-grown fellow adepts had teased him for it when he was young. But no memory of her existed in his mem-coils. The datasaint was the mother of the whole forge world, though. She was sacred in a way not even Mars would countenance. She had walked with the Omnissiah in ancient days. She could never leave.

The Bore went down into the liquid mantle of Uzurmandius, perpetuated by technologies long ago fallen out of the knowledge of even the most august lords of the Adeptus Mechanicus. In that adamant vault the datasaint could be sealed off, safe and unknown. Of no strategic worth, but incalculable value nonetheless. But the Bore was six hundred miles away. They went quickly, but there were days yet to go.

A column of oxide-blue dust blossomed to the east and the particulate wafted in upon the winds. Once orange but now black with battle grime, Rur-Arplex's robes snapped about him like pennants. He scrolled through several sets of augur lenses, trying to account for the fog of dust that descended. One of the dragoons drew near, the stilt legs of their mount bearing signs of corrosion from the elements. The rider's hood bellied and flapped as the dust storm grew in power.

<Lord manipulus, a possible contact,> the dragoon sent over the noosphere, knowing their voice would be stolen in the gale. They gestured eastward.

<Investigate.>

The dragoon loped east into the murk, the other rider veering west to cover. The spindly forms of the Ruststalkers fanned out, transonic blades humming with power. The electro-priests paired off and, like the dragoons, disappeared into the skirling miasma. Rur-Arplex established data-tethers to them all, elevating his cogitation matrix into battle mode.

He cast a reverential gaze over the datasaint. Worry not, holy one, he thought. I shall see you safe.

They kept moving. The data-tether to the more distant electro-priests and dragoons kept ghosting in and out, flashing crimson then returning to emerald. The storm was high now, wind over a hundred miles an hour. A pulse of jade thunder flashed soundlessly. The noosphere exploded.

<Contact. Forty yards, bearing zero five eight.>

<Contact. Fifteen yards, bearing two zero…>

<Contact. Engagi–>

<Kkkkkkkrrrrrrr…>

A dozen sendings came through simultaneously. Auroras of red, angry energy strobed in every direction as adepts veiled by the storm opened fire. Rur-Arplex collated the data in an instant to establish where the attack was coming from.

Everywhere.

It was an unhelpful conclusion. His electro-priests had already lost half their number. One detonated in a ball of actinic light. Rur-Arplex activated his suspensor harness and lifted slowly off the ground, drifting contrary to the wind so that he hovered some fifteen feet above the bulk of the datasaint. He adopted an overwatch configuration, spreading his mechadendrites so their simple machine eyes gazed in a three-hundred-and-sixty-degree arc. He hung in the howling tempest like some cephalopod hunter, keeping still in storm-tossed waters, fully alert. His kill-clade took five points around the datasaint, the frequency of their blades reverberating through the flensing gale.

<Lord manipulus,> came a brutish sending. A dragoon, radium jezzail glowing with repeated discharge, rode close out of the dust clouds. <The datasaint is in imminent danger. Permission to–>

The dragoon plummeted abruptly, legs swiped out from under them. A thin scream drifted on the wind. Rur-Arplex dropped into the plume of spiralling grit, magnarail lance cycling up at his side. He descended just quickly enough to see the dragoon, ejected from his mount's saddle, yanked beneath the datasaint's shadow.

Another scream.

Rur-Arplex dropped to the ground, weapons ready. The dragoon mount lay where it had fallen. A splash of blood and fluids darkened the dirt. The rider's body was gone.

<Interrogative,> he sent to the killclade princeps. <How did the enemy bypass your cordon?>

<Unknown, lord.>

<Locate them.>

One of the Ruststalkers lurched spasmodically, then its upper torso flash-boiled into slag, weapon arms falling, severed stumps glowing with heat.

<Melta bombs,> sent Rur-Arplex. The Ruststalkers, frustrated by the lack of visual data, ignited head-mounted lumens and panned the beams into the whickering grit. Rur-Arplex's augur suite picked up a faint contact and he launched himself after it, ducking beneath the datasaint and out the other side.

Gone again.

Rur-Arplex vented a flush of human frustration. He shouted. 'Scum!'

He stared into the dust storm. Then an atonal *thrum* echoed both into the wind and across his noospheric link. Then another. A rhythmic pulse of sound. The datasaint's integrity alarm, he realised. A hollow sensation yawned within him. He spun around in time to see another Ruststalker fall. He saw the attacker clearly this time.

Midnight-blue power armour bedecked in barbs and jutting spikes. Eyes glowing red like hel-pits. The attacker held a knife in each fist and danced with a grace that belied his heft. Each whipping strike slashed and pierced the organic inner structure of the assassin cyborg. The Ruststalker thrashed, but their muscles were failing them. The dying skitarius registered poison, Rur-Arplex saw over the noosphere. The Ruststalker's life-signal flatlined. The adept slumped, and the attacker was gone. It had taken less than a second.

Thrum.

The datasaint! Rur-Arplex sprinted back to the datasaint, and saw with mounting horror the slashes and gouges across her metallic skin. He jumped on top of her floating form and saw the round hatch that led to her amniotic vessel. It had been torn free and cast aside. He swept towards the ragged opening and stared into an empty stasis cradle. Bloody fluid swilled in its basin, umbilical hoses cut and thrashing. Something strange washed over Rur-Arplex then. Something almost forgotten from his earlier, more human days.

Panic.

He whirled around, unable to cogitate. His floundering logic capacity sent shockwaves across the noosphere as every member of the escort comprehended their failure at the same precise moment. Then, inexplicably, the attack stopped. Rur-Arplex stood on the datasaint's inert metal body. Two Ruststalkers endured, and possibly a dragoon. The noosphere was lousy with interference and his own discombobulation. A shape loomed before him. He sensed the survivors of the killclade steel themselves for another attack. Commendable.

With jerking, stuttering motion, the other dragoon waded towards them from directly in front. As it stepped out from smears of wind-born dust, Rur-Arplex saw its rider was broken and shredded. It lumbered its unthinking way towards them.

Then he saw the datasaint. What remained of her. She had been fastened across the calipered legs of the dragoon mount. She had been crucified and gutted. Grey, atrophied organs hung like ropes from her corpse-form. Her fleshless face was drawn tight into a silent scream, jaw pinned open with a blade. Her body was the reason the dragoon mount jerked. With each perpetual stride the machine took, more of the datasaint's bones ground and cracked as she was dragged and stretched by the walker's legs.

Rur-Arplex, who had not eaten via his biological mouth for decades, vomited. Black slurry oozed down his front and he tried to take a step, but faltered. The two Ruststalkers ran forward to free the datasaint from her desecration. A jet of invisible heat sliced one in half as a deadly accurate burst of bolter fire decapitated the other.

Rur-Arplex was paralysed with revulsion and terror. Feelings he had considered himself long since rid of now overrode his faculties utterly. His magnarail lance shorted as he mishandled its power draw protocols. He fell to his augmetic knees. Parts of him began to shut down involuntarily. A dozen power-armoured figures converged upon the carnage, emerging slowly from the storm like phantoms. One with a cloak of flayed skin and a long-handled chainglaive directed the others as they began pulling apart the felled Mechanicus warriors, dragging whatever components seemed undamaged from the heavily modified bodies.

Rur-Arplex watched, unseeing, as his comrades were disassembled for scrap. The leader leapt onto the hovering bulk that had formerly been the datasaint's carriage, still bleating its rhythmic alarm *thrum*. The Heretic Astartes approached the paralysed manipulus, hel-pit eyes glowing from a helm surmounted with red bat wings. He leant in closely and whispered to the tech-priest.

'Our blades yet thirst.'

The heretic slashed with his chainglaive, and the pious devotion of Rur-Arplex-9-4 was ended.

Chapter One

He would have been a monster in any other place.

His Mk V power armour bore its centuries of existence with ill grace, the ink-dark blue of it marred by scars. Each piece was silver-edged with razor or barb, corrosion blackening parts of the metal. A baroque power pack hunched between his shoulder blades like a whispering gargoyle, and from it hung a bleak testament of his atrocity. A pleated curtain of hides, cured and tailored with grotesque care. Each a different shade of discolouration, each the pelt of a human victim. Some slaves, some warlords, every one of them had been alive when their flaying began. Some had even survived its completion. A cloak of victory and of depravity. He held his helm in one hand, the crimson eye-lenses dim for now, a pair of heraldic wings sweeping up on either side of the crown. Each pinion was a venous ruby colour, and not feathered, but rather membranous as the chiropteran hunters of night's dark. His garb suggested the horror he could inflict, but it was his face that promised it.

Sallow skin drawn tight across sharp cheekbones, and eyes so deep-set as to be utterly black, like beads of jet. Half a scalp of dark locks fell like a veil, the other half shaven to the skin, hive-gang electoos fading below the pallor.

Dalchian Rassaq. The Skin-Taker. Commander of the VIII Legion warband the Blades of Atrocity. What was left of them, at least.

He would have been a monster in any other place. But here? On the bridge of someone else's voidship he was just another commander. Just another servant of the Great Powers whom the stagnant, consumptive, cankerous Imperium dared label *heretic*. Dalchian could not summon much bile towards the Imperium at that moment, though. There was a more pertinent object of his rage, though he fought hard not to show it.

Gorelord Thelissicus of the Crimson Slaughter slouched in his throne as his warband commanders gave him their reports. Bronze banding vied with arterial ceramite for prominence across his broad bulk. A fur-trimmed cloak of rich indigo furled around his armoured shoulders, a trophy from a long-dead planetary governor whose recidivism Thelissicus had punished in an earlier century when the Crimson Slaughter had been the Crimson Sabres, loyal Adeptus Astartes under the yoke of Terra's corpse-lord. The cloak was still immaculate, Dalchian noticed. The Gorelord's head was hairless and ritually scarified, and his gaze was fixed upon the figure speaking before him.

Urdamas Grensch of the Flylords oozed in his corpulent Terminator armour, his phlegm-ridden barking barely intelligible to Dalchian. Not that he was listening too intently. Dalchian's warband was lately the smallest in Thelissicus' alliance, and so Dalchian would be last to debrief their overlord. His gorge rose at the Gorelord's theatrics. *The piece of shit thinks he's a king,* thought Dalchian, not for the first time. He wanted to spit.

Leil Jathok stepped forward next. Sorcerer lord of the Abyssal Kindred, Jathok inclined his head deferentially and spoke in quiet basso. He appeared quite proud of his endeavours, reminding the council, and the Gorelord, that the subjugation of Uzurmandius had been his own suggestion. *Mewling sycophant.* After him, the cowled figure of the Bonesage Vilyas, emissary to the enigmatic Warp Ghosts, stepped forth and droned at length. Then Xerclon of the Sons of Malice brayed and scowled. At long last Dalchian had leave to address Gorelord Thelissicus. Dalchian cricked his neck and forced an even tone.

'My Lord Thelissicus. The machine idol has been desecrated.' Dalchian thumbed a rune on his gauntlet and his armour's cogitator parsed pict-capts and vid-feeds of his most recent raid to Thelissicus' throne. The Gorelord scrolled through the images, indulgent joy showing with the teeth of his grin. Filed to points, black like obsidian.

'Ah, Skin-Taker.' The Gorelord's tone dripped with malicious glee. 'Trust you to make such a pleasing mess. You have my admiration.'

'That is gratifying, Lord Thelissicus.' Dalchian clenched his jaw. 'I would ask of you, lord… Such raids are enjoyable diversions, but they offer little in the way of plunder.' Quietness descended on the bridge save for the mumbling of lobotomised servitors and the ever-present hum of the strike cruiser's power systems. 'We have need of more worthy prey.'

Thelissicus' indulgent smile remained as the Gorelord appraised Dalchian like a psychotic father considering his errant child. Dalchian kept his dark eyes on Thelissicus, allowing some of his true self into them. Thelissicus' smile widened. Dalchian's predator-senses kindled. Combat stimms ignited in his body. He fought to maintain stillness.

'Is the honour insufficient, Skin-Taker?' Thelissicus affected a wounded tone. 'That sack of ancient, rotten bones was beloved by the priesthood of Uzurmandius. You have wounded them deeply.'

Dalchian's blood ran molten in his veins. 'I fight for spoils, Lord Thelissicus. The same as any other.' He glanced at the other commanders, who stood impassive.

'The same?' Thelissicus breathed a coil of laughter. 'Your party is all but extinct.' He sighed obnoxiously. 'As much as I wish it, we are not equals, Skin-Taker. My two hundred to your… ten remnant Blades?'

Twelve, Dalchian thought through a haze of fury. He said nothing.

'Your service to my cause is a priceless gift to me, Skin-Taker,' Thelissicus said, his tone overtly declaring the opposite. 'I have opened my home to you in recognition of your loyalty. Would you abandon such generosity?'

Dalchian knew he was beaten. His Night Lords had nowhere to go. The ceramite of his gauntlets creaked in fists that he managed to keep from shaking. Just.

'No, Lord Thelissicus.'

'Of course not, Skin-Taker.' Thelissicus beamed. 'You are wiser than that.'

In the bilges of the *Torrent of Hatred* narrow corridors and duct-ways extended for miles, twisting around numberless knots of machinery in convoluted labyrinths of plasteel and corroded mesh. The vast voidship's plasma heart thumped through the ancient superstructure, saturating the stagnant air with rever-beration. The rusted caverns dripped and steamed, forgotten townships of wretched humans scraping an existence from the charnel leavings of the ship's masters on high. Here, the mer-curial systems of the huge craft waxed and waned; illumination faded for months at a time; the maze lurched from infernal heat to skin-cracking cold. The people here had no comprehension of the makeup of the galaxy. No awareness of the Imperium or the Crimson Slaughter's hatred for it. They knew nothing of what went on beyond the twisted plasteel of their habitat. They were human vermin, feeding on scraps and occasionally culled lest their numbers impinge upon the tasks of those above. They were feral and base beings.

And they were terrified.

Dalchian watched a clutch of the ragged waifs huddle against a heat-exchange manifold, crouching among the bulbous conduits, pressing themselves into the darkness. They whispered in pidgin-Gothic amongst themselves, gesturing and wiping away tears with grubby fists. The Skin-Taker watched their blood pump beneath their skin, saw the thin haze of their exhalations. The section was pitch black. The gritty crimson of his preysight painted each mortal in vibrant hues. He lowered himself from the girder-work above the manifold, dropping onto the inspection gantry soundlessly. He slithered down around the manifold into a looped space adjacent to the mortals' hiding place. They remained oblivious. He cycled through his preysight modes until he could see the shadows of bone structure through their fragile human flesh. He took his time deciding upon the specimens that represented the greatest potential. Then he slowly drew his skinning knife. He allowed the delicate sound – *shick* – and the mortals froze. They sprang from their hiding place, but the Skin-Taker was on them. He whirled and slashed and grinned, subsumed within their screams of horror.

It was two hours before Dalchian resurfaced from below decks, fresh trophies hanging from the chains at his waist. Pink bones and strips of flayed hide. The heat and acridity of his temporary arming chamber bestowed upon him vastly less succour than the dank hunting ground of the bilges. He laid down his trophies on a bench and began to process them.

'Feel better?' Zorean's voice grated.

Dalchian looked up to regard his second-in-command. Zorean was long-limbed and skeletally gaunt, a shade taller than Dalchian. His face was a thin-stretched thing of ashen skin and close-cropped hair.

'I shall feel better when I can do this to Thelissicus himself,' Dalchian replied as he pared loose flesh from a skull.

'Perhaps you should have done so already.' There was little bile in Zorean's voice. Dalchian knew his second was only voicing the same impotent frustration that all his Night Lords felt. His remnant Blades, as Thelissicus had mockingly called them. *Not inaccurately, the murdering bastard.* Dalchian felt a moment of wry self-awareness as he named the Gorelord a murderer, a fresh human skull dripping in his hand. There were varying degrees of murder, though. *For Thelissicus to murder legionary allies,* he thought, *that is a curseling's bitter jealousy, not simple sport. This mortal means nothing. My Blades mean everything.* Meant *everything.*

He ached to murder again.

'Perhaps I should have,' he admitted. 'But then what? You and the rest of the Blades would be butchered by his commanders. We would gain nothing.'

'We would have vengeance,' Zorean hissed.

'Obliteration is not an adequate price for revenge. Not for me. I anticipate living to savour our satisfaction.'

Zorean inclined his head in acceptance. 'As do I, Skin-Taker. But some of the others grow weary of such… pragmatism.'

'Have you nothing new to tell me?'

'As to that, it would seem not.'

'Mm?'

'Our… *hosts* seem to be utterly without sentiment regarding our presence. I hear them speak of the other warbands, but our names do not cross their lips.'

'Thelissicus knows better than to let loose tongues open a chink in his underbelly.' Dalchian nodded to himself.

'That is what I surmise. He maintains a tight grip around the throats of his men.'

'Do I hear admiration in your voice, Zor?'

'Recognition of the quality of our foe, Skin-Taker.'

Dalchian clenched his jaw and stalked away from his trophies on the bench. Zorean gave the remains a look as he stepped past them. Dalchian's quarters were standard fare for a strike cruiser such as the *Torrent of Hatred*. Spartan and gloomy, there was a small antechamber with two portals. One led into a dormitorium with an ablution point and a low rest pallet. The other led into a larger arming chamber with weapon racks and an inbuilt maintenance servitor, long defunct and rotting where it hung. Dalchian went to the ablution point and splashed brackish water over his scarred and uneven face. Thelissicus kept his ship infernally hot within, and Dalchian allowed himself a moment of remembrance for his destroyed frigate.

The *Abjuration* had been Dalchian's haunt for nearly half a century. He had known every corridor and gangway, every alcove and every cogitator. He had led his Night Lords on uncountable savage assaults from its embarkation deck, and there was enough of his blood soaked into the ship's plasteel for it to be all but family. After the disaster at the Serpessa Nebula, Dalchian had been the obvious heir to Veilmaster Iccrom, slain by the repulsive drukhari. From then on, the Blades of Atrocity had been Dalchian's to command, and with them the *Abjuration*.

For not nearly long enough. His command now seemed an eyeblink in time. A temporary rush of murder and glory ended long before it should have. Ended by the jealousy of Gorelord Thelissicus of the Crimson Slaughter.

Dalchian had sought assistance from the Gorelord, feigning

ignorance of the brute's responsibility for his humiliation. And now, in the very house of his betrayer, he keenly felt the pressure to wreak his vengeance. But the pressure to stave off extinction was just as keen. His warband was twelve surviving of the near fifty it had been when he had taken command. A paltry few whose lives he would not sell but for the very dearest price.

There was a small looking glass above the basin, cracked, fogged with grease and blood. Dalchian glared into his own eyes. Despair beckoned. A terminal morbidity of spirit that would see him, his warriors, and all his legacy destroyed by the pettiness of one commander who should have been an ally. The basin squealed as Dalchian's fingers deformed the metal. He relaxed his grip and closed his eyes.

He would not suffer to be extinguished.

'Keep listening, Zor,' he said. 'If there is a chance for advantage, I will not have it slip away from us.'

'Yes, Skin-Taker.' Zorean turned to leave, but paused. 'My lord, what of Krutaan?'

Dalchian took a considered breath and let it out slowly.

'Do not concern yourself with Krutaan.'

The arena lights were painfully bright. Formerly a barracks for mortal serfs in a prior century, three whole decks had been hollowed out to form a plasteel amphitheatre under glaring flood-lumens. The braying audience of Crimson Slaughter warriors watched from above as two figures clashed on the arena grating. Unwilling participants of future spectacles watched from below the grating, forced to crouch in the inches-deep soup of old blood and viscera that swilled there, sluiced in from above. The hot flood-lumens raised a rank humidity from the foetor.

The gladiators seemed well matched. Both were Chaos Space Marines and both were almost naked. One, hugely muscled and wielding a vast square-tipped sword, was the audience favourite. *Durveist! Durveist! Durveist!* his fellow Crimson Slaughter chanted. He trailed ropes of spittle from his gurning mouth, roaring as he swung his blade with horrifying speed and power. The challenger was leaner, though still with the engorged physique of his kind. His skin was bone white and the snarling grille of a rebreather was sutured over his nose and mouth. In his hands a glaive of graceful alien steel glimmered. A trophy looted from a drukhari bodyguard warrior.

Krutaan.

Krutaan was the faster of the two. He moved more, dodging or parrying where Durveist would block heavily, using his bulk. Krutaan ducked low and lunged under a sweeping cut of the great blade, and Durveist had to slam downwards with his weapon's hilt to divert the attack. Krutaan spun away, a monstrous upswing chasing him as he did. He crouched in guard position and Durveist deftly switched grip, the heavy blade flicking over to threaten the challenger's off side. Durveist leapt in uncannily fast, the blunt end of his blade bizarrely stabbing straight towards his opponent. Krutaan read the intent and dived beneath the strike rather than dodge to the side. He slashed his drukhari weapon and made to fillet his enemy's thigh. The big warrior snatched his feet away, over-extending his lunge, but avoiding the low attack. Krutaan pistoned upwards, driving his shoulder into Durveist's belly. The two rolled once together then smashed apart.

They fought for almost an hour. Constant movement, strength matched against speed. Knees, feet, elbows, foreheads bludgeoned in, splitting skin, cracking bone and loosening teeth. But neither could land a weapon through the other's defence. First blood drawn from the torso would end the bout. Bruises blossomed and ragged scrapes shone pink, but no blood ran between neck and waist. The crowd had grown as the fight went on. They stamped on the deck and bellowed their encouragement and derision in equal measure. Midnight figures clustered in the sea of crimson plate.

Saryuz was at the centre of the knot of legionaries. Normally wielding his baroque meltagun with savage proficiency, he went unarmed in the stalls, as they all did. Unhelmed, his alabaster pate was covered with a deep cowl that wafted in the arena's furnace heat. Cruel eyes glinted from its depths. Beside him was the broad shape of heavy gunner Zhikarga, whose face was hidden behind his snarling bronze helm. His arms were crossed in front of his breastplate, the heft of him like a fortress bulwark. Opposite Zhikarga loomed Dagardis, vaunted executioner of the Blades of Atrocity and tallest of the midnight-clad, his spiked power pack seemingly barren without the enormous power axe usually mag-locked to it. Dagardis laughed as Gamarth, a willowy Night Lord with an enthusiasm for chainblades, muttered something to him. Vellet, the sharpshooter, watched through his augmetic eye, his stillness characteristic but unnerving the Crimson Slaughter brawlers around him, who eyed him, sidelong, with suspicion. In the row in front, Ang Heltris' skull helm flicked from one combatant to another and back again, the knifeman unable to veil his excitement at the contest. His gauntlets moved endlessly, fingers practising blade grips and deft manoeuvres without conscious guidance. Keth Naa and Olokro conversed, relishing the fight, horned helms under their arms. Keth Naa's icon was absent from his power pack, stowed safely away while embarked. Something he said made Olokro grin, the warrior's sharpened teeth shining in the glare. Only Zorean and the surgeon-Apothecary Qi Umshar were absent. Dalchian watched from an upper tier, disappearing into the shadows among Crimson Slaughter champions and commanders.

Durveist peered through a swollen, blackened eye, stance favouring the foot that was not obviously broken. Krutaan's breath sawed in and out of his crumpled rebreather, one ear mangled into a lump. Even the prisoners in the misery below could not help but watch the awesome contest.

Krutaan zigzagged in with undiminished speed, his weapon a blur. Durveist slid aside and swung a massive arm around Krutaan's neck from behind, pinning him in place at last. Durveist's face split into a gory grin as he reversed his blade in his free hand to administer the winning cut to his transfixed opponent. The crowd was silent.

'Challenger wins!' An amplified voice rolled around the arena like cannon fire. Durveist stopped, incomprehension clouding his abused features. Slowly he looked down to where a neat incision traced a line over his ribs, from where a drizzle of rapidly thickening blood oozed. Still with the Night Lords warrior in his grip, Durveist stared at his wound, then slowly, deliberately, began to laugh.

The crowd erupted, slamming fists against chests and thighs to show their appreciation. It had been a rare fight. Durveist released Krutaan and the two battered gladiators clasped wrists in the manner of warriors through time eternal.

'A beast, him,' a Crimson Slaughter champion with an augmetic jaw said to Dalchian as the crowd began to thin. Dalchian accepted the compliment with a nod. As the red-armoured warrior turned away, the bas-relief of a daemonic face on his pauldron throbbed and grimaced. Dalchian made a face to himself. The Great Powers were useful in their proper place and time, but such willing association with the warp-born was not something the VIII Legion had ever seen advantage in. The things from the immaterium were capricious tools to be used with astute selectivity, as likely to be an obstruction as an aid. To have such a presence, however petty and inferior, trapped within one's armour bordered on the sickening.

And Krutaan was spending more time with these tainted ravagers than his own Legion brothers. Dalchian waited for him in a companionway between the arena and the defunct hangar where his Blades were billeted. Krutaan was enjoying an account of his own fight as told by Saryuz in graphic detail as the Night Lords ascended the steps. They stopped and fell silent as they beheld Dalchian on the stair above them.

'I will speak to Krutaan alone.'

The other warriors filtered away, only Saryuz looking Dalchian directly in the eye as he did so. Dalchian gave Krutaan a heartbeat to speak first, but the erstwhile Nemesis Claw leader waited in silence for his lord to address him.

'The Blades have need of you, Krutaan.'

'The Blades?' Krutaan stepped slowly up the companionway towards Dalchian. 'The Blades are ended, Lord Skin-Taker.'

'Truly?' Dalchian had foregone his helm to look his warrior in the eyes. Krutaan's battered, bloodied form stopped level with him and the discontent burned in Krutaan's exhausted features. Dalchian expected the former claw leader to laugh his question away, but Krutaan was utterly earnest. Dalchian took note of that.

'What have we remaining to us, Lord Skin-Taker?' Krutaan spread his arms, indicating the abundance of nothing that their warband now possessed. 'We are finished.'

'Such despondency has no place in my murder-kin, Krutaan.'

'You will punish me then?' Krutaan looked unconvinced.

'The others take your example.'

'And what of your example?' Krutaan said it, and took a breath as of someone freshly unburdened of some great weight. *We come to the crux of it, then,* thought Dalchian.

'What *of* my example? Criticise openly, so I may judge the value of your words.'

Krutaan leant in close, the acid stink of his recent exertions filling Dalchian's nostrils. The claw leader's whispers hissed into his soul.

'We were sacrificed as pawns in a power game, our ship destroyed by those we called allies. And here we are, in the bosom of our tormentors, and you do *nothing*! Your leadership is an edgeless thing. We are finished because you cannot summon the strength to take what steps must be taken!'

Silence reigned. Krutaan had laid Dalchian's turmoil bare, and if Krutaan saw it, others would too.

The claw leader was not finished. 'The ambition of the Crimson Slaughter may have cost you your command, but I will not allow it to rob me of my purpose. They are strong and ruthless, Lord Skin-Taker. As you once were.'

Dalchian absorbed this for several heartbeats, reaching past his fury, groping for full understanding. Grasping for options. The rightness of Krutaan's criticism rang him like a bell. But yielding to one of his underlings meant death, in his position. Perhaps not immediately, but certainly in the end, once his authority had faded away to nothing. Dalchian's lot was not to satisfy his warriors' simplistic expectations. A lord among the exalted of the Great Powers delivered his warriors glory, but only in reflection of his own. A lord delivered victory.

'I forgive you, Krutaan,' Dalchian said. 'For mistaking my patience for hesitancy.'

The claw leader's eyes widened, then narrowed again. Dalchian gambled that Krutaan still hungered for the same thing he did, and if given the opportunity, would dedicate his fury to the resurrection of their warband. Krutaan's penetrating look bored into him, weighing; considering.

'What, then?' Krutaan hissed. 'For what do we bide so interminably?'

'Our spoils hunting at the whim of the Gorelord have been

meagre,' Dalchian said. 'But they may finally provide us with an opportunity. We can take a ship for ourselves, Krutaan, and raid and plunder and murder our way to greatness again.'

'Can we?' Krutaan scoffed. 'Make me believe it, Lord Skin-Taker.'

'You must play your part.' There was flint in Dalchian's voice. He stared in silence. At length, Krutaan spoke again.

'What part?'

The fleet was restructuring its orbit again. Gorelord Thelissicus watched the slow dance of vessels on the *Torrent of Hatred*'s oculus, the rune marks registering changes in declination, altitude and velocity. He let his gaze linger on the rune marks, knowing their manoeuvres before they made them. Watching his deployment become reality on the oculus before him filled him with a deep gratification. It never mattered the specific nature of the plans that he made; all that mattered was that he watched them unfold flawlessly, according to his own meticulous design. He had arranged the ships of his alliance so that the majority of Uzurmandius was continuously observed, but shifting the greater concentrations of his forces to focus on one target location at a time. His methodical approach was yielding vast spoils, and his opening gambit had crippled the forge world's capacity to respond. It was all so very satisfying to watch.

An intake of breath from one of the mortal bridge crew drew his attention. He waited for the frail human to speak, knowing the number of seconds it would take them to summon the courage to do so.

'Your excellency,' the officer croaked, precisely on time.

'Speak.'

'Empyreal auguries are displaying… anomalies, your excellency.'

Thelissicus leant forward and the human withdrew fractionally, despite sitting ten yards distant from their master's spiked and riveted throne. Thelissicus grinned.

'Incoming?'

'Inconclusive, your excellency.' The officer swallowed. 'The anomaly is faint and irregular, your excellency.'

'Watch it closely.'

'Of course, your excellency.' The officer quickly sank back into their pit and the emerald glow of their rune screens. Thelissicus toyed with the brass rings on his fingers. The Imperium would not tolerate the wholesale harvest of even a lesser forge world such as Uzurmandius for long. Their challenge was inevitable, but, if this was that challenge, the speed with which it came was surprising. His alliance had beset Uzurmandius for barely three standard Terran months. He had planned for double that time, at least. No matter, there would be a way to manipulate the situation to his advantage. There always was. He was still toying with his brass rings when a figure in midnight armour stepped onto his bridge.

'To what do I owe the pleasure, Skin-Taker?' he asked without looking.

'I come with a proposal, and I am not Lord Skin-Taker,' Krutaan replied.

CHAPTER TWO

Zorean recognised the smell by now. This was the third Crimson Slaughter blood-rite he had attended, and the experience was always an overwhelming one.

Snarling Chaos Space Marines in grime-streaked crimson plate stood in the temple in disordered throngs. Some were partly armoured, others garbed only in the form-fitting bodyglove that lay beneath their suits of ceramite. All faced towards a stage of black granite at the temple's farthest reach. On the stage was a rack of chains above a huge bronze basin. Beside the rack and basin stood a warrior-priest in burnished armour, fetishes and human skulls hanging from chains wrapped about his chest and shoulders. He wore a crown, of sorts, fashioned into the angular sigil of the God of Rage and Murder, that shadowed all of his face but for the mad glint in his eyes. Zorean blinked a handful of times and looked away from the crown. Its form made him unreasonably angry.

The crowd paid Zorean no heed. They were snarling among

themselves, and the temple stank of aggression pheromones and the acidic spice of combat stimms. Weapon pommels clanked against armour in an arrhythmic, subconscious expression of dormant fury. Then the priest began to speak.

'Blood,' he said, and the crowd rumbled in anticipation. 'That is the currency of Khorne Who is Greatest.' A snarl of assent from the Crimson Slaughter worshippers. Then the priest uttered a string of guttural syllables in a language Zorean had only heard within this temple. A brand of glowing hate lanced into his mind and he instinctively reached for his knife. The noise of the crowd swelled and heavy cutting blades were raised into the hazy air. Zorean fought to replace the heat of the ritual's sudden rage with his own cold malice. It was difficult, but he managed, as he had done twice before. The priest spoke again.

'Khorne Who is Greatest demands tribute!' The priest raised a serrated blade reverently before him and the Crimson Slaughter brayed in appreciation. He spoke more harsh syllables and Zorean took deep, steadying breaths. The crowd began to shift and crush, hoarse barks and animal roaring lifting from the throats of the devoted. 'Who among his servants will offer their own blood-spill to the glory of Khorne Who is Greatest?'

'I!' shouted one of the assembled warriors, raising his fists. A surging roar of bloodlust rolled around the temple, Crimson Slaughter stamping and snarling their approval. The volunteer was dragged and heaved forwards and nigh thrown onto the granite, where he shivered with barely contained adrenaline. He grinned, open-mouthed and wide-eyed, raising his fists above his head again. The crowd howled, and the priest nodded, chains jangling.

'Submit,' the priest said, gesturing to the rack of chains. The Crimson Slaughter warrior stepped into the chains, securing them about his partly armoured form. The priest affixed manacles to the volunteer's arms, legs and neck, tightening the restraints that the warrior himself could not reach. The rack shuddered upwards by several feet on pistons, leaving the volunteer suspended above the basin. The priest turned to the crowd again.

'Blood for the Blood God!'

The devoted mass roared in rage-drunk adulation.

Gather as much intelligence as you can. That had been the Skin-Taker's order to Zorean. The devoted at the first blood-rite he had attended had nearly killed him, but he had worked hard to assuage their suspicion. The Blades' second-in-command now went largely unnoticed by the red-clad warriors, so normal had his wanderings become. They had let him in, and he dared not squander such an opportunity.

He looked on at the volunteer with the rest, only his regard was cool detachment, unlike the thirsting need of the others. The priest would make a thousand cuts and the basin would fill with blood. If, after the rite was complete, the volunteer yet lived, then he would be awarded a position within the ranks of Crimson Slaughter Chosen. If not, he would be a willing sacrifice to the glory of their patron. Zorean had witnessed two sacrifices so far.

Zorean would find a way to reinstate the Blades of Atrocity to their rightful place. That need consumed him, he knew. He would find the way, whatever it took. He allowed himself to imagine his warband in the ascendant again. He allowed himself to imagine the eventuality that he longed for.

He smiled to himself as the cutting began.

The hangar where the remnant Blades had made their temporary home was blissfully dark and cold. Desiccated corpses had filled the space when they first arrived. Long-dead victims of some mass slaughter. The Blades had hung the withered cadavers from the bulkheads in homage to their customary tradition, and the empty, shrivelled eye sockets stared at Dalchian as he crossed the deck plates. Dim lights shone from either side. Empty magazines and defunct machine shops had been commandeered as arming chambers for the legionaries. Many held themselves in quiet solitude, maintaining equipment or sparring notional foes.

Ang Heltris was honing the edge of one of his knives with the same bearing as a mother caressing her newborn. He nodded to the Skin-Taker as he passed. Qi Umshar was busy with an array of instruments. The quiet legionary had always had an affinity for the medicae kits Dalchian had insisted each of his claws carry, but in the wake of their humiliation, Qi Umshar found himself appointed surgeon-Apothecary. Dalchian was impressed by how many tools of his new trade the Night Lord had bartered from their hosts. He even wore a bandolier of empty progenoid containment amphorae, and Dalchian was reminded with a jolt of the genetic inheritance that had been lost in the suicidal assault on the templum-capitalis of Uzurmandius. Looking away, Dalchian saw Vellet at a trestle. The sharpshooter spent his life breaking down, cleaning, then reassembling his relic bolter as if it was his sole duty beyond killing. Only Zorean and Krutaan were absent of his dozen remnant Blades. *So few. So pitifully, depressingly few.* Unclenching his jaw, Dalchian continued walking.

At the far-distant reach, near the colossal blast door beyond which lay the void, a bulbous shape loomed. In its shadow a figure fussed and fiddled, occasional shrieks of pneumatic tools or the crackle of a welding rig echoing across the hangar's corroded deck plates. Dalchian cast an eye over the asymmetric bulk of the grav-lifter. Once he would have scoffed at the baseness of such a craft. Once he would have dismissed it, confident in the enormous superiority of his beloved Thunderhawk, veteran gunship of a score of centuries, a ruthless predator whose machine spirit matched the barbarity of its master.

His Thunderhawk had died on the surface of the world below them. One of the too-many Night Lords casualties from the initial planetary assault, and not the least in Dalchian's eyes. Had the promised second wave of Thelissicus' alliance arrived, then the Blades of Atrocity would not now be extinct and Dalchian's Thunderhawk may yet persist. But the Gorelord had used the Blades of Atrocity as a distraction, a murderous feint while his main force descended upon Uzurmandius' primary military fortress. Thelissicus had sacrificed Dalchian's warband for his own gain, destroying the Night Lords' raider craft in orbit too, lest any escape the surface and seek redress. None of the other warbands of the Gorelord's alliance had seemed unduly troubled by the development. Most said nothing, taking the lesson implicit from the Gorelord's actions, whose own Crimson Slaughter so outnumbered the other warbands. Rumours abounded that Urdamas Grensch of the Flylords, in an unguarded moment, had expressed deep satisfaction at the Night Lords' humiliation.

Swallowing his pride, Dalchian had feigned ignorance of the Gorelord's betrayal, instead seeking refuge with the Crimson Slaughter who had so misused him. Dalchian had thrown his remnant Blades upon Thelissicus' mercy, and the warp-cursed princeling had graciously offered them his hospitality. Dalchian knew Thelissicus would suspect his motives, as well he should. But that mattered little for now. Dalchian's warband endured, even when some of them would rather not, it seemed.

The wrongs will be righted, in time. Dalchian slowed his breathing, calming himself. Ruminating on their predicament was useful at times and needlessly aggravating at others. *My opportunity will arise if I but position my pieces with care.* In the wake of his Thunderhawk's demise, the fat-bellied grav-lifter was their chariot now, and its warden was an unexpected asset.

Theta-Ibriel-7-4 had been a mid-level tech-priest in the

templum-capitalis of Uzurmandius. As a prisoner of the VIII Legion, he had swapped masters in exchange for continued existence and the safeguarding of his precious datastacks. Dalchian had assumed his loyalty would be fleeting and his utility short-lived, but the tech-priest Ibriel had become a feature of the Skin-Taker's small contingent with curious ease. His skill piloting the lifter was a prominent factor, but not the only one.

'How go the adjustments, priest?' Dalchian's helm visor suppressed the sunspot glare of the welding rig. Ibriel disengaged the rig and turned to his master, many lenses whirring beneath his capacious hood. *Has he enlarged his cowl since we took him?*

'Progression rate is suboptimal, but I am reaching scheduled increments with acceptable regularity.'

'Slowly but surely, then.'

'Y-yes. Slowly but surely. My lord.' Ibriel almost forgot to add the courtesy, as always.

'And your… new toy?' Dalchian had been cautious with what he and his warriors said aboard the vessel of his adversary for the first few days, but after a short time Ibriel had assured him that all vox-thieves had been detected and disabled. Some of the Blades had not believed the tech-priest, but Dalchian saw no reason for him to lie. The Crimson Slaughter had no need of one such as Ibriel, so would easily find an excuse to kill him out of hand. The VIII Legion needed him. He was safe with them so long as he was useful.

'The instrument has been installed without undue difficulty. Only a live test will establish whether my amendments to the craft's power distribution have been adequate to take the increased load. For obvious reasons, this cannot be performed currently.'

Ibriel had agreed to aid Crimson Slaughter repair parties in exchange for equipment and ammunition for the Blades. He had surreptitiously liberated more than one choice component from their hosts during some of the expeditions, and the lifter was now home to a good number of non-standard faculties. One such device, secured by means utterly beyond Dalchian's comprehension, was the melta array from a ruined assault ram left to rot in one of the *Torrent*'s bilge decks. Dalchian tried to spot evidence of the powerful weapon, but could not. Ibriel had cloaked his modifications well.

'If the oh-so Great Powers deign, we will have an opportunity soon,' he assured Ibriel.

'The strategy you shared with Krutaan?' Ibriel said. 'My lord.'

Dalchian raised an eyebrow. 'You've been spying on me?' he asked coldly.

'Indeed,' Ibriel nodded. 'Pursuant to your request that I collect–'

'Order.'

'Mm, indeed, my lord.' Ibriel's mechadendrites twitched nervously. 'Pursuant to your *order* that I collect as much information from accessible systems as possible, I have indeed begun recording datalogs from the armour cogitator units of your warriors.'

'Good, what else?'

'Little, I am aggrieved to admit,' Ibriel said with a frustrated shrug. 'The systems of this voidship are heavily warded.' A pause. 'My lord.'

'What of the Crimson Slaughter themselves?'

'Regrettably, I do not have their noospheric ward-signum, so I could not establish a viable downlink. I tried many times. My lord.' His regret was authentic.

'Keep trying.' Dalchian suppressed the feeling of being stifled. 'Where are the datalogs from the Blades' armour?'

Ibriel produced a datacrystal from his robes and Dalchian slid it into his vambrace to review later.

'I took the liberty of placing them in order,' Ibriel said. 'Krutaan's and Saryuz's logs are primary, Zorean's the ultimate entry.'

'Very well.' It made sense, he supposed. 'I assume, given that you observed mine and Krutaan's discussion, that I need not specify your next task?'

'Correct. I have selected the relevant articles from your stock of spoils. My lord.' Ibriel handed Dalchian a dataslate upon which he had highlighted a particular registry file from their manifest, presenting the information for Dalchian's appraisal. Dalchian had extracted one of these components from the lumbering warrior tech-priests on their most recent hunt, and knew there were several more in the Blades' trove. There were six, now. *Six will have to be enough.*

'These are all tested and functioning?'

'That is so,' Ibriel answered, pride in his voice. 'My lord.'

'Good.' He handed the dataslate back to Ibriel. 'Begin making the necessary modifications.'

'I am yours to command, Lord Skin-Taker,' Ibriel said with an earnestness that surprised Dalchian. The tech-priest had long since proved his usefulness. Now he was dangerously close to proving his loyalty. Dalchian refused to let his guard down, but it was a promising sign.

Leaving the tech-priest, Dalchian took to his arming chamber and began reviewing the recorded conversations of his own warriors. Many commanders would have baulked at the blatant mistrust implicit in such an action, he knew, but other, more intelligent commanders would forego nothing in search of an advantage. Just weeks ago he would have found it almost impossible to imagine a conspiracy against him, with more than fifty Blades of Atrocity strong and vicious and feared. But since the disaster on Uzurmandius, since the wasted deaths of so many of his murder-kin and the loss of the *Abjuration*, he had come to believe such a mutiny inevitable.

Krutaan's datalog was sparse. The former claw leader spent relentless hours in the sparring cages with the Crimson Slaughter berserkers. When the lightning-claw-wielding Night Lord fought with his helm, Dalchian also had a visual feed to watch the bouts. Krutaan's violence was stunning, but so was that of the Crimson Slaughter. His edge was his cunning. He would feign an overreach to draw his opponent in, or flick a blade across the cage to sever the power cables, plunging the chamber into darkness, where he could hunt best. He never used the same trick twice. Dalchian found himself enjoying the fights, watching through Krutaan's helm lenses. *Could I beat him?* The question formed in his mind with a jolt. He was disconcerted to admit that he genuinely did not know. He skipped the sparring that followed until he found an audex file.

'You seem content with your diversions.' Saryuz's rasping tones were immediately identifiable. There were other sounds, clangs and thumps of armour pieces being shed. The whirr of a servitor.

'Their novelty wears dangerously thin.' That was Krutaan's voice. *'If the Skin-Taker makes no move soon, then he must be replaced.'*

'To speak so openly of such a thing!' marvelled the sibilant tongue of Olokro. *'Just get it over with, if you're so determined.'*

'Why do you wait?' Saryuz asked.

'Why do you?' Krutaan countered.

'Because I cannot divine what best serves my own purpose.' Saryuz's tone was bitter.

'And I extend our ailing lord a courtesy,' Krutaan replied. *'He may yet have some strategy. We all know his ways.'*

'Ah, noble,' Olokro mocked. *'But how many chances does this courtesy allow?'*

'Quiet,' hissed Saryuz. There was a pause, followed by the sound of approaching bootsteps.

'And what are we conspiring about today, then?' Dagardis rumbled.

Dalchian listened and watched for several hours. The sentiment bubbled beneath the surface among Krutaan, Saryuz and

Olokro mostly. Zhikarga seemed receptive to conspiracy, but would become non-committal when the discussion sharpened. Dagardis' datalog started with an audex recording of him and Ang Heltris, and Dalchian smirked as he listened. He tried not to acknowledge the depth of his relief.

'I'd love to see one of those crows raise a blade against the Skin-Taker,' Dagardis snorted.

'Krutaan is a fine murderer,' Ang Heltris offered.

'Oh, absolutely,' Dagardis agreed. 'But he's no Skin-Taker. I'd very much enjoy watching that fight.'

'And I.' Ang Heltris' smile was audible. 'And I.'

Dalchian was partway through Vellet's datalog when the Gorelord sent his summons.

The bridge of the *Torrent of Hatred* was heaving. Officers relayed streams of orders throughout the patchwork fleet while servitors flesh-melded into their stations mumbled unending screeds of augury and surveyor information and cogitators clicked and whirred and flashed. The mortal crew, ragged and pale, diligently kept their distance from the commanders of the Crimson Slaughter, whose numbers swelled on the platform before the Gorelord's throne. Baroque projector domes had been dragged in front of the dais too, and the hololithic silhouettes of the other warband commanders flicked into ethereal life. All had been summoned.

Dalchian knew better than to push his way to the front. Instead, he leant on the balustrade overlooking the augury pits and the frantic ministrations of the mortals below. Most were cruelly well trained by their masters and knew better than to cast their gaze upwards. One young officer, a new addition Dalchian guessed by her comparatively healthy complexion, chanced a look at him from her post near the master of ordnance. Her tanned skin turned ashen and she fixed her gaze back onto her lectern, hands shaking. Despite the unfavourable nature of his current predicament, Dalchian was heartened by the terror the officer had let show. To watch a sentient creature cower from his appraisal made him remember what it felt like to be a true son of the Night Haunter for an instant. *Gods, but it's been too long,* he thought. The machine-minded populace of Uzurmandius were slow to emotion, and while Dalchian relished the challenge of terrifying them, the immediacy of the deck officer's dread had offered him a taste of the human distress that fuelled his Legion so potently. He decided it was a good omen.

Thelissicus drawled at his commanders, issuing them their orders and reminding them of their oaths to him. Dalchian remembered the promises the Gorelord had made to him in exchange for the Blades' fighting strength. Empty promises. Bitter heat, long present but deliberately suppressed, flared anew in his gut. The bastard's sermon washed over Dalchian, but he forced himself to register the important details. A hostile fleet had not long translated in-system. An Imperial retribution flotilla. The Chaos commanders snorted with derision at the idea of Imperial retribution. As Thelissicus distributed deployment instructions via databurst to the commanders, something caught Dalchian's eye. In the augury pit below him a grey-skinned servitor watched a long-range oculus screen that showed the dispersal of the Imperial fleet. While class and threat could not be reliably determined at this range, Dalchian recognised an aggressive attack formation of a simple but effective type. As he absently watched the small screen, he saw the rune marker of a single vessel detach itself from the formation and descend below the ecliptic plane with blistering speed before disappearing altogether. The servitor logged the craft's departure, but continued to prioritise the hostile fleet's movements.

Dalchian's eyes narrowed. A lone ship, unescorted in an enemy-held star system? Rarely would even a Legion vessel tempt fate so brazenly. And the speed! Dalchian had the profound notion that he had just witnessed something of mighty significance. He thought for a long moment, careful to maintain a disinterested bearing among the other Chaos commanders.

The Gorelord had clearly finished, as the hololiths sputtered out of existence and the Crimson Slaughter cadre of under-lords and champions bared their teeth and growled with anticipation. Dalchian saw some of his Blades at the bridge threshold, Krutaan included, awaiting whatever ignoble orders Thelissicus had concocted for them. Dalchian studied his deployment databurst, then he snapped his head around to regard the Gorelord on his throne. Thelissicus' face was split with his black-toothed grin. Dalchian skimmed the order of battle once again to make sure he had not misread.

'Boarding action, alongside your veteran Chosen,' Dalchian stated, the question implicit.

'Yes, Skin-Taker.' Thelissicus beamed. 'I took to heart your plea for glory, and I would be a discourteous overlord indeed to deny such a fervent request.' Dalchian nodded in a gesture of cautious thanks. Behind his helm visor his eyes bored into those of the Gorelord. *And?*

'Also, your able champion here.' Thelissicus waved a clawed gauntlet at Krutaan, who had stepped forward onto the bridge. 'He was a most accommodating negotiator, and persuaded me to involve your… warband with the most gracious compromise.'

'What compromise?'

'Only that your warriors spread themselves across my squads and attack craft.'

Dalchian looked at Krutaan, then looked back at Thelissicus. With great care, Dalchian grasped the wings of his helm and pulled it off his head. He did not speak, but he allowed his repugnance of the Crimson Slaughter lord to show in the set of his shoulders, the inferno of his stare. Thelissicus continued to smile beneficently. Krutaan took another pace forward.

'Lord Skin-Taker,' the claw leader said. 'This strategy allows us more coverage, that any one of us may better leverage opportunities to–'

'Be silent.' Dalchian did not take his eyes off the Gorelord. 'Tell me, Thelissicus, is it not enough that we endure at your disposal? Have we not been decimated enough, that now you would splinter those who remain?'

'I only offer you the glory you seek, Skin-Taker. Seldom do I bow to such… sentimental demands from my subordinates.'

Subordinates! Dalchian allowed the malignancy of his hatred to fester and swell in the face of the Gorelord's superciliousness. *Warp take the scum!*

An officer addressed the Gorelord from their pit. 'Ninety minutes until the enemy are in engagement range, your excellency.'

'Good. More plunder to harvest.' Thelissicus sat back in his throne and focused his attention on the oculus and the confrontation to come. 'Accompany my assault wave, Skin-Taker, or skulk in your hole. It matters not to me.'

Dalchian left the bridge, bypassing Krutaan without a glance, leaving the former claw leader looking at the Gorelord, who was engrossed in his fleet dispersal.

Dalchian made a point of splitting his warriors at the very last moment. Twelve Night Lords strode onto the embarkation deck together, barbed armour bolted in place, ammunition strapped across their chestplates, belts hung with bladed weapons. Like everywhere on the Crimson Slaughter ship, the embarkation deck was illuminated to an absurd degree, the brightness bleaching out all but the most saturated colours. The Blades of the VIII Legion had their eye-lenses set almost utterly opaque.

The Crimson Slaughter were a contradictory breed. Some units were in parade ground rank and file, waiting to embark beneath the back-swept winglets of assault boats. Then, next to loading cradles where Dreadclaw pods swayed, other red-clad brutes clamoured and brawled with each other like animals. This juxtaposition existed in the bearing of their champions, too. Some were bedecked in horns, chains and hooks, barely controlling their own violence, let alone that of their warriors. Others seemed utterly robotic dedicants of the bolter like nothing so much as hollow, soulless Imperial Space Marines.

The whole Chapter had once been loyal to the carrion throne of Terra, Dalchian reminded himself, whereas he had been born on a sunless hive world, a vassal state of the true powers. The Legion had raised him. He considered himself unsullied by prior misplaced devotion.

Splitting my Blades sullies me, he thought.

'Stay mindful of our task,' he said.

'This ruse better suits the serpents of the Alpha Legion,' Dagardis opined over their closed vox-channel. His fists compulsively tightened and loosened around the haft of his massive power axe.

'Deception is a legitimate strategy,' Zorean shot back. 'Our very existence is at stake.' Dalchian nodded his thanks for the support.

'Find your places,' he ordered. 'Gift our foes with murder. Our blades yet thirst.'

'Our blades yet thirst,' some of them echoed. Only some.

Dalchian and Ang Heltris were assigned to an ageing assault ram with Durveist, the Crimson Slaughter arena champion, and his squad of Chosen veterans. On the spectrum of soulless to bestial, most of them existed at the latter end. One, addressed as Razkash by his comrades, literally loped along on all fours.

Those who were able to remove their helms did so and dragged sharpened gauntlet fingertips down their faces, letting ursine claw marks of blood to seep from their flesh in ritual preparation. Ang Heltris hissed, the sound ghosting through the rebreather grille of his skull-masked helm. His gauntlets endlessly went to the knives sheathed across his chest. Dalchian looked forward to the inevitable slick of gore that Ang Heltris would be drenched in. Not because he was a cleaving butcher like Dagardis, but because he knew which arteries to kiss with his razors to most gracefully exsanguinate his prey. There was profound art to Ang Heltris' murder.

My knifeman is as beastly as any of you brutes, and tenfold as cunning.

The assault craft were fully fuelled and servitors dragged away the umbilicals as the customary anticipatory tension exerted its grip upon the gathered warriors. Dalchian brought up the datafeed that the Gorelord – no doubt begrudgingly – had ordered be fed through to his armour systems. Dalchian was an experienced battlefield commander, after all. The Skin-Taker accessed a void auspex that gave a grainy, imprecise account of the two fleets as they approached one another. The *Torrent of Hatred*'s active void shields made the signal even shakier, but it would satisfy his desire for context that was usually absent from the interior of a ship during void action.

The Gorelord's alliance fleet had spread themselves into an uninspiring formation of presented broadsides and aligned lance batteries. It was the absolute opposite formation for their chosen strategy, and Dalchian's brow furrowed. Then he saw the offset, the array of ships bellying slightly out towards their enemy rather than concaved inwards. He smiled. The spread of the Imperial fleet showed close-up intent and by presenting a facing of gunnery, Thelissicus was tempting the lapdog armada to fan out and bring their own guns to bear before drawing into boarding range. If they did that, Dalchian guessed, then the Chaos fleet would leap between the ribs of the Imperial beast and drive its ships apart. It was a bold plan.

The Imperial fleet kept a tight wedge as they passed within the twenty-thousand-mile mark. The *Torrent of Hatred*'s rune marker flashed and Dalchian felt the monstrous shudder through his boots as the strike cruiser fired a brace of rounds from its prow bombardment cannon. At this range, the searingly fast projectiles would take many long minutes to reach the Imperial ships, and a successful hit was very unlikely. But the gesture mattered.

The battle had begun.

The reality of such a battle often defied the assumptions of those who had never set foot aboard a voidship. Dalchian knew from a century of murder in all its forms that a void battle was like an avalanche. The lead-up was nerve-shredding in its slowness, the impending upheaval only hinted at by a faint groan here, or the trickle of dislodged grains there. He watched the stolen auspex data as the time dragged by. After grudgingly admiring Thelissicus' strategy, his thoughts strayed to his own. He was not a pious soul, as a rule. The Great Powers' influence could be wielded if strength and skill allowed, but it was not in the teachings of his Legion to rely on such fickle potency. Even so, he mouthed a small prayer then. He knew he would need all the help he could get.

As each fleet drew closer, resolved clearer in the instruments of their foe, small adjustments were being made. Dalchian's sputtering auspex feed was blind to such minutiae, but the heft of the Crimson Slaughter strike cruiser swayed beneath him as the fleets danced. At the ten-thousand-mile mark the *Torrent* unleashed another bombardment salvo. Dalchian's thoughts turned to the ghost ship he had seen break from the Imperial fleet on the long-range augur screen. If it was some assassin-craft with fleet-crippling capabilities, well, there was nothing any of them could do about it now. But his instinct counselled him otherwise. It hadn't felt like a knife in the dark when he'd seen it, more like poison in the well. He put it from his mind. There were to be other concerns imminently.

A blaring signal echoed across the embarkation deck and, like a monster surfacing from below calm water, the assemblage of Chaos Space Marines shook off their spell of stillness. Assault craft began turning over their engines. Armoured feet thundered up crew ramps and access gantries. Hulking beings that were once man-shaped roared their gore-thirst.

Dalchian, Durveist and the rest filed into the twin booms of the ram, both armoured hatches grinding shut with a *clang*. Inertial braces clamped around their greaves and pauldrons, fixing them in place. The loping Chosen warrior howled as the arrangement agonised his hunched form, but he chewed his way through the pain. Visceral red lighting flooded the compartment, turning the Night Lords' midnight plate utterly black. Vapour oozed around their feet and condensation gathered on the tarnished bulkheads. Dalchian's hijacked datafeed became almost unreadable, so he shut it down.

Blind again.

The strangling confines of the assault ram as it waited on its launch rail seemed to squeeze Dalchian. He watched Ang Heltris rolling his neck in the inertia throne in front of him. Proximity to one of his most valued warriors should have relaxed him, but instead it just threw into sharper relief the absence of the rest of them. That, and the ridiculousness of the gamble to come. *Perhaps we all die today?*

Fragmentary details of the *Torrent of Hatred*'s situation filtered through into the assault craft. Manoeuvre alarms keened for several seconds at a time, their wailing deadened by inches of armour. The clamped-in Chaos Space Marines endured lurching adjustments as the strike cruiser tipped and rolled on its axis. Its bombardment cannon fired twice more, but then fell silent. Dalchian assumed they were now too close. A ripple made the ram shudder. The *Torrent*'s broadsides had opened up.

Dalchian tried the datafeed again. The runes were barely visible through the static wash, and he could parse little sensible information from it. Two vessels had died. He couldn't tell if they were Chaos or Imperial. *Gods, what a mess!*

The Gorelord's strategy had partly worked. His alliance had veered together at the last moment, it seemed, judging by the spear formation they now adopted that had penetrated into the Imperial spread. But the Imperials were still mercilessly tight. If they had spread to use their own guns, Dalchian could not see it. The two forces were now folding themselves together into a point-blank scrum.

What both fleet commanders had wanted.

There was no countdown; no warning klaxon. The assault ram accelerated like a bullet, squealing down its launch rail. The squealing vanished and Dalchian felt a contradictory push-pull in his gut as the ram passed out of the *Torrent of Hatred*'s gravity well and through its void shields. Curiously, the details of his datafeed sharpened. He read the *Torrent*'s rune marker, determined the Imperial vessel the assault must be targeting. A Naval battleship, Oberon-class.

The ram jinked and veered as it travelled. A mortal would have been violently ill within moments, unconscious soon after. Dalchian took steady breaths, feeling the fire of combat stimms ignite his metabolism.

CHAPTER THREE

There was something utterly primeval about void boarding actions. In the halcyon epoch of the Golden Liar, before His hypocrisy had been laid bare, for this very purpose had He made the first Space Marines. Inured against mortal frailty, enhanced beyond mortal capacity, excised from mortal morality. Brutal tools of dominion. Dalchian had made murder in a thousand cities, from gilded palatinates to foetid hive-spires. He had stridden across deserts and through jungles, captured slaves from ocean outposts and flayed prisoners at the top of mountains. He had made war under skies of every hue, and stars both living and dead.

But little compared to punching through a warship's adamantine hull and the close-quarters slaughter found within.

Their target vessel was climbing out of the battlesphere. Dalchian presumed it was gravely wounded. The ram pitched up to keep the battle cruiser in its arc. The Imperial vessel abruptly disappeared from the datafeed. Then everything became a blur of apocalyptic shaking and spinning. Alarms snarled and the red interior lighting of the ram stuttered and blinked. Dalchian's neck strained as his head crashed from side to side and front to back. Weapons that had been locked in racks and internal plating that had been riveted in place dislodged, flying around the interior on crazy trajectories, pounding Dalchian, Ang Heltris and the Crimson Slaughter warriors like ordnance shrapnel. One of the red-armoured Chosen, bellowing, came loose from his inertia throne and was smashed to pieces in the tiny space. Bits of him dented and sliced at the others. Gobbets flicked and danced.

Then everything wrenched forwards. Loose debris and remains shot to the front hatchway and plastered itself on. Dalchian's cloak of human skins snapped around him like a shroud, then slowly fell away.

They had stopped.

Dalchian was battered, nauseated and disoriented. It took him a moment for his vision to clear. Then the internal lighting steadied and a deep rushing sound began to build at the prow of the assault ram. The temperature climbed rapidly, and Dalchian realised the ram must have locked on to something. Now its melta array was eroding a way inside. His datafeed was dead.

What have we hit?

The other warriors regained their wits. Ang Heltris looked at the obliterated remains of the berserker who had come loose and let out a relieved snigger. Durveist, at the fore of the single-file boarders, grunted.

'Prepare yourselves.'

The sound of the melta array had reached zenith pitch. The heat was stifling. The hatch glowed a faint cherry colour. There was a slow, glutinous explosion outside and the ram shuddered. The internal illumination turned emerald. Their inertia thrones unlocked in a series of pops. The hatch blasted open.

Mag-locked boots prevented them from sliding down the deck. The ram was almost vertical. Below them, the slag and wreckage of their violent ingress had fallen on the heads of a Naval gunnery crew. Offal from the Crimson Slaughter casualty slopped down to steam and bubble on the molten pile. From his occluded perspective at the rear of the ram's hold, Dalchian presumed the gunnery crew, the men and women writhing thirty feet below as their flesh burned away, must be screaming.

Nobody would hear them, though. The gunnery deck stretched either side for hundreds of yards and the noise of it was total. Auto-lifters shunted cannon shells the size of battle tanks from magazine hoists where teams of Naval ratings dozens strong hauled on chains to lower them into gaping breeches. Propellant particulates and water vapour combined in an opaque smog that oozed across greased uniforms and under vast steel gun carriage wheels. Overseers screamed directions from their places on a gantry platform that spanned from one end of the deck to the other. Pneumatics howled and generators brayed.

A petty officer who had watched in horror as his gun crew had disappeared beneath a pile of liquid hull fragments stared, petrified, at the opening above him. Durveist put a bolt pistol round into his open mouth and the man's head evaporated, his body collapsing.

'Gantry,' Durveist ordered simply. 'With me.'

Keeping their boots mag-locked to the vaulted ribs of the gun deck's ceiling, they made their way quickly above the overseers' platform. Awareness would be slow to spread in the clamour of the gun embrasures, but that was no reason to dawdle. They dropped onto the platform, crushing two overseers and a servitor as they landed.

'There is only one ship in their fleet with a gunnery deck this large,' Durveist said.

'The *Divine Approbation*,' Dalchian replied over their vox. 'Oberon-class. Their flagship.'

'Indeed.'

Some Naval ratings hefting clubs started converging on them across the platform, but slowed to a halt as their enemy came into view. Terrified indecision showed on their sweating faces. Durveist turned on them and pulled out his chainsword, its teeth whirling and snarling. Some of the ratings fled, but some held their ground. The Crimson Slaughter fell on them without need of a command. Chainblades and axes ended the ratings swiftly. The gantry had emptied of overseers and crew. By now the alarm would be raised, and the anti-boarding parties would be flooding through the corridors towards them.

'Forward,' Durveist grunted.

'We make for the bridge,' Dalchian said. Durveist looked at him as they advanced towards the sternward bulkhead.

'That is idiocy. The bridge of this vessel will be a fortress. We are too few. We can disable their systems with less difficulty.'

'Your lord demands spoils, does he not?' Dalchian unlimbered his chainglaive from its sheath at his back as they moved. They reached the bulkhead and paired off, covering each other as they advanced through the arched hatchway into an arterial corridor. Naval breachers with void armour and shotguns were racing towards them down the passageway.

Gunfire echoed in the tiny space, blasts of shot pinging and whining from the Chaos Space Marines' armour. The Chaos warriors sent bolt rounds back, but their advantage was maximised at close quarters. They piled towards the breachers, who attempted to shore up a defensible line across the width of the corridor, but the speed of the Crimson Slaughter and Night Lords was inhuman.

Dalchian knocked aside a breacher's shield and loosed a blast from his plasma pistol into their helmeted face. Stepping over their corpse as it fell, he raked his chainglaive across the back of a retreating breacher, splaying ribs and drawing a scream. Ang Heltris darted beneath an axe swing and needled one of his knives into the axeman's gut. The Imperial stiffened instantly, then slowly toppled to the deck, where he twitched and shuddered. Durveist roared as he cut a defender in half at the waist with his chainsword. Gore fountained. The loping Chosen, bestial features helmless, grabbed a breacher's shoulders and bit their neck so deeply he all but beheaded them. The tight corridor filled with misted blood and screams. The boarders finished the surviving breachers with gauntlet and blade. Durveist for the joy of it; Dalchian, to conserve his ammunition. And partially for the joy of it.

'Not the bridge,' Durveist bellowed, blood-madness starting to sound in the hoarseness of his tone. 'The generatorium.'

They made their way down the passages and companionways. Mortal crew and serfs largely hid from their passing, but hatches and blast doors had been sealed at every intersection. Suel'ginn of the Crimson Slaughter carried melta charges for the heavier barriers, and the lesser ones yielded to persistent chain weapons.

It all took time. The boarding party relied on imprecise schematics of known Oberon-class configurations, as well as their combined centuries of experience, but a void-going battleship was a vast labyrinth in any case, and the ancient craft had borne millennia of refits and modifications. Klaxons keened and ochre lights strobed throughout the decks. Dalchian felt certain that the Imperials were clearing the way for them. The implication was not encouraging. The ambush was near.

The first Crimson Slaughter that died to enemy fire did so on the subsidiary arterial on deck forty-eight. A heavy round of tracer fire removed his head and he took two more steps before he fell. The glowing shots blinked down the arterial, ricocheting from bulkhead plating. Dalchian took a glancing blow on his pauldron. The impact made his entire left torso numb for a second. At the end of the arterial a junction had been closed off. An adamantine barricade had risen from the floor and dozens of Navy personnel armed with lascarbines and shotguns waited at the fire step. On a raised, shuttered platform behind them, an autocannon pumped its tracer fire in a steady rhythm. *Chak chak chak.*

The boarders crashed behind what cover they could. Reinforcement stanchions down the side of the arterial were better than nothing. Dalchian primed a choke grenade and threw it down the passageway. The thick gas pumped into the arterial and the Chaos Space Marines instantly broke cover. Autocannon rounds stabbed at them but the gunner's aim was fouled with smoke. Defenders in Imperial Navy uniforms reeled from the stinging clouds, and in the precious heartbeats it took for them to recover, the boarders had vaulted the barricade and were on them. Dalchian's plasma pistol spoke again, the bolt of superheated matter reducing a rating to glowing sludge. He gutted a petty officer with his chainglaive, flicking her writhing body from its teeth before moving on. Durveist wrenched the barrel of the autocannon from its crenellation and swung his heavy chainsword into the crew, who writhed as they came apart. The Navy personnel died in agony.

They were bait.

The trap had worked.

Bolter fire crashed into them from behind. Another Crimson Slaughter warrior died as his abdomen exploded. Durveist bellowed, arms and chainsword dripping with vitae. Another mass-reactive round took off Ang Heltris' left hand and one of his knives with it. He hissed as he spun around. Dalchian turned and discharged his plasma pistol even as he registered what he saw.

A squad of warriors in black armour marched in disciplined lockstep towards them, unleashing withering volleys of bolter rounds. Their armour described exaggerated feminine forms. Scrolls, reliquaries and holy trinkets dangled from chains and glinting rosaries. Simultaneous voices intoned a prayer of acid hatred as they came on.

Adepta Sororitas.

Sisters of Battle. Unhinged zealots clad with an arch veneer of piety. The Chaos intruders steeled themselves against the advance, turning the thickest parts of their power armour into the gunfire. Flakes of ceramite whickered off as the bolt rounds' explosive warheads dug beneath the layers. The Chosen of the Crimson Slaughter brought their own bolters to bear, and their volleys were telling. But so were those of the Sororitas.

A Crimson Slaughter warrior unloading with twin bolt pistols disintegrated as he was riddled with rounds, atomised tissue puffing into the air. A Battle Sister's head disappeared in pink mist and she fell beneath the feet of her comrades. Dalchian took a hit to his shin, his greave armour cracking as it absorbed the detonation. He loosed more plasma, but the venerable pistol keened a warning as its heat sinks reached capacity.

Razkash, the loping Chosen, devoid of ranged weapons, charged. He howled as he galloped, craters appearing in his armour as rounds thumped into him. A shot tore off his right foot, but he barrelled on, bloody stump slamming onto the deck grating. He pulled two frag grenades from his belt and leapt the last ten yards, roaring.

The grenades blew a gap in the Sororitas gun line and Durveist took huge lunging strides to exploit it, the remaining Crimson Slaughter yelling their blood fury and surging after him. The

Battle Sisters distracted, Dalchian looked for an escape from the dead end. The door lock was biometric.

'Ang Heltris,' Dalchian said. 'Their commander.' The knifeman nodded his understanding, glad to let the Crimson Slaughter bear the brunt of the Sisters' wrath. The legionary heaved through the pile of corpses, stray bolt rounds from the ruck just feet away blowing geysers of congealing blood out of them as he searched. He found the uniform he was looking for, and with a levering hack of his knife, removed the officer's head, throwing it to Dalchian by the door lock. Dalchian caught it, pulled open its eyes and jammed it against the reader lens. The doors ground open.

'Durveist!' Dalchian shouted. The Chosen champion glanced up from his butchery, the interruption unwelcome. Then he saw the open door and, after an instant, bellowed a laugh of triumph.

'Slaughterers, with me!' He withdrew from the melee, tearing his chainsword free of the corpse of a Battle Sister. Only two others remained with him. The Crimson Slaughter appeared to have surrendered strategy in favour of sheer blood-letting, accepting the fact they would likely not escape. Dalchian admired their brutality even as he sneered at their fatalism.

One of Durveist's Chosen lifted the autocannon from the deck as they ran. He turned it towards the Battle Sisters as he crossed the threshold and brayed with joy as he unloaded the heavy weapon from his hip, tearing into the advancing line of Sororitas. Brass bounced and clattered on the deck, and as the hopper emptied, Dalchian applied the severed head to the locking mechanism and the doors slammed shut once more. Suel'ginn jammed his last melta charge into the toothed sliding track of the door, and the blast fused the metal into an unyielding lump. Durveist had torn a bolter from one of his victims, and he threw it to Ang Heltris without a word. The knifeman sheathed his blade and snatched the weapon from the air in one deft movement, nodding his thanks.

'The generatorium?' Dalchian said.

'Let us see how close we get,' rumbled Durveist, chest heaving, the air around him exuding combat stimms. The arterial on this side of the door was blessedly empty, and Dalchian knew the next trap awaited them. He ground his teeth in irritation.

'We have an obligation to try and take the ship, Durveist,' he said.

'Our obligation?' Durveist grunted. 'We kill Imperials, Skin-Taker.' After that he said no more. Dalchian could hardly argue. *Sounds like something Krutaan would say.*

As they drew nearer the generatorium, the sounds of combat returned, echoing through the passages and companionways. And the smell became stronger. Several stairwells converged on a mezzanine deck that led into the generatorium proper through a thirty-foot-tall archway. The archway was stoppered with a monolithic blast door bearing the skull-cog device of the Mechanicus, and the mezzanine was in turmoil. Nine Termina-tors of the Flylords warband had teleported directly on board and were now trying to smash their way into the generatorium. Their hulking forms seeped and oozed. Ossified growths split their streaked, once-burgundy armour and splashes of unname-able fluid marked their bootsteps. Fat flies swarmed the space in great, billowing clouds.

For all the crusted malignancy of their wargear, they were nonetheless deadly. Bolt rounds thundered and acrid, clinging flames belched from their combi-weapons. Their foes were unarmoured, and Dalchian thought them to be cannon-fodder slaves at first. But as he and the rest of his boarding party vaulted down the stairway into the fight, he saw the apparently frail combatants for what they were: Sisters Repentia. *More warp-damned zealots.* Corded with muscle and scar-marked by a lifetime of combat, the Repentia were wrapped in rags and devotional parchments. Many wore masks, hiding their faces from the light of the Emperor in shame for whatever transgressions they judged themselves guilty of. All of them wielded improbably large and baroquely filigreed eviscerator chainswords with a surety that was astounding to see up close.

Dalchian beheaded a rag-draped warrior with his chainglaive as he charged. One of her comrades smashed his blade aside with an enormous sweep of her weapon. Durveist barrelled into her, spiked pauldron impaling her in three places. Roaring like a carnodon, she slashed the whirring teeth of her eviscerator across his back, damaging his armour's power plant and tearing into his collar flesh. He wrenched her from his armour and closed his fist around her neck as they disappeared from view into the heaving melee. A Flylords Terminator swept in with a notched power axe.

An eviscerator lunged straight for Dalchian's face. He whirled aside and the blow plunged into the helm of Suel'ginn behind him. The teeth blurred as they shredded the meat of his head, spraying lumps across Dalchian and the masked face of the Repentia. Dalchian kicked her in the midriff, struggling to bring his long-handled weapon to bear in such close confines. Organs pulped and bones broke and the Repentia yelled in agony, but she did not stop. She tore her weapon free and swung it at Dalchian. He ducked the strike and cut her in half with an upswing as he stood. Alchemical flame turned one of the Sisters into a torch that wafted choking brown smoke. Still the Battle Sisters came on.

With Dalchian and the Crimson Slaughter appearing at their

flank, though, the balance of the fight shifted. One of the Flylords near the blast door had enough room to swing his power fist now, and the deck and bulkheads shook with its impact. A crackling dent appeared in the middle of the skull-cog. He swung again.

Dalchian checked his chrono. It had been almost an hour since they launched their wave of assault craft from the *Torrent*. The lack of vox-contact with any of the other Blades was vexing him. His ploy was quite simple, and he hoped that went in its favour. The Blades had been split into six pairs among the Gorelord's assault craft, so their being separated in the tempest of battle was almost a certainty. Now that was the case, every pair was to fight alongside their respective party of Crimson Slaughter until the right opportunity presented itself, whereupon the Blades would regroup thanks to Ibriel's technical administrations. Dalchian knew such an opportunity was impossible for he and Ang Heltris aboard the *Divine Approbation*. The Imperial flagship was simply too big and too well defended. He could only keep fighting; keep surviving. His Blades would not fail him. They *must* not fail him.

Adamantine teeth ground as he locked blades with a Repentia whose mouth moved in constant recitation. He pushed her weapon away and stabbed in, but she slid aside. The follow-up almost penetrated his guard and he growled.

'Just die.'

'The lord God-Emperor is the strength of my arm and the fire in my belly. He maketh me great in His splendour and I flinch not from His divine command. Suffer not the heretic...' Her litany seemed unending. Parrying her eviscerator, Dalchian swept forward and punched with his empty hand. Her jaw almost came clean off, but she barely faltered. Rage showed in her eyes through the sheeting sweat and blood. She jumped forward, raising her blade for a diagonal cut.

'You're insane,' he told her as he severed both her arms above the elbows. Her hands clenched the trigger of her eviscerator as it fell, skidding across the deck and fountaining sparks. She dropped to her knees, slurred, shapeless prayers spilling ceaselessly from her broken mouth. She closed her eyes, welcoming death, and Dalchian decapitated her. Beneath his dinted helm, he grimaced.

'Insane.'

The Flylords Terminator with the power fist had been distracted from his breaching work. A Repentia covered in electooed scripture had dodged through the melee and engaged him. He blasted with his combi-bolter, blowing her legs to pieces under her. She fell, and the Terminator resumed his assault on the door, but the Repentia was not done. From the deck, she drove the howling chainblade point first into his bulging gut. Putrid, tumescent horror rained down as his abdomen came apart. She pushed further, the five-foot-long blade disappearing entirely into the trunk of the armoured beast. He twitched as a rain of filth cascaded from the rent in him. Dalchian marvelled at the amount of it.

A double-hairline of rippling energy passed through the tumult. It struck another of the Flylords who had stepped forth to avenge his comrade's suffering. The Terminator stilled, two fist-sized holes punched clean through him leaving molten armour and sizzling flesh. Like a building whose foundations had given way, he slid and toppled slowly backwards. A phalanx of Sororitas reinforcements descended one of the stairwells. They were festooned in the gaudy array of their ilk, and in their gauntlets were heavy weapons as deadly as those of any Space Marine. A multi-melta steamed from its barrels and the helmless Sister wielding it sneered with savage derision.

Dalchian leapt behind a Flylords Terminator as gouts of fire filled the chamber from the muzzles of two ornate heavy flamers.

Heavy bolter shells whipped spiralling patterns in the inferno. Immolating Repentia screamed prayers of absolution even as their lungs charred.

Durveist charged, his armoured form wreathed in fire from head to foot. Dalchian stayed behind the Terminator as it waded into the conflagration. More Sororitas were appearing, adding enfilading bolter fire to the tempest. A part of Dalchian's mind acknowledged he may be about to die. A mortal would have quailed with the realisation, but Dalchian registered the unhelpful information with cold detachment. Little could distract a legionary in the midst of battle.

Something else did distract him, though.

A blinking rune on his visor showed his armour diverting power. His cogitator unit had registered a predetermined signal-burst and was responding autonomously.

'Ang Heltris!' he roared as loud as he could over the din. In answer, his knifeman appeared from beneath a pile of burning corpses where he had avoided the worst of the flames. Ang Heltris ducked beneath the streaming bolter fire and leapt next to his lord.

'Now, my lord?' he asked conversationally.

'Now.'

'Thank the Powers for that. This is getting boring.'

A whine of building charge keened through the noise of the chamber. Durveist, still aflame, turned from his carnage and addressed them.

'Blades!' he bellowed. 'Stop skulking! Come and die with honour!'

'A tempting proposition, Durveist,' Dalchian replied. 'But, alas, not this day.'

Durveist cocked his head; Dalchian could picture his slab-features creased in incomprehension inside his helm.

'What do you–'

There was a blinding flash and a sucking reverberation of displaced air. And the two Night Lords were gone.

Chapter Four

Dalchian had endured personal teleportation infrequently in his time. The practice was better suited to those clad in Terminator armour, for the sturdier systems and greater protections afforded by that war plate were more able to offset the abhorrent violence of the process. Physically, it was like riding a missile through a hurricane. Even a genhanced transhuman legionary could not avoid nausea and dissociation as a result. But the fallout was more subtle than mere perturbation of the senses. The translocation lasted scant seconds, but Dalchian was immediately psychologically exhausted, as if he had spent years desperately evading a predator. He felt stripped of his armour and his vigour both. Subjected to the regard of some monstrous voyeur. A coldness gripped his heart and his guts. He shook off the effects as his auto-senses unscrambled.

He stood on an engraved teleportarium dais with Ang Heltris and six other remnant Blades, etheric vapour slinking from their armour. The chamber was miniscule. The barbed tips of their armour adornments scraped the ceiling. Vent louvres in the bulkheads inhaled the last greasy fumes as indicator lights flickered around them.

'Welcome aboard,' Qi Umshar said with a smile. He stood on the deck plating in front of the dais. His horned helm was gone and he bore the patchwork injuries of the recently embattled. Dalchian dropped from the dais and grasped his surgeon-Apothecary's wrist in greeting.

'Impeccable timing, Qi,' he said. 'Though this is a somewhat smaller teleportarium than I had envisioned.'

'The craft may be the smallest among the wretched Imperial battle line, my lord.'

'Well, that may have its advantages. Our strategy is a success, thank the Eye.' Dalchian cricked his neck. 'Is there kill-work yet to be done?'

'Aye.' Qi Umshar inclined his head respectfully. 'Krutaan and the Crimson Slaughter assault the bridge as we speak, lord.'

'Then our blades yet thirst.' Dalchian cast a look over the others who had arrived with him. Every one of them bore the abuse of battle. Dagardis flicked dripping gore from his axe blade, breath hammering like a promethium generator. Saryuz was kneeling and had been on the verge of firing his meltagun. Fibre bundles in his armour graunched as he stood. Keth Naa holstered his bolt pistol, the icon atop his power pack bent. Vellet had his bolter shouldered and knife drawn. Zhikarga spat blood and dropped the severed arm that had translocated with him. Zorean had escaped the worst, it seemed, though he was completely out of ammunition. Dalchian tossed his plasma pistol and Zorean caught it deftly, checking its charge level and heat sink capacity. Dalchian turned back to Qi Umshar.

'Show us the way.' Only now did he register two human operators seated behind the enormous control terminal of the teleportarium.

They looked like they might be sick. One's eyes bulged as he stared at the hideous new arrivals he had helped aboard. The other had their gaze fixed on the dials and readouts of the terminal.

The *Red Galentia* was one of three venerable destroyers attached to the Imperial retribution fleet. Of its squadron siblings, the *Gold Galentia* had been lost to a lance strike in the early void-clash and the *Black Galentia* was now vox- and astropath-silent. An assault boat disgorging eight Crimson Slaughter reavers along with Krutaan and Qi Umshar onto the *Red Galentia* had been more than enough to take several key decks of the modest vessel, including the teleportarium. A fifth of a mile long with less than three thousand crew, the destroyer was of the lesser-most order of Imperial voidcraft. Designed for needlepoint strikes against the weakest parts of enemy capital ships, the *Red Galentia* gave over a third of its total tonnage to the twin lance turrets on its ventral spine and their power and control systems. All other weapons on the vessel were close-in defence and ordnance countermeasures. Dalchian was frankly astonished that such a tiny ship would even have a teleportarium. But the array of voidcraft abroad in the galaxy was colossal, and all bore the variance of differing shipyards, the ever-changing requirements of centuries, and the whims of Mechanicus refit overseers. Dalchian decided being thankful for the good fortune was enough for now. A squad of Chaos Space Marines was an unignorable threat to a voidship of any size. Now they were reinforced to almost double, the fate of the small destroyer was all but a foregone conclusion.

There was only one way onto the bridge. The corridor was tight and the embrasure was sealed off by the interlocking leaves of a heavy blast door. *Another gods-damned blast door.* Dalchian sighed to himself. In front of the door was a whole platoon of Naval breachers in void-sealed armour with a veritable arsenal of weaponry. A portable twin heavy bolter turret had been anchored to one side of their position and the gun barrels were pounding tearing bursts of mass-reactive fire at the attackers. The breachers were armed with their customary shotguns, and whenever the Chaos boarders tried to storm them, their volleys were infuriatingly precise. The pocked corpses of two Crimson Slaughter lay on the deck, one in the corridor and one at its mouth in the strategium, where the rest of the boarding party gathered. Krutaan stood on the starboard side of the low-ceilinged space, extended lightning claws sparking as their energy fields flash-burned the blood that covered them into black flakes. The Crimson Slaughter were lurching and swaying with their need to be killing. But they were stalled. Out of grenades, and with no flame weapons between them, they could not get close enough to the mortal defenders to tear them apart with their blades and axes.

As Dalchian and his Blades appeared in the strategium Krutaan nodded his approval. The Crimson Slaughter champion's helm snapped around, his weapons reflexively pivoting towards the newcomers, expecting an attack. The champion took an instant to process the presence of an entire claw of Night Lords legionaries, seemingly conjured from thin air at his back. Dalchian imagined the champion was torn between the relief of reinforcement and the unease of those reinforcements being entirely the Skin-Taker's murder-kin. *How will he greet us, I wonder?* Dalchian thought.

'Your Blades are a heartening presence, Lord Skin-Taker. We have reached an impasse,' the champion said.

A smart one, this one. Dalchian smirked.

'Executioner Glausius,' he added by way of introduction. Dalchian ignored him.

'Grenades,' he ordered as his Blades approached the corridor mouth. Zorean tested the resistance with a swift glance. Instantly, heavy bolter shells and a crackling volley of shotgun fire reached down towards him, and he wrenched his head away. The Blades gathered a bandolier of frag and choke grenades between them.

'Dagardis, your arm is best.' Dalchian beckoned the axeman forward. Dagardis mag-clamped his power axe to his back and took the bandolier, priming the explosives. As he leapt across the mouth of the passageway, punishing shotgun fire chased him, blowing craters into the plasteel of the opposite bulkhead. The strategium hololith table had long since been obliterated. Dagardis slammed behind the bulkhead on the far side, armour peppered with smoking dents, hands now empty.

A rippling avalanche of flame and acrid gas filled the corridor. The grenades killed a dozen breachers and filled others with forge-hot shrapnel. Screams echoed in the smoke. The heavy bolter turret overturned, blasting uselessly into the deck plates until its autoloader decoupled. As the debris settled, a knee-high tracked automaton trundled forward, aiming its cracked vid-capt lens into the gloom.

Fourteen Chaos Space Marines exploded from the smog. The automaton crumpled beneath sprinting boots. The armoured figures filled the corridor. They eclipsed the glow of the lumen strips and made the deck tremble as they charged.

First to the breachers, Krutaan lifted a defender by the midriff, one claw sunk deep into their guts as he slashed another's head from his shoulders. A breacher staggered upright from behind the ruin of the broken heavy bolter turret. Dalchian took him in the chest with a thrust of his chainglaive. Glausius, crimson-clad executioner, brought his broad axe down through the collar of a multi-las gunner. The breacher stared in mute horror as their side pared away like fruit rind, arm going with it.

The assault could not be denied. Thirty Naval troopers died in as many seconds and the corridor, still shrouded in swilling gas, steamed with a charnel-house humidity.

'Saryuz,' Dalchian growled, clearing chunks from the teeth of his glaive. The melta gunner cycled up his weapon and braced his feet as he aimed at the centre of the blast door. He fired and the shrill hiss-whistle of superheated ignition gas accompanied the blossoming of a flowerhead of glowing, molten plasteel in the door. The orange-hot fissure widened as Saryuz fired again. The mechanics of the blast door tumbled apart within, and Dagardis and a Crimson Slaughter champion heaved the doors open.

Glausius and Dalchian leapt through first. Five breachers stood behind the door, shotguns raised. The executioner and the Skin-Taker felled them like coppice-wood, only two shotgun reports attesting to any attempt at resistance. The boarders flooded the bridge. Some of the mortal deck crew shouted in alarm, but most remained frozen at their stations. An aged man with a neat beard and the uniform of a Battlefleet Odovokan lieutenant commander drew his sabre and roared.

'Get off my ship, heretic scum!'

It was an admirable display of defiance. Zorean melted the man's head with an almost point-blank plasma bolt. A few other officers had drawn sidearms. Each was blasted apart with precision bolter shots, then stillness and silence fell.

'Who commands here?' Dalchian barked. His amplified voice filled the bridge space like a thunderclap. He let his glowing vermilion eye-lenses scour the deck crew. Most flinched and stared at the floor or clamped their eyes shut. Dalchian descended from the raised command platform to the lower level, filled with augur pits and control lecterns and petrified Naval officers. Despite weighing half a ton, he moved almost silently. His mantle of human hides hushed and whispered as he went. 'Who steps forth into your murdered captain's place?'

With surpassing reluctance, a younger man with sore-looking

eyes and a bald pate raised his head and stepped out from behind his lectern.

'You?'

'I… I am next in command,' the man stammered.

Dalchian advanced slowly towards the mortal until he towered over him, only inches away. He stared down into the mortal's puffy face, seeing how the bloody glow of his own eye-lenses reflected from the man's pale, perspiring brow. The officer shook with fear, but kept his gaze level and focused in the middle distance.

'How long until we're back in engagement range?' Dalchian asked quietly. The *Red Galentia* had circled out of the immediate battle in the hopes of dealing with its boarders before rejoining its fleet.

'S-seven minutes, sir,' the sore-eyed man replied, making a fair attempt at an even tone.

'My lord,' Zorean snarled from the platform where the other Chaos warriors watched. The officer turned even paler.

'I'm sorry, my lord. Seven minutes, my lord.'

'And remove that filthy perversion,' Zorean added, gesturing to the embroidered aquila at the officer's breast. The man dug thin fingernails beneath the stitching, trying to work the device free. Several others of the deck crew began to do likewise.

'Your name?' Dalchian purred.

'Sub-lieutenant Efrahim Scallen, my lord.'

'Assign your deck crew, *Captain* Scallen.' Dalchian turned away from the man, the mortal's heartbeat hammering audibly to his transhuman hearing. As Dalchian ascended back up the command platform stair, Glausius turned squarely towards him, both fists tight around the handle of his axe, fellow Crimson Slaughter at either side.

'I appreciate your assistance in taking this vessel, Lord Skin-Taker,'

Glausius said, his voice leaden with intent. 'This ship belongs to the Gorelord now.'

'This ship belongs to the Night Lords,' Zorean husked.

'Step aside,' Dalchian said.

Glausius pushed his chin forward, lifting the grimacing mask of his Mk VII helm. 'Regrettably, the Gorelord gives me other orders, Lord Skin-Taker. You are without authority here.'

'If you insist,' Dalchian sighed and gestured. Vellet, faster than a thought, raised his bolter and put a round into the eye-lens of a red renegade. Dagardis' axe smashed away the notched sword of another before cleaving his torso in two. Ang Heltris swept up behind the last of them and thundered his knife into the Crimson Slaughter warrior's throat again and again and again, dragging him backwards. Dalchian rested his chainglaive at Glausius' neck as Zorean wrenched away the executioner's axe.

'I once commanded a warband of fifty Night Lords, Executioner Glausius.' Dalchian's voice dripped with bitterness. 'Do you know what happened to them?' There was a set to Glausius' shoulders. He knew what was coming.

'I do.'

'I once commanded a Denouncer-class raiding vessel. My old master Iccrom named it the *Abjuration* after he took it from the Word Bearers. Do you know what happened to it?'

Glausius sighed through his rebreather grille. 'You would have done the same were you in my master's position, Lord Skin-Taker.'

'Incorrect.' Dalchian allowed himself then to feel every iota of the grief and fury he had spent the last weeks burying. He let the hatred course through him and pictured Thelissicus' grinning face. 'I would do much, much worse.' He gunned his chainglaive, sweeping it through Glausius' neck. The executioner's head skittered away and his body took several long seconds to fall sideways onto the decking with a *clang*.

'Any others?' Dalchian directed his question at Krutaan after a few heartbeats. The lightning-claw-armed legionary looked down at the dead in crimson plate before answering.

'Two more, likely in the enginarium, my lord.'

'Find them and kill them, all of you.' Dalchian turned away from his Blades. 'Zorean, remain here with me. Qi, secure the infirmary.' The Night Lords who had struck without question – Dagardis, Vellet, Ang Heltris – they moved with purpose. Others were slower to respond; had showed less vigour against the Crimson Slaughter. Saryuz, Keth Naa, Zhikarga. Dalchian knew he had work to do.

But he had a ship again.

'Any news of Gamarth and Olokro?' Dalchian asked Zorean as he went to stand at the bridge transept.

'Their assault boat was destroyed in flight by the Imperial fighter screen,' Zorean replied. Dalchian's armoured fingers dug into the balustrade at the answer.

'We are ten, then.'

'We are, Skin-Taker.'

'You.' Dalchian pointed at an officer near the environmental controls. 'Kill internal illumination above minimum necessity and drop the temperature by fifteen degrees.' They nodded dumbly and obeyed. 'Scallen.'

'Yes, my lord?'

'Send a communique.' Dalchian transferred a databurst to the master of vox's terminal that contained the frequency and the wording of the message. The *Red Galentia*'s new captain gestured a young ensign to the vox-terminal. The ensign moved like a servitor, her face impassive.

'Communique sent, my lord,' Scallen said after a moment.

'Good. Time to engagement range?'

'Four minutes, my lord.'

'Hail the Crimson Slaughter flagship *Torrent of Hatred*. Tell them Skin-Taker of the Blades of Atrocity commands this vessel now. Then target their bridge with both lance turrets, maximal fire.'

'Not the… the Naval flagship, my lord?' Scallen asked, referring to the Imperial command vessel. His discomfort warred with bafflement at Dalchian's orders.

'Must I repeat myself?'

'N-no, my lord! At once, my lord.' Scallen issued the orders, his newly rearranged deck crew retreating into the false comfort of practised movements, not questioning why the Archenemy targeted his own. Not daring to question.

'Is this the time, Skin-Taker?' came Zorean's voice over their private vox-channel.

'I can think of none better,' Dalchian snarled back.

The oculus filled with rune markers as the *Red Galentia* arrowed obliquely across the battle lines. Its attack vector was clearly aiming for the Chaos fleet, so the Imperials paid the destroyer no heed. Ships burned, lambent points of flickering light, each a thousand miles distant. Bulk transports shirked the violence, burning vacuum towards the beleaguered forge world that hung like a malignant bauble in the black, its atmosphere smeared with twists of vapour pollution. Would-be liberators, sounding their silent charge through the void.

The *Torrent of Hatred* hung above the battlesphere. Gashes in its blood-red hull plating showed where lances and torpedoes had done their work. Its complement of attack craft swirled about it, invisible but for their sparking demise as thrice the number of Imperial interceptors winnowed them away. The *Divine Approbation* closed in, only a few hundred miles between the two huge war vessels. Abeam of its Chaos counterpart, the Oberon-class flashed volley after punishing volley. The *Torrent* replied, macrocannon broadsides seeking to overload the *Approbation*'s void shields so that probing lance turrets might deal a lethal blow.

The *Red Galentia* swept in like a small fry bothering a kraken, engulfed by the shadow of the looming strike cruiser.

'Incoming hololith request from the *Torrent*, my lord,' Scallen said.

Dalchian nodded the signal through. The hololith dome suspended above the bridge transept stuttered to life, and the enthroned figure of Thelissicus appeared in shimmering ghost-light.

'What says the Gorelord?'

'Ah, *Skin-Taker.*' Thelissicus beamed. *'Congratulations on your success. Quite how you gathered your remnant to you was a fascinating work of deception. Bravo, Skin-Taker. Truly, I'm impressed.'*

'You promised me a share of the spoils in exchange for my loyalty, Thelissicus. I am glad to reward your betrayal with my own.'

'But spoils you had, Skin-Taker! In fact, your tin pet has just blown a hole in my stern hangar bay doors.' The Gorelord laughed, but Dalchian saw the fury deep in the Crimson Slaughter leader's eyes. Dalchian allowed himself his cruellest smile.

'That was but a foretaste.' Dalchian gestured to Scallen, who cut the link before Thelissicus could respond. 'Lances ready?'

'Aye, lord.'

The metal cliff faces of the battleships turned as the *Red Galentia* powered by them. Dalchian watched the magnified images as the *Divine Approbation* let fly another soundless cannonade. The *Torrent*'s void shields wavered and blinked.

'Fire.'

The lance turrets inflicted no recoil on the *Red Galentia*, but the energy they drained from the ship's systems slurred everything for a moment. Lumens dimmed and the oculus splintered into patches of readout, part moving, part frozen. There was a flurry of rune markers as the destroyer's auspex registered the hit, then its systems recovered.

'Hit confirmed,' the gunnery commander called from her lectern. 'Hull penetrated, target venting atmosphere.' Dalchian felt a rush of vengeance.

'My lord,' Scallen said. 'A Mechanicus cargo vessel is aski–'

'Open the shuttle hangar. Let him in.'

'Aye, lord.'

'As soon as he's aboard, feed all power to the engines and make for the system's gas giant.' Guelphos orbited close to the Uzurmandius star and its prodigious magnetosphere would make them less visible to prying augurs.

'*Lord Skin-Taker.*' Krutaan's voice, ragged with exertion, came through Dalchian's helm vox. '*We have murdered the last Crimson Slaughter aboard…*' He hesitated.

'But?'

'*We tried to stop them, lord, but they killed the Navigator.*'

Dalchian took a steadying breath and closed his eyes. *Warp curse them!* He turned and strode to the command throne, seating himself upon the blocky plasteel.

'Thank you, Krutaan. Stand the Blades down.'

'*Is the battle over?*'

'For us. For now, at least.'

'*We are running.*' Krutaan's voice was dark. Dalchian clenched his jaw.

'Yes, Krutaan. We must recover our strength.' He cut the link. *By the Eye, but he wants for death? Perhaps the Crimson Slaughter blood-madness has claimed him.*

'My lord, the Mechanicus cargo lifter is aboard,' Scallen said.

Dalchian acknowledged with a nod and Scallen wisely said no more. The *Red Galentia* accelerated hard. A vox-hail from one of the other Imperial vessels came through the bridge augmitter horns.

'*Red Galentia*,' a deep voice said. '*This is Admiral Blenken. I commend you on your valiant efforts, that was a sound blow. Now, return to formation at once.*'

'Cut vox,' Dalchian ordered. A palpable cloud of tension rose from the deck crew, hesitancy in every movement. They yearned to serve their Imperial masters. Dalchian went to the headless corpse of the ship's late captain and pulled the sabre from his nerveless grip. It looked like a toy in his hand. He stepped down into the nave of the bridge and approached the master of the vox, who began to shake uncontrollably in her starched uniform.

'Cut vox,' he said again, just as another signal started to transmit.

'*Red Galentia, this is Blenken, do you–*'

The master of the vox drew her hand along the line of switches, silencing the system.

'Good,' Dalchian said, and ran her through, pinning her to the vox-console. She gasped, clutching at the sabre in her belly and floundering as Dalchian returned to the command platform.

'Station the Blades around the ship,' he said to Zorean. 'Instruct them to ensure loyalty among our new crew by whatever means they find most appealing.'

'With pleasure,' Zorean grinned.

The void battle raged. The *Red Galentia* speared away under full power, urgent requests for vox connection blinking at the side of the oculus. A Sons of Malice light cruiser broke from the Gorelord's fleet and began to give chase, lance forechasers searing against the *Red Galentia*'s stern void shields. The smaller destroyer was faster, though, and rune markers indicating flights of Imperial strike craft harried the light cruiser. Eventually it broke off its pursuit and, one by one, the *Red*

Galentia's proximity alarms disengaged. The battlesphere began to fall away. Dalchian had salvaged opportunity from extinction, but once the initial void clash concluded then whoever was left was coming after him, be they Imperial curs or those of the Gorelord's alliance.

To compound the obstacles ahead, Krutaan's tone had soured Dalchian's sense of victory considerably. He ground his teeth. There was still much work to do.

He cleared the ward room of the last vestiges of the ship's officers, appropriating the low-ceilinged chamber for his own quarters. Dalchian removed his helm for the first time in days, placing it on the darkly varnished table at the centre of the room. His skin felt raw and new. The air of the ship was recycled like that of his armour, but the voidcraft's atmosphere still felt comparatively fresh. He saw his reflection in the table's lacquered surface. Weltering bruises and split flesh criss-crossed his face, his superior physiology barely keeping up with the punishment of the last few hours. His half-scalp of lank hair hung, swaying like a sheet. His own helm caught his attention, and he leant down, knuckles on the mahogany, to inspect it. It was battered and dented and burned. Scratches and flaking paint showed the ceramite beneath. A gobbet of flesh had lodged in a vent opening and begun to cure. Dalchian pulled it free, flicking it away.

And then he perceived it again. The roiling serpent in his core. The beguiling urge to accept the extinction of his warband and surrender to thoughtless violence. Not a berserker's rage, but sterile. Not the labyrinthine scheming of a psychopath, but rudderless. To empty the vessel of his being and let whatever else fill it. He knew the source of such temptation. Every soul that acknowledged the Great Powers knew it.

He spat a string of congealed blood. His remnant Blades would rise again. There was no other path for Dalchian Rassaq the Skin-Taker. *He* would rise again, whatever the cost.

Two hours passed in which Dalchian pushed his new command as hard as he could. The destroyer powered in-system, leaving the forge world's sphere of influence and burying itself in the black of interplanetary space. Dalchian ordered his Blades onto rotating watches across the ship, knowing even transhuman servants of the Great Powers need to rest, but knowing just as well that leaving the mortals unmolested for any amount of time would invite disaster. When Krutaan's time came to be off watch, the sound of boots hammering on deck plates echoed into the ward room.

Krutaan thundered into the room and slammed to a halt, glaring at his lord.

'Not only did we run from battle, but we fired upon the Crimson Slaughter as we did so.'

'That was my order, yes.'

'Are we simpering Imperial herd-beasts, now?' A pause.

'Control your tone, Krutaan.'

'I do control it!' The claw leader took an involuntary step forward, tendons taut down his neck. 'You asked me to speak openly my criticisms. You gave your word we would regain our strength. I conspired with you so the Gorelord would think us weak and loosen his grip upon us. I believed you wanted what I want. Now I ask if we have utterly abandoned our cause to do the work of filthy Imperial vermin for them *before their very eyes*! To turn on our own when lapdog prey was ripe for the butchering?'

'The Crimson Slaughter are not our own.'

'They are more so than the wretched, idol-blind Sororitas!'

'Thelissicus was almost the end of us! You seem keen to forget that truth. His treachery demanded redress.'

Krutaan balled his fists. Combat stimms inflamed Dalchian's nervous system as Krutaan snarled. 'It is you who are the end of us, lord, if you cannot summon the strength to *lead*!'

'Your words are mutiny, Krutaan.'

'Then denounce them and execute me!'

Dalchian had propped his chainglaive against some trophy cabinet on the bulkhead, within easy arm's reach. In a fluid motion he seized the weapon and swept it around in a blistering arc. Krutaan dropped aside, the heavy sawtooth blade passing within a hair's breadth of him. Krutaan spun in low, lightning claws ringing as he spread the digits apart to strike. Dalchian dodged back, spinning his glaive around his offside and hammering it down from above. Krutaan rolled and kicked, smashing Dalchian back and making him stagger. Krutaan pistoned his legs, launching himself into the air to fall onto the Skin-Taker, claws wide. Dalchian braced his glaive square above himself, fists gripped wide apart on its haft. The polearm stopped Krutaan's descent and the claw leader slammed his weapons in from either side. Dalchian levered his glaive haft, pitching the other legionary away, Krutaan's lightning claws shaving curls of ceramite from his rerebraces as he tumbled. The claw leader crashed to the deck and Dalchian was upon him, one boot keeping the left claw pinned, the butt of his glaive fixing the right one. They both drew deep breaths, eyes locked as several weighted seconds passed.

'I will not deprive the Blades of their best,' Dalchian said at last. 'We cannot afford the loss. What I do, I do for the good of this company.' Krutaan stared up in disbelief. 'Kill Imperials we shall. The moon colonies of Guelphos lie hence, and they are fat with the resources we need. Our blades yet thirst.' With that, he snatched away his glaive and turned his back on Krutaan, leaving the claw leader lying alone on the ward room deck.

CHAPTER FIVE

The moon colonies of Guelphos were a long, hard burn towards the core of the Uzurmandius System. But Dalchian had a suspicion that something else lay that way, too. The phantom ship that had sidestepped the void battle so deftly. Its engines and capacity to shroud itself from augurs alone made it a worthwhile trophy, but the Skin-Taker felt in his bones that there was more to the mysterious craft than mere speed and subtlety. He yearned to know its true nature. The flotilla logs of the *Red Galentia* listed only such craft as had joined the battle, and try as he might, Dalchian could source no further clues from the ship's datastacks or cogitator archives. He caught himself praying for some insight, and reminded himself that the Powers only granted boons in exchange for sacrifice. Indulgently, he decided he had sacrificed enough already.

The bridge was cleared of the dead. The warriors of the Crimson Slaughter were stripped of their arms and armour and piled in an air gate to be flushed when the destroyer next made orbit, incinerating them with atmospheric entry heat. In a quiet moment during a night cycle, Dalchian let himself into the air gate and removed the progenoids from the dead as discreetly as he could. Such a profound taboo would usually be beyond even him, but they had precious few bargaining pieces, and he needed every advantage he could get. He packed the organs in a stasis casket in Qi Umshar's infirmary, and if the surgeon-Apothecary suspected the contents, he gave no indication. For his part, Qi retrieved Glausius' head from where it had come to rest in a dark corner of the bridge, replacing his own lost helm with that of the executioner.

Ibriel performed similar reparations to the rest of the Blades' suits of armour. Ruined segments were replaced with looted red ceramite, scattering patches of crimson throughout their midnight. Ang Heltris' amputated hand was replaced with a threaded socket onto which he could screw a knife that Ibriel had modified for the task, and the knifeman seemed happy with the augmentation. The tech-priest's newly retrofitted melta array had performed without fault, facilitating his escape from Thelissicus' flagship, and his bulbous cargo lifter and its precious store of Mechanicus secrets was now clamped into the destroyer's tiny shuttle bay.

'The repairs are done?' Dalchian asked as he strode into the destroyer's compact armorium forge. Ibriel looked up from a gauntlet he had been melding back together. The finger segments were a random scattering of blue-black and scratched red. The gauntlet belonged to Saryuz.

'Affirmative, as of this moment.' Ibriel admired his work as he stowed the welding rig. 'My lord.'

'Then you may begin collating an inventory of weapons and equipment on board.'

'Most of the *Red Galentia*'s small-arms are las-based or one of several patterns of shotgun,' Ibriel responded without missing a beat. 'There are some crates of explosives, frag and smoke grenades, mostly. The stockpile does boast a considerable sufficiency of heavy bolter ammunition though, so I have salvaged one of the weapons from the turret the Imperials used to defend the bridge. Administering the necessary adjustments, it should be hand portable, by one of your legionaries, at least.' To punctuate his summary, Ibriel produced a dataslate where the inventory scrolled in tight lines of text. Dalchian was impressed, but did not show it.

'Good. Zhikarga's bolter suffered terminal damage during his boarding action. The heavy weapon will serve him well.' Dalchian could readily picture the glee with which Zhikarga would accept such an upgrade.

'*My Lord Skin-Taker*,' Qi Umshar's voice crackled through the vox. '*Shake-down of the infirmary is complete.*'

'And?'

'*Most of the supplies are irrelevant to us*,' the surgeon-Apothecary said. '*That which is largely for mortal first aid and other petty concerns. However, there are several vitacopia apparatus.*'

'That's a reassurance,' Dalchian replied. The complex medicae instruments allowed for induced coma of both mortals and transhumans in which serious injuries might more effectively heal. Qi Umshar closed the link.

'The *Red* yields itself to you,' Ibriel said, his reverence for the huge machine evident. The Blades had begun referring to the ship simply as the *Red*. 'How does it compare to your prior vessel?' The tech-priest's question came from nowhere and Dalchian's gut tightened in sudden grief and rage.

'Not even close,' he growled. Ibriel's mechadendrites twitched and Dalchian took a steadying breath. 'It's a hundredfold better than rotting in Thelissicus' bilges, though, I'll give it that.' It did feel good to once again command a ship, he admitted to himself. The Blades' resurrection could finally begin.

Bootsteps echoed at the armorium portal as Zorean and Saryuz entered the chamber, the latter missing a gauntlet. Saryuz stared at Dalchian as he strode past without speaking. Dalchian clenched his teeth, keeping his back to the melta gunner as Ibriel reattached the final piece of armour with whirrs of a pneumatic fastener. Zorean stood with his helm in his hand, one eyebrow slightly raised, some vague amusement haunting his expression. He said nothing. Saryuz stepped in front of Dalchian again, flexing the digits of his new repair.

'The next prey, Lord Skin-Taker?' Saryuz asked.

'The hunting ground draws near,' Dalchian replied. 'So too does our rightful ascendancy, Saryuz.'

The melta gunner nodded, stepped past Zorean and left without another word. *Mountains climbed and mountains yet to climb*, Dalchian thought, the contempt of his murder-kin weighing upon him. They sorely needed some unity. He hoped that hunting together away from the complications of warband rivalry would provide it.

'The Blades will rise again,' Zorean offered through a skeletal half-smile as the two Night Lords left the armorium.

'We're a long way closer, now we have a ship again,' Dalchian said, biting back his own choler.

'And what of the crew of that ship?' Zorean asked. 'Their loyalty will need securing, too.'

'You think the mortals ignorant to the consequences of infidelity?'

'I think they will try their luck, Skin-Taker.'

Zorean split off towards the quarterdeck, where the Blades had established a makeshift sparring pit, leaving Dalchian to head towards the strategium. The passageway connecting the *Red*'s main arterial to the strategium was not a long one.

Dalchian was halfway down it when the ambush came.

A small canister clattered across the deck plates and choke gas spewed out into the narrow corridor. Dalchian unlooped his chainglaive with practised ease and peered through the fuming morass. His helm was in his arming chamber, so he relied on his genhanced eyes. A sound made him spin around. A volley of gunfire hammered into his back. The noise and impacts could only be bolt rounds. Dropping to the floor, Dalchian turned and wrenched himself towards his ambushers as the rounds crashed over him. Through the swilling gas he saw five mortal crew in environment hoods blasting away. The bolters were jury-rigged sentry guns with knots of cabling where their triggers should be. They were mass-produced things, smaller calibre than Astartes weaponry, but still capable of killing. More importantly, they had been absent from Ibriel's inventory.

Duplicitous little wretches, Dalchian thought. They paused to reload and he leapt to his feet in the acid fog. The mortals scattered down two companionways to either side. Dalchian dived right, flattening one of the crew into the bulkhead with his armoured mass, killing him instantly. He ran the next one through with his glaive as they tried to jump down the grating steps. He tore them back and swung, inertia dragging them from the chainblade and slamming them into the far bulkhead with a fatal crunch. Then he vaulted down the companionway to crush another beneath his boots. He sprinted after the rest.

Unfortunately for the remaining ambushers, they had encountered Zorean at the foot of another companionway. He had suspected what was taking place as soon as he heard the gunfire above, and had come running. He pinned both crew to the bulkhead with his hands, crushing their own bolters into their chests. Unable to move, the crew cried out as the breath was squeezed from them. Dalchian rounded the intersection, chainglaive revving absurdly loud in the tight space.

'Consider your timely advice heeded,' Dalchian said to his second-in-command. 'Let them down.'

Zorean kept the pair pinned for an extra moment, the desire to end their pathetic lives clear in the tilt of his head. He let them fall, snatching their guns from them as they did.

'What shall I do with them, Skin-Taker?'

'Bring them.' Dalchian's fury was a palpable thing. 'We have need of answers.'

'With pleasure, Skin-Taker.' Zorean's grin added sibilance to his already hoarse voice as he cast aside the modified bolters and seized the two mortals, dragging them along. One was unconscious, but the other began to flail and yell. Dalchian spat the residue of rancid choke gas from his mouth before opening his vox-link.

'All Blades, to me.'

Scallen's face told Dalchian all he needed to know. The man screamed a wordless protest as Dagardis dragged him from the command deck. Krutaan and Ang Heltris rounded up all the other bridge crew and fastened them in chains. Across the decks of the *Red*, divisional commanders and petty officers were herded together by the towering, daemonic forms of the Skin-Taker's Blades. The Night Lords were ungentle in their work. Dozens of mortals were cut down for uttering the slightest imprecation. It took nearly two hours, but eventually, every member of the crew above rating rank was packed into the aft magazine, which after the battle was practically empty of its usual point defence ammunition. Over two hundred humans sweated in the space, despite its frigidity.

Such a number demanded an efficient brutality. Dalchian, Zorean, Krutaan and Ang Heltris made their way through the crowd, laying open torsos and tearing off sheets of skin. The crowd filled the cramped space with screams and flowed away from the circling torturers like a gestalt organism, squeezing itself against the bulkheads, pulling the chains that bound them taut against one another. Bones broke, people were crushed in the swell. The other Blades stood like baroque sentinels at the fringes, blasting back the heaving mass of humanity with precise bursts of bolter fire. Blood flowed across the deck plates, splashing and clotting.

And over the whole hideous pogrom blared the artificially amplified voice of Dalchian Rassaq the Skin-Taker.

'Who was involved? Who among you plots? Tell us what you know, and you will be spared.'

Dagardis held Scallen on an overseers' gantry, forcing the slight man to watch the massacre of his comrades. He writhed and squealed and soiled himself, Dagardis' axe, its power field disengaged, resting coolly against his neck. He held out for five minutes, then:

'Please, in Throne's name, STOP! I'll tell you anything! Everything!'

And he did. Upon the gantry with Night Lords standing over him, Scallen poured out the plot to kill the Skin-Taker. He yelled the names of the conspirators, most of them already dead in the horror below. The slaughter and desecration abated as he talked, the surviving crew shaking and weeping and keeping themselves as far away from the vengeful legionaries as they could physically get. One man stood and shouted at Scallen, calling him weak and a traitor. Krutaan grabbed the man by his neck and disembowelled him with slow, deliberate sweeps of his lightning claws, the bladed digits sharp enough for the work without needing their sheaths of crackling energy. Eventually the man stopped screaming.

Scallen howled in misery. Dalchian demanded details of the Imperial fleet – its composition, its order of battle, its captains, and their weaknesses. Scallen overflowed with information, the flood unable to be stemmed now it was underway. He told Dalchian every detail that was asked of him about the Imperial Navy fleet. And then Dalchian asked him of the phantom. Scallen writhed and Dalchian nodded to his Blades. They hewed down mortals, ripping flesh from bones and filling the chamber with screams. Scallen broke. He told Dalchian of the phantom ship. It did not take long, for he knew little.

A ship from the Sol System. It broadcast no ident codes, and could remove itself at will from the augur readouts of the other Imperial vessels. All the Imperial admiral in command of the battle group had said was that it was an envoy vessel of the Adeptus Astra Telepathica.

Dalchian's hearts kept a steady pace, but his mind churned. Scallen told them that the Imperial retribution fleet had mustered at Sigma Velarnum for the warp jump to Uzurmandius, and there it had been joined by a shrouded barque bound for the same system. Scallen was convinced that the vessel had waited at the muster point and timed its translation to coincide with that of the Imperial fleet to better hide from the Chaos forces.

Dalchian knew that this was the very last information Scallen would have divested. The man was empty. Dalchian gestured and Dagardis hewed the *Red*'s most recent commander into pieces, Scallen's lifeblood oozing through the gantry into the mire of gore below.

Over two hundred had entered the aft magazine chamber and just under thirty left it. The Night Lords marched the surviving crew back to their posts in chains, the wretched humans covered in the blood of their fellows and trembling, ashen-faced. The rest of the crew were chained at their stations, the balance of their relative liberty reweighed after the attempt on Dalchian's life. Of the dead from the magazine, the Blades dismembered the corpses and spread them across the ship.

Limbs, skins, heads, entrails: all were mounted on bulkheads and above workstations as a stinking reminder to the crew of the cost of perfidy. Ibriel was tasked with programming wafers for servitor clades with rivet guns and pneumatic bolt-tighteners to carry out most of the work. The tech-priest was deeply unenthusiastic about such a task. He did it, but remained silent and sullen as he did.

Dalchian oversaw the efforts with a distracted air. Somehow, he had known the spectral contact he had seen on the *Torrent of Hatred*'s long-range augur was important. He could not put his finger on how he had known, but his certainty had been immediate and unyielding. Now he had a glimpse of its true nature and he felt vindicated.

An Adeptus Astra Telepathica ship from the Sol System. Its providence begged further questions, and Dalchian hungered to answer them.

The bridge was practically empty of non-lobotomised humans. The systems ticked and whirred away on pre-determined rotations. Servitors mumbled and slurred every now and then. Dalchian had brought Scallen's head with him, and jammed it onto one of the finials surmounting the transept balustrade, where it was visible from every part of the bridge. Scallen's hide would be added to the curtain of trophies hanging from his power pack, the Skin-Taker had decided. For his audacity, if nothing else. Bootsteps sounded behind him, and he recognised them as those of Zorean.

'The *Abjuration* spoiled me, Zor,' Dalchian said. 'That crew was naturalised to its fate, had long acknowledged the dominance of the Legion. These vermin still think of themselves as Imperial military.'

'Understandable, perhaps, given the suddenness of their repurposing?'

'Understandable, yes,' Dalchian admitted. 'But unforgiveable on my part.' There was a long silence.

'That is how some of the Blades see it, no doubt,' Zorean said at length. He seemed loath to give voice to the sedition fomenting within the warband. Dalchian turned to regard the gaunt legionary. They were both splattered with drying blood, their much-repaired armour still a scraped, denuded panoply. They were princes of a shattered regime whose only subjects were now dregs and mutineers. Dalchian could not stem the despair as it filled him to his fingertips. His dark eyes closed against the futility of it all, unable to parse the all-encompassing shadow. A door in the foulest reaches of his mind cracked, a sliver of unlight shining through.

'What do they see, Zorean? Tell me the very worst.'

Zorean looked askance at Dalchian's tone, suspicious. After a moment, he spoke.

'They see you as the one who cast our primacy to the warp-weft. They see you as a spent blade, dulled by a command position of which you are now unworthy. They… they see you spare the lives of Imperials at the expense of our own Legion-kin.'

At this last accusation, Dalchian winced. *Can I deny it?* He could practically hear Krutaan's voice saying the words in his mind.

The Skin-Taker opened his eyes, and his gaze settled on the oculus where the coordinates for the Guelphos moon colonies still ticked gradually closer. There was a pleasing callousness to the runes; an absence of agenda in their winking existence. It was information, nothing more. Data. Dalchian felt the hand of logic reassert its grip on the tiller of his psyche. The foul door closed, reluctantly. Information to guide him towards an enigmatic prey.

A ship from the Sol System.

Dalchian examined the long-range auguries. The Imperial fleet and the Gorelord's alliance were a distant cluster of rune markers. He had a head start, but that did not mean much, and both would come looking for him, he knew. Neither could suffer him to reave the system's backwaters and pose an ever-present threat. In an idealised fiction, Dalchian would have plenty of time to reforge his warband and regain his strength, but the reality was brutally opposite. He wanted the phantom ship. He yearned to trap it and uncover its secrets with a primal avidity, but to do that he needed a more powerful bite. He needed crew and materiel.

And he needed not to be snared by his enemies.

'Take command of the ship, Zor. Find a capable deck crew from the survivors. We raid again in four hours.'

Chapter Six

Guelphos was enormous. Two hundred and eight per cent as massive as the Sol System's Jupiter. Storm bands girded it, striations of green-yellow near the equator gradually blending into turquoise and indigo near the poles. Thousands of moons clustered around it, most collected from the asteroid belt whose orbit overlapped that of the gas giant. Not only would Guelphos' colossal magnetosphere smudge the *Red Galentia*'s signature from passing ships, but there were dozens of Imperial colonies scattered across those moons. Mineworks, refineries and hydrocarbon extractors, all dedicated to the vast task of keeping Forge World Uzurmandius fed with raw materials. Added to that the bastion armouries, void dock workshops and fresh mortal crew, the colonies had much that the Blades required.

Void dock 12/Epsilon, designated *Larel's Haven*, hung above one cratered moonlet like a rusting pitchfork. The tines of its docking piers were empty of all craft and its long boom, comprising mostly cargo space, was nearly full. The magna-haulers were due any cycle now, but Watch-Ensign Edal Baradoz had heard about the enemy ships, so he wasn't surprised the schedules had slipped. *Larel's Haven* did not possess its own astropath. All communications had to come via vox-link from the Administratum citadel on Guelphos Quaternary, and that rock was on the far side of the massive gas giant at that moment. Watch-Ensign Edal Baradoz was not overly concerned. The Adeptus bloody Mechanicus could certainly take care of itself, he knew. The raiders would be gone soon, and the schedule would get back on track.

Baradoz drifted from one side of the oversight bubble to the other, enjoying the lack of simulated gravity. Most of the dock fell within its own artificially generated gravity well, but here at the end of the auspex mast everything floated in microgravity, including whichever operator was on duty. The other dockers told him he was childish, but the novelty had still not waned for Edal Baradoz. The armaglass bubble was four yards across and the cogitator lectern and restraint throne filled most of it. But Edal was a slight figure, and he pushed himself back and forth, back and forth between the fronds of cabling. What in Throne's name else was there to do?

'Larel's Haven *harbour-master, this is the Imperial Navy gunboat* Red Galentia *conveying intent to dock for resupply. Make ready for our approach.'*

Edal blinked and stared at the vox-horn as he drifted.

'Larel's Haven *harbour-master, acknowledge our approach.'*

Edal started like someone brushing against both terminals of a powercell. Flapping to right himself, he fastened the headset over his ears and engaged his vox-tube.

'*Red Galentia*, this is *Larel's Haven*, we acknowledge your approach. Please transmit your particulars for validation.' His heart hammered in his chest. A warship, here! A warship, here? The Naval destroyer's specifications came through as a screed of runes on his viewscreen. As his initial rush of excitement abated, Edal remembered there were protocols for this sort of thing. He dredged his mind for the procedures that had been hammered into him during longshore orientation at the fleet collegium on Guelphos Septenary.

'We see you, *Red Galentia*, please make for docking pier secundus.' Edal racked his memory. An unscheduled warship must always be treated with utmost caution, his old instructor had barked many times. '*Red Galentia*, please be advised that atmospheric sluicing is in effect so boarding gangways will be depressurised.' There was a pause of a few moments.

'*Acknowledged, harbour-master, we'll be sure to hold our breath.*' The vox clicked off.

Edal's pulse throbbed in his ears. He opened a hardline to the dock commandant.

'*What is it, Baradoz?*' Merdal Jai Shin was audibly angry to be so abruptly awoken.

'Enemy inbound, commandant,' Edal coughed.

The pale young sub-lieutenant looked up from her vox-lectern and nodded at Dalchian, who stood at the bridge transept. A smile spread across his face.

'They take the bait,' he said.

'I envy you your imminent sport,' Zorean offered. Dalchian laughed before striding from the bridge.

'Look after the *Red* for me, Zor.'

'Our blades yet thirst, Skin-Taker.'

'Our blades yet thirst.'

Ships never approached straight in. In the event of a power outage or overshoot they would collide with the junction modules of the void dock. The *Red Galentia* came to a dead stop directly above the gap between docking piers primus and secundus. Then, once its position had been confirmed, tiny needles of directional thrust gas gently eased the dagger profile of the destroyer down between the spars. More bursts of attitudinal control and directional thrust flared from gargoyle mouths across the crenellated outer hull. Ever so slowly, the *Red Galentia* stilled, equidistant between the grimy trusses of each pier. Gigantic servo-arms reached out and closed locking jaws around cleats along the flank of the warship, holding it fast. A telescopic gangway extended from pier secundus, its end veering across the *Red Galentia*'s hull buttresses until it found one of the destroyer's air gates. A locator lug engaged with a socket above the air gate, the *clunk* registering through the superstructures of both warship and void dock, and the armoured collar of the gangway screwed tight over the air gate portal.

There was no atmospheric sluicing. The code phrase was used throughout the subsector by Imperial outposts and way stations to establish the presence of pirate raiders. Given the warning code response by the Naval vox-operator, an Administratum security detail of twenty now deployed into the gangway, backed up by five Adeptus Arbites. There was a system-wide border control sub-divisio within the reaches of Uzurmandius, but the garrison was minute, boasting only a dozen or so arbitrators spread thinly across the fragmented civilian outposts. Commandant Jai Shin had been relieved to learn that such a significant Arbites force was on a routine patrol stopover aboard *Larel's Haven*, and had requested their assistance immediately. Boltguns, shotguns, flamers and grenade launchers all levelled at the air gate portal, even before the hard-lock had been confirmed. The Arbites personnel in their black armour deployed portable plasteel barricades, their segments spreading out on clanking pneumatics, and knelt behind them, guns ready.

Flushes of vapour billowed and an indicator rune above the

portal lit up. The gangway echoed to the sound of slides being racked, weapons made ready.

The air gate opened, two door leaves sliding laterally, two more sliding vertically. Dull red light silhouetted a handful of enormous shapes, taller and wider than any baseline human. The shapes of chainswords and bolters hung from their hands and red eyes glowed from their faces.

'Open fire!' the Arbites proctor roared.

The gangway filled with gunfire. Bolts streaked forth, blowing holes in air gate and silhouettes alike. Shotguns crashed, clods of lead punching wide dents and shredding flesh. A frag grenade sailed between the giant silhouettes with admirable precision, filling the air gate with razor shards and sparks. The flamer unit stepped forward and poured burning promethium into the air gate, roasting the towering forms where they stood and making the gangway atmosphere thick with smoke and vaporised condensation.

The figures did not move. The gunfire and shot pounded into them, tearing pieces off and garbing them in flames, but they did not acknowledge the punishment. A chainsword fell as the hand holding it was severed by a bolt round detonation. Gradually, the gunfire abated. The security detail and their Arbites superiors held off, guns lowered, cautious. The enormous figures had still not moved. As the smoke and vapour cleared, thin lines became visible around the huge shapes. The proctor nodded a subordinate forward to investigate. Shotgun tight in their grasp, the arbitrator took careful steps across the gangway deck plates. The hulking forms remained static. As the arbitrator stepped closer, they saw the long-dried wounds gaping in the grey flesh of the figures. They saw the plasteel cabling that held the figures upright, the ends plasma-bonded to the air gate ceiling. Red lights glowed in eye-sockets that had been hollowed out by the strokes of a scalpel. The giants were dead. Cadaverous puppets held aloft by grim rigging. Their weapons were broken and useless. The arbitrator felt a surge of relief and turned to their proctor, taking a breath to call out.

The gangway sheared in half. A crash of explosives rent the metal, and heat and fumes washed over them for a split second. Then everything was sucked from the gangway with a hurricane inbreath. The security detail and the Arbites were torn from the deck and spun out into space in a cloud of sparks and wreckage, smashing into torn plasteel edges as they went. The arbitrator tried to shout in alarm as they spiralled through the debris, but there was no sound and their lungs collapsed suddenly and excruciatingly. Absolute coldness seized them in a vice. The two halves of the gangway reared over them; the last thing they saw as their vision went purple then failed completely.

Dalchian's Blades stood mag-locked to the gangway exterior, waiting out the swaying reverberations of the breaching charge that had torn the structure in two. Vellet put a few void-silenced rounds into some of the flailing Imperials as they drifted away. The marksman could not help himself. Spheres of flash-frozen blood droplets expanded around his victims as they came apart. One of the Administratum troopers wore a rare suit of void-sealed armour and they pounded their limbs against the ebbing rush of expanding atmosphere, the swimming motion all voidfarers hoped never to have to use. Astonishingly, after a few heartbeats the trooper had managed to arrest their drift and began slowly moving back towards the breach. Dagardis stood closest and watched as they came on, inch by furious inch. The Night Lord reached out his hand and the mortal, stupefied with their own terror, grasped for it madly. Dagardis took a firm grip of the mortal's wrist and gently spun them over his head, releasing them to drift directly away from the void-dock and into the unadorned black of space.

The Blades clambered onto the half of the gangway still attached to the void-dock. Boots mag-locked again, they made for the portal that had closed automatically when the gangway was breached. Dalchian carried a small, tracked automaton in his hand. A reconnaissance unit from the *Red*'s breacher contingent. The unit extended a dataspike and engaged with the portal control panel.

'How long to unpick the lock?' Dalchian voxed Ibriel back aboard the destroyer.

'*That will depend upon the… um–*'

'What?'

'*It seems the portal is not locked,*' the tech-priest said in bafflement. '*My lord.*'

'Really?' Λ pause.

'*Indeed.*'

Dalchian shrugged and pressed the rune key on the control panel. The portal slid open and atmosphere blasted from the gap. Dalchian shorted the door controls with a punch, then the Night Lords waded into the torrent. Pieces of cloth and paper whipped past them. More security troopers were in the corridor beyond, arms folded through handrails and hands clutching riveted panelling against the airstream trying to throw them out.

'Knives,' Dalchian voxed. The legionaries advanced, stabbing and slicing at the personnel who were unable to defend themselves and hold on simultaneously. Mortals fell and tumbled towards the portal, blood spattering and flicking in the gale. All the dead and some of the living slid out into space. After a minute or so the rush of atmosphere faltered and stopped, the whistling replaced by the silence of vacuum. Dalchian dropped the breacher automaton unit, feeling it land with a *clunk* through his feet, and the little robot trundled gamely forwards.

The next portals were locked, but that was little hindrance to Ibriel's remotely accessed efforts. More typhoons of venting atmosphere followed as the Blades emptied the void dock of human life. Some mortals in void-armour fought back. Some with lasguns but most with wrenches and hammers. Their resistance was admirable but pathetic.

After three hours, the void dock was nearly empty, and Dalchian stood at the forward port-side air gate, watching pitiful mortals trudge aboard the *Red* in a line, each miserable figure bound to the next with plastek cordage.

'How many?' he asked Qi Umshar, who had directed the enslaving.

'Just over two hundred,' the surgeon replied. 'We found a locked hab-module full of off-duty longshore personnel.'

'Not enough to replace our losses,' Dalchian said. 'But a good start.' A screed of text appeared on his helm display. A list of weapons and ammunition.

'Inventory of the arsenal complete, my lord,' came Saryuz's curt vox-message.

'You have done well,' Dalchian replied. Saryuz severed the link without saying anything further, and Dalchian clenched his fists. Qi Umshar said nothing.

'Ibriel,' Dalchian opened a new vox connection. 'Progress?'

'The last load is aboard,' the tech-priest said. *'My lord.'* Ibriel had descended with his lifter to the void dock cargo bays that had been ratcheted open and begun ferrying goods back to the *Red Galentia* before the assault was even complete.

'Good.' Dalchian looked at Qi Umshar. 'Imperial scum or the Gorelord's lapdogs could be on us any moment. Let us not tempt fate any longer.'

'Aye, lord.'

The *Red* thrust hard forward, tearing free of the dock's coupling arms and forcing its ploughshare bow through the superstructure.

The void dock crumpled like paper, its trident berthing spars folding and snapping. Fire bloomed, and as the *Red* pushed through, the dock's vox-mast splintered off and began to slowly spin away, leaving Edal Baradoz, the last surviving crew member of *Larel's Haven*, pressed horrified against the armaglass of the oversight bubble at the mast's end.

Master of Executions Glausius and his fellow Crimson Slaughter had played their part faultlessly. Their bodies remained strung up in the air gate, blasted and abused by their short service as decoys. The destruction of the gangway had damaged the air gate's outer seal, so Dalchian left the corpses where they hung, exposed to the void.

The slaves were put to work and mortal crew were redistributed. Some of the humans did a great deal of screaming and crying, but the senior ranks of the *Red* recognised the value of new labour and fresh supplies, so cooperativeness grew by degrees. Most of the void dock's cargo was plasteel stock and promethium products bound for Uzurmandius' forge complexes, as well as basic mechanical and electrical components, oils and lubricants, and stacks of synthetic and reconstituted foodstuffs. Ibriel tasked clades of servitors with further ship repairs and engaged in the thankless task of fabricating replacement weapon parts and bespoke alterations to the Blades' power armour. The work was not so arduous, however, that the tech-priest had no time to construct some alterations to his own mechanical form. Within just hours of the raid Ibriel had created a mollusc-like shell for himself that fitted his entire cache of tech-lore mem-stacks within it. He declared himself off limits for a quarter cycle as he reconfigured himself, data-embedding the mem-stacks into his own mechacortical architecture.

On the bridge, there had clearly been a fatal disagreement. More of the deck crew were absent, and fresh blood was drying on the grating. Dalchian raised an eyebrow at Zorean.

'Trouble?' Dalchian asked.

'Nothing beyond my capacity to address.'

'Good.' Dalchian looked around the mortals. Silent faces hung in despondency, hunger showing in the prominence of their bones. 'Loyalty is such a curious thing,' he mused aloud, directing his voice across their pits and alcoves. One mortal flashed a wide-eyed, pleading glance up at him before looking back down to his viewscreens. Zorean growled.

'So it is, Skin-Taker,' the gaunt Night Lord husked. 'But I have secured theirs beyond doubt.'

Two more void docks and a crew exchange relay fell victim to the Blades' predations over the following standard day. Threading through the orbital tracks of Guelphos' abundant satellites was a challenge, especially given the auspex disruption inflicted by the huge body's magnetic eccentricities, but each prize surrendered more and more valuable resources, and the crew exchange relay filled every empty post left on the *Red Galentia*. Dalchian had deeply enjoyed using the destroyer's lance turrets to sever the colossal chains holding the relay in formation with two binary lumpen moonlets. As the spired structure pinwheeled away, its lights dimmed and the Night Lords went to work. Over a thousand souls, including forty children. Dalchian harboured a dream of returning his Blades to their full complement, and some of the children were of age to begin the elevation process. But as it was, he had hardly enough resources to keep his pitiful remnant in the fight, let alone that to meet the material requirements of fresh recruitment. Bitterly, he set his aspiration aside and all the mortals were put to work. Ibriel's servitors ceaselessly forged chains and manacles for the new arrivals, while the tech-priest continued to modify his cargo lifter until it bore little resemblance to the craft it had once been. The *Red* was almost back to full operations, minus the frustrating lack of a Navigator, but the Blades had more potency than any time since their betrayal on Uzurmandius.

And Dalchian could breathe.

Krutaan came to him after the exchange relay raid. Dalchian had expected that he would, sooner or later. He was leaning over the mahogany table in the ward room, tallying manifests of plunder from the dataslates spread before him when the claw leader ghosted in.

'When do we rejoin battle, Lord Skin-Taker?'

Guelphos had made long-range auguries patchy at best, but fragments had still come through to them. The Chaos alliance held and running battles between them and the Imperial flotilla were continuous. It had become an attritional back and forth. Felid and rodent. Such contests were laced with risk.

'Our raiding bears fruit. These colonies are rich. You wish to leave the rest unharvested?'

'We have greater than we need, and not the capacity for more.' A sound point of which Dalchian was acutely aware. 'The screams of murdered Imperials take up no space but are a hundredfold more valuable to harvest.'

Dalchian suppressed a sigh. *There speaks that damned berserker in you.* Krutaan's eyes, ever intense, bored into him from beneath scarred lids. The claw leader's breath *shushed* gently in and out of his rebreather unit.

'There are many ways to hurt the Imperium,' Dalchian said quietly, mind drawn inexorably back to the idea, the suggestion, of the phantom ship. Krutaan's eyes darkened and his brow twisted in a sneer, misunderstanding his lord's words.

'These tiny way stations will die unnoticed. Even once the mewling Throne-lovers realise they're gone, they will simply ship in more resources. More people. This hunt is unworthy!'

Dalchian was about to clarify what he meant when klaxons began to bray and ochre lumens flashed. Both Night Lords looked up at the sounds.

'Skin-Taker,' came Zorean's voice over the vox. *'The cursed Imperials have found us.'*

'I'm on my way.' They both left the ward room and made for the bridge, Krutaan's relish clear in the crease of his eyes.

'Perhaps, now the fight has found us, you will choose to regain a measure of the respect of which you demand too little.'

Dalchian stopped. 'Meaning?'

'Even Zorean should call you *lord*.' Krutaan threw the words over his shoulder as he stalked off. After several long moments Dalchian started again on his own way to the bridge, and in his mind a familiar doorway cracked open once more.

The Imperial patrol had dogged the trail of blood and horror left by the Night Lords. Amid the technical disruption of Guelphos' sphere of influence, it had been arduous work plotting the next likely victim and drawing any information from the wider colonial directorate. The patrol had waited in vain twice for a heretic raid that never came, gambling on their information and losing. But, at last, their diligence had paid off.

The *Vizier of Arandeep* led the patrol, the light cruiser's macrocannon decks forming the backbone of the patrol's offensive bite, supported by the interceptor complement and plasma batteries of the frigate *Prideful*. The two formidable ships were escorted by a pair of ancient but effective destroyers, each with the capacity to deliver melta torpedoes with unerring precision at short range.

The Imperial ships were fourteen thousand miles away and closing fast. Dalchian analysed the tactical hololith displaying the patrol's identities. The vessel wore their colours proudly and did not baulk from broadcasting their capabilities. Capabilities that were wretchedly in excess of anything the *Red* could bring to bear. If the fight started, Dalchian knew, then it could only end in the *Red*'s destruction and the death of all his hopes.

'I shall prepare the Blades for boarding,' Krutaan growled and made to leave the bridge.

'No.' Dalchian stared at the hololith.

'What are your orders, Skin-Taker?' Zorean asked.

'Lord.'

'What?'

'I am your *Lord* Skin-Taker, Zorean.'

There was a weighted moment. Zorean narrowed his eyes, calculating. Krutaan's desperation to fight dripped from him. Dalchian could almost see the forking paths before him, the expectations of his warriors pulling at him, trying to drag him into different futures.

'Generatorium,' Dalchian called. 'Direct as much power as you can to the engines. Get us far, far away. I want these starch-collared bastards left with nothing but our plasma trail.'

'Aye, lord,' one of the mortals replied.

'No,' Krutaan breathed.

'Return to your posts,' Dalchian ordered. 'I have the bridge.'

'No!' Krutaan roared. 'We will not run again! I will not have it.'

'Return to your post.'

The *Red Galentia* shifted under them. Plasma coursed through its systems, feeding the vast engines at the stern. Vibrations rattled teeth in their sockets as the ship accelerated away from the Imperial patrol.

Krutaan howled his fury as he charged.

Dalchian brought his chainglaive up just in time to turn aside Krutaan's first lightning claw, then managed to duck the second. Krutaan recovered immediately and brought both his sets of energised blades raking down from above. Disruption fields parted Dalchian's ceramite, but the armour robbed force from the blow. The Skin-Taker kicked out, sending Krutaan reeling.

'There is no choice here, Krutaan.'

'Always there is a choice, and always you choose cravenness!' Krutaan tensed and sprang, colliding shoulder first with Dalchian's midriff. He raked his claws across the Skin-Taker's back, but Dalchian pinned one arm under his and brought the chainglaive down onto it. Krutaan blocked with his free arm, and whirring teeth tore loose and ricocheted as the chain track ground against the keen-edged blades. The fighters crashed apart, turning and rebalancing. Some of the mortal deck crew cowered behind their lecterns or in their pits, the violence of two Chaos Space Marines in close combat utterly overwhelming their senses. The bridge stank of overworked fibre bundles and the fleshy musk of transhuman exertion.

The two Night Lords connected again with a knell of armoured bulk, chainglaive spinning and slashing, lightning claws leaving scratch-mark afterimages on the retinas of anyone misfortunate enough to watch.

'Our enemy are *there*!' Krutaan's voice cracked a little with desperation. Dalchian might have felt a sliver of pity then, but countering Krutaan's assault took every iota of his concentration. 'What is our purpose, but to inflict death upon them?'

'And die in turn?'

'If that is our fate!'

Krutaan knocked Dalchian to the deck and fell upon him, claws outstretched. Dalchian rolled aside at the last instant and Krutaan's claws sank into the plasteel plating. Dalchian sprang up, kicked Krutaan in the side and spun his glaive into a downward grip. Krutaan withdrew his claws and snatched his legs, flipping himself upright in a smooth motion. Dalchian brought his toothed blade up, but Krutaan read the hesitation and kicked the glaive away.

'If you truly lead this band, Dalchian, then I must die. For else I shall kill you and take command myself!'

'Two-score Blades have I lost already, Krutaan. I do not wish to lose another.'

'*Weakness!*' Krutaan screamed. 'The cursed False Emperor rotting on his liar's chair, the Great Powers, the galaxy itself – none of these things care what you wish!' Spittle began to ooze from his rebreather as he flexed his claws, stance low. 'Be lord or be slave. Or be nothing, Dalchian.' Krutaan swept in again and for an instant Dalchian beheld a face at the door ajar in his mind. A grinning face.

He smashed Krutaan's attack away, leaning into the charge. With a low sweep he tripped the claw leader, who tucked as he fell so he could roll away. But Dalchian whirled his glaive two-handed and drove it like a spear into Krutaan's back. He heaved down upon it. The teeth scraped and juddered as they pierced armour, flesh, bone and deck plating.

Pinned face down, Krutaan slashed behind him. Dalchian stood on one of the claws, using all his weight to cease its flailing. The Skin-Taker drew a flaying knife from his belt and, holding it with both hands, pushed it through the soft armour joint at Krutaan's elbow and sawed through the tendons of the joint. Krutaan made no sound but he still fought, kicking and swinging his other arm. With great deliberation, Dalchian repeated the process on the other side, and with that, Krutaan fell still.

The claw leader's breath was astonishingly calm through the dented rebreather. He kept his eyes open and focused as Dalchian placed an armoured boot on the back of his head and tore the chainglaive free from his back.

'I am your *Lord*,' Dalchian said. 'Skin-Taker.'

He severed Krutaan's head with one blow, and in the same moment Dalchian heard the door in his mind slam shut.

Dalchian could not remember Saryuz, Qi Umshar, or any of the others arriving on the bridge during his fight. He only noticed them when he stood up, holding Krutaan's open-eyed head in one hand and his chainglaive in the other.

'Know this,' he said at length. 'The price of mutiny.'

CHAPTER SEVEN

Qi Umshar embalmed Krutaan on the ward room table at Dalchian's request. The dead Night Lord's progenoids were removed efficiently and without ceremony, and then Dalchian took lone vigil, sending all others away and placing Zorean in command of the ship. The Skin-Taker showed no anguish. He stared at the dead; he stood in silence; he turned over thought after thought in his mind.

He felt relief to be rid of a mutineer, but the feeling was a distant one. A practical conciliation trying and failing to supersede the conflict in his hearts. Krutaan had been a supreme warrior, capable of murder and horror the likes of which some VIII legionaries would hunt and die and never have attained. But he was broken. The Gorelord's treachery and then the feckless butchery of his bloodhounds had unmade Krutaan's nature as a Night Lord, cast him as some unthinking animal, blinded to the need of nuance by undiluted rage. No, Dalchian did not mourn the Krutaan he had killed, but the Krutaan that

Thelissicus had robbed him of. The death had served some purpose, though, and that gladdened him. The Blades had looked upon him with the light of renewed respect in their eyes. Even Saryuz, who would resent the killing of his comrade, would recognise the inevitable power that Dalchian Rassaq the Skin-Taker still possessed. *Your death serves the Blades,* he told Krutaan in his mind. *Your death paves the way for us to be stronger, just as you rightly demanded.*

After a time, he took up Krutaan's left lightning claw and slowly, deliberately removed it from the corpse's armour. Disengaging his own gauntlet, Dalchian slid his hand within the claw assembly, its fibre bundles locking on to those of his own armour instantly. It felt like someone else's weapon, but it also felt exactly right that he should wield it. After all, had he not always been told the Night Haunter himself favoured such blades?

Dalchian felt the heritage of his Legion as a brittle thing, then. *What do I truly know of the primarch? What do I know of his legacy beyond that poured into me by my own old masters?* He flexed the bladed fingers, acclimatising to the new wargear. *Am I as blind and hollow as the deluded Imperial herds? Perhaps Krutaan was right about the rest, and all we can do is dash ourselves against the guns of the Imperium. What is it that I fight for?*

The phantom ship. The resolve flared and Dalchian curled the claw fingers together, residual power in them sparking at the contact. *I must discern its nature,* he thought. *A ship capable of such stealth and speed! The havoc I could wreak, but I must know what it is I hunt.* The claw sparked again, and Dalchian felt something in his mind shift. All his doubts disappeared beneath a deluge of insight as he realised what the phantom must be. The only thing it *could* be.

Scallen had been told it was an Adeptus Astra Telepathica envoy.

That arm of the festering Imperial bureaucracy that portioned out humanity's psykers among the branches of the Corpse-Emperor's domain. Be they battle-psykers of the Astra Militarum hordes, glorified vox-casters the Imperium called astropaths that sent messages back and forth across the galaxy, or the countless uncontrollable mutants that they fed to the Golden Liar himself to keep his immaterial beacon shining in the warp. Such an institution needed a constant supply of raw psykers to meet their vast need, and rumours of Black Ships plying the interplanetary routes collecting a tithe of human mutants were as old as the Imperium itself.

A Black Ship.

An unseen vessel, faster than any warship, full of psykers of incalculable collective value, with unfettered access to a million Imperial worlds. The implications of his revelation stunned Dalchian to stillness. There were no more doubts in his mind. There was no other path for him, other than the hunting of this prey.

Dalchian went to the shuttle bay where Ibriel made his lair. The tech-priest loomed in his new form, his mechadendrites animated with a newfound prehensility. Ibriel was making yet more adjustments to his craft and his bulk swayed within the hold. Dalchian stepped up the ramp into the vessel. He was about to ask a question when something caught his eye. Tucked in a stasis alcove was the casket of Crimson Slaughter progenoids he had placed in Qi Umshar's care. As he gazed across the storage racks, he saw a variety of the most important apothecarion gear neatly stowed.

'Why do you have that?' Dalchian asked. Ibriel's hands continued disconnecting and reconnecting cables in the bulkhead, but his cowled head rotated completely around to regard the Night Lord and the object of his question.

'Qi Umshar is upgrading some stasis systems and has requested that I keep safe the most critically important components until the work is done.'

Dalchian nodded, remembering the surgeon-Apothecary mentioning such an upgrade.

'Well, make sure you do keep them safe.'

'That is a redundant repetition of Qi Umshar's request… my lord.'

'No. It's my order.'

'Acknowledged.' Ibriel bowed his reversed head. It was a curious sight. 'Have you come with a query?'

'I have.' Dalchian passed a gaze across Ibriel's spiral shell of bronze and ebon. 'I wonder if, in your capacious new repository, you might have the means of helping me find something that wants not to be found?'

Ibriel's lenses spun and whirred. 'I deduce you wish to seek the phantom ship the late Captain Scallen spoke about.'

'Not seek. Seize.'

'Acknowledged.' Ibriel shifted his bulk, closing the access panel in the bulkhead as he did so and sliding into the pilot throne of the lifter. His head never stopped looking directly at Dalchian. 'There is a sixty-six per cent probability that applicable data might be found within one or more of my ancillary mem-stacks.'

'Start cogitating.'

'Acknowledged.'

As Dalchian stepped off the lifter's cargo ramp, a scrambled vox-transmission shrieked in his helm. His brow creased and he blink-clicked to try and clear the signal. When another discordant burst of static sounded, Dalchian turned back to Ibriel to demand assistance, but before he could speak the shuttle bay door began to open.

With a thought, Dalchian activated the mag-locks in his boots, fixing him to the hangar deck. Atmosphere screamed through the widening sliver at the base of the door and unsecured detritus bounced across the bay floor. Ibriel's hands were a blur over several tethered dataslates as he fought to access the ship systems.

'I cannot close the door,' Ibriel squawked. 'I shall attempt the atmospheric containment field.'

Abruptly the storm deadened as a film of transparent energy stuttered to life across the bay entrance. The door continued its grinding ascent.

'Zorean,' Dalchian called over the vox. 'What in the Eye's name is happening?'

There was no response. A shape was resolving in the darkness beyond the containment field, and Dalchian felt a lurch in his guts. He blink-clicked his new lightning claw to life as he stalked towards the opening. The bay door completed its yawning with a *clang*. On bursts of vector thrust, a Thunderhawk gunship in black-and-turquoise livery loomed through the containment field, only its armoured nose fitting into the tiny space. The assault ramp lowered and thirteen figures marched down it, one at the fore and the other twelve in perfect lockstep behind. Their power armour was the same gloss black and turquoise as their gunship. They came to a halt and the figure at the front stepped forward. The Chaos Space Marine wore a long robe of crimson over his armour and leant on the icon-topped staff of a sorcerer. His dark face was bearded and his cranium was scattered with crystalline implants. Leil Jathok, sorcerer lord of the Abyssal Kindred warband, smiled beneficently and spoke with a deep rumble.

'I claim this vessel in the name of the Gorelord Thelissicus.'

Chapter Eight

Dalchian had not risen to command his Blades by throwing himself against insurmountable odds. Indeed, that very trait seemed to have stood him in poor stead with his own legionaries of late. So, as the sorcerer Jathok strode casually onto Dalchian's ship with an entourage of warriors and claimed it for the Gorelord, Dalchian's incisive notion of when to fight and when to wait for the right moment was the only fragile dam holding back his tectonic rage. It took him several moments before he trusted himself to speak.

'How did you get on my ship?' Dalchian growled. Jathok looked around, the cables of his cranial implants twisting and creaking.

'Through the shuttle bay door, Skin-Taker,' he said in a tone that conveyed worry for Dalchian's state of mind.

Dalchian nearly flew at him then. Fury bubbled in the Night Lord's veins. *Insolent filth.* There was a clanking whine from the ramp of Ibriel's lifter, and they both turned to see the tech-priest, who had deployed an enormous gun barrel from his shell-form and was aiming it firmly in Jathok's direction. From the crackling fizz of its ready state Dalchian guessed it was some sort of rad weapon. *Where did he get that?*

'My lord surely poses the interrogative, by what means did you initiate the opening sequence of said door, and, undoubtedly, how has your vessel converged upon our own without triggering our proximity augurs? Is that correct… my lord?'

'Close enough.'

The sorcerer's smile slipped on sight of the tech-priest's armament. 'You may kill me, machine-man, but my bodyguard would tear you and your lord to pieces.'

'A hypothesis I would gladly test.'

'Just answer the question, witch,' Dalchian said.

The sorcerer gave Ibriel a lingering look before turning his head back to Dalchian.

'Sedition,' he said simply. 'One of your Night Lords invited us.' He waited a heartbeat for Dalchian to assimilate the information. 'He made all the arrangements for your usurpation, Skin-Taker. Perhaps you have an inkling?'

The revelation that one of the Blades had orchestrated Dalchian's downfall from afar was a difficult tonic to swallow. Had it been Krutaan in anticipation of his own death? Dalchian considered killing Jathok and forsaking the situation entirely. Perhaps the Abyssal Kindred could be strong-armed into his service?

That was a folly, and he knew it as soon as the thought occurred, but it made him take a second look at the sorcerer's guardians, still in rigid formation at the foot of the Thunderhawk's ramp. Twelve warriors in the gloss-black and deep turquoise of their warband. Their armour was ancient, far more so than Dalchian's own, and what he had first perceived as the horns so common on the helms of Chaos Space Marines were in fact tall crests, barred ebon and jade. Tabards the colour of dried blood creased across their fronts, mad iconography and words of twisting scripture filling every inch of the ragged, stained cloth. He knew their shape, but had to dredge the name from distant memory.

Rubricae.

His brow creased. *Puppet automatons of the exile?* He knew the myths better than any Imperial herd-creature, and had met veterans of the Long War in his time who told unbelievable tales of a unified humanity and more familiar tales of broken promises. Ahriman, that was his name. The exile. *Where did Jathok hijack these walking phantoms?*

'I safeguard many secrets,' the sorcerer said archly, seeming to read his mind. Dalchian sneered and his dislike of sorcerers, nominally considerable, grew further. Without warning, his helm-vox started working again, erupting into garbled voices.

'…just marched straight in!'

'…another squad in the aft air gate, deck fifteen…'

'…frigate holding formation with weapons primed…'

'…caught like a bilge-rat in a snare.'

The voices belonged both to Blades and newly commissioned crew all across the *Red Galentia*. Without a shot being fired the Abyssal Kindred had taken the destroyer that Dalchian had worked so hard to make his own. New vitriol surged. Could this be the doing of Krutaan? A final insult to the lord he wanted dead? The lightning claw around his left hand twitched and Dalchian wanted to tear it off. Krutaan's hatred of him had been absolute, in the end, but the dead legionary had worn his hatred openly. This stank of scheming whispers. Dalchian regretted never revisiting Ibriel's secret datalogs.

'My new bridge, Skin-Taker?' the sorcerer rumbled.

With clenched teeth, Dalchian turned and stomped towards the hangar portal. Jathok followed and the Rubricae fell neatly into files behind him as they went. Ibriel withdrew into his lifter, pointedly raising and locking the ramp from within.

The way to the bridge seemed tremendously long. Several times he was close to fighting, the nihilistic core of him seeping into his thoughts and almost convincing him he may as well. What could possibly come after this? Thelissicus would kill him and his remnant Blades for attacking the Crimson Slaughter ship. Dalchian knew he was doomed, so why did he go along?

'Why don't you just kill me?'

'The Gorelord has demanded you captured hale to face his judgement. If I'm honest, I'm surprised you haven't fought tooth and claw like the animal you are.'

'This animal uses every weapon available to him.'

'Most wise.'

'Don't mock me, witch.'

Dalchian could sense Jathok smiling behind him, but the sorcerer said nothing more. *Most wise.*

The rest of the Blades had been gathered in the strategium and were being guarded by a score of Abyssal Kindred, cramming the small chamber with spiked armour and bared teeth. These were not Rubricae but warriors of flesh and blood, and there had clearly been more than one fight. Several of Jathok's Kindred sported wounds and damaged plate, and both Dagardis and Saryuz were bloodied. Dalchian found it curious to see Saryuz, Krutaan's closest confidante, among those who had resisted the boarders.

'We are betrayed,' Qi Umshar hissed. 'Again.'

Dalchian said nothing as he passed them by. Not all his Blades were present, and a feeling of disjointedness was stealing over him.

He entered the bridge, where more Abyssal Kindred stood, weapons drawn. *Warp's spit, how many warriors does the cur have?* Dalchian threaded between them until he came to the command throne and its occupant, and Dalchian looked him dead in the eye.

'Our future is secured, Skin-Taker.' Zorean smiled through grey teeth as he spoke. Dalchian stood in silence for a long moment.

'You forfeit us to our enemies.'

'I deliver my murder-kin from your dismal clutches, Skin-Taker.'

'And this is the manner you choose?'

'Deception is a legitimate strategy. Our very existence is at stake.' Zorean grinned. It was the happiest Dalchian had ever seen him. 'You have bled us dry and cast us to the wind. New alliances had to be made, a new path beaten. For the Blades.'

'For the Blades?' Dalchian whispered. Curiously he felt no urge to strike Zorean. Fury, yes. Wrath. Abhorrence to be betrayed by his own Legion kin. But no violence sprang forth from him. Zorean stood before him and Dalchian perceived in him not the pride of an artful murderer or the joy of inflicting terror on a pathetic mortal soul, unable to defend itself. Instead Dalchian saw preening self-aggrandisement. No harm Dalchian could visit upon this turncoat could make him lesser or hollower than his own, gutless contrivance.

'Lord Zorean has been a most assiduous negotiator,' Jathok purred. 'Any of your band that choose to may submit themselves alongside you.' Jathok was beaming at the notion. 'All else, this ship included, go with him.'

'*Lord* Zorean?' Now it was Dalchian's turn to grin. 'Lord of whom?'

'The Blades, Skin-Taker,' Zorean sighed as if indulging the idiot questions of an infant. Dalchian nodded slowly, equitably. Then he turned and picked his way back through the Abyssal Kindred and off the bridge.

'Let us see, *Lord* Zorean,' he said as he left.

The rest of the Blades were still on their knees, the weapons of their captors hovering, promising a swift and terminal retribution to any who might seek escape. Dalchian glared at the Kindred, warp-touched and swaddled in arcane scripture.

'Your lord extends me the courtesy,' he roared, 'that my loyal murder-kin may remain by my side.' He turned his gaze down at the beaten, excoriated, pathetic survivors of his once mighty warband. The unhappy few of his remnant Blades. 'This choice is before you, then, sons of the Night Haunter. Submit yourself to bondage with me, the lord to whom you owe your oaths. He but for whose efforts none of you would now live, all having been rent by the blow of treachery. He but for whose conspiracy none of you would have taken a ship of your own again, as we have done even in our weakest state. He but for whose bitter dedication your very kinship as legionaries would be sundered thrice over.

'Submit yourself to bondage with me, and remain my Blades, keen and deadly.' He held up Krutaan's claw, grinding the digits together in a razor fist. 'Or pledge fealty to Zorean, who, amidst the agonies of our rebirth, abandons us to seek his own regard among daemon-lovers and the prideless.'

The newly anointed Lord Zorean stood in the portal to the strategium. Two Abyssal Kindred flanked him, emphasising his newly unveiled allegiance. In the silence following Dalchian's ultimatum he began to clap. Dalchian looked only at his warriors as the traitor mocked his earnestness.

'They are wise, Skin-Taker,' Zorean husked. 'They will–'

'Silence,' Dalchian whispered. Zorean went silent, seemingly surprising himself.

Steady and logical, Qi Umshar did not move his head as his eyes flicked between Dalchian and Zorean from where he knelt. Saryuz stared at the deck plating, the working of his mind almost audible. Most of the others looked straight ahead in consideration. Dalchian expected to feel trepidation, an angst for what his warriors may decide. He expected to see the paths branching before him once more as he had done prior to killing Krutaan. Surprisingly, he beheld no forks in the road, only the inevitability of fate unseen. He felt no trepidation. He felt free.

At length, Dagardis stood, tense muscles cracking, bloodied face sneering. Slowly, he clomped over to Zorean and faced the self-appointed lord. Dagardis opened his mouth, but instead of speaking he hawked a rope of bloody slime at Zorean's feet before turning and coming to stand beside Dalchian. Ang Heltris snorted with laughter and came to stand by Dalchian as well. Qi Umshar stood, nodded something like an apology at Zorean, and likewise aligned himself with the Skin-Taker. Keth Naa and Vellet looked at one another as they stood and, coming to some unspoken agreement, slid beside Dagardis and Qi Umshar. Zhikarga growled to himself, bronze helm wheeling from Dalchian to Zorean and back. With a grunt of frustration, he stepped towards Dalchian's group.

'The unwise or the unworthy,' he snarled. 'You, Lord Skin-Taker, are the least of those two evils.'

Dalchian accepted the conditional support with a nod. No other could hold him to account more stringently than himself now. Zhikarga would learn the rightness of his choice in time. Only Saryuz was left. Krutaan's old ally stood and flexed the fingers of a damaged gauntlet.

'Krutaan demanded strength,' he said. 'Krutaan demanded that the lord of the Blades act as one befitting the title.' Saryuz threw a dark gaze at Zorean. 'The wind of fortune has folded you like a tower of cards, *Lord* Zorean. Krutaan defied the Skin-Taker openly and was defeated. For the basest coin you sell your own warband – your own *Legion*!' Saryuz turned a vicious look at Dalchian. 'Your flaws are manifold, Skin-Taker, but of pride and shame?' He turned again to Zorean. 'You have neither.'

With that he took his place beside his murder-kin, and Zorean stood alone. He stared at the warriors whose loyalty he had presumed would pass to him. Slowly the taut skin of his face turned into a petulant grimace.

'You mindless ingrates!' he spat. 'I hand you the ship we fought for and the prospect of winning back all that we lost – the prospect of murder and plunder beneath a mighty banner! What madness possesses you? It was the Skin-Taker who nearly ended us!'

'It was treachery that nearly ended us,' Dagardis grunted. 'You conniving bastard.'

'Ironic, wouldn't you say?' Ang Heltris asked lightly.

Zorean's features twisted even more and his dark eyes flitted as he fought to comprehend the scale of his misjudgement. 'Get off my ship,' he said at last before turning and skulking back to his lonely command throne. Dalchian's eyes bored into his back as he left.

'Our blades yet thirst,' the Skin-Taker uttered, lip curling.

The Abyssal Kindred were the breed of Chaos Space Marines that Dalchian had learned to loathe. Their flagship, the *Ikhtheos*, was filled with the malign esoterica of warp worship. Nauseating presences slithered through the plasteel of the vessel's superstructure. Incense lingered in noxious wisps and devotional scripture had been etched into every stanchion, every bulkhead, every deck plate. Tapestries depicted scenes and beings whose form, while clearly illustrated, defied rational interpretation. And every inch of the hideous warship whispered and promised and teased. Dalchian was continually dismissing the sensation that someone was standing directly behind him, sighing and grinning.

Leil Jathok's warriors relieved the Blades of their weaponry. Ang Heltris fixed the Abyssal Kindred with the burning gaze of his skull-helm as he laboriously unscrewed the prosthetic blade that replaced his amputated hand, dropping it to the deck contemptuously. Dalchian made a note of the obvious fury bleeding from the knifeman, usually so cold and calculating. Ang Heltris had wanted to fight. So had Dagardis and Saryuz. Dalchian kept them on a tight leash, though. The Abyssal Kindred were a potent band, and Dalchian had counted at least fifty separate warriors, with no doubt more going unseen. His remnant Blades would fight well and die quickly against such odds. Dalchian was enamoured of unfair fights, but only those in his favour. All else demanded patience. And cunning.

The line warriors of the Kindred carried themselves like monks, heads down, voices chanting. They looked like any other renegade Dalchian had seen, armour banded with thorny metal, helms decorated with horns or barbs, but they reeked of warpcraft. Unseeable daemon-spoor billowed in their wake, and the Blades instinctively kept a ready distance. They were marched to a brig on the starboard flank of the *Ikhtheos*. The cage was brutally strong, designed and forged to hold transhumans in check. If they tried to break out of it they would only break themselves, Dalchian knew. He kept the thought to himself. The sting of Zorean's betrayal was potent, and sharing his mind openly was not a practice he felt inclined to repeat. Perhaps the need for confidantes and naysayers was beneath a lord of Chaos Space Marines after all.

'You,' he barked at the studded helm of one of the Abyssal Kindred who guarded them. 'Bring your master. I will speak with him.'

'He is at prayer, my Lord Skin-Taker,' the warrior replied, respectfully enough. The Blades snorted in derision from behind Dalchian and he held up a gauntlet to quieten them, suppressing his own scorn.

'Lord Jathok's adjutant, then,' he hissed.

'I will convey your wishes to the exalted Endagur,' the warrior conceded, his helm clicking as he opened a vox-link. After a few moments and a few more clicks, he addressed Dalchian again. 'The exalted Endagur will attend you.'

Dalchian did not deign to speak further, turning his back on the guard.

The Blades shuffled like penned vultures, looking at one another, at the bars of their cage or simply at nothing at all. They chafed against the physical confinement. Predators in a too-small net. Saryuz fixed Dalchian with the scarlet glow of his eye-lenses.

'Is this what Krutaan died for?' the gunner said over the vox. All the Blades heard, and deathly stillness fell. 'For us to languish as prisoners, once again?'

'Krutaan died for his mutiny,' Dalchian replied, his meaning inescapably clear. Ice-cold rage filled his mind and hearts. Breaths, sawing through a damaged rebreather, echoed in Dalchian's ear. He knew it was a sound only he could hear. The breaths began to laugh softly. Dalchian felt the claw of Krutaan throbbing with bloodlust, even though he did not wear it. He sensed the weapon nearby, the dislocation of the feeling a new one for him.

'Krutaan betrayed the Skin-Taker,' Dagardis said, interposing himself between Dalchian and Saryuz. 'Just like Zorean did.'

'You condemn them,' Saryuz hissed at the axe wielder. 'Why? Why should they find contentment in Skin-Taker's service?' The bitterness dripped from him.

'Because the Skin-Taker freed us from the Gorelord's clutches and won us a ship,' Dagardis said matter-of-factly. 'Because he had the foresight to negotiate with our treacherous allies and buy us time, rather than wasting our lives in a doomed attempt at vengeance. Because the Skin-Taker keeps us feebly alive rather than gloriously dead. Shall I go on?'

Dalchian stood motionless. He had come to accept Dagardis' easy loyalty, though in truth he had never understood it. But the axeman spoke facts, and Dalchian saw the truth of them, too. It gave his hunger for redemption a keen new edge.

'Skin-Taker may be the death of us,' Saryuz retorted, his prior confident rebelliousness knocked.

'Or our salvation,' Ang Heltris added. 'The *Torrent* was a bigger ship than this, and the Crimson Slaughter far more numerous than these Abyssal Kindred.'

Dalchian knew the guards would be watching, knowing some disagreement took place. For all that he resented Saryuz's discontent, he was thankful the gunner had challenged him over the vox-net and that the Abyssal Kindred could not hear their words.

'How would you hunt a spire-bat, Saryuz?' Dalchian asked, the unexpected question derailing the competing egos as he knew it would. Saryuz thought the question through and immediately recognised the point Dalchian sought to make. Slowly, reluctantly, Saryuz answered.

'Discern what it has an appetite for,' he said. 'Bait an isolated nook within its hunting range, and wait.'

'Just so.' Dalchian allowed his smile to be heard over the vox. 'You will find contentment in my service, Saryuz. Of that I am certain.'

Bootsteps sounded and Dalchian turned his back on his Blades who, thankfully, returned to sullen silence as two Abyssal Kindred strode into the brig.

The exalted champion Endagur was as tall as Saryuz and clad in gloss-black and pearlescent turquoise armour. Silver filigree edged every plate, a rack of ossuary trophies surmounted his purring power pack, and a long broadsword was sheathed at his waist. But none of these things were his most noticeable feature. Endagur's face stopped at the bridge of his nose, the lower portion utterly absent, leaving a raw, knotted gape of flesh that tapered sharply to his neck, where the open end of his trachea bubbled and sighed. Above the horrific wound were sharp, calculating eyes of deep blue and a cranium flecked with auburn stubble. The other Abyssal Kindred warrior wore a horn-crested helm and seemed to speak Endagur's thoughts for him, the champion remaining understandably silent.

'You requested the presence of exalted champion Endagur?' Horn-helm said. Dalchian looked only at the half-faced champion as he replied.

'You imprison my Blades like cattle,' he said. 'You have taken our ship and our weapons. Release us from this unnecessary confinement.'

'For you to steal a craft from our hangar deck and flee?' Horn-helm said without a pause. Endagur stared at Dalchian expectantly.

'I suspect we would not get far.'

'Exalted Champion Endagur agrees.'

'Then what have you to lose?' Dalchian gestured behind him to his Blades. 'Let my warriors spar in your cages, let my surgeon work in your infirmary.'

'Allow you to spy and plot?'

'You have more eyes and ears than we,' Dalchian argued. 'Set as many to watch us as you choose, but release us from this cage.'

With deliberate movements, Endagur lifted his helm and set it onto his armour's neck seals with a snap, covering what remained of his face with a snarling beast-visage.

'Exalted Champion Endagur will consider your request,' Horn-helm said. 'Anything else?'

'Yes,' Dalchian bit. 'Let me speak to the sorcerer.'

'Lord Jathok will be approached.'

With that, the two Kindred left, leaving the Blades with only their guards once more.

'What in the Eye was he about?' Dagardis asked over the vox, his incomprehension making him angry.

'Lord Jathok is a subtle creature,' Dalchian answered. 'He'll warrant careful handling.'

'Best leave that to you then, my lord,' Saryuz said. Dalchian made no reply.

I'll be ready, Jathok. Whatever your scheme, you bastard, I'll be ready.

Half an hour later they were moved to a billet deck with arming chambers. A score of Abyssal Kindred guarded the portal to the billet and the corridors beyond, but the portal itself remained unlocked. Their weapons were not returned, but Dalchian still felt strangely certain that Krutaan's claw was close by. A guard addressed him once they had arrived.

'Lord Jathok will see you now.'

'Dagardis.' He summoned the brute with a nod towards the portal, and then after a moment added, 'Saryuz, you too. The rest of you, behave yourselves.' The three of them stalked from the barracks into the warship, five Abyssal Kindred falling into step behind them.

A short corridor led to a steep companionway, at the summit of which was one of the vessel's arterial transitways. Mortal slaves in pairs or small groups averted their eyes, whispering tremulous prayers to themselves as they scurried past, keen to avoid being noticed by the Night Lords. The piteous dregs were garbed in devotional robes and most of them sported ritual branding or electoos. Some had their eyes sewn shut, the haphazardness of the stitching suggesting it was self-inflicted. One wretched, gibbering wraith of a man wept and drooled beneath the weight of an enormous, bronze-hasped tome that was chained to his back, bending his spine almost parallel to the deck.

'This place is ill,' Saryuz growled.

'Ripe with witch-stink,' Dagardis agreed. At every junction or diverging companionway a censer hung, filling the atmosphere with smog that was either so sweet it was gorge-raising or acrid to the point of suffocation. Dalchian was grateful for his helm's rebreather systems, but even they could not remove the stench entirely.

They reached a long thoroughfare that ran fore and aft through the frigate. The narrow space was tall, the fluted columns and ceiling vaults hung with parchment and fetishes, the once Imperial brutality of the ship's creation subverted to a sickening, unnatural grandeur. Dalchian's disgust faltered and an equally unwelcome sensation swelled within him.

Envy.

The *Ikhtheos* was a warp-infested fane of a craft, the slick filth of daemon worship drenching it, but beneath that veneer it was also a powerful warship, savage and efficient. Dalchian had known command of a vessel like this before, and the loss of that command sat in his guts like a block of ice. A six-legged servitor trudged past pushing a cart of ammunition towards the prow flight deck. A knot of mortals hushed each other and fled before the midnight-armoured murderers, their steps echoing in the sepulchral corridor, their robes setting delicate spirals of incense smoke spinning in their wakes. The slaves darted into a portal off the corridor just to one side of a long flight of steps that led aft and upward. Dalchian gestured and the Blades began to climb. At the summit was an arched doorway, and their guards indicated to Dagardis and Saryuz to wait while Dalchian entered.

Beyond the doorway was a dorsal observation blister. The armaglass hemisphere projecting from the *Ikhtheos'* hull gave him a spectacular view of absolutely nothing, the dead black of empty voidspace, but it also gave him a half-obscured perspective on the *Red Galentia* as it sailed fifty miles off the *Ikhtheos'* port side.

Dalchian had never been one to dwell on misfortune. His ilk were bred to keep striving and never look back, to be furious and remorseless in pursuit of their objective. The dagger lines of the *Red* drew his attention like an open wound, though. The second ship he had lost in less than a standard year. Veilmaster Iccrom, erstwhile lord of the Blades of Atrocity, would have had him flayed and his bones bleached for committing such an offence just once, let alone repeating it. The Veilmaster was dead, though, and Dalchian was not. He stared at the destroyer, its tiny lights winking with the distance, imagining his gaze could flense away the adamantine and part the plasteel to show him the turncoat Zorean. He bared his teeth, rage seething inside him. For a moment he could hear the talons of Krutaan's claw ringing in atonal knells as his fingers swayed and flexed; he could hear the breath of Krutaan grating in his ears, the sound soothing his wrath somehow, feeding him a sense of profound balance.

After a moment he remembered the claw was sealed away, and noticed that his plain gauntlet was moving of its own accord. He clenched his fist to cease the motion and turned his gaze back to the *Red* in the distance. Back to Zorean.

Loyalty is such a curious thing.

'I trust my guests are keeping well,' came Jathok's bass voice from behind him. Dalchian did not turn.

'Guests indeed.' Dalchian finally tore his eyes from the *Red*. 'My thanks for allowing us out of our cage. I should kill you now, daemon-lover, to show you the error in your accounting.'

'Please, try.'

Leil Jathok was exactly as he had been when he boarded the *Red*, his black-and-turquoise armour swathed in a deep cloak, dark face smiling beneath his crown of crystalline implants.

'Do not tempt me,' Dalchian said.

'I sense temptation has already visited you,' the sorcerer said. 'And I sense you have already given your answer.' Jathok glanced pointedly at Dalchian's hand where he would have worn the lightning claw. Dalchian remembered the door in his mind that had shut when he killed Krutaan. It had stayed blessedly shut. He narrowed his eyes at the lord of the Abyssal Kindred.

'I have a proposition,' Dalchian said, ill at ease to be in such proximity to the warp-touched. Jathok's white beard split into a smile and he laughed softly.

'Out with it, then.'

Dalchian kept a vice grip around his temper. *Politic*, he told himself.

'This galaxy offers few guarantees for a servant of the Powers. Our myriad scattered brethren seldom share any bonds greater than those of convenience. The fate of my own ship and most of my murder-kin stands testament that the alliance of the Gorelord is a fractious thing, full of schemes and conspiracy.' Dalchian let the self-evident truth hang in the air, and Jathok's smile contracted slightly.

'Go on.'

'We could be valuable allies.'

'Or dangerous rivals.'

'That also.'

Jathok looked sidelong at him. 'A poor bargaining chip.'

'You know not what I may offer.' Dalchian loaded his voice with intent.

'There is nothing you could offer me, Skin-Taker.' The sorcerer seemed to be trying to convince himself as much as Dalchian, and it was the Night Lord's turn to laugh. A play of vague irritation and then acceptance danced across the sorcerer's features, and he spoke again.

'Alas, I never gained the capacity to lie convincingly. Honesty is one of my more perplexing faults.'

'You'll have no trouble telling me your true answer, then,' Dalchian pressed.

Jathok gazed out of the blister into the firmament beyond and stroked his greying beard, the ceramite of the gauntlets carved with skirling patterns and eye-wringing sigils.

'If I do not return you to the Gorelord then the favour of my company is forfeit. I face threats enough, Skin-Taker. I'll not give Thelissicus a reason to want me dead, too.'

'I am merely breathing oxygen onto the ember of a possible future in the hope the flame will take,' Dalchian said. Now was his time to gamble. Time to test what the spire-bat had an appetite for. 'We may have a prize in common, Lord Jathok.'

Dalchian let the image of the Black Ship coalesce in his mind, and he felt Krutaan's absent claw *clink* as the blade fingers curled. The sorcerer turned sharply to the Skin-Taker and looked him in the eyes, searching.

'Is that so?' Jathok asked.

'Certainty is elusive, I'll admit,' Dalchian said. 'But in one thing I am convinced. Treat with me, Leil Jathok. Let us be allies.'

'I will not let you go.'

'Allies within the confines of Thelissicus' snake-pit, then.'

There was a long silence before Jathok spoke again.

'I will consider it.'

Ah, the spire-bat catches his scent.

'Do not wait overlong,' Dalchian said. 'The Imperial Navy hunt this void, and the Gorelord will be impatient for your return.'

'I am grateful for your concern,' Jathok said with a raised eyebrow. 'Was there anything else you wished to discuss?'

'I have a request, as it happens.' He returned the sorcerer's intense gaze. 'Aboard my old ship is a tech-priest and his shuttle. Bring them into your custody here.'

'This I will do.' Jathok bowed his head respectfully and, sensing the consultation was at an end, turned to leave the blister.

'And don't be so modest,' Dalchian added over his shoulder as he looked back out into the void.

'Mm?'

'You're as good a liar as any.' Dalchian knew the sorcerer was grinning as he strode away.

CHAPTER NINE

Ibriel's cargo lifter took up little space on the *Ikhtheos'* hangar deck in comparison to that of the *Red*'s minute shuttle bay. It seemed to shrink in the looming shadows of the two Thunderhawk gunships that dominated the space. The *Red*'s tiny shuttle bay had been a solitary refuge for the tech-priest, but aboard the Abyssal Kindred craft there were ground crews of haggard mortals who, when not administering to the attack craft, were always skulking nearby, filling the air with fractured whispers, the shuffling of feet and the grinding of teeth. Worse than that, though, the Abyssal Kindred Warpsmith made the place his haunt.

'You,' Cyren Narltsa barked from his plasteel throat. He was lying prone, arm shoulder-deep in a conduit gulley beneath the grating of the hangar deck. His huge armour was streaked with the oil and grime of decades, obscuring the turquoise heraldry and etched scripture equally. Only the bald back of his head betrayed a biological form beneath. His face was a plasteel skull, boxy and startling in proportions. 'Run a diagnostic on that coolant management cogitator. It's taking too long to flush during turnaround.'

One of the litter of gargoyle-tipped mechatendrils that emerged from his power pack like a nest of serpents jabbed at an alcove in the bulkhead where an interface screen flickered. Ibriel was cataloguing again. Attempting to make sense of the vast quantities of data and crystalline memory that, theoretically, he could now access. The process required concentration, and he had stolen himself as far away from the Warpsmith as possible, but the armoured giant sent his growling voice directly at Ibriel over the grav-carts and fuel hoses of the hangar deck.

'Respectfully, I am not one of your serfs, honoured Warpsmith,' he said.

'You're a tech-priest, aren't you?'

'I was.'

'Then you know how to run a coolant management diagnostic.' It was not a question. Fully distracted now, Ibriel cancelled the cataloguing processes and turned towards where the Warpsmith worked.

'I am a–'

As soon as Ibriel started speaking, a gush of vapour engulfed the Warpsmith, boiling from a rent in one of the conduits he was working on. The huge Chaos Space Marine cursed floridly, sending a mechatendril down the crawlspace to twist a stop-valve shut. The vapour ceased pouring and gradually dissipated. Naritsa's armour was rimed with frost when the receding drifts finally revealed him again.

'What?' he bit.

'I am a prisoner of your master,' Ibriel said. 'Here at my own lord's request. I am not obliged to follow your directives.'

Naritsa neither stopped his work nor looked up. 'Two hours

your fat little boat has sat on *my* hangar deck, unmolested. I am more than in my rights to strip the thing for parts.'

He let the fact hang. Ibriel's mechadendrites *clinked* together in a twitch, then with a whirr of ocular lenses he strode over to the coolant management cogitator.

'Better,' Naritsa said.

The coolant management array had a sticky valve. Once Ibriel had fixed that, Naritsa had him run an authority check of both Thunderhawks' control surfaces. More tasks followed and Ibriel sullenly applied himself to the work. It took Ibriel far longer than it should have to realise Naritsa was complimenting him. The Warpsmith had few acolytes among the Abyssal Kindred themselves, and judging by his manner towards his mortal helots, Ibriel concluded Naritsa was a perfectionist, jealously protective of his dominion of machines. Some of Ibriel's resentment transmuted into smugness. Naritsa had not double-checked Ibriel's work once.

The ranking Mechanicum adept on board the *Ikhtheos*, a bloated squid of a mystek called Aggannazor who drifted about the ship on humming suspensors, tried to bar Ibriel from the ship's crucial systems. Gyren Naritsa and Aggannazor embarked upon a heated exchange, the Warpsmith little hiding his contempt for the mystek and the impenetrable layers of coded etiquette within which Aggannazor operated. The mystek's plasteel tentacles flared in affront, but they finally unlocked vital cogitation datacores, clearly dismissive of Ibriel's stated capabilities and expecting him to fail.

Afterwards, Ibriel and Naritsa upgraded several of the frigate's main command systems. They purged phantom rune lines from the machine animus of the ship's void shield generator, increasing its surge-deflection envelope by a factor of one point zero nine. Many more of the longest-running issues aboard the vessel were either solved outright or mitigated for in ingenious ways thanks to their combined efforts, a development which saw Aggannazor quietly retreat to the generatorium. Ibriel and Naritsa's shared technical acuity was vast, but it soon became evident that each valued solving machine problems far above comradeship. Their respective considerations of one another morphed from hostile suspicion to outright enmity.

'Stop trying to outdo me,' Naritsa said from the arched alcove of the plasma generatorium authority shrine.

'I am not attempting to *outdo* you, honoured Warpsmith,' Ibriel replied, three of his now four hands hastily tapping at the screens of a suite of tethered dataslates floating before him on suspensors. 'I am merely finding more efficient solutions through application of novel tech-lore.'

'I thought your lot despised anything novel?'

'I was sanctioned for my beliefs many times.'

'What a shame.'

'At least in my previous life my contemporaries seldom stooped to sarcasm.'

'How admirable.'

Ibriel realised too late he was being baited. As he applied finishing touches to the last binharic catechisms, Naritsa had already engaged a plasma distribution engram of prodigious complexity to the generatorium cogitation matrix. The throbbing superstructure around them shook as it adjusted to the new regime, lumens dipping and flickering. Then, the disruption settled, and the generatorium throbbed with a smoother cadence. Naritsa's metal face betrayed no emotion, but Ibriel perceived self-satisfaction in the set of the Warpsmith's shoulders.

'Stop trying to outdo me,' Naritsa said again.

'In eighty-three point six per cent of circumstances, solutions derived from my own cogitations have been more efficient than yours. Plasma regulation is a speciality of mine.'

'You are welcome to rewrite the engrams at your leisure,' Naritsa sneered. Ibriel cast an internal projection of Naritsa's rune-work into his cortical visualiser. It was a formidable piece. He estimated it would take him at least five days to unpick it, now that it was enmeshed with the generatorium's governing architecture.

'I shall.' He turned back to his dataslates.

'You'd really do it, wouldn't you?'

'Correct.'

There was a long silence as Naritsa's metal face stared, eyes glowing like embers. Finally, he took a rasping breath.

'How about a real challenge, if you're so capable?'

Something in Naritsa's tone gave Ibriel pause and he turned away from his dataslates to look at the Warpsmith.

'What manner of challenge?'

'Follow me.'

The great, dark shape hung among hooked chains and loops of frayed cabling. No lumens worked in the chamber, but a dim red glow emanated from nowhere that Ibriel could identify, underlighting the curved armour and steel banding of the thing. Ritual scrolls hung in their hundreds down the smeared bulkheads to either side and a censer of foul aromatics filled the space with serpents of thick smoke. Ibriel and Warpsmith Naritsa could not avoid the charred bones that coated the floor, and their tread crunched as they slowly, reverentially approached the looming mass.

Ibriel sent a mechadendrite forth to interface with the sarcophagus' dataport, but Naritsa's hand shot out and grasped the segmented appendage, stopping it dead. The Warpsmith shook his metal skull slowly, then released the mechadendrite.

'Very well,' Ibriel said with a confidence he did not totally possess. 'Indirect interface only.' At this the Warpsmith nodded.

Ibriel unfolded an uplink spider from his wrist, and the tiny brass thing *ticked* its way across the pitted surface of the inert Helbrute. It found the dataport and slid its tined face into the opening, lights stuttering to life on its abdomen. Screeds of transmitted data tracked across Ibriel's vision. He followed it at inhuman speed.

'It does indeed live, as you say,' Ibriel whispered, the sepulchral feel of the chamber quieting even him. 'Castra Ferrum pattern originally. Legion attribution Seventeenth. What Legion bears that numerical?'

'The Bearers of the Word,' Naritsa rasped.

'Ah.'

'Continue.'

'Well, it seems magenta-grade fail-safes of ancient origin have been engaged.' Ibriel's lenses whirred, data flashing by in front of them. 'The subject was not… It is unclear. The subject was either not interfacing with the machine animus or…' he faltered.

'Or?' Naritsa prompted.

'Or the subject had *overridden* the machine animus. That cannot be.' He spooled through the data again. 'A pan-spectral inversion of the machine animus was performed after subject interment. The animus was… *expelled*, in favour of… of something else.'

'We call it a truesoul. Or Neverborn. The Imperium calls it something else.' Naritsa was enjoying the varying levels of confusion and anxiety wafting from the tech-priest.

'Daemon,' Ibriel whispered. 'You already know all this.'

'I do.'

A biological digestive system Ibriel barely used any more constricted in acid revulsion. Up to that moment, Ibriel had regarded Naritsa as merely a corrupted mirror of the Techmarines of the Adeptus Astartes – a data-wrangler and fabricator of weapons and armour. But then, in the chamber with an archaic relic of daemon worship slumbering before them, cultic enthusiasm bled from Naritsa's pores. The warpcraft clearly named in his rank surfaced in his hideous, glowing eyes, and Ibriel experienced a deluge of doubt and hesitancy.

But his thirst for knowledge was unquenchable.

'Why is it inert?'

'I do not know.' Naritsa seemed thrilled by his own ignorance. 'All I know is that I've been trying to disengage the fail-safes for nearly six years, standard. Nothing I tried has worked.' He gazed up at the dangling war machine with awe and hunger somehow showing on his unmoving features. He reached out and almost rested his gauntleted fingers upon the ancient armour. Almost. 'How's that for a challenge?' he asked, withdrawing his hand.

Ibriel scrolled through more and more of the data. His mecha-dendrites twitched as the rune-lines became less logical, more chaotic. No, more Chaotic. The screeds slashed past his vision faster and faster. Bile crept up his oesophagus.

The uplink spider sparked and blew out, fragments clattering into the bones at his feet.

'Well?' Naritsa said.

Ibriel studied the arcane brute for a long time, then, taking a breath, he deployed a replacement spider. 'It will take time.'

Dalchian marvelled at the changes the tech-priest had wrought upon the once humble cargo lifter. Exotic circuitry glowed in every corner of the craft; curious amendments were everywhere, neatly welded or bolted into the most unlikely places, cables of varied hues snaking from them into the panels and case-work of the lifter's internal skin. The pilot throne had been greatly adjusted to account for Ibriel's new bulk, extended and tucked within a nest of displays and interfaces. The tubular masses of multiple gunship-grade weapons systems intruded on the cargo compartment like tumorous growths. Incredible though the modifications were, Dalchian was still irked. Ibriel was not here. Dalchian needed the tech-priest if he had any chance of finding the Black Ship, but the wretch was absent again. No doubt ensconced in some warp-curdled bilge with the Abyssal Kindred Warpsmith. At first Dalchian had felt reassured that the tech-priest was ingratiating himself, for the Blades might be able to leverage the reflected glow of his high regard if it came to it. But Ibriel had taken to scurrying off early every cycle, and on the occasions when Dalchian had seen him, it had been obvious that something was captivating the tech-priest. Ibriel was obsessively pursuing some project outside the aegis of Dalchian's confidence, and the Skin-Taker had been betrayed too many times to ignore such a thing.

Footsteps sounded on the deck plating, and Dalchian took a breath in readiness to bring his errant tech-priest back to heel. But the steps were not Ibriel's.

'Lord Skin-Taker,' Gyren Naritsa greeted him. 'I did not expect to find you here.'

'Whereas I did expect to find my tech-priest. Have you seen him?'

'Yes, my lord.' Naritsa held himself with caution, and Dalchian decided to test this Warpsmith.

'I hope you haven't killed him.'

Naritsa's plasteel head drew back a fraction. 'Of course not, my lord. He assists me with a technical problem.'

'He assists you?' Dalchian asked. 'Yet you are here and he is… where?'

'My armorium, Lord Skin-Taker.' Naritsa hesitated, then seemingly made a decision. 'In truth, my lord, he now does work far beyond my understanding. He has sent me here to fetch some components he requires.' The Warpsmith indicated the lifter. Dalchian smiled, surprising himself.

'Sent Gyren Naritsa, honoured Warpsmith of the Abyssal Kindred, on errands, has he?'

'It would seem so, my lord,' Naritsa said, nodding. Dalchian stood aside and the Warpsmith clambered into the craft, checking a dataslate for storage coordinates. Along with new machinery, the place was also bedecked with compartments, stowage nets, drawers and mag-clamped boxes, which Naritsa now searched through for items listed on the dataslate register.

'What is the problem for which Ibriel's expertise so eclipses your own, then?' Dalchian asked.

'A machine relic, my lord,' Naritsa grunted.

'Oh, he'll love that.'

'Indeed.' The Warpsmith collected an assortment of things in a small crate held aloft by one of his segmented mechatendrils. 'I have rarely seen such insight regarding techno-arcana. He works like a master of old.' There was honest admiration in the words, and the statement, free of subtext or ulterior intent, struck a chord within Dalchian.

'He is quite good,' he admitted.

'Good?' Naritsa withdrew from the lifter and sealed the crate, items accounted for. 'Lord Skin-Taker, Ibriel is a rare gift. Worth protecting.' Something in his tone made Dalchian narrow his eyes.

'From whom?'

Naritsa took a breath, the air sounding odd as it sucked between his metal jaws.

'Lord Jathok is mighty,' he said. 'But he is hard on the tools he wields.'

'As a lord of the Powers must be,' Dalchian replied icily, defending the position rather than the man.

'Without doubt, my lord.' Naritsa bowed. 'I apologise if I spoke out of turn.'

'That is for your lord to decide,' Dalchian said, and Naritsa's shoulders stiffened. 'If you choose to share it with him. What business is it of mine?'

'You are gracious, Lord Skin-Taker,' Naritsa said bluntly. Dalchian let out a bark of laughter.

'Now that is something I have never been called before!'

Naritsa inclined his plasteel head and strode from the hangar bay carrying Ibriel's requested items.

An honest warrior, Dalchian thought. *How refreshing.*

CHAPTER TEN

Ibriel had worked exclusively upon the Helbrute problem for nineteen uninterrupted hours. He knew Dalchian would demand an explanation, so he had prepared his, should he have to face his master's interrogation.

The arcane data he had taken from the ruins of the templum-capitalis on Uzurmandius was vast. The lines of rune hymnal code ran into the quadrillions, and the knowledge stored within was more priceless than any other relic stack he had ever had the privilege to parse. But the architecture was ancient. His engrammatical processing capacity was of a vastly inferior order to that of his purloined datastack, so he had to take every opportunity to refine his own algorithms and match them to its requirements. Dalchian had tasked him with finding an unfindable ship, and Ibriel was certain the lore was in his grasp, but translating such hugely complex and powerful information into usable data might very well kill him. The Helbrute represented a trial run of the experimental – his former fellow adepts would no doubt say *heretical* – data transcription pathways he had devised that posed his own cogitation much less risk. Less, but not none. That would be his justification to Dalchian, and every part of it was absolutely true. The only detail he omitted was the sheer joy of the technical challenge.

A flutter of anticipation ran through him as he made last-minute adjustments to the whirring equipment scattered across the boneyard deck of the Helbrute's sepulchre. Sorcerer Lord Jathok had arrived with his Master of Possessions, Vurdomal. The hooded Kindred was taller than his lord, and he wore a fanged helm reminiscent of a deep ocean predator. Ritual smoke coiled from the hollowed skulls atop his power pack. Gyren Naritsa stood stock-still, metal face intractable. Ibriel had worked long and close enough to the Warpsmith now that he could tell the Kindred was deeply torn. Fury at being bested in so short a time at something he had been attempting for half a decade wrestled with mad delight at the prospect of seeing his project finally bear fruit. Ibriel tried to ignore the Warpsmith's looming presence.

'You are certain of the wards, Vurdomal?' Jathok asked the hooded Kindred, who bowed deeply.

'I have never wrought such strength into a binding, your lordship.' The Master of Possessions exuded confidence in his work. 'A greater Neverborn itself could not work its way free.'

The ancient Dreadnought chassis had been bound by yet more chains. Plasteel rings as thick as a mortal thigh fixed the suspended beast in a cruciform of rigid mechanical limbs. Braziers flared lurid alchemical flame and fresh devotional pictograms had been worked into the ceramite skin of the monster itself. The chanting had begun two hours ago. Ibriel had no idea where the voices came from, and Naritsa had offered no explanation. The tech-priest tried to ignore them, too.

The fail-safes within the machine form were cyclopean in scale and vastly older than anything Ibriel had ever worked upon. Surface categorisation of some of his stolen tech-lore had revealed potential solutions, and it had taken him many refinements to identify the precise rune hymnal within his mem-stack. The data was deep and well embedded. Ibriel had never run such a complex cogitation without the need for additional neural processing support, but the data was part of his mechacortical architecture now. In theory, he should be able to run the hymnal unaided.

In theory.

He took a last look at the Abyssal Kindred lords. Jathok and Vurdomal simply stared in expectancy at the hulking Helbrute. Naritsa stood impassive. Ibriel's mechadendrites twitched. He took a breath and readied himself to enter the data-trance. Cables ran from beneath his robes, plugging into various pieces of machinery surrounding him. Code amplifiers, surge controllers, noospheric broadcast plates. A heavily reinforced uplink spider had been welded into the Helbrute's dataport. Ibriel had lost nearly forty of them before perfecting modifications that made them resilient enough to handle the binharic load. Mnemo-chants sank him into the rune lines, and he began.

The path was unlaid. He arranged access protocols following the experience of the prior weeks, tunnelling his way into the machine animus like a prospector, propping the narrow entryway open with multiple overlaid code-locks. He worked diligently, as fast as he dared but assiduously triple-checking each new step before feeding the rune lines in. The venerable animus began fighting him. He pried open the data vaults of his stolen lore, fending off aggressive animus cancel sequences with virtuoso skill.

The stolen tech-lore was exactly correct. Ibriel felt a swell of triumph as he let the arcane rune lines move through him. They slammed into his psyche like a grav-train. Technomantic psalm-keys as old as the Imperium itself bludgeoned their way through his adapted brain, lancing into the spiralling data pulses of the Helbrute's machine animus. It was like watching lava erupt on the floor of a night-dark ocean. The ancient code flowed where it willed, congealing into new forms, and flattening the long-standing fail-safes like brittle corals. Ibriel tore himself back out of the collapsing code-locks, painfully aware of the mechacortical scarification he was enduring. He hoped the damage to his own form would be minimal.

The Helbrute glowed with tectonic power, splits migrating across the ceramite of its mighty form then knitting again. The plasma-like weapon at its side throbbed and keened as the coils ignited into sickly unlight. Bone protuberances tore through the beast's armour and bloomed into razor hooks or knuckles of syphilitic spongiform. The deeply recessed helm of the thing grinned, fleshy mouth yawning wide, vomiting forth concentric rings of fanged gums that grew and withered, grew and withered. The chains around it snapped tight and groaned, the intricate runes and pictograms worked into every link seeping acrid smoke as they fought to contain the immaterial creature and its physical host form. After a shuddering few moments, the initial pangs of rebirth quietened, and the Helbrute relaxed into its confinement, glowing eyes bulging and extending to observe its new surrounds.

'Success!' Ibriel bleated through sheets of blood that cascaded from his facial orifices. It seemed the damage to his own form was more significant than he had expected. He turned to Naritsa and grinned, before dropping onto the deck and contorting in a violent seizure. The last thing he processed before losing consciousness was the sound of Dalchian's voice roaring from the hatchway.

'What have you done to my tech-priest?'

* * *

Qi Umshar and Fleshwright Ophis had the warp's own job of stabilising Ibriel's careening vitals. After two hours of relentless work with chirurgeon, vitacopia and countless drugs and conjurations, at long last Ibriel descended into the stillness of induced coma. In the depths of the *Ikhtheos'* night cycle, the attending warriors gradually retired, leaving the tech-priest to the ministrations of the auto-systems, until only Dalchian and Leil Jathok remained in the otherwise empty apothecarion.

'Well?' Dalchian demanded.

'He acted entirely of his own volition. In doing so, he achieved a great work.'

'Your Warpsmith lured him in, witch.'

'My Warpsmith initially wanted him off our ship.' Jathok was unconcerned with the fate of the tech-priest. The sorcerer was simply indulging him for the sake of their so-called alliance. 'I am mightily glad you brought him here. He has gifted us a weapon I have long sought.'

'Good for you.'

'He is your servant. My gratitude for his efforts extends to you, by rights.'

'Gratitude for a gift I did not know I was giving? I see through you, witch. More lies within lies.' His determination to be politic escaped him as Ibriel wavered close to the edge of death.

Jathok heaved a sigh and turned his gaze from the somnolent tech-priest to the Skin-Taker.

'You were born in the Nightspires of Tathaxes, were you not?'

Jathok's question took Dalchian aback. He knew the fact, but remembered nothing of the time.

'Yes.'

'Your Legion raised you, so your hatred is pure. That is to your credit. But you do not know the Imperium as I do. I was born on Nega Viltra, among the shrines and cathedrals. I still remember my birth-parents, albeit in a fractured, echoing way. They were both Ministorum preachers, proving beyond doubt that the Great Powers have a sense of humour. The Ardent Spears Chapter took me and began preparing me for elevation, marked for service within their librarius. With them I imagined I would possess grand power. Ah, Skin-Taker, the crude pyrotechnics of the Imperium are the weapons of a frightened child. Only we have the courage to wield the immaterium itself. Then the Thousand Sons Legion raided the Ardent Spears' fortress-monastery, taking me and all the other infant recruits. They cast us in their image, those of us that survived. That was a lifetime before I founded my own Abyssal Kindred, but I understood then. Do you know what it was that the Imperium took from me?'

'What?'

'Everything!' The sorcerer's bellow echoed from the apothecarion's plasteel surfaces for a long moment. 'All the promise and the power I should have had, forfeited in the name of dumb servitude to a dead god. You rage so assuredly against all who share your state, but you level no revilement at the architects of our subordination!'

Dalchian saw the faltering lines of his own determination in his mind's eye. He beheld his multitude of failures afresh; heard in Jathok's venomous words the voice of Krutaan, desperate for glory once more. The claw at his left hand lurched. He heard Krutaan's breath saw in and out of his old, battered rebreather. Dalchian's eyes had closed. He was not sure when. He opened them again and looked square into the face of Leil Jathok. The sorcerer went on.

'We renegades…' Jathok had his momentum now. 'We *heretics*. All we have left to us are the great desires. Our lives and deaths can be for naught but want of the highest vengeance, the pursuit of ultimate retribution against a putrid order that forged our very natures, then denied us our destiny! Wrath is the only worthy answer to those who betray you, but surely all betrayals pale before the colossal arrogance of Imperial *excommunication*?'

Dalchian's mind churned. He hated the sorcerer, and resented his potency; he was furious at Ibriel's incapacitation. But most of all, it turned his guts to fire knowing that Jathok was right. All the vitriol he had projected at Thelissicus, at Krutaan, at Zorean: none of it mattered. His existence had only one purpose.

'A Black Ship,' Dalchian said after several minutes of silence. Jathok looked at him, deep eyes darting as he comprehended what Dalchian had said. Understanding dawned across the sorcerer's features. Understanding, and relish.

'Here at Uzurmandius?'

'Indeed.'

'That explains many things.' Jathok turned to leave, but hesitated. He looked Dalchian in the face, then abruptly held out his gauntleted hand. 'Shall we cement our alliance in the old way?'

Dalchian appraised the sorcerer with his hand outstretched, and a twist of perception brought his fate into sharp focus for the first time. He knew what lay before him, and the knowledge made him smile. He grasped Jathok's hand in accord.

'Allies,' he said.

Chapter Eleven

The *Ikhtheos'* strategium was a temple fane, with pews radiating from an ebon altar, and glassaic depicting cavorting un-creatures. The trophies of defeated enemies hung from iron chains. Banners, skulls, weapons and tokens, all bought with blood and fire by the Abyssal Kindred in war.

'The Gorelord Thelissicus is a subtle creature,' Jathok said. 'Despite the image he cultivates.'

'I had reached that conclusion.'

'His subtlety is greater than you know.' Jathok laid a dataslate upon the altar and slid it towards Dalchian. 'Do not mistake yourself as the only victim of his duplicity.'

Dalchian read the text on the slate before him.

'What are these names?'

'They were my seers. Boramora, there, was my Navigator.'

'Thelissicus killed them?'

'Mostly.'

'Then the Gorelord is intolerant of psykers.' Dalchian played along. He needed to know what Jathok wanted to tell him. 'A position for which I have some sympathy. So, why does he tolerate you?'

'Thelissicus' subtlety is greater than you know,' Jathok repeated. 'Such intolerance is a useful distraction to the Gorelord, who, rather than exterminating wielders of the immaterium, harvests them instead.'

'Harvests? What for?'

'Leverage.' Jathok scrolled the dataslate along until it showed a vid-feed, clearly from the pict-capt gargoyles within the corridors of the *Ikhtheos* itself. It showed crimson-armoured Chaos warriors crashing into an octagonal chamber where a coterie of seers was chained to amplification thrones. The red butchers tore through the psykers in a hail of gore, wrenching frail bodies apart with orgiastic glee. 'Eleven of the sixteen were so badly dismembered and mutilated that it took my medicae helots weeks to discern that the bodies of the remaining five were not among the remains. To this day, I don't know how the Crimson Slaughter smuggled them from my ship.'

'How could you allow such an overstep on your own ship?'

'How could you allow almost your entire warband to perish?' At Jathok's goad Dalchian glared, but said nothing. 'A detachment of his Crimson Slaughter were aboard while we raided the convoy lanes of the Pleurotus Nebula. This was before your Blades joined the Gorelord's armada. They purported that my seers conspired with my Navigator to send us off course and corrupt our communications.'

'You have proof otherwise?' Dalchian asked, and Jathok ground his teeth.

'Proof? No. The seers were flaccid creatures, usable only in the bluntest sense, but usable nonetheless. They couldn't have conspired to steal a ration carton. Boramora, though. She had been with me for decades. We had navigated together – shared the holy vista of the immaterial plane. She could no more have betrayed me than cut out her own heart.' The depth of sadness in Jathok's voice unnerved Dalchian. 'I have no proof, but I do have certitude.'

'And after Thelissicus' brutes had finished their rampage?'

'The *beneficent* Gorelord leased me a new Navigator and clutch of psykers.'

'Who no doubt owe fealty to him rather than you,' Dalchian said, beginning to understand.

'Fealty might be too strong a word,' Jathok sneered. 'They are but his puppets. Nothing more. As long as the commands I give them reflect the will that the Gorelord has branded onto their thoughts, they behave themselves. If I diverge, they weep and bleed and jabber, and all their works lead me astray.'

'An effective leash,' Dalchian said.

'One with which he reins in his whole *alliance*.' The resentment was a cold and heavy thing in the sorcerer's voice, and for the first time, Dalchian felt a pang of kinship with the Abyssal Kindred lord. That is, before remembrance tempered his sympathy.

'Perhaps I should be grateful that he simply annihilated my ship in orbit, rather than install his own psykers on board?' There was acid on his tongue.

'I do not seek pity, Skin-Taker. Merely to convey to you the… poignance of your own discovery.'

'If we secure the Black Ship, then we can rob from the Imperium's chattel-tithe more psykers than Thelissicus could ever dream of harvesting.'

'Just so.'

'Do you think he knew the Black Ship would be here?'

Jathok considered the question. 'It went unlooked for by him when the Imperials translated in-system, you say?'

'Indeed. None of the Crimson Slaughter seemed overly attentive to the makeup of the fleet. It was sheer fortune I saw the undesignated rune-marker, and that I later tortured an Imperial captain who lacked the spine to take some choice information to his grave.'

'His dead god's adulators will curse him for that shortfall,' Jathok said with a smile. 'No, I don't believe the Gorelord knew of the Black Ship's coming, but I cannot prove that. Certainly, it is strange. For a Thronescum Black Ship to be here means there must be psykers in the system to take.'

'Making it a fine coincidence that a warlord prepossessed with seizing them should be here concurrently.'

'When you have plucked the strands of fate for as long as I, Skin-Taker, you are forced to surrender all but the most ironic perception of coincidence.'

'There is an inevitable question, then,' Dalchian said after a pause.

'How do we find a Black Ship?' Jathok's tone betrayed his hopelessness as he voiced the conceit out loud. 'And how do we commandeer it once we have?'

A dark look crossed Dalchian's face as he considered his answer, prior hostility threatening to surface once again.

'The best chance for doing so,' he said icily, 'is in a coma in your apothecarion.'

Dalchian went to see Ibriel once the tech-priest had regained consciousness. The robes Ibriel used to wear, fouled with blood, mucus and hydraulic fluid, had long since been cut away and replaced with a black shift. Nutrient paste oozed along feed tubes, and medicae regulators and auspex arrays beeped and hummed around him. Two slabs had been joined to support the swollen shell of his data storage, and the tech-priest was curled like the biomechanical parody of a foetus. Dalchian realised with a lurch that he had never seen Ibriel without his hood, and an absurd sensitivity urged him to look away and preserve the tech-priest's modesty. He crushed the notion.

'You survived, priest,' Dalchian greeted him with coarse humour. Ibriel's head was uncannily elongated with silver and bronze, his biological face almost entirely excised in favour of a dozen or more lenses of differing sizes and hues. The lenses bleared up towards Dalchian as he approached. The tech-priest shuddered pitiably.

'Archmagos, I am sorry...' he ghosted, head sagging.

'Archmagos?'

'It... I... My lord,' Ibriel stuttered. 'There is... I am suffering.'

It was all he could manage. Cold angst gripped Dalchian's insides. *Is he undone?* His concern was at potentially losing his chance of finding the Black Ship, not potentially losing a comrade. It did not occur to him that such a thought was callous.

'Has your technomantic experiment rattled your wiring, Ibriel?' Dalchian tried to make his voice sound light so as not to upset the tech-priest. Ibriel gazed up at his lord, head swaying, primary arms closed around himself.

'I'm sure I will recover,' he gasped.

In that moment, Dalchian was unconvinced. 'Be sure that you do, priest. We need you.'

'Wh... what for?'

'Many things, Ibriel. You have value.'

'That is... gratifying to hear.' Ibriel wound his jaw in figures of eight, flexing fingers and mechadendrites. 'My lord.'

After another week, Ibriel was upright and ambulatory, though the impact of his delving into the deeper secrets of his stolen cache was still evident in his dissociative manner and occasional lapses into mute torpor. Dalchian instructed him to rest as much as he could, only performing the least taxing of tasks.

'You must save yourself, priest,' Skin-Taker said as Ibriel settled into the enclosing confines of the lifter's pilot throne. 'There are trials ahead.'

'That is ever the case,' Ibriel rattled. 'I shall limit my exertions. My lord.'

Dalchian nodded, then turned and walked away.

Leil Jathok encouraged the Skin-Taker to be present for the ritual, as a courtesy and in recognition of their new accord. Dalchian appreciated the gesture, but not the experience. The strategium fane of the *Ikhtheos* had been bedecked in votive offerings and the air was rank with spiced smoke. Kneeling mortals in robes arranged themselves in concentric patterns with Jathok and the altar at their centre. Dalchian was all but invisible in the shadows of the chamber, his winged helm in the crook of his arm.

'Could you not have done this alone?' Dalchian whispered as he glared in overt contempt at the frail mortals crowding the deck. Even his quietened voice echoed from the bulkheads.

'I could,' Jathok replied. 'But this way is easier. There is less risk… for me.' One of the mortals closest to Dalchian swallowed, but did not move.

'What if it fails?'

'In the extreme case? We all die instantly.'

'That seems an excessive gamble.'

'I am a weapon they do not possess. My gifts offer us an advantage that would be naïve to overlook.' Jathok's voice was becoming fractious. Dalchian could not suppress his vindictive enjoyment as he pressed the psyker, disrupting his concentration. *You're an abomination, witch-breed.* He stopped before making the sorcerer too angry, though. They both needed this to work.

'Just don't ask me for help,' Dalchian said.

'You could not assist me, in any case.' Jathok laid out several small items atop the altar with obsessive precision. Dalchian grunted.

'What are those?'

'Symbols.' There was an Imperial Naval rank pin, a spent bolter casing, a tin cup of dark liquid that Dalchian's transhuman olfactory sense told him was blood. These things he could divine the symbological value of, but the rest was beyond him. A sherd of primitive pottery, the stub of a burned-out tallow candle, a pair of bone dice. Dalchian looked away as Jathok kept producing more curios to arrange. *What nonsense. A clean whetstone and the screams of my prey are the only rituals I favour.* Krutaan's claw *clacked* involuntarily again, and Jathok looked up sharply.

I must have Ibriel look at that.

At great length, the sorcerer raised his hands over the array on the altar-top and started chanting. The mortals began a simultaneous drone, slowly lifting then dropping their heads in sinuous rhythm. Bile rose in Dalchian's throat. The air was dead still, but flaming torches in the wall sconces shuddered and hanging banners fluttered at their corners. Dalchian watched the ritual build and tried to keep a firm grip on the disgust swelling within him.

The VIII Legion were not a proud brotherhood. Seldom had their exploits served any purpose other than plunder or ruin, as Dalchian well knew. But of their vanishingly few philosophical convictions, rejecting the rot of daemon worship was as close to a unifying belief as anything they possessed. Yet here he was, in a temple dedicated to the yawning madness of the immaterium, beseeching the unknowable entities of that impossible plane for assistance, albeit through the proxy of Leil Jathok. He had told himself it was necessary; that it was a tool he must use, as the sorcerer himself had said. *Was this the strength that Krutaan demanded? Have I forfeited my soul and that of my Legion?* The doubt curdled and festered in his mind as the chanting around him grew in volume. He considered what his old master, Iccrom, might say, and his sneer deepened. He needed the path before him clearing, that was certain. *Is this truly the way it must be done?* He looked at the sorcerer swaying in devotion for as long as he could stomach, suddenly revolted by the notion of their alliance. *Is this truly the way?*

He turned from the ritual and left without looking back.

Zorean was continually surprised that he still had teeth, given how much recent time he had spent grinding them in thwarted frustration. The crew of the *Red Galentia* were plentiful, but practically useless. He had killed over forty of the pathetic waifs so far in his tenure as commander, and he suspected his temper would get the better of him again sooner rather than later. All the fresh souls taken in Skin-Taker's raids attended their stations and suffered under the whips of the Night Lords' most enthusiastic converts, but their lack of training echoed in every stuttering system and delayed order. Even the stubborn Mechanicus adepts that the Skin-Taker had thrashed into line were starting to waver. Zorean had no choice but to execute so many. Lethal enforcement to ward against the spectre of mutiny. The absence of his murder-kin did not soothe matters. He considered his abandonment by the rest of the Blades. There was no sense to it; no logic. They should have flocked to him, grateful to be unburdened of so tragic a liege lord. Instead, they had spurned him and made his victory bittersweet, robbing him of all his most capable potential new underlings into the bargain. He was one master amidst a sea of slaves and wretches.

And the command throne was cursedly uncomfortable. He shifted to favour one side, then shifted to the other. With a grunt he stood and strode forwards to rest his hands on the transept balustrade. He decided he would have the throne melted down into scrap and replaced with something more befitting.

A chime sounded in his helm-vox. Zorean raised an eyebrow when he saw the vox request came on a channel reserved for communication between suits of Legion power armour. He opened the link.

'How fares the traitor?'

'Skin-Taker?' Zorean could not hide his surprise. 'What an unexpected joy. I was convinced I would never hear from you again. To what do I owe the pleasure?'

'The pleasure, scum, is all mine.' Dalchian's voice was bilious but fatigued. *'The knowledge that you sit there, alone, brooding about all your life's injustices even in your state of triumph exceeds all personal gratification I would take from flaying you alive myself.'*

'Now, now, Skin-Taker.' Zorean smiled. 'Somehow I doubt that very much.'

'No, I suppose you're right. Please transfer to the Ikhtheos *so I can make a thorough comparison.'*

'It is curious to hear you making threats to me, Skin-Taker, given your imprisonment.'

'You have imprisoned yourself irredeemably, Zorean. If you don't recognise that, you're less astute than I ever gave you credit for. The Blades and I are but temporarily waylaid.'

'If believing that makes you feel better, Skin-Taker, then by all means.' Dalchian was full of defiant sentiment, but he sounded worn-down, perhaps even defeated. It was pathetic really. Zorean revelled in it. 'So, I ask again, why is it you have contacted me? In fact, firstly, how have you contacted me? Our helm-vox should be well out of range.' Zorean eyed the *Ikhtheos'* rune marker on the oculus, fifty miles distant.

'Oh, that? But the work of moments for my pet tech-priest. Have you forgotten his utility so quickly?' There was an ember of relish in Dalchian's words, and Zorean's teeth rasped against one another.

'Luckily, I have no need of that simpering wretch. I'm glad

his parlour tricks keep you entertained.' With an effort, Zorean loosened his fingers from the balustrade. He had looked forward to unpacking the machine-man's secrets at his leisure, but the sorcerer had ordered Ibriel moved to his own ship before Zorean's vivisection could begin. No matter.

'*If you must know,*' Dalchian went on, his voice deadening again, '*I was simply curious. What did these daemon-lovers and warp-whisperers offer you in exchange for your duplicity?*' There was the faintest, most delicate thread of despair in Dalchian's voice, and on hearing it a thrill went up Zorean's spine. This was the heart of it, then.

'Lordship of the Blades, Skin-Taker,' he replied, deciding that the truth would be more painful for Dalchian to hear than any contrivance. 'A chance to repair the catastrophe you wrought upon us.'

Dalchian did not reply at once.

'*Such a prize was not theirs to grant.*'

'And yet here I am, free to reave and plunder.'

'*Without the Blades whose lordship you claim.*'

'I am not to be blamed for the intransigence of others.'

'*Nor I the* treachery *of others.*'

A long silence followed. Zorean had the curious sensation that his victory was a slippery thing, and even a momentary lapse could see it fly from his grasp. He wished Dalchian was dead. At least then it would explain why Zorean felt so haunted by him.

'Is that all you wanted to ask me?'

'*Your answer was incomplete. Why these curselings? Their ways are filthy and their dedications malignant. How could you favour them with your conspiracy rather than simply mutiny against me? You would have found ready ears among the Blades, I think. That is, before you sold them all out. Now they will only kill you if they can, regardless of whether you once might have swayed them.*'

The question stung Zorean. It had occurred to him to seek allies within his own warband, but he had chosen not to pursue that avenue. He refused to admit to himself the reason why. A notch of opportunity caught in his mind, though, as he considered Dalchian's words.

'You are not enjoying the company of your hosts, then?'

'*What?*' Dalchian spat. '*Of course I'm not! This ship reeks of their witchery and every one of the bastards mumbles and chants ceaselessly. My patience with them is at its limit.*'

'I am deeply saddened to hear that, Skin-Taker,' Zorean said, grinning to himself.

'*Not yet, you're not.*' Dalchian's voice gained a flint edge. '*The Blades and I have had enough. Jathok is not so strong as he appears. In truth, I wanted to give you what you denied me. Fair warning. I will be master of the* Ikhtheos *soon, and when that happens, it would be in your interest to be very, very far away.*'

'Ambitious, Skin-Taker,' Zorean jibed. He still smiled to himself, but unease kindled.

'*You have no idea.*'

With that, Dalchian cut the vox-link, leaving Zorean to his thoughts.

A slippery thing, indeed.

Dalchian found Ibriel back in his ship on the *Ikhtheos'* flight deck. The tech-priest's biological parts were pallid and clammy, and his mechadendrites lurched drunkenly. Ibriel reclined in his pilot couch, hands drifting by his sides.

'You are repaired?' Dalchian's boots clanked across the deck plates. Ibriel swivelled his head slowly.

'I am. I think.' His head drooped then jolted up. 'My lord.' Droop. Jolt.

'What in the Eye's name were you doing?'

'Applying some of my d-data cache to a novel conundrum.' Droop. Jolt. 'My lord.'

'And that was dangerous?'

'It would seem so. Parts of my mechacortex have realigned in ways I c-cannot entirely categorise, and some of the archeotech rune-lines I utilised appear to have enmeshed with my para-sympathetic subroutine b-binharic.' Ibriel glanced pointedly at a lone mechadendrite rooted in his abdomen. The segmented extremity was jumping and skipping in strange patterns, as if it was sketching shapes onto the air with an unseen stylus. 'That motion, for instance, is entirely involuntary. It is fascinating.' Droop. Jolt. 'My lord.'

'I've no doubt.' Dalchian looked sidelong at the skittering mechadendrite. 'Are you capable of addressing the task I set for you prior to your little distraction?'

'The B-Black Ship,' Ibriel said. Dalchian nodded. 'It is unlikely I would have any success in my c-current state, for which I apologise… my lord. I will have to stabilise myself further.'

'How long?'

'Seventy-two hours, I estimate. P-perhaps a fraction longer.' Droop. Jolt.

'Begin stabilising.'

'Acknowledged.' Droop. Jolt. 'How proceeds your other d-designs? My lord.'

'In motion. There may be… excessive disruption while you *stabilise*.' Dalchian turned to leave. 'Seal yourself in here. Remember, tech-priest, you have value.'

'Acknowledged.'

Zorean scuffed his boot along the deck where the old command throne had been. The servitors had made a decent job of the repair, for he could barely see the scars in the metal. Twelve hours had passed since his conversation with the Skin-Taker and his erstwhile lord was starting to feel quite distant again. Thank the Powers. A blood-streaked and skeletally thin ensign croaked to him from the communications lectern.

'Communication from the *Ikhtheos*, my lord.'

He nodded. A grainy hololith of Leil Jathok materialised before him, the light of the projection skipping and fractured.

'We have a situation.'

'What sort of situation?'

'The Skin-Taker…' Jathok seemed unwilling to give voice to his predicament. *'We cannot locate him or any of the Blades.'*

'Cannot locate him?' Zorean's hackles rose. 'Were they not securely detained?'

'I saw little need to confine them.' Jathok's unease was palpable, even over the fraying hololith connection. *'The forces at my disposal should have provided ample deterrence to any… ill-conceived behaviour.'* At this Zorean hissed through his teeth.

'Then you have committed the sin of underestimation, Lord Jathok.' Anxious rage frothed within him. He would not let the inadequacy of the Abyssal Kindred or their commander lead to his own undoing. 'How long since you last had contact with them?'

'The Skin-Taker attended a ritual of mine, half a cycle ago. He left before it was complete. None of my vassals have caught a trace of him or the others since.'

'Twelve hours,' Zorean husked. 'It is likely already too late, Lord Jathok.' Zorean looked towards the mortal officer, barely able to stand, at the ship's helm. 'You. Order the generatorium to commit all available power to the engines, and make ready for a course adjustment.'

'Aye, lord.'

'What are you doing?'

'Securing my command.' Zorean snarled as he stabbed a new bearing into the command console that had been fixed to the balustrade. The sequence flashed onto the helm officer's rune screen and the mortal began applying the adjustment. The *Red* groaned as its nose shifted a few points starboard. 'I have learned my lesson, Jathok. Dalchian Rassaq, curse his name, wields more power than I credited him with, and the Blades will follow him into ruin without complaint. He has little left to lose, sorcerer, so he will play his full hand whether the prize is a fortune or a pittance. That you allowed him to beguile you rather than simply delivering him to the Gorelord proves, frankly, that you deserve whatever he has in store for you.'

'*Watch your tone, Night Lord.*'

'Consider my words valuable insight into the nature of the thing that hunts you. Have you lost control of your environmental systems yet?' Jathok's silence was all the answer he needed. 'Then he has already begun. I wish you the luck of your foul gods, Jathok. By the Eye, you're going to need it.'

'*How dare–*'

The audio feed of the projection cut out and the hololith shuddered. Jathok lurched to one side, arms snapping up to arrest his fall. He stood back up into reception range of his holo-caster, helm moving as he evidently spoke to Zorean, unaware of his being silenced. A mortal chained into the *Red*'s augur pit spoke.

'My lord, the *Ikhtheos* is experiencing power fluctuations and system-wide transmission anomalies.'

Zorean stared at the sorcerer's glowing silhouette for a second longer. Jathok was looking around himself, perhaps directing queries at his bridge crew. Zorean growled and cut the connection. 'What of their propulsion?'

'It appears to be faltering, my lord.'

'Farewell, Leil Jathok,' he murmured before rasping his orders. 'Full speed ahead. We leave the *Ikhtheos* to its fate.' It took the inept crew far too long for his liking, but after a minute or so, the *Red* tremored with plasmic potency, and the *Ikhtheos'* rune marker on the oculus screen began to fall away behind them. The smaller destroyer could outpace the larger frigate in an even race. But the *Ikhtheos* had, or at least was about to have, a very terminal disadvantage.

I will be master of the Ikhtheos *soon,* Dalchian had said. *And when that happens, it would be in your interest to be very, very far away.*

Zorean was grateful for the advice.

On the bridge of the *Ikhtheos*, Jathok stood impassive as the machine spirit of his ship squealed and grated in discomfort. The cogitators lurched in and out of operation; lumens flickered and popped; alarms brayed briefly before auto-cancelling. His ship was in rapidly escalating turmoil.

'Well,' the sorcerer said as he watched the *Red*'s rune marker accelerate away. 'The Lord Zorean is most obliging.'

'Miserably so,' Dalchian sighed.

CHAPTER TWELVE

Six hundred millennia before, the hungering gas giant had dragged its smaller neighbour into a deathly embrace. For protracted centuries as they orbited their hot red star, the two bodies grew closer and closer, each near pass plucking and tearing at their surfaces. The condensed gases of the giant swelled and rippled with gravitational turbulence while the just-cooled skin of the inferior orb split and cracked, hurling globules of molten rock into eccentric, elliptical orbits where they cooled into glittering chains of asteroids. When, finally, the two planets converged in an act of violence few sentient races of the galaxy had ever had the power to imitate, skeins of the gas giant's liquid mantle unravelled across the orbital track, drifting inexorably away from the bulging, convulsing chimera planet the Imperium would one day name Guelphos. These clouds of irradiated gas and microparticulate would ebb and surge for aeons before settling into the gravitational sanctuaries at Guelphos' Lagrange points. Like their emancipated parent, these clouds harboured exotic energies and heightened levels of radiation, making them ideal haunts, in latter millennia, for void-faring craft that wished to go unnoticed.

Zorean took the long way through the gas cloud. The agglomeration was a minor detour on his course back to Thelissicus and the rest of the alliance, but it would provide a more-than-adequate mask against Dalchian's revenge. He hoped the Abyssal Kindred would be proof against Dalchian's coup, but there was a strong chance they would not be, so Zorean took all the precautions available to him. The *Ikhtheos* had abruptly vanished from his long-range augurs three days ago, and he had no appetite to be ambushed.

The *Red* now had a new captain, which was making Zorean's ordeal slightly more bearable. Irun Sibilla had been on the directing staff at the Imperial Naval scholam they had raided among the asteroid colonies, and she was at last applying some sort of discipline to the pathetic dregs of humanity that wept at their stations. She had also ordered the senior tech-magos out of his burrow and onto the bridge where he belonged. With the ship better operated than it had been since he took command, and the prospect of long hours transiting a signal-impenetrable radiation cloud, Zorean gratefully retired to the ward room and removed his helm. He sat on a cushioned bench seat where dried blood crisped in flakes, and allowed his thoughts to unspool. Come warp or high ruin, he would survive whatever the galaxy was going to throw at him.

A pealing klaxon tore him back to consciousness from half-dreams of witchcraft and betrayal. So seldom was the need among transhumans for true sleep that to have descended into the sequential neural shutdowns of a catalepsean cycle took Zorean bitterly off-guard. He crushed his exhaustion and opened a vox-link to the bridge.

'Sibilla, report.'

'Contact, my lord. We've exited the radiation cloud directly into an ambush.'

'Skin-Taker,' Zorean snarled.

'No, my lord. The Imperial Navy.'

Zorean blinked, then snatched up his helm and careened out of the ward room.

'How did they find us?'

'Unclear, my lord.'

In moments he was on the bridge. Sibilla turned stiffly towards him, most of her frame still in medical support devices due to the injuries inflicted upon her during her enslavement. She was biting off orders to her deck crew and the *Red* swerved beneath their feet. Zorean stared at the oculus. An Imperial light cruiser filled the screen, the augurs showing it as less than ten miles ahead. Point-blank. The image swept up the oculus and to port as the *Red* dived beneath it.

'Renegade destroyer Red Galentia,*'* thundered a voice from the bulkhead augmitters.

'Signal incoming from the enemy ship,' strained the vox-officer unnecessarily.

'This is Canoness Commander Beatrizi Dostevska of the Adepta Sororitas, patrol commander and acting captain of the Vizier of Arandeep. *In the name of His Immortal Majesty the God-Emperor of Mankind, surrender or be destroyed.'*

'Ready dorsal lances,' Zorean ordered.

'Should I respond, my lord?' the vox-officer whined. Zorean swept down from the transept, bellowing at the gunnery station as he went.

'Ready dorsal lances!' He pounced towards the vox-officer who was transfixed, wide-eyed as the towering nightmare enfolded him. Zorean drew his skinning knife and with two deft flicks, severed the carotid arteries and jugular veins on both sides of the man's neck. Zorean grasped the officer's thin hair in his fist. Blood jetted from his neck, drenching his epaulettes, and rapidly soaking into the frayed uniform beneath. The man scrambled to put his hands over the wounds, but the manacles at his wrists were chained to the console before him and he could not lift them far enough. He began to shriek.

'Lances ready, my lord,' came the tremulous voice of the gunnery operator.

'Target their engines,' he rasped, his transhuman voice carrying across the shrill screams of the dying vox-officer. Zorean kept the man's face angled directly towards his own; saw the crimson glow of his eye-lenses reflected in the whites of his prey's eyes. 'Fire at will.'

The *Red* shuddered with energy discharge as it continued to avoid the firing solution of the Imperial ship. The vox-officer's screams began to fade, his hollow face starkly white. The blood had soaked his entire torso. It was pooling in his lap and dripping onto the deck plates.

'Lance fire ineffectual, my lord,' the gunnery operator wheezed. 'It was absorbed by target voids.'

'Keep firing. Generatorium, disable safety protocols and burn the engines to their very limits. Get us away.'

'And get our damned void shields up,' Captain Sibilla added. 'Second contact, my lord.'

Zorean dropped the now silenced vox-officer and looked at the tactical readout on the oculus. An Imperial frigate was closing obliquely, cutting off their escape trajectory with enviable voidsmanship. As the *Red* did its best to peel away, the frigate slewed nimbly abeam to present its compact but menacing plasma broadside battery.

'All hands, brace for impact!' Sibilla yelled into her vox-horn. Zorean mag-locked his boots to the deck and took a sharp breath in.

The bridge heaved around him. Deck crew and servitors were torn from their thrones and pits and niches. Bodies dashed against bulkheads. Bones crunched and blood spattered. Sibilla broke across the balustrade, her medical bracing tearing loose. Zorean was nearly dislodged, but his armour held him firm. Alarms wailed. After a few moments damage reports began to flood the oculus readout. Shields down; dorsal lances hit; six decks breached to the void; fires across several sections. Zorean roared orders at whoever was still alive to hear them. He pulled the shattered remains of the helm ensign from their station and directed the ship himself. A mortal sheeted with blood from a head wound wrenched an unconscious comrade from the augur lectern and took their place.

'Enemy frigate launching boarding craft, my lord!' they shouted over the klaxons. Zorean took up Sibilla's vox-horn.

'All hands,' he snarled. 'Prepare to repel boarders.' He threw the horn aside. He grabbed a hunched officer by the neck and lifted him from his pit, placing him before the helm. 'Get. Us. Away.' With that, Zorean drew the Skin-Taker's old plasma pistol and turned to leave the bridge.

'My lord!' The bloody mortal at the augur console pointed a quivering finger at the oculus. 'New contact!'

'Another?' He glowered at the mortal, then stared in disbelief at the oculus.

The *Ikhtheos* surged down from the apex of the battlesphere. Leil Jathok's ship cut between the *Red* and the oncoming frigate with bravura skill, the *Ikhtheos*' point defence emplacements shriving the wave of Imperial assault boats as it passed, blasting more than two-thirds of them into blotches of expanding dust. The Imperial frigate twisted and sheared to port, passing within half a mile of the Abyssal Kindred vessel.

'Assault craft in the void, my lord,' the augur crew croaked.

'The *Ikhtheos* is boarding the light cruiser.' Zorean watched as the sorcerer's vessel threw dozens of assault craft towards the looming *Vizier of Arandeep*. Not Naval assault boats, these craft. The tactical readout marked two Thunderhawk gunships and fifteen assault pods. Chaos Space Marines sped across the soundless void in their armoured craft, autocannon rounds and low-yield las fire merely scorching their hulls. The Imperial light cruiser poured everything it had at the assault wave, to no avail. The *Vizier of Arandeep* was a formidable line breaker, but without flight decks the large ship was vulnerable.

'*You're welcome, turncoat,*' Dalchian crackled over the vox. Zorean was speechless. '*Keep that frigate busy, Zorean. Make your wretched hide worth a damn.*'

There was no reply. Dalchian gazed intently at the tactical hololith guttering in the Thunderhawk's cockpit. He watched with hatred as the *Red* powered away from the battlesphere, forsaking the fight utterly. He watched with hatred, but not surprise.

'So it is,' he spat.

'He runs?' Jathok asked, his already deep voice made positively tectonic by the modulation of his helm augmitters.

'He runs.'

'As would I, in his position,' the sorcerer said with a shrug.

The gunship heaved again. They were through the worst of the point defence envelope, but there were ultra-close-range cannons nestled within the buttressed flank of the cruiser. Another burst flashed across the canopy, the impacts staining the armaglass with scuds of yellow soot.

'Ten seconds,' the pilot called. Dalchian replaced his helm and the two commanders descended into the crew compartment. Half of Dalchian's remnant Blades stood in a line on one side. The others were led by Saryuz aboard the second Thunderhawk.

Jathok's Rubricae formed a line of statuary down the centre of the compartment and a demi-squad of Abyssal Kindred armed with chugging chainblades were hunched behind the ramp, their champion spinning his barbed maul over and over in his hand. Jathok placed himself behind his squad while Dalchian stood at the head of his Blades.

'Five seconds.'

A swathe of runes across Dalchian's visor told him the assault pods had already latched on and bored through the feet-thick pla-steel skin of the *Vizier*. The cacophony of close-quarters combat erupted into his vox-feed as the Abyssal Kindred committed wholesale to the taking of the Imperial vessel.

Over forty Chaos Space Marines in total. Dalchian's pulse quickened and an involuntary grin split his face. To the warp with Zorean. To the warp with Thelissicus. From the depths of ignominy, the star of the Skin-Taker would now begin its ascension. His tragedy was told; now would come the triumph.

'Three.'

Dalchian felt cleansed by his ordeal. His path had already been laid before him, and every step he had taken since had only resolved it the clearer.

'Two.'

Once, his name had been spoken with terror across the sub-sector, even by those who fought at his side. It would be so once more.

'One.'

He let forth a pitiless laugh. Now was his time again.

'Brace!'

Chapter Thirteen

The impacts of the boarding craft were indistinguishable shivers of plasteel within the humming, groaning strategium of the *Vizier of Arandeep*, but Canoness Commander Beatrizi Dostevska felt them as blows against her soul.

The Adepta Sororitas commander was lean, wiry and nearly six feet tall. Her armour was charcoal black, the stylised goblet full of flames on her tabard declaring her of the Order of the Ebon Chalice. The teeth of her lower jaw were gleaming plasteel, the mandibular bone having been crushed decades ago in a tank battle and replaced with an augmetic. She sucked her breath in through those metal teeth as she considered her position.

The lone heretic vessel had been an obvious target. Such a craft of the reviled Heretic Astartes – may they burn eternally – would usually boast only five or six of the warp-rotted scum amongst numberless mortal slaves. Formidable, but far from incontestable for a force the size of her patrol group. She had driven her ships close, accepting the risk of boarding in exchange for the hammer blow her broadsides could deliver.

Then the heretic frigate had launched several assault pods and two gunships. It could be a feint. She hoped it was. And the alternative? If all those craft were full of genetically superhuman, daemon-worshipping power-armoured nightmares? She closed her eyes and offered a prayer to the God-Emperor of Mankind. She would confess to the sin of recklessness once the battle was done. If she lived.

'Point defences ineffective,' a servitor declared from an augur niche, without inflection. 'Enemy boarding craft have full contact.'

'Let them come.' Captain Lom Tarignal sneered. 'Let them die.' The porcine man's captaincy was new, as was his ship's secondment as an Adepta Sororitas duty vessel. He seemed determined to prove his intolerant piety. He sat at the head of the strategium hololith table, watching the latticework projection of his own ship as rune markers showed the deployment of his voidsmen-at-arms and breacher teams. He exuded satisfaction. If he had asked Dostevska for her input then, she would have dutifully pointed out the sloppiness and inconsistency of the crew's efforts, and the many weak points in the defensive cordon. He did not ask.

'You have remarkable confidence in the capacity of your troops, captain,' Dostevska said. Tarignal smiled, mistaking it for a compliment.

'Naturally.' Tarignal ran ringed fingers through the curls of his beard. 'Even the lowliest rating of mine wouldn't suffer a gutless heretic bastard to walk these deck plates if they still had the fight in 'em.'

'Your crew will adequately repel this assault, then?'

'Fear not, honoured Canoness,' he said. 'This ship won't be captured today, I swear it.'

Dostevska nodded, months of void-borne travel with Tarignal

more than enough time to learn what sort of a commander he was.

'Oaths are not to be sworn lightly under the gaze of the God-Emperor,' she said. Tarignal looked up from his hololith for a moment, a twitch of unease creasing his jowl before he blinked it away.

'On my life,' he doubled down. 'And that of my crew, Canoness.'

'The almighty God-Emperor knows your dedication, Captain Tarignal.' Dostevska saw some of the rune markers on the hololith turn crimson, indicating hull breaches and enemy engagement. She gestured to her Palatine, Agnetta Gaulos. The Battle Sister second-in-command stepped forward and dipped her head respectfully. She was head and shoulders taller than her superior, her devotional bob dyed platinum where the Canoness' was natural silver. Agnetta's gauntlets rested at her side, one on the pommel of her power sword and one on the holster of her inferno pistol.

'Order the cutter ready for emergency launch,' Dostevska said. 'If the battle goes ill, I want as many Sisters as possible aboard and returning to the main battle group.' Tarignal's head snapped up, the colour draining from his face as Agnetta nodded.

'The materiel stowed in the hold?' the Palatine asked.

'Hmm.' Canoness Dostevska knotted her brow. 'No way to transfer it now. Throne forgive us, but it must be sacrificed.'

Agnetta nodded again and turned to leave, but stopped when Tarignal shouted.

'What in blazes is this, Canoness?' The man was standing, eyes popping. 'The cursed Archenemy are blasting their way onto my ship and you turn to flee like common cowards!'

Palatine Agnetta stepped towards the captain, partly drawing her blade so that a few inches of its gleaming length showed. She spoke quietly.

'Have a care, captain.'

Dostevska had not moved. She regarded the captain with open curiosity.

'Do not misunderstand my intent, captain,' she said. 'But did you not this very moment swear your crew were more than up to the job of repelling this attack?'

'Yes,' Tarignal ground out. 'With Adepta Sororitas support, naturally. You've a whole damned commandery embarked. Not to mention a thousand Frateris illiterates!'

Palatine Agnetta took another half step, another few inches of her sword blade emerging. Dostevska sighed.

'Do not misunderstand my intent,' the Canoness repeated. 'I shall deploy my Sisters and the Frateris Militia among your defensive troops, and they will sell their lives dearly to protect this ship of His Immortal Majesty's Imperial Navy.' At the clarification, Tarignal's bluster abated slightly. Dostevska was not finished. 'But we are here to liberate the forge world Uzurmandius. That is *our* oath, captain. While this patrol endures, I shall command it, but if this ship faces certain ruin and I can serve my divine obligation elsewhere, then that is what I must do. Is that clear?'

Tarignal's chins scraped against his starched collar as his gaze flicked from Canoness to Palatine. With supreme effort, he swallowed his panic and remembered his station.

'Of course, honoured Canoness,' he said. Sweat beaded at his brow. 'Please excuse my lapse in decorum.'

'Naturally.' Dostevska nodded. 'Now, direct your defence from the bridge, Tarignal. A crew should see their captain.' She tried not to let her relish show as she asserted her command. Poor Tarignal had yet to see her at her most direct. He blinked in surprise and then fled the strategium, muttering as he went, 'Quite right, Canoness Commander. Quite right, too.'

Once he was gone Palatine Agnetta replaced her blade and turned to Dostevska.

'We may abandon the *Vizier*, Canoness, but what stops it falling into Archenemy hands once that oaf inevitably surrenders?'

'It's a concern,' Dostevska admitted with raised eyebrows. 'You have a suggestion?'

'There is an insurance I would implement, yes, Canoness.'

'Good.' Dostevska took a long breath. 'You have my complete trust. Whatever your *insurance*, see it done. But first, I want you in the gun line directing the Frateris. Let's see if we can't hoist this situation out of the privy before committing ourselves, hmm?'

'Grace of the Emperor be with us, Canoness.'

'Never doubt it, my child.'

A petty officer and six ratings stood on the gantries that ran high across the starboard hold. Crude void suits were lumpy beneath uniforms of slate grey with yellow piping, and bulbous helms gave them the proportions of infants. Stacks of containerised materiel stretched out in all directions below them. Dehydrated rations and plastek-wrapped uniforms were bound together on pallets; stationery, toiletries and bunk linen filled boxes and bins; machine components, lubricants and fixings were crammed tight into locked cages. The veteran crew team had almost tuned out the relentless blare of the *Vizier of Arandeep*'s general alarm. They were as ready as they could be, knowing that the cargo decks were unlikely to be the target of a boarding action, but attending their posts diligently nonetheless. Not often did the Archenemy behave the way a sane foe might.

A mighty explosion bloomed through the inner hull, sending glowing chunks of plasteel into the cargo stacks. The defenders barely kept their feet. Atmosphere started to seethe out of the breach, whipping up a tempest around them, when a second impact quaked the superstructure. Now they all fell. Vacuum alarms began to keen, and new crimson lumens flashed their warnings from bulkhead sconces. The Naval team could not see the boarding craft over the ramparts of cargo. They regained their feet quickly and clanked along the gantry for a better vantage.

The gunship was enormous, its centreline-mounted turbo-laser having cored a glowing rend in the hull of the cruiser. The black-and-turquoise craft was streaked with grime and burn marks, and its assault ramp hung open, the compartment within unnervingly empty. The petty officer ordered three of his team down the ladder to investigate and kept three high as top cover before sprinting back along the gantry towards the hardline vox-set to report the breach.

About halfway, he came to an abrupt stop as if he had run into a solid obstacle. Confused, he cast his gaze around before coming to stare in disbelief at the huge, armoured hand that was clutched against his chest. In the skirling atmosphere and the darkness irregularly lit with crimson warning lumens, he could barely see the silhouette of the hand's owner perched on the edge of the gantry like some daemonic acrobat. The silhouette was titanic. Sharp edges glinted in the palsied light, and the silhouette slowly withdrew its armoured hand.

The petty officer gaped, unfeeling, as bladed fingers, each over a foot long, unsheathed from his torso flesh with a barely audible *slick*. He watched his own blood slide in ropes from the blades, and a bitter coldness stole over him. His blood frothed from the incisions in his void suit, the rapidly dropping pressure in the cargo hold sucking it greedily from him. The bladed gauntlet swept across and he flinched. Both of his forearms fell to the deck and began to roll in the gale, skidding along the grating towards the hull breach. Then he saw his belly hanging open, shreds and loops of pinkish grey organs fluttering out and forming a wet pile that sagged through the gaps in the grating. He screamed and his legs gave out.

Dalchian dragged the still-screaming man to where his top cover stood at the gantry railing. The Skin-Taker did not rush, enjoying the body language of the three Naval crew as they stared at him and the writhing form of their disembowelled superior. A sharp scent on the rushing air told him at least one of them had soiled themselves. Dalchian stopped ten feet from them and lifted the lightning claw whose power field he had not even bothered to activate yet. The three Imperials followed the slow motion of the claw as it rose, then Dalchian clenched the blades together.

One of the Imperials disintegrated in a shower of gushing fluids as Dagardis struck from behind, putting his axe through the mortal from collar to pelvis. Spinning in shock, another of the Naval crew watched Qi Umshar's skinning knife, hypnotised as the blade pushed through their rubber visor and into their mouth. Qi Umshar lifted the mortal with his blade through the roof of their mouth. Dropping their lasrifle, they shuddered and jerked as they died.

The last Imperial, admirably, levelled his shotgun at Dalchian and fired. The shot ricocheted from the curved mass of ceramite, barely marking the blue-black livery. Keth Naa hauled himself over the railing behind the last crew member and simply picked them up with both hands. The Imperial squealed as Keth Naa hurled them bodily from the gantry to bounce from the Thunderhawk's armoured fuselage and be sucked out into the void through the still-glowing entry wound.

A conveyor rattled up to the gantry level from the deck below. The mesh screen rolled back and Jathok, his Rubricae, and the Abyssal Kindred shield-bearers stepped out. The sorcerer looked at the dripping mess of two dismantled crew and watched as Qi Umshar slid his blade out of the third cadaver's face.

'Welcome aboard,' the sorcerer said. Dalchian strode level with him and gestured towards the portal ahead.

'Shall we?'

The *Ikhtheos* had driven a wedge between the two Imperial ships, and now, with its predatory payload delivered, it capitalised on its position. Simultaneous broadsides stretched out to either flank, hammering the gracefully veering starboard stern of the *Vizier* and the glowing engines of the sharply banking Imperial frigate, named *Prideful*. The immediate threat that the *Ikhtheos* had to contend with, though, was the pair of Asp-class destroyers that accompanied the Imperial splinter fleet. The smaller, more manoeuvrable craft were sweeping in and rapidly lining up on the *Ikhtheos*, whereupon they would loose their melta torpedoes and watch the Abyssal Kindred vessel be torn asunder. But the will of the Chaos frigate's crew was not to be underestimated. Rather than break from the destroyers to run, or turn its heavily armoured prow towards them to soak up the barrage, the *Ikhtheos* tracked steadily about, staying abeam of the two Asps and running up a surge of speed. The destroyers did as the Chaos Space Marines had hoped, letting their torpedoes fly in a hurry. The *Ikhtheos* powered across the acquisition solution of the torpedoes' simple machine spirits, swiftly crossing out of their engagement arc. The torpedoes streaked off into the outer dark with no targets to latch on to.

Now the *Ikhtheos* yawed hard, letting its own forward lances speak. The Asps diverged their courses hoping to force the *Ikhtheos* to choose between them, but the Chaos lances were hot and hungry. Threads of scarlet light blitzed across both destroyers, making their modest shields falter and fail. The destroyers continued their manoeuvre for an instant longer before one detonated in a violent sphere of pearlescent fire. The other simply broke, twisting from its own thrust-line and shedding armour, plasma and human lives as it went. There could have been no finer execution of strategy on the part of the *Ikhtheos'* crew, and had the clash been a great fleet battle then such quality would have been marked and studied by the ever-prying Imperial strategos. Perhaps even cited by the educating staff of the illustrious fleet collegia on Cypra Mundi or Hydraphur in centuries to come. But the battle was not a grand affair, and none aboard the Imperial ships were currently of a mind to record the tactical acumen of their hated enemy for posterity.

The *Prideful*, given room to adjust by the destroyers' vain attack run, let fly a plasma broadside into the *Ikhtheos'* starboard bow. The Abyssal Kindred ship's shields flared, the competing energies forming a pyrotechnic display that clung to the *Ikhtheos'* gunwales as it tore through them. The *Ikhtheos* rounded on the frigate and began to chase it, but the heart of the void battle was now within the very hull of the Imperial patrol leader, the *Vizier of Arandeep*.

For the Blades of Atrocity and the Abyssal Kindred meant to take it for a prize.

The *Vizier of Arandeep* adhered to a common pattern of construction among the Imperium's staggeringly vast armadas of voidcraft. Though a light cruiser by class, the veteran warship's bulk was still leviathan in scale, and its Battlefleet Odovokan livery was faded and scarred across its flanks from aeons of battle.

But the newest wounds shone proud.

Dalchian's Night Lords and the Abyssal Kindred had made the orlop deck with little encumbrance. Another Naval fire-team at the companionway had died messily, and now the Chaos Space Marines threaded their way in darkness between huge drums of berthing chains, tightly wrapped while the *Vizier* was underway, far from void dock. A sealed corridor across the deck was the only way onwards. The boarders approached the wide portal, four leaves locked tight. They spread out and Dalchian nodded Keth Naa forwards to use one of his melta bombs, but it was unnecessary.

The portal grated open and a mob of mortals poured out.

Gunfire erupted. Shotguns and autorifles crashed in the fists of the defenders as Night Lords and Abyssal Kindred bolters roared their deafening reports.

Jathok's warriors sprinted forward, using their armour-clad heft like a battle tank's dozer blade. Mortal forms were slammed aside and pitched into the air. The Kindred champion's maul sank into skull after skull. Dagardis was next in, hewing limbs and torsos, barking laughter. Jathok's Rubricae unleashed metronomic volleys of jade tracer fire, their rounds leaving charred flesh and weeping metal where they struck. Dalchian swept in, Krutaan's old claw reaping lives as the razor digits slashed across exposed throats and faces. The frail humans fell like wheat under a scythe.

Dalchian killed and killed and killed, wondering just why the mortals seemed so eager to throw themselves onto the Chaos weapons. The dying masses were robed in vestments and everywhere he looked was the glint of rosaries and devotional icons. *Ah, of course. The Sororitas are feeding us their prayer-drunk pets rather than risk themselves.* Frateris Militia. Formerly civilian dedicants so consumed with religiosity they took up arms and joined the fundamentalist crusades of the Imperial war machine. Dalchian had used screaming, gibbering cultists before in battle and these fools were no different, save for the name of the deity on their lips.

The slaughter quickly began sapping the impetus of the Frateris assault as dozens died. The Chaos Space Marines had been slowed a fraction, but the mortals could do nothing to stay their advance. The armoured monsters went where they willed, slaying and mutilating and letting blood flow in thick rivers across the corroded plasteel of the deck.

Then the true attack came.

From open blast doors on the right flank of the access corridor, the streaking hiss of a missile launcher sounded. The projectile seared into the melee, detonating in a blast of light and heat. A handful of mortals fell, riven by the blast. Concerningly, one of the Kindred also fell, the krak missile breaking the Chaos Space Marine's armour in two. The Kindred struggled to rise, blood heaving from the splayed ceramite across his chest, but the swarm of howling mortals bore him down. Bayonets and shivs found the gaps at his neck and armpits and groin. One mortal screamed, an armoured gauntlet crushing his face, but the Kindred died of a thousand wounds beneath the mob.

At the blast doors stood a gunline of militia, their devotional robes hung with flak-jackets, Militarum-grade weapons in hand. At their centre stood a hugely tall Adepta Sororitas warrior, directing their gunfire with sweeps of her drawn power sword. One militia veteran reloaded the missile launcher while another steadied the tube on her shoulder. She fired again.

Another blast echoed in the plasteel darkness, shining momentarily like a flood-lumen. Keth Naa flew back, breastplate and pauldrons rent, helm blown from his head. The icon on his power pack swung and broke, the bat-winged skull with a bone-saw in its teeth skittering beneath a drum of chains and out of sight.

Fury boiled in Dalchian's belly watching another of his Blades felled, but also at seeing the icon of the Blades of Atrocity cast down. The Skin-Taker roared like a berserker and cannoned through the press of praying, screaming militia. Another krak blast reverberated through the chamber, but he hardly noticed. Leaping like an animal, Dalchian fell on the group of mortals nearest the sooty dent in the deck where Keth Naa had been hit. He tore a lean man to shreds with a single sweep of Krutaan's claw and kicked the tatters into the faces of a pair of scurrying militia. Blinded, they tripped and fell to be mulched beneath his razor-edged boots. A decapitated head spiralled before him, and Dalchian saw that Dagardis was also making vengeance-murder with his lightning-wreathed axe. A woman ran at him, prayer-scrolls trailing behind her as she charged. He gunned the throttle of his chainglaive and hewed her at the waist and she dropped, cleaved messily in two.

The Blades unleashed months of degraded, denuded wrath against these willing prey-scum, drenching themselves in gore and peeling the life from shrieking victims. More blasts sounded along with disciplined volleys of las fire, but Dalchian was in the murder frenzy. Nothing mattered. The cocktail of burning hair, body odour and blood filled his olfactory senses. An old man pawed at the organs that fountained from his belly. A keening girl's skull emptied as a bolt round hit her in the eye. One mortal so fouled as to be indiscernible from a corpse knelt and prayed, the furore of the death around them leaving them miraculously be. Until their spine shattered under the Abyssal Kindred champion's maul.

'Skin-Taker!'

Dalchian kicked the feet out from under a mortal as they fled from him, pinning them to the deck with his claw-blades as he carved his glaive into their back. He stood and went after another man who had dropped his shotgun and run. Dalchian grasped the man's head in Krutaan's claw and yanked. The man's shriek quavered piteously as his face ribboned. He lunged and grabbed the foot of a woman as she tried to crawl away, severing her leg with a flourish and basking in the horrified yelping sound she made.

'Lord Skin-Taker!'

'What?' he demanded, looking Krutaan dead in the eye. They stood before one another, surrounded by empty blackness and silence. Krutaan, armour immaculate, took a step towards his lord.

'This is good, Dalchian,' the claw leader said, nodding.

'What is?'

'Your path is laid for you,' Krutaan said. 'You see it yourself.'

'Why aren't you dead?' Dalchian knew Krutaan should be dead. He could not remember why, but Krutaan should definitely be dead.

'Who do you see, Dalchian?' Krutaan asked. 'When I speak, whose voice do you hear?'

'Enough games, Krutaan.'

'Ah!' The claw leader's eyes widened in comprehension. 'The mutineer. Yes, that makes sense. This is very good, Dalchian.' Krutaan's rebreather began to stretch, the smile beneath contorting the metal. Did its grille look like fangs?

'Don't call me that,' Dalchian snapped, unsure why.

'Call you what?' Krutaan said, grinning. 'Dalchian?'

'*Dalchian!*' Leil Jathok's staff hammered into the side of his helm, and the madness vanished. He blinked twice and looked around at the charnel ruin of the orlop deck. The mortals were dead or fled. Over a hundred corpses steamed in the darkness.

'Witch,' Dalchian said fuzzily. 'Keth Naa.' He turned to the fallen Blade. The icon bearer was on his back, struggling to rise. His exposed face was a pulverised mess of singed meat, but his trunk was worse. Half his chest armour had broken away, and the partly cauterised chasm in his side was a soup of exposed bone and quivering organ tissue.

'I live, my lord,' he said thickly.

'Good,' Dalchian nodded. His thoughts were like strips of silk in a gale. He snatched for them. Jathok stood before him and fixed the Skin-Taker in his gaze.

'Are you fit, Skin-Taker?' he asked quietly so no others would hear. Dalchian swallowed his disorientation.

'Aye, witch.' *What in the Eye was that?* 'The fury of battle, nothing more.' *I saw Krutaan. I think… I…* He looked briefly at the dripping fingers of Krutaan's claw. He felt the looming threat of indecision and spoke aloud before it claimed him, mag-locking his glaive to his power pack. 'We go onwards.'

The image of Krutaan flashed in bright negative colours every time he blinked, the picture clear but wrong, somehow. The blades of the lightning claw flexed rhythmically without his direction. He felt a hollowness like deep hunger, but the sensation was in his hand, not his belly. *How odd.*

The few Frateris survivors had evacuated the orlop deck access corridor completely. The blast doors at the far end grated shut as the Chaos boarders filled the tight avenue with their looming bulk.

'We'll be fortunate if our melta bombs breach that,' Qi Umshar said. He had managed to lift Keth Naa and was half-carrying the legionary whose lifeblood dribbled in a trail behind them.

'Fret not, sawbones,' Jathok replied. There was hurried movement on the far side of the misted armaglass vision slit as the sorcerer advanced towards the heavy door. The booming *clangs* of locking bars engaging shuddered through the plasteel, an indicator lumen turning bright crimson on the bulkhead above. Jathok placed his palm onto the door and shut his eyes, the Rubricae forming a cordon around him.

Dalchian ground his teeth. One Kindred dead was a steep price for this early stage of the assault, but Keth Naa seemed soon to follow. Qi Umshar propped the injured Blade against the corridor bulkhead. Keth Naa, pieces of his shattered bolter still hanging from their strap, drunkenly pulled a bolt pistol from his belt with the arm that still functioned. His blood-filled eyes wandered and lumpen gore pooled beneath him.

A depressurisation alarm began to keen. The atmosphere whirled and sucked around them. Dalchian went to a control terminal on the bulkhead.

'They're opening the fairleads.' The holes in the hull through which the berthing chains fed while in void dock were sealed with armoured plugs during transit. The defenders of the *Vizier* were unstopping those plugs, opening the orlop deck to hard vacuum. Dalchian jabbed the rune board as he tried to close the portal into the access corridor. 'And they've disabled portal controls,' he said pointedly in Jathok's direction.

'Give me time,' the sorcerer murmured, eyes still closed, hand against the plasteel of the blast door.

'You have seconds, witch,' Dalchian snarled. The Frateris corpses began to bubble and seep as the pressure dropped still further.

'My lord,' Qi Umshar's voice called from where he knelt by Keth Naa. Dalchian looked at him. Keth Naa's ruined face was straining. The crater in his side bubbling and spilling fragments of tissue.

The pressure display on Dalchian's helm display plummeted, and he felt the temperature going with it. The fringes of Keth Naa's pool of blood and bits was already rimed with frost. The legionary's throat was snatching at breaths that would not come. A gene-forged anatomy could withstand short spells exposed to vacuum, the implanted mucranoid embalming it in biochemical waxes to offer temporary protection. But only while it possessed most of its physiological function, and it was clear to Dalchian that Keth Naa's did not.

'If we can get him inside, I may be able to stabilise him,' Qi Umshar said.

'Witch!' Dalchian barked. 'How long?'

Jathok grunted in frustration, the hand resting against the blast door clenching into a fist.

'As long as it takes!' The sorcerer opened his palm again. The storm winds had all but abated and an airless quiet descended. They spoke by vox.

Dalchian could ill afford to have his surgeon shackled to a nigh-dead legionary. They had to maintain the momentum of the assault, and he needed every able-bodied warrior he had. Keth Naa had slid to the deck, his eyes and tongue bulging from his skull, and his catastrophic wound was voiding entrails into the vacuum with every second. Dalchian stalked towards the blast door, his back to his Blades and the dying Keth Naa. He edged between the Rubricae, who showed no sign that they noticed, and placed himself before the enormous plasteel slab.

The vision slit was speckled and blurry, but a narrow slice of the corridor the other side showed clearly enough. A figure stood there, and Dalchian looked her up and down. Clad in power armour that was a refined, more elegant echo of his own, she stood almost as tall as he did, which was immensely rare for a genetically un-altered human. Fluted pauldrons of obsidian lacquer were filigreed with the carrion Corpse-Emperor's haughty raptor. A melta pistol was holstered at her hip, and she rested a hand on the pommel of a sheathed power sword. Her face was as scarred as any veteran warrior's, a sharp brow shading dark brown eyes. Washed-out electoo scripture covered her face, greening with age. Her neat bob of hair was a uniform ivory colour.

And she was smiling. Dalchian leaned his glowing red eye-lenses forward until his helm's silver banding came to rest on the armaglass.

'Witch?'

'Wait,' Jathok answered, brow creased with concentration. The blast door's lock was stubborn. The mechanism ground and boomed as the sorcerer coerced it with psychic brute force, the sounds unheard, but felt through their feet instead. The indicator lumen remained crimson. There was a pause.

'End his suffering,' Dalchian ordered.

'But, my lord,' Qi Umshar protested. 'He may yet endure.'

'End him.'

The silence stretched. Dalchian stared at the smiling Adepta Sororitas warrior. Krutaan's claw ground its blades together in a fist, swaying back and forth.

'A reckoning awaits you,' he whispered to her.

The Battle Sister placed a sallet helm over her head and disappeared. Dalchian backed away from the door where Jathok still worked his witchery, then turned to his Blades. Qi Umshar had not moved. Dalchian leant down and took the bolt pistol from Keth Naa's shuddering, nerveless grip.

And shot him through the temple with it.

Dalchian fixed his glowing eye-lenses on Qi Umshar, who said nothing.

'Too often of late have I needed to repeat myself,' Dalchian hissed. 'I am your lord, surgeon-Apothecary.'

'Yes, my Lord Skin-Taker.' Qi Umshar bowed his head. Dalchian let the moment linger for several heartbeats.

'See to your task,' he said.

'Aye, lord.' Qi Umshar immediately knelt beside Keth Naa's corpse and began drilling through the icon-bearer's abused armour to access the organs of his gene legacy. When the locking lugs of the blast door finally withdrew, he was all but finished, another vial full at his belt.

A new hurricane raged as the great door slowly lifted, gritty atmosphere battering them. The Sororitas warrior and any others were long gone, and the corridor was empty. They passed through and, exhausted, Jathok closed the door behind them.

He used the control panel this time.

CHAPTER FOURTEEN

The billet held forty ratings in tightly bunked cots, with a small shrine, kit stowage, washroom and mess table at each corner. The crew were off watch, but during a boarding action all hands made ready for close-quarters combat, so they stood by their bunks with short-barrelled shotguns and a variety of improvised clubs in hand. They awaited the orders that would direct them anywhere aboard the ship to bolster defences. The atmosphere in the billet was tight as a drumskin. Some of the more experienced ratings voiced jibes at the expense of their enemy or quips of gallows humour to ease the fear of their young comrades. Anxious murmurs of laughter only threw the tension into sharper focus.

The lumens in the billet stuttered and then failed, dropping them into total blackness. There was a scurrying sound. Then emergency lighting saturated the chamber with a bloody glow. The ratings held their breath and blinked. One of the older crew gurgled from where he hung off a high bunk, a plasteel snare around his neck and fastened to the cot frame. The emergency lights failed.

A handful of wet thumps sounded and a rating screamed. The sound of blades piercing meat echoed from all corners of the billet and the ratings erupted into violent, horrified anarchy. Screams and shouts filled the air and the spinning illumination of handheld stab-lumens glanced from glistening, skinless flesh to weeping faces to the pointed edges of enormous monsters made of shadow. A few shotguns crashed in the darkness; pulses of lightning that imprinted frozen tableaus of gore-drenched misery onto the retinas of the mortal crew. Their screams became animal howls.

In less than a minute, all forty ratings were dead.

The champion Endagur led the Abyssal Kindred forward into the billet with his toothed power sword drawn, the Night Lords having cleared the way. The daemon-worshippers had committed their fair share of carnage in their time, but the obscenity they waded through in the wake of Saryuz's Blades made even their twisted hearts skip a beat.

'The way is clear,' Saryuz said unnecessarily, the grin audible in his voice. Endagur looked around and, as was his custom, said nothing.

The crew billets emptied quickly. Hundreds of the lowest dregs of the Imperial Navy personnel cohort fled the indefensible section, yelling and tripping over themselves. They barrelled their way towards the gun decks to the fore, shouting for armed comrades, breachers and officers. At an intersection between them and the gun decks stood a ship's commissar, plasma pistol humming. Seventeen ratings fell, incinerated by the energy bolts, before the flood of crew came to an uneasy halt.

'The Emperor expects,' growled the commissar in a voice that was low but carried down twenty yards of corridor with astounding clarity. 'He expects that every one of you do your duty. Face the enemy! Or face the Almighty God-Emperor Himself.' The tight-packed column of men and women slowly turned, the grips on their improvised weapons tightening.

Fifteen Heretic Astartes rounded the far bend. The horns and knotted hair surmounting their helms scraped the very ceiling, amber eye-lenses smouldering in the half-light. Turquoise livery formed sinuous veins of brightness across the gloss black of their hulking armour. At their head was a giant with a beastly visage worked in ceramite over the face of his helm. A rack of jangling bones, scrimshawed with migraine runework, hung from the iron spikes atop his power pack, and in his left fist he held a toothed power sword, its disruptive energy field sending tendrils of lightning down the blade. Some of the crew prayed; some of them felt tears run; all of them trembled. Warp-spawned nightmares advanced in front of them and the divine wrath of Him-on-Terra stood implacably behind. They would stand and they would die.

'Be not afraid,' the commissar intoned. 'Glorious instruments of His will. Your service is your honour, your sacrifice is the price of victory, willingly paid. Though you stand in the shadow of the servants of evil, you shall be not–'

He stopped mid sermon. Some of the crew had started to allow a fatalistic detachment to steal over them, the commissar's words doing their work. The rear rank turned hesitantly, curious why their commissar was silent.

Ang Heltris peeled the heavyset man like a fruit. Equal parts leather trench coat, starched epaulettes, and clammy skin came away as the knifeman's prosthetic blade worked in practised sweeps. The Night Lord had his other hand so tight around the commissar's neck that the political officer's hat had fallen off, the veins of his temple bulging horrifically. His plasma pistol lay steaming in a pile of skin and cloth.

Saryuz stepped out behind Ang Heltris, skinning knives ready. Vellet wore his marksman's bolter over his shoulder, a baroque chainsword in his hands for the close work of boarding. Zhikarga stomped forth, his heavy bolter racked and ready. The heavy gunner's bronze skull-helm grinned at his prey as the belt of ammunition swayed below his monstrous gun.

'Be not afraid,' he said in a mocking hiss. Then opened fire.

His disciplined bursts blasted apart anyone with a stripe on their uniform, petty officers and midshipmen explosively disintegrating under the assault. With a collective shriek, the group recoiled from the braying weapon and surged towards the larger force of Endagur's warriors instead, who drew blades and revved chain weapons. The mortals shuddered, the desire of each outward-facing rank to withdraw crushing those trapped in the middle. Zhikarga ceased his fusillade, allowing his murder-kin to stalk forth.

The Night Lords fell on the mob with glee.

On eight separate decks of the *Vizier of Arandeep* heinous combat broke out. Junior ratings, rapier-toting officers and cloaked Mechanicus adepts engaged the heretics with desperate fury. A Dreadclaw of Abyssal Kindred had bored into the aft weapons locker and was in the process of destroying the platoon of Naval breachers that tried to hold it. Another boarding party gained access to the plasma redirection conduits feeding one of the vast engine stacks, severing the huge pipes and forcing a partial shutdown of the *Vizier*'s propulsion systems. Off-watch crew were positioned at vital intersections, only to be butchered and burned by Abyssal Kindred weapons. Sections of the light cruiser's defence collapsed in sequence as the Chaos Space Marines skilfully, mercilessly advanced on the bridge and generatorium. By turns, the inevitability of the outcome became more obvious to both attackers and defenders.

Palatine Agnetta Gaulos, nursing catastrophic injuries to her torso and left leg, staggered into a conveyor alone and descended through the decks, bleeding but smiling.

Dalchian and Jathok smashed their way onto one of the *Vizier*'s gun decks. Their warriors carved through the ratings with distasteful ease, the press-ganged crew choosing to turn and run rather than fight, but dying just the same. A party of Naval breachers blasted the Chaos Space Marines with shotguns, but Jathok's melee warriors ran them down. The sorcerer's implacable Rubricae laced the Imperials with warpfire, the unearthly bullets passing through four or five bodies before detonating in a loop of emerald flame. Ang Heltris leapt across the armoured blast screening between each gun team, his huge mass seemingly forgotten. He fell upon petty officers and gang-bosses, filleting them and throwing them, shrieking, down into the wells of the macrocannon embrasures where the wheels of the vast gun carriages slid back and forth with their constant recoil. Qi Umshar worked his bolter, gutting and dismembering mortals rather than killing them outright so their screams added to the terror and confusion. Dalchian and Dagardis formed a deadly pairing, chewing a spear tip through the ramshackle defence.

A huge conveyor designed to caddy replacement parts up from the hold to the gun deck shuddered to a halt nearby. Tall cage doors rolled back and half a dozen Sororitas surged out, rinsing the Chaos Space Marines with automatic bolter fire. Another shape loomed behind them in the darkness. Abyssal Kindred flames washed towards the Battle Sisters as Jathok's shield-bearer rounded on them. Ang Heltris dropped among the Sororitas, his blades flashing.

The looming bulk of a Penitent Engine lumbered from the conveyor behind the Sisters, piston limbs stomping it forwards.

Two huge disc saws whirred at the tips of the battle walker's arms, an iron maiden encasement on its torso showing where the engine's operator was incarcerated, the wretch's furious repentance driving the engine's motion and weapons. Strips of prayer cloth and reams of devotional parchment hung from the engine's frame and it carried with it the scents of myrrh and gore.

Flames billowed from projectors on its arms, engulfing Chaos Space Marines and Imperial crew alike. Dalchian and Dagardis waded through the inferno towards it. A cone of psychic power spun into existence about the walker, sealing the gouts of flame off from the boarders thanks to the sorcerer's efforts. Qi Umshar's bolt shots hammered the iron maiden, further torturing the soul within.

Dalchian slashed his claw across a spinning disc blade. The energised talons were for carving meat and sinew, not cleaving metal, but nonetheless the disc blade shattered, sending whistling shards in every direction. The engine slammed its wounded arm forwards, knocking Dalchian from his feet and hurling him into the melee where the Abyssal Kindred chainswords were hewing into Adepta Sororitas plate.

Dagardis hacked his axe at the engine's leg armature, severing hydraulics and causing the thing to sag. It batted his next swing aside with its broken arm and ploughed its second buzz saw into Dagardis' flank, severing the Blade's right arm and grinding into his torso armour. The Night Lord brayed in pain. Then the *Vizier* quaked with tectonic violence. The Penitent Engine, with Dagardis still lodged on to its saw blade, tumbled from the deck and into the well of the macrocannon embrasure, disappearing into the smoke and dust below.

Dalchian snarled as he smashed into the Sororitas, killing one with his impact alone. The Imperials folded, the last Battle Sister roasted by one of Jathok's flamers. Dalchian cast a swift glance below the massive ship's gun, into the shadow beneath its wheels. His teeth made grinding noises as he grimaced in fury. Then he cast his gaze around. A long, tall companionway threaded the inner edge of the gun deck, describing a path up to the gallery decks that led towards the bridge.

'Onwards!' he roared.

Deeper within the *Vizier*, Endagur's boarding party mowed a bloody trail, the champion's serrated sword ripping baseline humans apart, their flak armour barely an inconvenience to its honed teeth. Saryuz fractured the helms and breastplates of overseers with his meltagun, its hissing blasts heralding agony and death. Their party had eviscerated the billet decks and pursued their mortal prey into a wide, richly carpeted officers' mess hall. Portraits of important figures from the battlefleet's history or the past crew of the *Vizier* itself filled the bulkhead arches; mahogany tables and chairs were arrayed with neurotic precision under hanging chandeliers of bronze and crystal.

Dark wood splintered beneath their tread, portraits holed and shredded by detonating bolt rounds. The Naval voidsmen-at-arms returned fire across the mess, upturned tables providing them the illusion of cover as they thundered volley after volley. Despite the defence the Chaos boarders crashed towards them like a tsunami, blades high, eyes glowing.

They obliterated the resistance in the mess hall, tearing apart mortals and treading them into the carpet. Beyond the hall was the *Vizier*'s main arterial, a huge corridor hung with battle honours where countless portals, companionways and conveyor shafts led all over the ship's anatomy. The open space was practically indefensible and lightly armed Imperials fled before the barbed assault of the Chaos Space Marines.

Paired doors to the port side of the arterial groaned open and a mob of Frateris Militia poured forth, easily two hundred of the self-flagellating fundamentalists. Cheap, die-stamped auto-rifles coughed and improvised explosives sailed over their heads towards the boarders. The Chaos Space Marines met the charge with devastating violence, but the mortals were too faith-crazed to acknowledge the hopelessness of their plight. They mired the power-armoured heretics in a flood of bodies, the dead held upright by the press of the living.

While Saryuz growled and barked at the insane humans, Endagur watched as a conveyor cage slid open. It was a huge conveyor, suited to shuttling tons of materiel up from the hold in a single journey. A handful of Adepta Sororitas stormed from the doors, pouring their firepower into the morass, uncaring if devoted Imperial fanatics fell as collateral. Then the arterial corridor filled with rumbling and the chemical tang of pro-methium exhaust fumes.

In all their combined years of fighting void war and pros-ecuting boarding assaults, none of the Chaos Space Marines present had ever witnessed what now confronted them. Saryuz watched in disbelief as a battle tank clattered from the conveyor, its armoured flanks satin like the rest of the Sororitas, religious fetishes clinking from where they hung against the ceramite.

The Immolator tank bore the ubiquitous Rhino chassis, the bluntly sloped faces of the design an ageless echo of human con-quest; a shape that had haunted battlefields and atrocities for ten millennia and more. The satin ceramite was banded with stripes of ruddy scarlet, and each armoured door frescoed with scenes of miracles and devotion, saints and martyrs rendered exquisitely in delicate enamel. A Battle Sister in black-and-scarlet plate sat in the wide cupola of the vehicle turret, gauntlets tight around her weapons controls. The fanatics raised their voices in devotional madness as the tank's turret adjusted its angles.

Still trapped within the heaving mass of humanity, Endagur hacked and hacked, silent but furious. Saryuz bellowed his frustration and hoped that Dalchian's boarding party were near. Realising that the Skin-Taker was the one warrior he wanted to see charging into the Sisters of Battle was a painful moment for Saryuz. To acknowledge his lord's capacity in his own mind, after so long spent disparaging him. It was almost as painful as what came next.

The mortals screamed in fervent ecstasy and the Chaos Space Marines howled their rage as white flame blanketed them all.

Another flight of attack craft blinked into life on the augurs.

'Ether's depths!' Warpsmith Naritsa cursed as he turned his metal face towards the readout. 'How many damned fighters do the bastards have?'

'This would be the seventh sortie,' Ibriel replied, bringing the information to the front of his mind without effort. 'Transponder idents associated with the attack craft indicate a complement of at least thirty interceptors aboard the *Prideful*, accompanying a possible forty fighter-bombers, most of which were destroyed as we–'

'Thank you, tech-priest.' The Abyssal Kindred Warpsmith, his throwaway rhetorical question answered in frustrating detail, had many things competing for his attention.

The *Ikhtheos* had been battered by attack craft. There were hull breaches on several decks and one of the port-side cannons had been taken offline by a close-range missile cluster. Naritsa spared no thought for the hundreds of serfs crushed and burned at their posts by such a blow. Most of the Imperial bombers had by now been accounted for by the *Ikhtheos'* formidable point defence armaments, but the lascannons and hypervelocity autocannon rounds of the *Prideful's* interceptors were still proving a distraction. Within the *Ikhtheos'* void shields, the tiny craft could snipe defence turrets and vital subsystems with infuriating impunity. It was all dragging his focus away from the bigger threat.

The *Prideful*. A terror frigate from the Imperial shipyards, with engines massively over-classed for its tonnage and a reinforced prow, it was an explosive javelin to be hurled at enemy fleets head-on. It was a line breaker, tasked with ramming the choicest foe and cleaving it asunder before disgorging a swarm of attack craft to sow misery and destruction in the back line.

The *Ikhtheos*, an Adeptus Astartes frigate, was perhaps the only class of human vessel in the galaxy that could match the *Prideful*, turn for turn. The *Prideful*'s flights of Imperial attack craft should have crippled the *Ikhtheos* out of hand, but the Abyssal Kindred were habituated itinerants, their arms and panoply long since adjusted to operating without support in the deep void. Furthermore, not only was the *Ikhtheos'* point defence abundant, but it possessed better than brain-wiped servitors at the controls of each turret. Malign intelligences from beyond the mortal plane had been courted and then imbued within its targeting arrays and surveyor banks. The ship cast tendrils of awareness out through the immaterium, glimpses of foreseen flight paths making their aim unerring. The Imperial bombers had swerved and died, but the interceptor pilots were a more even match.

The *Prideful* and the *Ikhtheos* stepped their lively waltz around each other, the Imperial frigate knowing it could end the smaller *Ikhtheos* in a blink if it lined up the correct ramming manoeuvre; the Abyssal Kindred vessel knowing its brutal gunnery could chip away at the *Prideful* until it was bleeding from too many cuts. But neither could gain the upper hand, and neither could break off. It was a remorseless dance towards oblivion, unless the paradigm changed.

Ibriel's working knowledge of the *Ikhtheos* had recently eclipsed that of Aggannazor, the Mechanicum mystek usually to be found on the bridge of the frigate, so it was now him engaged via data-port and umbilical to the generatorium overview station. Scrolling rune-lines and flashing status alerts filled his vision, the function of the ship occupying most of his attention. But not all. A virtual hololith shone in his tertiary eye-lenses, the tactical playout of the engagement around him.

'I can regain the initiative, acting captain,' he offered after a few seconds of consideration as the *Ikhtheos* barrelled away from the oncoming *Prideful* for the umpteenth time.

'How?'

'My lifter can penetrate their fighter screen and deliver a decisive payload.'

'That thing?' Naritsa said in disbelief. 'It's a fat-gutted wallower.'

'I have made considerable modifications.' Ibriel heard a seam of curiously human emotion running in his own words as he spoke. It took him a moment to recognise it as stung pride.

'No, tech-priest,' Naritsa rumbled. 'Your post is here.'

A plasma leak on the deck five manifold demanded Ibriel's attention for a few seconds. Two compartments scoured clean. Crew complement: minus twenty-one. He shored up the leak and logged it for running repairs once the battle was done. On his virtual hololith a wave of fighters circled back, their ident runes flashing with proximity. The shimmer of defence turrets lit up across the readout, but the enemy fire scored hits nonetheless. Ibriel briefly redirected more power to the manoeuvring thrusters as Naritsa demanded an achingly tight turn to keep the Imperial frigate in the *Ikhtheos'* broadside arc. Ibriel took a few microseconds to extrapolate the fifty most likely outcomes of the engagement. The results were not favourable. Ibriel made the decision. He issued a summons to Mystek Aggannazor in the generatorium, then, accessing the hangar deck command cogitator, set into motion a series of automated readiness sub-routines. Finally, he sent a rune-hymnal to another system.

The *Prideful* screamed past the *Ikhtheos*, easily within half a mile. In void combat terms they were practically on top of one another. The Imperial vessel's short-range plasma batteries drenched the *Ikhtheos'* under-hull in liquid energy as it rolled away violently.

'Warp's spit!' Naritsa leant into the roll, the ship's inertial dampening fields straining against physical laws. More alarms howled, but the damage was not critical. Naritsa ordered the *Ikhtheos* to burn away, knowing it had scant seconds before the Imperial warship realigned and came on again. 'Well, at least we have their attention,' he consoled himself. He allowed his gaze to flick briefly to the ident rune of the *Vizier of Arandeep*, enduring its own private massacre, he thought, smirking. The light cruiser was lending the odd flurry of gunnery to the *Prideful's* efforts, but the *Vizier* was clearly struggling as it slowly diverged from the two smaller vessels and their vicious contest. A launch alarm burbled, and Naritsa's attention went back to the *Prideful*, expecting another wave of attack craft. But the source of the launch was the *Vizier*. Berthed until now within the light cruiser's shuttle bay, a sizeable cutter had made an emergency egress and was engaging its plasma engines to run from the battle. The cutter bore a transponder ident of the vile priesthood of Terra, the Adeptus Ministorum.

'Get us after that cutter,' Naritsa barked. If they were escaping this battle, then they were important, and if they were important then Gyren Naritsa wanted them in chains in the *Ikhtheos'* hold.

'We can't break away, my lord,' the executive officer bleated, the mortal's robes clinging to him as his attention flicked from station to station.

'Do it.' Naritsa knew it was unlikely, but he would be damned if he did not try. The mortal nodded, issuing orders to his deck crew.

'Enemy ship coming about,' came the call from the surveyor pits.

'Engines at ninety-four per cent.'

'Cutter is underway, my lord.'

'Enemy ship directly abeam, starboard side.'

'Do we chase the cutter, my lord?' the executive officer asked.

'Cutter accelerating hard.'

'Enemy ship closing fast! Bearing zero four seven by negative zero zero six.'

'My lord?'

Naritsa's adamantine teeth screeched together, the Warpsmith staring with glowing red eyes at the competing priorities on the oculus.

'Abort pursuit,' he growled at the last moment. 'Evade, and bring our guns to bear.'

The bridge exploded with activity, the anxiety of the mortals bound in servitude there only eclipsed by the frustration of their transhuman commander. The *Ikhtheos* veered up and to port, robbing any potential ram of its ship-snapping angularity. The *Prideful* brought itself up short, wisely allowing the Heretic Astartes frigate to bank rather than coming too close to its still-ferocious broadside. Naritsa turned his full attention back to the battle, the cutter forgotten as it powered away into the darkness.

The bridge portal hissed open and Mystek Aggannazor floated in, mechatendrils swaying.

'What are you doing here?' Naritsa asked. Ibriel had apparently vacated the generatorium overview station and the mystek was inserting themselves into the throne.

'The honoured mystek is here by my request,' Ibriel said.

'Regretfully, I feel I must join battle in my personal craft, acting captain.' Ibriel had already edged almost completely out of the portal and Aggannazor recommenced their mumbling commune with the ship's systems.

'Priest!' Naritsa snarled. 'I ordered you to–' But Ibriel had already left, and the *Prideful*'s plasma battery was sweeping closer again.

'Ether's depths.'

Ibriel arrived at the hangar deck just as the clade of servitors completed their installation procedure. His cargo lifter, formerly a commonplace burden-craft of the Adeptus Mechanicus, was now an ovoid agglomeration of hull plates, signal-relay spikes and knuckles of tightly knotted conduits. The rear hatch closed and Ibriel seated his own equally modified form into the pilot couch. The craft was fuelled and ready.

'*You abandon me, priest,*' came Naritsa's voice over the vox.

'I am capable of turning the tide, Warpsmith Naritsa,' he replied. 'If you do not allow me to try, I'm afraid I will force the issue.'

There was a long pause. The *Ikhtheos* continued to lurch beneath him, the faint *thrum* of defence turrets accompanying the rippling shudder of a broadside volley. Naritsa's answer came by way of the hangar doors slowly beginning to open.

The gallery ran along the spinal atrium of the *Vizier* three decks above its mosaicked floor. High arches filled with stained armaglass set a diffuse kaleidoscope across the grating, and Dalchian looked down through the leaded windows in disbelief.

A Sororitas battle tank had been brought out of the ship's hold; fuelled, armed and then placed in the line of defenders across the great aisle of the arterial. Its grumbling engine could be felt even over the ever-present vibration of the ship's own power systems.

A sea of flame writhed and licked in front of the tank, its immolation flamers drenching a throng of figures in liquid rage. Scores of human shapes contorted in the inferno, spasming into broken sticks of ash. Beyond those figures were the silhouettes of Chaos Space Marines, locked equally in blazing torment, their armour slowing the voracious flame but not able to stop it. Bolter-armed Sororitas flanked the tank and their salvoes bracketed the boarders, pummelling back into the fire those who tried to drag themselves free.

As Dalchian watched, the toothed blade of Endagur, glowing ruby and blanketed in sheets of flame, came spearing through the air to impale two of the hateful Sororitas front to back. Their bolters dropped and they fell aside, ignored by their comrades. Dalchian chewed against his admiration for their discipline, just as he longed to break it. He tore his final krak grenade from his belt and flicked the primer stud, ready to blow the armaglass pane and drop down into the mess below.

He stopped himself. He disarmed the grenade and replaced it. They had to go on. Jathok with his remaining Rubricae and warriors caught up with the Blades. The sorcerer stared for a brief instant at the unconscionable scene, the coruscating flame underlighting his short beard and craggy features. Dalchian saw Jathok's eyes take in the Sororitas skewered by Endagur's blade. He saw the tiny mote of grief flicker across the sorcerer's face.

'Nallath,' said Jathok, addressing the champion of the shield-bearers. 'Circle your warriors back and find a way down. Punish them.' He glowered at the Adepta Sororitas.

'Yes, my lord.'

'Qi Umshar,' Dalchian said. 'Go with them. Do what you can.'

'Aye, Lord Skin-Taker.' Qi Umshar took a breath. 'I would ask for the use of that krak grenade, my lord. Yours was the more direct path.'

Dalchian smiled and handed him the oval device. Nallath looked at Jathok, who nodded. The Abyssal Kindred shield-bearers lined up behind the Blades' surgeon-Apothecary.

'Our blades yet thirst, my lord,' Qi Umshar said.

'That they do.'

Qi Umshar blew the arched window, sending glistering shards onto the armoured heads of the Sororitas below, who did not notice in the violence. A flaming Chaos Space Marine, heraldry indiscernible through flakes of blackened armour, burst through the barrage of bolt shots and swung a chainsword whose mechanism was defunct, but whose heft and teeth could still adequately maim. A Sister fell under the attack and her squad covered each other as they withdrew from the burning, howling beast. Qi Umshar took that moment to drop with great precision onto the closed rear hatch of the Immolator, rocking it on its hydraulic suspension. The Abyssal Kindred followed in quick succession.

Dalchian wanted to watch, but they had to keep moving. He, Jathok and the Rubricae went on, the abruptly changing sounds of the battle below echoing through the shattered archway behind them.

Ibriel hauled on the flight controls of his lifter, the craft performing like a forge-fresh atmospheric interceptor in total contrast to its shape and mass. The void between the *Ikhtheos* and the *Prideful* glittered with razors of debris and flashed with blossoming spheres of detonating munitions. Imperial parasite craft chased him through the vacuum, but the agility of his lifter baffled their targeting matrices, hammer blows of vectored hypergolic thrust jinking him out of their crosshairs whenever they locked on to him.

The *Prideful* loomed in the dark, gunwales alight with the discharge of plasma batteries, spotlights mounted on point defence turrets swivelling and tracking madly in the gloom. The cliff face of the frigate's sloping prow thundered past him as he burned hard for his target. Closer in to the ship's hull, fewer turrets could draw a bead upon him, but those that could were much closer, so their hypervelocity ammunition was far more densely packed within their firing solutions. It was a fine balance.

Ibriel dived beneath a plasma cannonade; the violet light bleached his cockpit for an instant as the clods of energised matter swept past in silence. Then he was beyond the gun decks, and he spun the lifter up over the spine of the frigate, matching the ship's swiftly changing vector with mathematical brilliance.

A lance beam from the *Ikhtheos* blinked for a microsecond off his starboard, penetrating the Imperial vessel's shield and birthing a geyser of ruptured hull plating and sparks that Ibriel had no choice but to plough through. The wreckage slammed against his lifter's skin, but its armour held.

A distant explosion suddenly illuminated the wide cathedral-face of the *Prideful*'s bridge, and Ibriel hoped the explosion had not been the *Ikhtheos*' demise. More lance fire whickered in, reassuring him that the Abyssal Kindred vessel still functioned. He pitched up at the last second, the bridge sweeping beneath him, its spires and domes vanishing in a blink as he jetted past it and then pulled a horrendously tight bank that crushed his organs within him. No unaltered human would have survived the manoeuvre. He blitzed his lifter down towards the dorsal hull just aft of the bridge, where the ship narrowed to a fin-like ridge. The hull was monstrously armoured here, given the proximity to the *Prideful*'s strategium within.

But Ibriel's lifter was no mere missile boat. Its melta array shrieked as he poured power into the weapon. So close, beneath the ship's void shields, the armour liquidised and sloughed away in glowing drips, the atmospheric pressure within pushing out against the failing integrity of the hull. Ibriel plummeted into the breach, slamming into the mess decks exposed to the void. He shot the explosive releases on the lifter's cargo bay ramp.

An inhuman roar echoed impossibly in the vacuum as the awakened Helbrute Ibriel had liberated from Naritsa's keeping tore its way free of the lifter and dragged itself into the *Prideful*'s guts.

Ibriel disembarked, rad weapon vibrating, and pushed himself through the airlessness until he reached a sealed portal. He engaged a mechadendrite with the control panel and the portal admitted him, atmosphere keening out as he passed. He closed the portal behind him and set about following the path of the Helbrute. It was easier than he expected.

He just followed the screams.

Canoness Commander Dostevska was the last to board the crew ramp of the Adeptus Ministorum cutter. Monstrous forms in black-and-turquoise ceramite had dogged their steps, with only the valour of her Battle Sisters keeping them at bay. Dostevska herself had cloven half a dozen of the Heretic Astartes, her continued lethality always a pleasing reassurance as she neared a hundred and forty years of age. *Thank the God-Emperor for juvenat drugs,* she thought, simultaneously chastising herself for the impiety.

The *Vizier of Arandeep* had no grand flight decks full of fighters like a Naval carrier, just the one shuttle bay for its tender craft. The cutter sat like a beached cetacean across the deck plates, its grey hull festooned in icons of the Imperial Creed. A servitor-guided aft-facing autocannon turret crowned the cutter's bulk above the stern ramp, and as Dostevska felt the ramp lift beneath her, the four barrels of the autocannon turret thundered.

Three huge transhuman warriors in ceramite battle plate sprinted through the portal onto the deck, dodging the turret fire. Two were unleashing streams of mass-reactive ammunition from their coughing bolters, the other was empty-handed. He wore a helm cast in the likeness of some sub-oceanic horror and skull braziers burned on his power pack. As Dostevska watched, his arms distended, ceramite cracking as the limbs swelled with bulging musculature. Gauntlets became grotesquely oversized hands with talons at each fingertip. The mutant heretic roared like an ursid and powered towards the ramp as it closed. Dostevska stood and glared her contempt, trusting the divine will of the God-Emperor that no bolt round would find her. The other warriors' explosive ammunition detonated within the crew bay, Sisters of Battle hunkering down as the shrapnel whined across their armour.

The great engines of the cutter began to roar. Under typical circumstances such a vessel would exit the shuttle bay under vector thrust, only igniting its main engines once voidborne. But these were not typical circumstances.

The heat wash knocked the two gunners from their booted feet, clanging onto the deck with great peals, before the building exhaust started baking them in their armour.

The mutant was faster, though.

He slipped between the roaring columns of fire and leapt at the closing gap between the ramp and the cutter's fuselage. The two massive hands jammed into the inches-wide gap, their ropy fingers flexing, talons screeching against the plasteel. The beast pried the gap an inch as the cutter lurched forwards. Dostevska saw a fleshy maw full of needle teeth bulging from where the Chaos Space Marine's helm should have had a rebreather grille. She raised her left hand, the plasma pistol in it whining up to full power.

'You are an abomination,' she said with an even tone. 'And I have killed your like before.'

She pulled the trigger and the beast's face exploded in a splash of white heat. The talons clenched reflexively, and Dostevska swept across them with the chainsword in her other hand. The teeth roared and her neat slice severed the digits in one. The ramp boomed shut as the cutter accelerated, mutant fingers rolling down onto the deck to lay oozing at her feet.

'Flamer,' she said. One of the Battle Sisters stepped to her side and, levelling her weapon, played a wash of fire across the disarticulated remains, reducing them to ash.

They sat in grav-thrones, the cutter pulling more and more as it cleared the shuttle bay. Beatrizi Dostevska felt the drag-lurch of leaving a ship's gravity well, and closed her eyes.

'Now I pray,' she told the seated warriors, her strong voice carrying across the crew bay of over a hundred Sisters of the Ebon Chalice. 'I pray for our noble Sacresants and the soul of Palatine Agnetta.'

Canoness Commander Dostevska began intoning the words and without hesitation the Sisters of Battle took up the prayer together.

God-Emperor forgive me, Dostevska thought, *but I'll never be so old I can't enjoy a damn good fight.*

Though a comparatively small vessel, the *Vizier of Arandeep* still possessed a grand stairway of carven granite that led up to the bronze double doors of its bridge. At the foot of the stairway a phalanx of Adepta Sororitas veterans stood with shields locked. The flanged heads of maces hovered above their visored helms, daring the boarders near, and at their centre one of the warrior women stood without shield or mace or any weapon that Dalchian could see. Instead, she held aloft a golden frame on a tall pole, within which was a frayed and smeared scrap of cloth the colour of varnished oak. On the steps above the Sororitas a score of Naval breachers stood, shotguns pulled tight into their shoulders.

All this Dalchian processed in an instant as he threw himself from the companionway shadows, lightning claw crackling, chainglaive buzzing. A wall of lead shot smashed into him. Ang Heltris lunged past, prosthetic blade outstretched, his other held low behind him. Dalchian cleaved a shield almost in two with his chainglaive as the unearthly glow of Rubricae gunfire lanced up into the breachers' ranks. Jathok stepped forwards, empty hand stretched out before him, fingers spread wide.

A discordant wail of unnatural energy fuzzed Dalchian's senses as a Battle Sister detonated in a gout of iridescent flame. Still charging, he caromed into the gap, Krutaan's claw tearing into black ceramite. A mace drove into his faceplate, sundering his helm and breaking his nose behind it. He spun his head, casting the ruined helm free, and cannoned the offending weapon aside with his chainglaive. But the Imperial warrior accounted for the off-balancing, letting the maul spiral away and sweeping up a bolt pistol in her other hand. Dalchian turned his head away as the pistol hammered on full automatic into his pauldron. The shuddering impacts pushed him back.

More warpfire shots speared the void-armoured mortals, twisting their flesh in hideous ways as the luminous rounds passed through them. Ang Heltris traded blows with a mace-wielder, her skill prodigious. Dalchian saw the Sororitas with the relic over the swinging weapons. She was serene amongst the carnage, a palpable sense of unassailability radiating from her. Near to her, none of the Imperials had fallen. Dalchian dearly wanted to turn away from her and kill someone else.

'Skin-Taker!' Jathok yelled, brow creased, fingers clawed. 'Bring the icon down.'

But she is unassailable, he wanted to reply for an instant. Then the feeling passed. He thundered into the Sororitas at her side. Shotgun blasts skinned the side of his face and raked the paint from his armour. A Sororitas mace arced towards him and he darted aside. The speed with which he moved stunned the

Imperial for a moment, so uncanny was it for a shape so massive. He rammed the buzzing chainglaive through her sternum, her moment of astonishment her undoing. She swung again, but there was little force, and Dalchian kicked her from the teeth of his glaive, crushing her helm beneath his boot as she fell.

The unarmed Sororitas warrior with the icon turned to face him, her face stern and haughty. He very nearly turned away, but his hatred swelled and he fixed her with a bloody stare. He crouched and sprang. A shield moved to block him and he slammed it aside with his chainglaive. He brought the claw up from behind him, then down over his head. His mouth was open and his teeth bare as he drove the bladed fingers through the Sister's cranium, through her skull, through her ribcage. She fell, shredded, and another Battle Sister cast her own shield aside to catch the icon as it began to slowly topple from the lifeless grasp of its bearer.

Dalchian caught it first. Krutaan's claw viced around the haft and severed it neatly. The framed scrap, presumably a piece of some ancient banner or tapestry, flicked and fell away from the Imperial reaching out for it. As the frame broke and the scrap fluttered onto the bloodied steps, Dalchian felt the hitherto unimpeachable resolve of the Sororitas tremble.

Jathok's eyes gleamed and he spoke a short word.

A sphere of misted luminance flashed from the sorcerer, the psychic pulse expanding like the shockwave of an explosion. The surviving Imperials were almost all blasted from their feet as the light hit, and then the Chaos Space Marines swept upon them. Breachers screamed as Ang Heltris butchered them and Rubricae blasted them apart. The Sororitas died in stubborn silence. Dalchian decapitated the last armoured zealot with his chainglaive as she struggled to bring her mace to bear. She toppled sideways, her helmed head bouncing away.

With the last of the defenders dead, their attention turned to the bronze doors between them and command of the ship. Alarms screeched and warning lumens flashed around them, as had been the case since the moment they first boarded. Distant explosions and reverberating deck plating told them the fight was still fully underway on other decks of the *Vizier*. Dalchian allowed himself a morsel of anticipation. Few battleships could withstand assault by nearly forty Chaos Space Marines, let alone this light cruiser. The Sororitas had augmented the resistance of the ship's company enormously, but it was likely they were all now dead. *It's not in those prayer-addled lunatics to run from a fight*, Dalchian thought, grateful for their indulgence.

Leil Jathok climbed the stairs, his smile broad and avaricious. When he stood before the great doors, he took a breath to steel himself, steadied his staff in one hand, then placed the other against the metal and closed his eyes.

Immediately the doors began to slide apart, a jagged gap appearing between their interlocking teeth.

'You're improving,' Dalchian said with a smirk, but the sorcerer was suddenly wary.

'That wasn't me.'

Chapter Fifteen

Palatine Agnetta dragged her ruined leg behind her as she worked, the pain of the burnt tissue only driving her onwards. A team of huge ogryn servitors trundled along in her wake on heavy track units. They were deep within the magazine of the *Vizier of Arandeep* and she was moving from section to section, directing the servitors to haul enormous cages out from their shielded compartments. Each cage held a dozen huge discs stacked together, each disc six feet thick and eighteen feet across with a skin of tightly woven fabric.

Macrocannon charges. Slabs of high explosive capable of launching multi-ton shells into the void at speeds of almost a mile a second. Their sheer energetic potential meant the chamber in which they were stored had to be the most obnoxiously protected section of the whole vessel. With bulkheads feet thick and millions of gallons of water held in its double-skin, the magazine made the charges as safe as they could be.

Agnetta had undermined every damage reduction measure in place. Blast-diverters had been lowered, pressure release vents closed; inert gas-fire suppression systems had been shut down. With her work finally at an end, and beneath the ceaseless din of klaxons, she dismissed the servitors and limped her way to the central compartment of the magazine and the armed cyclonic warhead on its trestle there. She grasped the improvised trigger unit in her right hand and knelt awkwardly, gasping at the agony, to pray.

Agnetta had watched with mixed sadness and relief as the majority of the Adepta Sororitas aboard the *Vizier* had boarded the Ministorum cutter that filled the light cruiser's shuttle bay and departed, their main force preserved so that one day they might avenge their fallen Sisters. The Heretic Astartes frigate had seen them and tried to give chase but was too caught in its duel with the *Prideful* to break off.

Her Sisters spared a wasted death in the void, now Agnetta committed her soul to the Emperor's side, praying that her efforts would find her worthy of His everlasting glory, and feeling a private, sinful indulgence that the Bell of Lost Souls on Holy Terra might one day, years, decades or even centuries from now, ring for her.

'By thy light,' she whispered. 'My soul shalt ne'er be cast adrift.'

She squeezed the trigger assembly and was instantly reduced to atoms.

Dalchian darted through the huge doors before they were fully open, curiosity burning in him. Jathok held back, wary of a trap. This was where there should have been the fiercest, most deadly resistance. This is where the ship's company of the *Vizier of Aran-deep* should have made their final stand; a last, desperate effort and final opportunity to reveal any ace cards they still held.

It should have been an inferno. Instead, the bridge was quiet, only the ever-present hum and rattle of cogitators and the consumptive wheezing of servitors. The deck crew knelt before him.

This cannot be.

As Dalchian stepped closer, he saw that the deck crew knelt because they had no other choice. Iron chains manacled them to each other and to the deck plates. The restraints enfolded their wrists, ankles and necks. Their trembling jangled the chains delicately. A hand-written strip of parchment hanging from the chains declared the Naval crew to be 'Defectum'. There were no weapons levelled at him, no crouching assassin waiting for him to get just close enough.

The *Vizier* was his.

He kept the triumph at bay for now. There were questions. Leil Jathok stopped level with the Skin-Taker and likewise stared at the pinioned deck crew.

'Curious,' he said.

'Indeed.'

The sorcerer approached one of the senior officers, who sobbed and twisted away. The chains ran between his teeth, too, gagging them. Jathok held his hand over the officer's head, what had once been a neat coiffure long since shaken to tresses. Dalchian, allied with the sorcerer though he was, drew away from the telepathic interrogation he knew was coming, a grimace ghosting across his ravaged face. But the interrogation was not needed. Jathok snatched his hand away as though burned, eyes wide.

'We have to go!' he said. 'Now!'

'What is–'

A seismic rumble echoed through their feet. Jathok spun around and launched himself towards the bridge portal. Dalchian activated his boot mag-locks out of instinct.

Then, the galaxy tore in half.

The deck below Dalchian swung up and to the side like wet parchment, taking him with it. He was slammed into the bulkhead and metal deformed around his impact. The blow knocked him almost senseless. Mortal crew-flesh spattered through the tears in the deck plate. A scourge of fire whipped across him, but almost immediately the skin-tearing cold of vacuum sucked it away. Inertial turbulence like he had never known threatened to pull the muscles from his bones as his armour's locked fibre-bundles fought against horrific g-forces. He vomited blood, which sprayed and froze, tiny gemstones spiralling in gaps in the tortured plasteel.

He felt a lurch of mindlessness; the appealing nothingness of catastrophic trauma. He fought. He disengaged his mag-locks and clawed his way through the metal decking. On the other side his purpling stare was transfixed by the serenely drifting shape of his chainglaive, weightless and lost. The weapon was thirty fathoms distant, and more with every second. Where it was headed filled Dalchian's barely working mind with awe.

Opened at the seams like a beautiful, nightmarish flower, the plasma core of the *Vizier of Arandeep* whirled and pulsed like the micro-star it was. Every visible colour, and many invisible ones, shone from the throbbing vortex of raw power. Superconductive ribs of magnetic alloys melted from its sides, unfurling to let the violent energies skip and jet out into space. Dalchian, mind rapidly numbing, felt the uncanny heat on his face. Loose edges of wounded flesh crisped and hardened in the radiative wash even as the deep, heatless bite of vacuum sank into his bones.

The *Vizier of Arandeep* had broken into dozens of pieces. Some large, many small. In the watery spotlight of the Uzurmandius star the deep shadows extended like the claws of death herself. Dalchian bid his chainglaive farewell, the boundaries of his perception fraying.

He pulled himself through the wreck. His exposed face meat screamed. Nodules of necrotising skin bulged from the dozen rents in his armour, the void earnestly teasing his insides out.

The bridge doors and their staircase were still intact. As his vision failed, he felt an armoured gauntlet, cold in a manner even more profound than empty space, grasp his forearm and drag him.

His consciousness faltered. Silence reigned.

He saw the *Abjuration*, his old Denouncer-class frigate, fresh as the day it put to void.

He saw Krutaan. The Nemesis Claw leader spoke without speaking.

Shut the door, Skin-Taker.

Dalchian's lungs felt full of rockcrete and broken glass. His breaths made squealing, ratcheting noises that he didn't like. With supreme effort, he blinked, the lids making audible scraping noises against his eyeballs. Vision spotted its way back to him, the imagery around him greyscale and happening in chunks. A hand was still clamped, vice-like, onto his arm. He bent his addled mind to seeing the figure. *Jathok,* he thought he said. *Is that you?* With a rush, a wave of perception crashed over him. The figure was kicking their way along the contorted stanchions of a voidship corridor, dragging Dalchian weightlessly behind. There was no up or down. Usually that would not have mattered, Dalchian's transhuman senses keeping him oriented, but he was operating very far from his normal capacity. Bits of gristly skin broke off his face and drifted away as he watched.

The figure was in Abyssal Kindred armour, but was not the sorcerer. A tall crest of barred metal surmounted its brow, and its baroque armour was almost utterly broken.

No. It *was* utterly broken. Dalchian stirred the sludge of his mind, trying to understand. Gaping rents bespoke ruinous damage across the warrior's form. Parts of its plate were completely missing, just burned and cracked edges belying where once they were. Dalchian's slowly recovering faculties almost aborted anew when he looked down and saw that the hand clutching him was floating free of the arm to which it should have been attached. Floating free, but still in perfect anatomical arrangement. Like the missing pieces of armour were just out of sight. The elbow was a shredded stump of blackened ceramite, and it should have ended there, but the hand was exactly where it should be, about eighteen inches away. And still holding Dalchian firm. The rents in the armour bore no flesh or blood. They were hollow and gritty, like a long-dried crypt. Motes of dust trailed from the gaps.

Rubricae, he thought he said.

Some more of his mind had returned by the time they reached the gun decks. He waved in front of the Rubricae's face and tapped the disarticulated gauntlet. The phantom warrior released him and they pushed on, making their way rapidly without the dragging encumbrance of gravity.

The gun decks were open to the void and Dalchian's already mutilated body shuddered at the fresh torture. As they drifted across the embrasure, Dalchian looked out into the firmament. Thousands of frozen corpses glittered in the dark. Huge pieces of the vast warship tumbled sedately. An oblong section of the *Vizier* loomed, casting them into shadow as it blotted out Uzurmandius' frail sunlight.

Dalchian's mind spasmed like it had been electrocuted. He slammed the Rubricae on the pauldron and the living spectre turned its half-hollowed helm. Dalchian pointed. They diverted at the next piece of jutting plasteel, pivoting to launch themselves directly out into the void. The vacuum was pulling Dalchian away again, the totally hostile environment quickly eating through his genhanced resilience. He refused to succumb. His fate was to commandeer an Adeptus Astra Telepathica Black Ship and wreak such horrors. His fate was to repay Gorelord Thelissicus for the near annihilation of his murder-kin. There were tasks left undone.

He refused to succumb.

After what felt like a year but also only a heartbeat, they clattered into an armaglass canopy, and as Dalchian fitted, his limbs jerking, he met Qi Umshar's stupefied gaze.

Shut the door, Skin-Taker.

CHAPTER SIXTEEN

Lacerating sensation drenched Dalchian's skin. He felt his eyes crackle open, but his vision refused to resolve. He shifted himself, acutely aware of the knifing pain all over his body, and indeed within it. *Good. Means I'm alive.* Nothing but fuzzed half-images of his surroundings settled into his swimming perception.

'Hchln.' Taking a slurping breath through his broken nose, he tried again. 'W-what…?'

'My Lord Skin-Taker,' a voice replied, filled with relief. 'I was unsure if you would regain consciousness. You are… substantially injured.' Dalchian recognised the voice, but could not recall the name. *The surgeon.*

'Wh–' Dalchian was racked by a fit of coughing which filled his head with exploding lights and noise. At length the coughing subsided. 'Where… we?'

'The gunship, my lord,' the surgeon said. *Qi Umshar, that's his name.* 'We're making our approach now.'

'*Ikhtheos* lives?'

There was a pause before Qi Umshar answered.

'The *Ikhtheos* lives, my lord, but we are approaching the *Prideful*.'

At this Dalchian hacked a mutilated laugh. 'B-boarding?'

'No, my lord.' Qi Umshar's voice became clearer, as if he had turned to speak directly towards Dalchian. 'The *Prideful* is yours.'

'No,' Dalchian said simply. 'Enemy.'

'By my blade, Lord Skin-Taker, I swear it.' Even in his ruined state, Dalchian recognised the thrill of victory that sharpened Qi Umshar's tone. 'We have taken the ship.'

Dalchian could not fathom how, so instead he turned his attention inwards, feeling the churn of his transhuman physiology as it desperately gathered the last scraps of his energy and bent it to repair. It felt as though he dropped into a deep sleep for hours, though only a few minutes went by. As the jolt of landing shuddered through his body and he heard the diminishing pitch of the Thunderhawk's engines, more of his mind began to function.

Power-armoured bodies were scattered within the Thunderhawk's troop bay. Most were the black-and-turquoise Abyssal Kindred, and a fair few were blackened and melted into anonymity. Half a dozen Kindred stood among the piled casualties, as well as Qi Umshar, bent down over a bleeding warrior. Dalchian was propped up at the foot of the ladder that connected the bay to the cockpit, and another midnight-clad legionary appeared in the small hatch, his pilot duties complete. The Night Lord tipped his lord a wry salute and the prosthetic knife attachment, now dulled and twisted, was unmistakable.

'Ang Heltris.'

'Back to life for more, my lord?'

'Always.'

With a huge effort and almost unbearable agony, he heaved himself upright. Ang Heltris cocked his helm in astonishment.

Qi Umshar swept over to Dalchian and clasped his lord's shoulders with both hands.

'You should not exert yourself, my lord.'

'Bit late for that,' Ang Heltris said.

'I am well enough.' Dalchian tried to brush the surgeon-Apothecary away and stumbled. His sense of balance freewheeled around him, and only Qi Umshar stopped him from hitting the deck.

'That is… fundamentally incorrect, my lord.'

Without observable motion, Dalchian's battered lightning claw was at Qi Umshar's neck.

'Must. I. Repeat. Myself?'

'No, my lord. Of course not.'

Dalchian's grip held for a moment, then he released the surgeon-Apothecary. There was a gurgling noise from the pile of dead and dying. 'See to them.'

'Yes, lord.' Qi Umshar returned to the others. Ang Heltris descended from the cockpit and indicated the ramp controls.

'Ready, Lord Skin-Taker?'

'Open the door.'

The flight deck on a Chaos Space Marine vessel was often a spare, functional affair, maintenance the purview of a few fully initiated warriors, or even just one, as on the *Ikhtheos*, and an equally slim handful of mortal serfs, with most taxing labour performed by servitors and slaves. They were normally sepulchral places, largely empty of life.

The flight deck of the *Prideful* was the antithesis.

People were everywhere. Mortal crew numbered in the thousands. There were technicians operating under the watchful gaze of tech-priest enginseers and teams of ratings dragging hoses or wielding fire suppression gear. A sortie command bunker jutted from the bulkhead thirty feet above the deck and the pale faces of officers peered through the observation slit. Two hundred and fifty yards away, the opposite side of the vessel was a mirror image, and on both flanks the egress doors were open to the void, only an atom-thick film of energy holding in the atmosphere. Holding in the heat and the stink. The egress door openings were not the vast maws of dedicated carrier vessels through which whole flights of strike craft could pass, but rather half a dozen narrow arches on each flank, only just wide enough to accept Jathok's Thunderhawk, through which the *Prideful's* boarding craft blasted when the moment of assault came, and through which they could return to be refuelled, refilled with voidsmen-at-arms, and launched once more into the abyss. Returned assault boats were scattered chaotically about the deck, as well as the paltry remainder of the ship's modest bomber and interceptor complement. The lumens were bright and the noise deafening.

Dalchian emerged from the ramp and silence descended instantly.

'Salutations, my lord.' Ibriel's engorged form met him at the foot of the ramp, primary and secondary arms wide, hood bowed deferentially. 'Welcome aboard your new command.' The tech-priest's greeting was confident and expansive, at odds with his usual demeanour. Dalchian's vox-bead crackled in his ear as Ibriel sent him a discreet communique.

'The cooperation of the crew is only momentarily assured, my lord,' he sent hurriedly. *'Please make your way to the bridge as a matter of superlative urgency.'*

Dalchian gave an imperceptible nod.

'Good work, priest.' He turned to the others within the gunship troop bay. 'Blades, Kindred – with me.' His vision swam, static roared in his ears, and every speck of him longed to collapse into a restorative coma.

'Perhaps my analysis was premature,' Qi Umshar said over

the vox, his slab-faced helm silent to the onlooking mortals. Dalchian looked at his Blades in turn, then addressed the Abyssal Kindred, hoping the absence of their own commander present would translate into obedience to him. All could be lost if they refused.

'Soldiers of the Great Powers,' he addressed them, forcing his riven voice to carry across the flight deck. 'Gather the officers of my ship in the mess hall. I shall bear witness to their oaths, as this ship shall bear witness to mine.'

Ang Heltris and Qi Umshar read the intensity correctly and immediately went separate ways into the crowd of mortals. Blessedly, the Kindred followed their lead. The officers on the flight deck were quickly herded together and, chaperoned by the loaded boltgun of an Abyssal Kindred warrior, made their way through the portal and deeper into the ship. The other Chaos Space Marines made for the companionways and conveyor shutters, their amplified voices demanding all officers be brought forth. Dalchian watched them go in silence, before he turned and jabbed the autolocking rune key on the Thunderhawk's ramp controls. The ramp lifted with a whine of hydraulics and the armoured gunship sealed itself with scorched, abraded dignity. The injured still on board would have to endure. *At least they'll be spared from filthy Imperials* interfering *with them.* He and Ibriel made their way towards the flight deck's aft portal, the frail humanity parting before them. Ibriel had the heavy tubes of his rad weapon visibly deployed. *Things really must be on a knife edge,* he thought. The tech-priest sent another silent message.

'*The mess hall, my lord?*'

Dalchian felt his flesh split as he allowed himself a superior smirk.

'*Would your victory not be more effectively completed from the bridge?*'

Abruptly, a different missive rattled into Ibriel's mechacortex. 'Survivors from the *Vizier* issue a distress call, my lord,' he said archly, out loud. 'What do you command?'

'Retrieve them,' Dalchian said, ensuring the mortals were listening. 'The *Prideful* no doubt requires its losses replacing. Bring their officers to the mess hall, too.'

'Your will be done, my lord.'

It took almost two hours for every officer on board the *Prideful* and the handful of those surviving from the *Vizier* to be rounded up in the mess hall. Over six hundred men and women of the Imperial Navy were pressed beneath gun muzzles into the frigate's main galley, where thousands of meals were prepared each cycle as crew came on and off watch at different hours. Most of the galley staff had been shut in a ration store for the duration, but Dalchian kept a few to attend the huge pots of boiling oil he had ordered them to prepare. The Abyssal Kindred stood as sentinels around the fringes of the galley, their obvious wariness filling the mortals lining the brushed plasteel with dread. Dalchian armed himself, Ang Heltris and Qi Umshar with hooks from the meat locker. Lifting the *Prideful*'s thrashing captain into the air with the butcher's implement, he made a simple request.

'Guarantee me the loyalty of this ship.'

After three hours the surviving Naval officers were peeling the Imperial aquila from their lapels and swearing their unending devotion to the Blades of Atrocity, the VIII Legion, and to him.

Unending devotion to the Skin-Taker.

Dalchian's armour was as brutalised as his body, and his cloak of leathers had been destroyed when the *Vizier* died. Chemicals were fetched from the quartermaster's stores and dozens of fresh hides were prepared and tanned by the victims' own comrades under the baleful appraisal of new masters. Dalchian directed the tailoring, admonishing the weeping mortals for every dropped stitch or snapped thread. It only took fourteen hides in the end, but Dalchian ordered the rest carefully stored for spares while the sturdiest of the remaining officer cadre secured the mantle of fresh pelts across his shoulders. The crew were finally released back to their posts, and a collection of polished skulls accompanied Dalchian and the others to the bridge to be stacked neatly around the command dais.

Loyalty is such a curious thing, Dalchian thought as he surveyed the efforts with a serene pride.

'Ang Heltris, you have the bridge.'

'Aye, lord.' The knifeman's arms were blood-slicked to the shoulder, the gore drying quickly in the recirculated atmosphere.

'Oh, sub-lieutenant.' Dalchian addressed a mortal at the internal vox-station in an offhand tone. The mortal's eyes were red from tears and she shook as if freezing to death. 'The audex feed from the galley was piped to all decks for the full cycle as requested, was it not?'

The mortal snatched part breaths and nodded weakly. 'Y-y–'

'Good.' Dalchian nodded. 'Qi Umshar, with me.'

'Aye lord.'

They strode from the bridge and threaded the decks and gangways of the *Prideful,* traumatised crew scurrying from their path. After a few minutes they reached the medicae bay.

'Out,' Qi Umshar barked, and the medics and orderlies fled. The surgeon-Apothecary locked the portal behind them and Dalchian nodded his thanks.

He was unconscious before he hit the deck plates.

Chapter Seventeen

Memory returned to him in jolts. The battle; the explosion; the *Prideful*. He tested his muscles and the squeaking wobble of vita-copia tubes answered his movements. His armour was gone. He was lying upon a medicae slab made for mortals, his calves and feet hanging off the end. The medicae bay was cool and silent. He sat in quiet solitude for a long while, the aggregate agonies of his body coming online one by one. Every movement was excruciating and the energy taken up by merely thinking made his insides heave. But he could move, and he could think. At length he decided to rise, and the slab creaked alarmingly as he shifted his weight. Placing a foot on the decking, he let out an involuntary cry. His bones felt like they were twisting out of his body. But they were not. He placed his second foot, steeled for the sensation, though still failed to suppress a grunt. With a juddering intake of breath, he stood, swaying. The vitacopia tubes connected to his skin crowded him and he pulled them out, the hunched machine emitting panicked beeps as he did so.

The chamber whirled around him as a medicae servitor trundled through the portal in answer to the vitacopia's alarm.

'Patient,' the lobotomised cyborg droned. 'You must sit. Patient, you must sit. Patient, you must sit.'

Dalchian slapped the thing away, dashing what remained of its brains on the deck. The strike rang his arm like a bell, his flesh howling in pain.

It is a good pain.

'My lord.' Qi Umshar appeared at the portal. 'You return to us.'

'Did you doubt it?' Dalchian quipped with false nonchalance. His voice was thick and wet.

'Yes, my lord,' Qi Umshar replied. 'Many times.'

'Hmm,' Dalchian coughed.

Qi Umshar began to check him over, reattaching a monitor node to his lord's temple. Another Chaos Space Marine appeared at the portal and Dalchian stared.

'You look as bad as I feel,' Dalchian said.

'You look worse, my lord.'

Dagardis' armour was freshly repaired. All Astartes, whether the limp-souled lackeys of the Carrion Lord or dedicants of the Great Powers, or any other for that matter, knew the business of power armour like they knew their own bodies. Dalchian recognised that while Dagardis' armour was hale now, more than half of it had been overhauled or completely replaced, the paint subtly different from piece to piece. Such a scale of work implied huge damage, and the bare head emerging from the gorget was torn and burned. Dagardis' shoulder-length hair was gone, as were most of his identifying features. Raw pink scar tissue stretched tightly around his eyes and lips. Dalchian looked pointedly at the other Blade's arm and Dagardis flexed it stiffly. The augmetic nature of the limb became obvious at the motion.

'Basic, but functional, my lord.'

'Your best qualities.'

Dagardis' ruined face twisted in a smirk, and Dalchian felt his own skin tear as he returned the expression.

'But I wasn't jesting, my lord.' Dagardis gestured to a looking glass that had been placed nearby. Dalchian hesitated for a fraction of an instant and hoped the others did not notice.

Dagardis was right, he was much worse.

His face was skeletal, most of the skin burned or eaten away, exposing lurid scraps of musculature that hung from his cheeks and brow. The whites of his eyes were violet and blotched. His hair was also gone, and dry bone showed in deep gouges across his crown. Beneath the medicae robes he was purple and yellow from neck to toe, and every few inches was a crater of dead flesh, burning as his metabolism tried to heal what was no longer there. Lumps showed where bones were reknitting; white patches where dead tissue was yet to fall away.

'And you've been in biological shutdown for twenty-two hours healing, my lord,' Qi Umshar said. 'Before this you looked...' He raised his eyebrows.

'At an end.'

'Indeed.'

Dalchian stared at the corpse scarecrow he had become for several moments longer before the concerns of the present surfaced once more. 'The humans remain obedient?' he asked.

'They do, my lord.'

'Good.' Dalchian took another step, his strength trickling back. 'My armour?'

'Restored to the best of Ibriel's ability.'

'Dagardis, fetch it to me. And convene a council in the strategium. There is work to be done.' The Blade bowed his head and departed to make the arrangements, leaving Dalchian and Qi Umshar alone.

Not alone. For the first time the other slabs caught Dalchian's eye. Power-armoured forms, blackened and twisted. Saryuz's plate was melted around him, the connective folds of reinforced plastek between the plates bubbled and cracked. Dalchian stared at the pitiful sight for a long time.

'He is trapped within?' Dalchian asked.

'All of them are.' Qi Umshar indicated Zhikarga and the five Kindred on slabs next to the Night Lords, all victims of the self-righteous flames of the Adepta Sororitas. Jathok's favoured champion Endagur was among them, the beast visage of his helm the sole remaining identifiable feature even though it had begun to slide and droop. 'They could survive a few minutes perhaps, if I removed it. No more. What systems remain are keeping their blood flowing.' Each Chaos Space Marine was connected to a ramshackle collection of medicae devices only engineered for mortals, but cajoled into serving an alternate biology over hours of Qi Umshar's incessant effort.

'Vellet?'

'Dead. Incinerated. I am aggrieved, my lord, for I could not secure his genetic legacy.' Qi Umshar bowed his head, and Dalchian's personal fury, dulled to a vague ember by his ordeal, flared. The Skin-Taker crushed his hands into fists, saying nothing. After the tide receded, he turned back to the recumbent Abyssal Kindred.

'What does the sorcerer say about our guests?'

'Very little. Lord Jathok yet sleeps at the mercy of his sus-an membrane. He remains critical, it seems.'

'Who commands, then? The Warpsmith?'

'Yes. Naritsa thanks us for our efforts, and wishes them brought back aboard the *Ikhtheos* when they are stable enough to be moved.'

'If.'

'Indeed.'

Dalchian rested a haematoma-riddled hand on Saryuz's deformed breastplate, the pumps hanging above him working hard to keep his comatose body oxygenated. *Prizes, and the sacrifice of claiming them.*

'At twelve Blades,' Dalchian said softly, 'I thought us a pitiful remnant. What are we, now we number but five... perhaps, soon, four? Is oblivion to be the sole legacy of my deeds?'

'Our violent death is predestined, my lord.'

'Krutaan once reminded me as much.' Dalchian stared unseeing at the softened edges of Saryuz's helm, the lenses cracked and dark. 'Krutaan demanded of me what I should have demanded of myself.' He looked the surgeon-Apothecary in the eyes. 'I will not err in this. I swore to the Great Powers, curse their names, that this is the time of our rebirth. None shall stand between us and the glory that we are due. Do you understand me, Qi Umshar?'

The other Blade bowed deeply, moved by the intensity of Dalchian's tone.

'I am yours to command, Lord Skin-Taker.'

Dalchian's gaze drifted across the supine Kindred.

'None shall stand between us and glory.'

The strategium of the frigate was the epitome of Imperial martial grandeur. Doric columns of veined marble stretched aloft to vaults of stained armaglass, beyond which the satin void hung. The table at the centre of the chamber was ten feet wide and twenty long and hewn from a single piece of dark, polished hardwood. Cogitators lined the bulkheads, viewscreens glowing emerald with rune lines and datascreed. The place would have been flawless, but for the jagged rent where the portal once sat and the sprays of dried blood that pooled in dents in the deck plating.

Dalchian had donned his newly repaired armour in the first hour of the cycle, and in it he felt more himself again.

Ibriel's repairs were magnificent, though Krutaan's old claw still twitched at curious intervals.

'The question of the moment, then, is how you came to achieve your victory, tech-priest?' Ibriel took a breath to speak, but before he could, Dalchian added, 'In simple terms.'

The tech-priest nodded.

'Upon launching from the *Ikhtheos* I undertook surveyor-baffling manoeuvres, utilising a signal scrambler of ancient design.' Ibriel nodded his vast, suspensor-lofted shell carapace, indicating the repository where such ancient designs dwelt. *What a mighty asset he has proven to be,* Dalchian thought as he listened. 'This allowed me close enough to the *Prideful* to bypass its void shields and defence turrets, whereupon I forced ingress to the bridge–'

'With a melta array,' Dagardis put in, enjoyment showing through his injuries.

'Mm, affirmative, with a melta array. Once within the bridge, I deployed my destructive payload, which performed beyond my expectations, winning the ship in your name, my lord.'

'I congratulate you. What destructive payload?'

'Thank you, my lord.' Ibriel hesitated. *What's this? The others seem amused.* 'The Helbrute, from the *Ikhtheos*, my lord. The survivors of the *Prideful*'s bridge crew negotiated surrender once it became clear the payload would work its way through the ship unimpeded, perceiving myself to be its operator. They surrendered, and the destruction… abated, my lord.'

'You can command this thing?'

'Mm, not *precisely*, my lord.'

'How did you cease its rampage?'

'A matter of serendipity, my lord.'

There was a weighted pause. Dagardis sniggered.

'It stopped by itself?'

'That appears to be the case, my lord.'

'Then call it the will of the Powers,' Dalchian said levelly. *You'll find that damned beast and remove it, you cog-gutted tinkerer!* 'The threat of it held our new crew in check until I could persuade them in a more permanent fashion. You excelled yourself, tech-priest.'

He would deal with Ibriel later. Dalchian noticed the ill-concealed surprise on the face of Nallath, the most senior Abyssal Kindred aboard the *Prideful* while Endagur was still felled.

'Does Warpsmith Naritsa know of your ploy, tech-priest?'

Ibriel's lenses seemed to retract into the shadows beneath his hood. 'Negative, my lord.'

'I see.' Dalchian turned to Nallath. 'In the interests of the alliance between our two forces, allow me to be the first to inform your lord of his… mislaid property.'

The Kindred champion was clearly angered at the slight on his warband's honour, but had enough respect for Dalchian Skin-Taker to acquiesce. *Politic.*

Following the conclave, Dagardis, Ang Heltris and the Abyssal Kindred went about the ship. They gleaned reports of ship systems, damage and supplies from the overseers of each section, as well as cataloguing the trail of destruction left in the Helbrute's wake. The trail stopped at a conveyor shaft that descended into the bilge decks. They were readying to follow further when the command came for the Abyssal Kindred to depart. Sorcerer Lord Jathok had awoken. Dalchian ordered his Blades back, and Ibriel instead sent a cohort of servo-skulls and arachni-drones below.

'He did what?!' Gyren Naritsa was visibly shaking, lumens reflecting off the angles of his adamantine skull shimmering in the hololithic projection.

'Here, now, Gyren,' Leil Jathok intoned from his place next

to the livid Warpsmith. The sorcerer was as battered as the rest of them. *'A disconcerting transgression, I'll admit, but look at what Lord Skin-Taker's tech-priest has achieved. I have no doubt that every effort is being made to return the article to the* Ikhtheos, *is that not correct, Skin-Taker?'*

Damned right.

'Just so. I assure you, had I been privy to the tech-priest's plans then he would not have carried them out. Perhaps it is a good thing I was not?'

'Loyalty among servants is a valuable trait,' Jathok said. *'As indeed among allies.'*

Dalchian considered the jibe for the appropriate time.

'Surely, Lord Jathok, our accord has never been stronger? Look at the bounty of our shared endeavour – I am in command of a voidship once more. A vessel I daresay as capable as the *Ikhtheos.'* Dalchian showed all his teeth as he grinned. 'Worth a little hardship, I think.'

'Certainly, Lord Skin-Taker.' Jathok smiled acidly through his singed beard. *'I am merely perturbed by the absence of my Kindred who, at this moment, lie inert within your med bay.'*

'Qi Umshar assures me the facilities are now adequate to warrant the title of apothecarion, Lord Jathok.' On separate ships, with a distance of space between them, Dalchian could sense the dynamic of their alliance changing, as he had known it would. They still needed one another, he and the sorcerer, but the equation had been adjusted. Now they were closer to equals. True parity, the Skin-Taker was keen to attain. Or exceed.

'Your apothecarion, then.'

'You recall the disorder of our escape from the wreckage of the *Vizier.* I sought to save as many of your Kindred as I could. In fact, were it not for Qi Umshar, your champion Endagur would now be desiccated flotsam.'

'*I meant no offence,*' Jathok said humbly. '*Nevertheless, I insist on their return.*'

'Then their return is agreed.'

'*You are gracious, Lord Skin-Taker. Permission to come aboard to collect them?*' It was an exaggerated politeness, but Dalchian let himself enjoy the fact he now commanded a ship that Leil Jathok could not just stroll onto.

'Granted.'

'*My thanks. As to the other matter of our shared interest?*'

'The work begins immediately.'

'*That is reassuring.*'

They broke off the hololithic connection.

'I see you, sorcerer,' Dalchian said to himself as he strode from the bridge of his new warship.

CHAPTER EIGHTEEN

The *Prideful*'s allocation of attack craft was considerable relative to the frigate's tonnage. Or at least it had been before the predations of the *Ikhtheos*. That formerly sizeable contingent, composed of venerable interceptors, lumbering missile strike craft and assault boats, had been stored between engagements across two hangar decks below the *Prideful*'s flight deck. Below that, necessary to support flights of parasite craft on long deployments, the vessel boasted an enviable armorium forge. The long complex of workshops and manufactorum units ran the entire length of the flight deck seventy feet above, and was replete with lockers-full of replacement pulse engines, lascannon focus tubes, armour plates and all manner of other materiel. After long months denied a true lair, Ibriel had seemed giddy as he commandeered the space, and he had quickly made his presence felt.

Dalchian picked his way through the armorium complex, edging between teetering stacks of caskets and pall-shrouded chunks of machinery.

'Priest,' Dalchian called. 'Where are you in this scrapyard?' A few hunched tech-thralls lifted their monocular gazes at the intrusion before returning to their tedious labours. Knots of activity gathered around the needle-bright lightning of lascutters or the rhythmic hammering of pneumatic pry-callipers. An arachni-drone *tick-tacked* across the ceiling, its skull thorax registering the Skin-Taker with a strobing lens. Dalchian met the thing's gaze. 'Emerge.'

'I am here.' Ibriel arose from behind the slumped frame of a Sororitas Penitent Engine. Dalchian saw the fleur-de-lys emblem on shredded armour plates that were neatly arranged in stacks. Tubes and gears had been pried free and sorted according to a perplexing system of categorisation. The war machine was almost completely disassembled, yet Dalchian recognised it nonetheless.

'Ah yes,' the Skin-Taker said as he eyed the construct's emptied chassis. 'You found Dagardis among the wreckage.'

'Affirmative.'

'I was not aware that you retrieved so much… materiel, while you were supposed to be retrieving survivors.' He looked around at the hoard of salvage gathered from the *Vizier*, from the Sororitas and from other, less obvious sources.

'I calculated it to be a beneficial additional application of my efforts. My lord.'

'Yes, I suspect you did.' Dalchian lifted a serrated disc that had formed one of the engine's devastating melee weapons. Some teeth were sheared off and a sharp-edged crack ran almost the whole radius. In a century of service to the VIII Legion Dalchian had encountered the Sisters of Battle several times, and even faintly recalled firing upon a similar Penitent Engine from a distance, once upon a time. Save for the action on the *Vizier* and this very moment, he had never been so close to one of the bizarre but deadly contraptions.

'Have you prepared me a replacement helm?'

'Indeed,' Ibriel nodded, sending an enginseer scurrying with a gesture. 'My lord. I hope I have adequately matched the colour.'

Dalchian looked down at his ceramite plate, every panel discoloured to a differing degree, burn marks, gouges and weld lines forming a dense patchwork across the silvered banding and night-dark blue. Even having been repaired, a legacy of abuse was writ large across its face. The enginseer scurried back bearing a bat-winged helm that looked, in comparison at least, practically forge fresh. Dalchian lifted the helm and examined it, and his lip curled, the skin there cracking again.

'And have you discovered anything worthy of note?' Dalchian asked as he mag-locked the helm to his waist.

'Many things,' Ibriel said, his excitement leaking into his vocaliser. 'One thing in particular.' He began lifting pieces out of his way, searching for something. 'My lord.'

Dalchian sighed as he watched the tech-priest rifle, but did not order him to stop. After a few moments, Ibriel lifted up a flat piece of circuit plate. At one end was a rat's tail of collected wires bound in a loop, and at the other was an articulated finger of metal tipped with a trident of loosely hanging barbs. Dried blood still caked around their needle tips.

'And this is?'

'It is an excruciatum locus, my lord.' Ibriel fixed his many lenses on the Skin-Taker. 'The Adepta Sororitas–'

'The corpse-worshipping lunatics.'

'Y-yes, my lord. Well, they utilise this Penitent Engine, and others like it, as a battlefield asset but also as a punishment for those they deem to have erred.'

'I know.'

'Quite. Well, they administer pain to the subject in a variety of ways in order to magnify its frenzied behaviour in combat.

The tines of this parasitic device are lodged directly into the subject's thalamus, wherein they deliver artificial pain signals at least two orders of magnitude higher than could be achieved through physical infliction. The agony I surmise to be exceptional without doing physiological harm to the subject.'

'Ingenious.'

'That was my conclusion too, my lord.'

'And what is significant about it?' Dalchian asked. The tech-priest seemed on the verge of dancing a jig.

'This component, my lord.' He clacked a metal fingertip against a tiny piece of circuitry. 'The pain regulation ordinator. It fascinated me because its crystalline structure follows a unique geometry I have not encountered before. I cross-referenced the manufactorum process required with known design signatures, and found that it is not derived from Adeptus Mechanicus construct patterns!' The cowled lenses leaned in at Dalchian, almost shaking with delight.

'I am struggling,' Dalchian said flatly, 'to be patient.'

'I never would have identified such an archaic design mode,' Ibriel blurted. 'Had it not been for my… liberated store of venerable tech-lore. The specific marker was interminably difficult to identify, but identify it I did, in the end.' The tech-priest took a breath. 'It is a Nostraman design!'

A few seconds passed as Dalchian stared at the excruciatum locus with fresh interest. He reached out his hand and gently took the device from Ibriel's manipulators, turning it over in his gauntlet. The thing was tiny in his grip. His genhanced sight picked out the tiny runes and numerals etched onto the ordinator component; a tiny flake of silicate in its miniature polycarbonate donjon.

The myths of his Legion's home world were known to him, as all Night Lords. The arch fable of a society tainted not by the power of the warp, but merely with the sicknesses of the human soul. How the Night Haunter, Konrad Curze, Dalchian's genetic primogenitor, scourged the cities in perpetual darkness, shrived them for their failings, and then raised his Legion of murderers from the best of those that remained. And how, in his absence, the world had backslid into misery and abuse under a torturous creed, diluting the martial grandeur of the Night Lords by sending the worst scum imaginable to meet the Legion's recruitment tithes.

Dalchian had never felt close to this irrelevant pre-history. The Legion took him, like it took them all, and made him into the reaver he was. There was no great purpose, no lofty ideal. Just the incontestable expectation that he plunder and murder and hunt in the name of the Legion. No prey was beyond consideration, no crime too sour to commit. Sevatar, Sahaal, Nostramo; Konrad Curze, even: these had never been much more than dull utterances to Dalchian, completely removed from the scope of his own terrorism.

But to now be holding a thing with provenance to Nostramo, however indirect – to know, to really know, that that sickening world had truly once existed, and that so must all the rest have done: it stoked a previously unfelt need within Dalchian. This knowledge, this new closeness, begat questions.

And as for the scabbed, verminous, bile-bellied Imperium? The filth of Terra had abandoned Curze to a protracted doom of madness and self-loathing even as they cast out all his sons to scratch an existence in the daemon-addled fringes of the galaxy. For them, for their supposedly most pious devotees, for those mewling sycophants, those miracle-proclaiming hypocrites to still use *Nostraman* technology in the name of their festering corpse idol!

Dalchian shook. Krutaan's claw was viced shut, the newly sharpened blades screeching against one another. Ibriel suddenly noticed that all his enginseers had taken a few steps back. Dalchian's black eyes, deep set within the excoriated ruin of his face, stared into the device and beyond it. Something wheeled behind his colourless irises. As the silence lengthened, Dalchian gradually returned to himself and to the armorium.

'My thanks for the gift,' he growled. Ibriel hesitated, betraying the fact that giving away the object had not been his intent. But he read the room.

'The honour is mine, Lord Skin-Taker.' Ibriel bowed deeply.

'We must discuss the next phase.' Dalchian's mien snapped sharply back to where it had been before seeing the locus. Deftly, he slid the bloody augmetic into a pouch at his belt, and Ibriel bid it a silent farewell.

'To which next phase do you refer?' Two of Ibriel's secondary arms began sorting through the pile of parts again, while another typed on the runeboard of a dataslate.

'You have not forgotten.' Dalchian sensed the distraction in the tech-priest, here among his precious hoard. Ibriel needed reminding of his duties. 'The tool to locate the Black Ship.'

'Mm, I now recall. There is a sixty-six per cent probability that applicable data might be found within one or more of my ancillary mem-stacks.'

'And you recall me ordering you to test those odds.' Dalchian allowed ice to form around his words. Ibriel had deferred commencement of his crucial work, and Dalchian would not allow him to prevaricate any longer. He had the Abyssal Kindred as allies, now. The sorcerer and his numerous warriors would no doubt prove useful. The Imperial Navy patrol group had sidetracked them, but he could not be overly angered, for the battle had brought its own boons. Now, he had the *Prideful*, and what a ship it was. More Blades had been lost, and the real prize went unclaimed, but every event had brought him a step further.

'You have a bounty of resources at your disposal, now, techpriest,' he said. 'Use them. Your time has come.'

Ibriel's secondary arms stopped sorting as his many-lensed face dropped a fraction.

'I understand, and offer my apologies.' A heartbeat. 'My lord.' The order had been given and no more need be said, but the Skin-Taker could not reconcile the gleeful abandon Ibriel showed among drifts of scrap with his unwillingness to indulge in the forbidden lore he so meticulously curated. *I am missing something.*

'What inhibits you?' Dalchian asked. Ibriel needed a moment of cogitation before he answered.

'There is…' Ibriel flinched suddenly and a burbling signal echoed in the depths of his hood, which he processed intently for half a second before turning his lenses back to Dalchian. 'Forgive me again, my lord. The Helbrute has been located.'

'Good. Secure it and get it off my ship.'

'Y-yes, my lord.'

Dalchian glimpsed the same reticence, but decided to ignore it. *Know your place, priest. I'll not have that thing tear this ship from under me.*

'I am uncertain of the procedure's duration. My lord.'

'For this, I can be patient.'

'Yes, my lord.' Ibriel realigned some of the conduit plugs in his torso compartment as he climbed out of the salvage heap. He holstered his dataslate and, with a *whirr* and a *click*, reconfigured some of the noospheric uplink antennae at his shoulder. The swollen shell of his datastore booted up, lumens blinking beneath the bronze carapace. Settling into the data-trance, Ibriel stilled as he detached his awareness from his own form and inserted it into that of one of his arachni-drones.

Deep within the bilges of the *Prideful*, in a narrow section full of redundant pipework beneath the atomic furnace of the engine stacks, the arcane beast-device crouched, rocking back and forth.

The Ibriel drone felt the inner hull skin deforming slightly with the huge Helbrute's motion. Waves of relief came over the tech-priest, thankful that the thing had not done more damage for which he would have been completely responsible. The drone *ticked* closer along the plasteel, and Ibriel felt the otherworldly heat of the daemon engine seep into his tiny form. A clamour of voices began to sound, quiet as if very far distant, and sibilant. Braving the infernal choir, the Ibriel drone jumped nimbly onto the armoured leg of the Helbrute. The voices grew louder and strange lights played over him. Lights with no source. The drone climbed, and then engaged with the dataport on the millennia-old sarcophagus. The armour just a few inches away wobbled and sweated, twisting with constant, metastatic growth. Ibriel gradually engaged the antediluvian rune-hymnals within his mem-stack, repeating the data infiltration he had performed once before.

And the real work began.

Dalchian watched as the tech-priest twitched and jerked. Random clashes of binharic jetted from Ibriel's vocaliser, and his mecha-dendrites shook, their lenses dilating and constricting wildly. Lumens danced on his mem-stack, and cogitation systems within the tech-priest's body sparked and hissed. After ten minutes or so Dalchian noticed a seam of smoke rising from Ibriel's collar, and the acridity of burnt silicates filled his nostrils. Ibriel's eye-lenses spun furiously and he issued a maddening litany of scrapcode as his body was racked with convulsions. Dalchian gazed on in rapt revulsion as the tech-priest shuddered from side to side, pivoting on his ankles like a carnival troupe performer.

At long last, Ibriel collapsed to the deck, smoke billowing from his robes. The datashell drooped gently on its suspensors, the crystalline cores within it cycling down into somnus mode. Subordinate enginseers approached Ibriel and, with undisguised reluctance, engaged their mechadendrites with his dataports to recite diagnostic code psalms. Tech-thralls clustered in to offer their motive force to their new lord's survival if needed. The enginseers worked away, and Ibriel's state seemed to stabilise by degrees.

Dalchian stood impassively watching it all take place, completely ignored by the Mechanicus adepts. Caught between disgust, curiosity and admiration, he allowed Ibriel all the time necessary to return to normative function. It took almost three hours.

'Quite the display,' Dalchian said as Ibriel regained consciousness. 'That Helbrute must be a formidable contrivance.'

'Mm, that d-difficulty you witnessed stemmed from accessing the mem-stack, not communing with the Helbrute.' Ibriel shook his hooded head in a jarringly canine motion. 'My lord.'

'The mem-stack?' Dalchian arched his shredded eyebrows and the pain made him wince. 'Just accessing data does that to you?'

'I am not merely accessing data.' Ibriel's mechadendrites twitched with affront and Dalchian smirked. 'I am engaging with an ancient wisdom, distilled into expansively complex rune-lines of sacred code. It is non-trivial to explain the process, especially given my fatigued state. I can prepare you a treatise to digest at your leisure, if you wish?'

'I do not.'

'I understand.'

'Though I'll admit to being baffled how a backwater forge world like Uzurmandius ever possessed such significant lore.'

'Well, prior to the Great Schism of Mars, Uzurmandius was home to the–'

'I am content in ignorance, Ibriel,' Dalchian interrupted.

'Mm, yes, of course. My lord.'

'Though I now see why you hesitate to carry out my order.' Dalchian delivered the accusation in a flat voice, and Ibriel said nothing. 'There is no escaping it, Ibriel. I demand this of you. Burn through as many adepts as you need, but find me the scent of our prey.'

Ibriel's mechadendrites twitched.

'Yes, my lord.'

The Abyssal Kindred Thunderhawk touched down on a much clearer, much emptier flight deck than it had done with Ang Heltris at the controls, hours earlier. A flight of interceptors hung at readiness in their launch cradles, but every other scrap of life had been locked away. Dutiful Legion serfs should be neither seen nor heard. The Thunderhawk's assault ramp lowered and Jathok stepped out, accompanied as ever by his Rubricae bodyguard. Dalchian momentarily tried to identify the one that had rescued him from the *Vizier*, but could not tell the spectral automatons apart. Their ancient armour had been repaired to as high a standard as their master's, and none betrayed the slightest recognition through their eerily lambent helm lenses.

'Welcome aboard the *Prideful*, Lord Jathok,' Dalchian said, new helm under his arm, his massacred face on show.

'A warship is a necessity for our kind,' Jathok said as he looked around appreciatively. 'You are restored to your proper place, my friend.'

Friend now, is it?

'My restoration is incomplete, but at least I have added teeth to my claws.' Dalchian was a little surprised as Jathok came close and offered a wrist to grasp. Dalchian met the gesture and Krutaan's claw twitched. Dalchian had brought no welcoming party and there was nobody else on the flight deck, so he concluded the courtesy was for his benefit alone. *He acknowledges the folly of rivalry; seeks to reinforce our cooperation. Very well.* 'Only with the Abyssal Kindred at my side could such a feat have been possible. You have my gratitude, Lord Jathok.'

'The trophy your pet tech-priest promises to deliver us will more than settle the debt, even once it is split between us.' *Ah, can't have me mistaking your help for altruism, can we?*

'He has already begun.'

'That is heartening news.' The avaricious gleam in Jathok's eyes was authentic and undisguised. 'The twin threats of the Imperial Navy and the Gorelord's ire loom close in our wake. Time is short.'

'I little need reminding.'

Less than an hour ago the proximity alarms on the *Prideful*'s bridge had begun to shriek. A Sons of Malice slave probe had keyed onto their position and started transmitting to its parent vessel. A storm of blitzing defence turret fire had obliterated the thing, but no one could be sure how much intelligence it had imparted before it died. The *Prideful* and the *Ikhtheos* had come to an oblique heading and put as much void behind them as possible.

'Though I'm curious,' Jathok continued. 'By exactly what mechanism does he expect to penetrate the veil behind which our quarry hides?'

'You'd have to ask him.'

'An excellent idea.' As Jathok beamed, another black-and-turquoise warrior stomped from the crew bay of the Thunderhawk.

'Lord Skin-Taker,' Gyren Naritsa said, nodding his greeting. 'Congratulations on the new machine.'

'Naritsa must monitor the armour systems of my casualties during the transfer, so he joins us, if that is acceptable?' Jathok asked, immediately followed by Naritsa himself interjecting.

'That, and I've never seen this frigate class from inside before.' The Warpsmith's plasteel skull gazed about, lenses flickering. Dalchian gestured to the bulkheads dismissively.

'By all means.'

'Thank you, Lord Skin-Taker.'

They descended on one of the deck conveyors, the oblong plate dropping slowly down through the hangar decks into Ibriel's armorium. Dalchian was a practical soul, not ordinarily given to displays of vanity, at least as far as he saw himself, but on this occasion he had demanded the mortal ground crew arrange the stored attack craft with parade-ground finesse. The dozen interceptors' sharp, chrome lines were polished and gleaming, and the last four missile craft reared on their stanchions, missile bay doors open, their snub noses leering. It was the assault boats that stood centre stage, however. Their toothed hammer heads yawned open to reveal rows of arrestor thrones, the straps of each harness folded identically to the last. The obsessive neatness was glaringly conspicuous, and Dalchian kept his eyes on the lord of the Abyssal Kindred as they descended. It was a statement of intent, and Jathok acknowledged it tactfully.

'You have prepared admirably for the trial ahead, Dalchian.'

'As, no doubt, have you.'

'We'll have a rare obstacle to overcome, make no mistake.' Jathok's injury-riven face creased with anxiety for a moment. 'I pray daily to the Great Powers that our joint forces are equal to the task.'

'And do the gods answer?'

'Their answer will be known to us through our victory, or through our extinction.'

'Your knucklebones offer you no clues?'

At this, Jathok laughed gently and Dalchian smirked.

'Where do you place your faith, Skin-Taker, if not in the will of the Primordial Annihilator?'

'Of course, the sorcerer asks questions to which he already knows the answer.'

'Sincerely, I am curious. In all your... misfortune, your certainty of triumph never dims. How?'

Is this a game, witch, or are you truly unable to tap my thoughts? If only you knew how dim my certainty has been of late.

'The only failure is death.'

'My, my, Dalchian.' Jathok shook his head, smiling. 'Such absolutism. For a moment there you sounded like an Imperial Astartes.'

The jibe was light and comradely, but Dalchian felt a moment of pure, incandescent rage to be likened to an Imperial Space Marine, the nadir of Terran hypocrisy. The image that, unbidden, blazed like a beacon in his mind was the Sororitas commander aboard the *Vizier*, stood on the other side of the blast door to him, smiling as the vacuum slowly dragged Keth Naa's life from him. Dalchian was not offended by her relishing the death of a foe; he understood that well enough. No, what curdled in his gut like burning promethium was the *superiority* of her expression. The total conviction of righteousness in the Sister's face, less than an hour before the Sororitas themselves condemned thousands of Imperial lives to a death as gruesome as any Dalchian could inflict. *What superiority? What warp-cursed difference between them and I? I embrace my monstrosity, that's the difference. To feign humanity in its absence is far worse than the absence itself. The Eye take the filthy delusionists!*

Exerting control over himself, Dalchian relaxed and took a breath. The blades of Krutaan's claw had clamped tight, and he opened them slowly, a distant hiss of laughter echoing in his skull.

'My certainty, Jathok, is purely practical. I will win or I will die. In any case, I need not fret.'

'Then I commend your directness.' If the sorcerer had noticed the impact of his words, he did not show it. 'I shall, nevertheless, keep praying that our two ships are enough.'

'They will have to be.'

The conveyor shuddered to a halt in the armorium receiving chamber, where dozens of attack craft too broken to fly were stacked against the bulkheads, halfway stripped for components. The party went aft towards the sounds of thumping machinery and pneumatic tools, and Dalchian noticed Naritsa becoming increasingly distracted as they traversed Ibriel's store of salvaged materiel.

A clade of servitors busied around a huge cylindrical engine, making alterations and adjustments under the light of fizzing lumen strips. Ibriel was hunched over one end of the engine, several limbs at full stretch within it. He noticed his visitors and wordlessly paused the work of his servitors. They withdrew their manipulators and stood to dumb attention, the generatorium units of their power tools winding down.

'Greetings,' he said, adding after a moment, 'my lords.'

'Lord Jathok here has requested some detail as to the nature of your schematic.'

'I am honoured. How much detail, precisely?'

'His visit is only brief.'

'Mm, I see.' Ibriel was a little crestfallen.

'My capacity for detail may eclipse that of Lord Jathok,' Naritsa said. 'Meaning no disrespect, my lord.'

'Of course not.' Jathok smiled. 'Your capacity far eclipses mine, Gyren. I shall ask the first question, though. How does it work?'

Ibriel accepted the question with a nod, then, unsure, swapped his gaze from Jathok to Dalchian and back.

'My humble apologies, but did Lord Skin-Taker not say you were *briefly* visiting?'

'Concisely summarise for Lord Jathok,' growled Dalchian.

'Of course. My lord.' Ibriel unfolded a hololithic micro-projector from his chest, and a technical illustration of something immensely complex smoked into glowing life in the air between them. The linework had several large gaps and many undesignated portions, and the floating image meant absolutely nothing to Dalchian. Jathok looked on, his expression unreadable, but Naritsa took a step forward and leant close to the projection, his metal face flicking from one detail to another, the hololith limning his fabricated features with emerald light. Ibriel, having clearly struggled with the idea of a concise summary, finally decided on a place to start.

'The basis of the device seems to share its energetic signature with Geller field distribution nodes, though quite how that interacts with long-range auspex or augur capabilities, I am yet to determine.'

'Its primary operational harmonic is etheric?' Naritsa asked.

'Mm, that much is certain.' Ibriel manipulated the hololith and zoomed in on a specific area. 'This is some form of channelling juncture, which is reminiscent of several patterns of warp-drive alignment array.'

'The biologic input?'

'I have yet to determine the… specific organic component required.'

'Organic component?' Dalchian asked.

'Quite,' Ibriel said. 'The machinery is an amplifier of some kind, in addition to other, less scrutable functions, but anything that operates in a psychic mode requires a biological sentience to function.'

'Or a Neverborn one,' Naritsa grunted. 'But the focal vertex is undefined?' The Warpsmith immediately addressed Ibriel again.

They went on like this for some time, their shared comprehension allowing for a robust back and forth. Dalchian and Jathok listened intently, inferring meaning from context when their knowledge was insufficient, which was frequently. A rudimentary understanding gradually inched closer in Dalchian's mind, but Jathok got there first.

'It's a psi-hound,' the sorcerer said, stare fixed upon Ibriel. 'A psychically prodigious mind, slaved to the task of sniffing out its kin.'

'Yes, my lord,' Naritsa replied. 'But a cyborganic construction. Incredible.'

'You're like a child with a new toy, Gyren,' Jathok smirked. Naritsa's gaze flicked to his lord. He said nothing.

'As I stated before,' Ibriel said, 'I have yet to fully develop the design from the lore to which I have access.'

'May I be privy to that lore?' Naritsa asked, and Ibriel froze. Dalchian read the abject fear that suddenly exuded from the tech-priest, and he tensed. Jathok felt the emotion as if it was his own and his stance subtly shifted. Krutaan's claw clacked. Naritsa rerouted seamlessly. 'Of course, I would not seek to divest any rare archeo-data from you, Ibriel. Our combined efforts brought success aboard the *Ikhtheos*, perhaps I could be of use to you here?'

'An excellent suggestion,' Jathok said, too quickly.

'Mm,' Ibriel mumbled as he regained his composure. 'Your assistance would be valuable, thank you, Warpsmith Naritsa.'

It took Dalchian an instant to understand what was happening, but Ibriel had already accepted the offer. The Skin-Taker looked at Jathok, who was nodding along. *You insidious bastard! Now I have a spy of yours aboard my ship to contend with, enmeshed in Ibriel's work, no less. You bastard.*

'I'm glad he'll be of use to you, tech-priest,' Jathok was saying. Dalchian had no reasonable way of reversing the agreement whilst maintaining the peace, so he created a diversion instead.

'We can make arrangements for you to return to the *Prideful* once your wounded are safely back on your ship, Naritsa,' he said.

'One of my enginseers can accompany the wounded,' Ibriel

volunteered. 'They have been maintaining the injured Kindred for some time. They are familiar with the systems. That would enable us to begin work immediately.' He waved a mechadendrite towards Naritsa. 'Progress will be greatly enhanced.' The tech-priest was visibly enthused by the thought. 'My lord.'

'Excellent,' Dalchian said. *By the Eye and the Eight Winds, priest! How mightily I wish you were not indispensable, for I would excise what remains of your skin with my bare hands!* 'You had best begin.'

'You are gracious, Lord Skin-Taker,' Jathok said.

'I'm no such thing.' He thought of his interaction with the Warpsmith in Ibriel's lifter. When Naritsa had called him gracious, he had meant it.

'And speaking of my wounded Kindred, I wish to see them now.'

'Of course.'

The trip to the medicae bay, newly enhanced to apothecarion status, seemed to Dalchian to go on for days. He and Jathok discussed the logistics of attack, exchanged information regarding boarding assault resources and attack craft numbers. Much of their strategising was theoretical, as neither of them possessed much information regarding the Black Ships of the League. Jathok had a fraction more context. As a psyker born on an Imperial world he had been collected by one as an infant, though his memories of it were scant and wholly subjective. They agreed emphatically, though, that as they were largely ignorant of what defences they might face they needed every weapon at their disposal. All the while they talked, half of Dalchian's mind was in the armorium where Jathok's Warpsmith revelled in Ibriel's arcane Mechanicus secrets. Dalchian found it surprising and unnerving to discover how possessive he had become of Ibriel and the advantage the priest's knowledge conferred. With an effort, he put his concerns aside once they reached the apothecarion.

'By the Powers,' Jathok breathed.

Qi Umshar had been ready for them and was standing at the foot of Saryuz's slab.

'It seems Saryuz and Zhikarga took the brunt of it,' the surgeon-Apothecary said. He gestured to the two Blades, still comatose even after the days that had passed since the battle on the *Vizier of Arandeep*. He had cleansed their armour as best he could, revealing miniscule flakes of unincinerated midnight paint on protected patches, where all else was bubbled and twisted ceramite. Zhikarga's bronze helm was marred with bands of green-blue discolouration, his lenses shattered. Saryuz had faced the flames head-first, and at the ruptured joins at his neck and arms there were glimpses of crisped, necrotic flesh. Qi Umshar indicated the slab next to them. 'Exalted Endagur fared little better, though he appears close to regaining consciousness.'

Jathok went and stood beside his champion, wincing at the fouled ruin of his beast-mask. 'Can you wake him now?' he asked. Qi Umshar looked at Dalchian, but the Skin-Taker waved the decision back to his surgeon.

'It would be preferable to wait until he does so by himself.'

'Endagur is unfathomably strong.'

'As you wish, Lord Jathok.' Qi Umshar adjusted the vitacopia attached to the Abyssal Kindred, then he swiftly tapped upon the dataslate connected to a port within the champion's power pack. 'It may take some time,' he warned.

'It may not,' Jathok replied.

Before Qi Umshar could say any more Endagur's back arched, lifting his chest from the slab with a crackle of tendons. The warrior's head lurched from one side to another, abused eyes visible through the shattered lenses. The surgeon-Apothecary administered a small dose of morphia and a lucidity stimulant through the vitacopia's cannula. Endagur relaxed a little, and his smashed eyes focused through the open rents where his helm lenses used to be, pupils differentially dilated within black-brown irises. He looked around, ragged breaths sucking wetly through his mangled rebreather. Dalchian thought about his first meeting with the champion and the huge injury that left half his face missing. Jathok leant over him.

'Calm, Endagur.' Beneath the figure of the sorcerer lord, the half-incinerated warrior began to nod stiffly. He lifted his hands with tremendous difficulty, wheezing as he did. He held the blackened extremities before his face and flexed his fingers, the agony obvious.

Over the course of nearly an hour, Endagur was brought first to sitting, then standing. Two more of the other six Kindred were conscious, not quite as badly mauled as their champion. The rest were placed onto grav-gurneys. As Ibriel promised, an adept in a crimson robe attended to them, monitoring those vital, life-perpetuating systems of their power armour and the apparatus connected to them.

As the Abyssal Kindred shuffled slowly from the apothecarion, Dalchian gazed at one of the roasted warriors, the pain evident across their forms conjuring in his mind. He grimaced.

'Look after these warriors,' Dalchian told the adept, who bowed deeply. 'They are valiant servants of the gods.'

After their guests had departed the chamber, Dalchian looked at the two Chaos Space Marines clad in derelict midnight plate, comatose on their slabs.

'Will they be ready for what is coming?' he asked Qi Umshar. The surgeon shrugged.

'I hope so, my lord.'

'But you cannot be sure.'

'There are no guarantees.'

Saying nothing else, Dalchian followed the cortege of Abyssal

Kindred back to the flight deck, where they delicately secured the wounded within the Thunderhawk.

Jathok addressed Dalchian as his gunship's engines began to howl. 'More preparation beckons.'

'I shall inform you of any developments with Ibriel's device.'

'As shall Naritsa, no doubt.'

No doubt. And with that, Dalchian was left alone on the flight deck, the downwash of the Thunderhawk abruptly diminishing as the craft passed through the energy shield and out into the void.

Chapter Nineteen

Apart from line-breaking, the *Prideful*'s secondary role was to harry enemy escorts, bursting their shields with volleys from its plasma obliterator batteries, breaking them over its triple-reinforced prow if it managed to line up such a strike or taking them via boarding action. Over half the voidsmen-at-arms of the *Prideful*'s breacher cohort had perished to the *Ikhtheos'* defence turrets during the battle for the *Vizier*, but that still left nearly six hundred. Combat specialists, trained exclusively in the arena of shipborne assaults and the horrific close-quarters battles they demanded. They were the most effective weapon the vessel could deploy, and the main reason such a ship existed at all. Veteran mortals, rare and driven.

Adequate grist for the mill, Dalchian thought as he stood appraising the neat ranks of personnel. He had summoned them to the quarterdeck, above and abaft of the flight deck, as this was nominally where the breachers would stand-to before embarking upon their boarding craft. The wide space echoed, marble and ouslite flags arranged in a checkerboard on the deck, the venerable stonework discoloured by old bloodstains and new.

With so few Legion murder-kin under his command, Dalchian was under no illusion that he didn't need to use every asset available to him. There might possibly be enough Abyssal Kindred to take a Black Ship, but no power in the galaxy could convince him that Jathok's warband would honour their part of the bargain unless he could apply his own leverage. He needed soldiers. Moments of introspection had him yearning for the *Abjuration* and his Blades of Atrocity as they had once been. Fifty predatory Night Lords in all their panoply. Rhinos, combat bikes, his beloved Thunderhawk. All destroyed on the off-chance Dalchian would return from a trap engineered to be his downfall. He had allowed the treachery of Gorelord Thelissicus to fade in his mind, for other concerns were more pressing, but he knew the agony of that disinheritance would never abate. The Gorelord would suffer under his attentions one day. But now was not a moment for introspection, so such thoughts he stowed away. Now, he had another task to fulfil.

The breachers, like all the crew, had removed the aquila from their uniforms, but Dalchian was not naïve enough to think they had removed it from their souls. The *Prideful*'s officers had witnessed the flaying of their compatriots and said their vows. The voidsmen-at-arms had not. If he deployed them aboard an Imperial vessel without oversight, then their defection was ensured. He had to guarantee that they would fight for him.

'You all belong to me,' he rumbled. He had left his helm in his arming chamber as he had found his uncovered face had a pleasing impact upon mortal constitutions. The exposed musculature around his eyes stung and the lack of one cheek lent his voice an accompanying hiss. 'But some of you will think you know better.'

Dagardis and Ang Heltris prowled across the flagstones around the ranks of soldiery, their staring helm lenses dissecting the mortals where they stood. Dalchian went to the rear rank, deliberately bypassing the voidmaster and sergeants-at-arms at the fore. It was an old but reliable tactic. Invert the hierarchy and the dissatisfied will emerge. Dalchian stopped before the breacher on the very end of the last file. The soldier stayed at attention, looking dead ahead.

'Look at me,' Dalchian hissed. The breacher flinched, but still did not move. Sweat beaded from beneath his tight, neat beret. A warrant officer with a cane who stood at the front of the company gave him a shallow nod, and he turned at once, drilled expression fixed through Dalchian, as if willing the heretic monster not to be there.

'Obeying your superior is commendable,' Dalchian said. 'Ignoring me is not.' He reached for the breacher but the mortal snapped up his hands, the laspistol previously hidden in his waistband suddenly drawn and readied. The muzzle levelled unwaveringly at Dalchian's left eye and the breacher pulled the trigger. Before the firing mechanism could engage, the pistol and the breacher's hands were dropping to the stone deck. The knife in Dalchian's fist shone with new blood. The breacher staggered, and another instinctively turned to help him.

'DO NOT MOVE.' Dalchian's voice was a physical force. Even the veteran voidmaster at the head of the company blanched. Someone emptied their bladder into their breeches. The breacher who had started turning recoiled upright like a plasteel girder suddenly released from tension. The handless soldier staggered again and gasped. Dalchian grabbed him, gauntleted hand entirely enclosing his neck, and slammed him to the floor. The mortal's skull cracked loudly against the stone flags, and he fell still. Dalchian ignored the pistol and severed hands lying on the deck, turning to the next breacher in the line.

'Look at me.'

The breacher turned and met his hideous gaze, her yellowed eyes wide.

'The task is simple,' Dalchian said. 'Declare that you serve me and only me. If your declaration is not convincing then you will be disposed of.' The breacher looked from Dalchian, to the dead breacher and back. Taking a deep breath, she jutted her chin and shook her head. Dalchian lifted her without effort and threw her, face-first, into the deck. Dalchian moved to the next breacher.

'Your declaration,' he prompted. The young man shook from head to toe as he looked up at his new master. After a heartbeat he turned and ran.

'Stand-to, trooper!' the voidmaster hollered, but the breacher continued pell-mell across the flags. Ang Heltris met him on the far side of the quarterdeck and dismantled him in a few short swipes. Dalchian took another step.

'Your declaration.'

'I serve Lord Skin-Taker,' the soldier said, kneeling.

'Don't you f–' the voidmaster snarled before the back of his skull blew out. Dagardis left his augmetic arm outstretched, the bolt pistol in his grip wafting a lazy curve of smoke from its muzzle.

'Good. Present yourself to the adept for branding.' Dalchian smiled as he spoke, and the man nodded as he stood. One of Ibriel's subordinates was off to the side. They had replaced one of their own arms with an extension armature bearing a wrought iron sigil upon its end, and the adept held the sigil in the heating chamber of a portable autoclave, waiting patiently for the breacher to approach. The next breacher spat at Dalchian and as he broke against the stone, an angry hiss echoed from the ceiling vaults and the air became suffused with a cooked meat stink. The man receiving the brand wailed in pain.

Their bleak choice now grotesquely evident, the process began to accelerate. Some breachers died under Night Lords blades as they tried to rush their would-be masters. Some surrendered their dignity, weeping and screaming. A lonely, broken few cocked hidden laspistols and ended their torment on their own terms. But, in the end, most submitted to the branding and joined Lord Skin-Taker's new foot-soldiers, who stood in a knotted mass, rank and file a distant memory. The mortals delicately touched the edges of charred, suppurating skin across their faces, the pattern repeated upon every single one of them.

The eight-pointed star. The icon of the Primordial Annihilator. Dalchian loathed the foul magicks of the gods of the warp, but invoking their names had its uses. The Black Ship would be crewed by the brain-cleansed and the superstitious, and no mortal bearing the mark of the gods would be suffered to live once on board. These soldiers would die at the hands of the Adeptus Astra Telepathica, and whether they fought back or not, Dalchian cared little. *Adequate grist for the mill.* He ordered the remaining sergeants-at-arms to draw up a revised order of battle, then strode from the corpse-strewn quarterdeck.

CHAPTER TWENTY

Ibriel's message was a text datapulse that flashed on his command throne's slate, requesting a meeting. Dalchian thought it odd Ibriel had not simply contacted him over the vox. Curiosity piqued, he acknowledged.

The tech-priest leant heavily on a servo-tractor, the bulky unit growling as its promethium engine powered it slowly around the overflowing scrapheap of his armorium. Ibriel's misshapen figure was hunched and bowed as he inched his way towards his lord, and Dalchian knew it was the task he had set that put Ibriel in this state. A robed ship's enginseer accompanied Ibriel, and as he drew closer, Dalchian saw a spherical device protruding from the crippled tech-priest's cowl at a point where Dalchian supposed Ibriel's mouth must be. Standing before one another, Dalchian nodded.

'How goes the great work?'

In answer, the spherical device at Ibriel's mouth issued a chattering sound and a ribbon of parchment came ratcheting out of it. The enginseer at Ibriel's side reached up and tore off the strip, reading it tonelessly.

'The data-gathering has briefly disabled most of my higher communication faculties.' Another ribbon stuttered out, which the enginseer tore off and read. 'I apologise for the temporary incapacity.' Another chatter of ribbon. 'My lord.'

'Data-gathering,' Dalchian said. 'Has construction begun?'

Chatter, chatter.

'Negative. It was necessary to collect as much specification data as possible before embarking on construction.' Dalchian felt the hot itch of impatience.

Chatter, chatter.

'Additionally, accessing my unconventional repository has not grown easier.'

Chatter, chatter.

'I require time to recalibrate between access phases.'

Chatter.

Dalchian suppressed his frustration. The longer they waited before making their move, the more likely was their discovery by the bastard Imperial Navy. And that was not the only factor that the Skin-Taker chafed at. Krutaan's claw clacked and the enginseer gave the weapon a wary frown.

'And the Warpsmith?' asked Dalchian. 'Is his presence useful?'

Chatter.

'Most assuredly.'

'Wonderful. What report of yours necessitated this visit, then?'

Chatter, chatter.

'Resulting from my data-gathering, it seems I require a Navis Nobilite abhuman in a sacrificial capacity.'

It took Dalchian an instant to comprehend the implication of the request. 'Navigator Osthol.'

Chatter, chatter.

'She is the only Navigator on board, is she not?'

'But if you use our Navigator in a *sacrificial* capacity, how then are we to adequately pursue our prey?' Dalchian and Jathok had already discussed their hunting strategy and, given their backwater hiding place and the likelihood of the Black Ship being near the planetary system's population centres, they had accepted that a short warp translation would be necessary to achieve the requisite surprise for an attack. For that, he needed his Navigator, or the risks were too great. Far too great.

Chatter, chatter.

'My data leads me to deduce that such an absence will not prove an obstacle.'

'Is that so?'

Chatter, chatter.

'The details remain unclear, but through the process I expect them to become less so.'

Chatter.

'My lord.'

'You ask much, tech-priest.'

Chatter.

'As do you.'

Chatter.

'My lord.'

'Do you need her now, or can she remain ignorant of her utility until she is needed?'

Chatter, chatter.

'I believe I can complete the construction without her, yes.'

'Good. Make sure this *requirement* does not become known among the crew.'

Chatter.

'Of course.'

Chatter, chatter.

'Additionally, the power demands will be too great to rely on sectional shipboard power relays, so the device must be wired directly to the plasma core of the ship.'

'I see.' *This is getting more convoluted by the moment.* 'Displace the generatorium overseer. Do what you must, but keep the ship battle-worthy while you do it.'

Chatter.

'Of course.'

Chatter.

'My lord.'

Dalchian sighed as he stood alone on the conveyor platform rattling back up through the decks. Not for the first time he wondered to himself whether Ibriel truly possessed the knowledge he claimed to, or was just wildly wrong. Or lying. The tech-priest had surprised him with what he could do up until now, but could his hesitation regarding the psi-hound mean something other than Ibriel had said? Could Dalchian really believe this lowly tech-priest from a half-forgotten forge world actually had the ability to track an Astra Telepathica Black Ship? His body was still very broken, and the stab of doubt was one of many in his gut, but the thought of the prize to be had if Ibriel spoke the truth was an enticing balm. True or not, he would make the attempt. What else was there to be done?

Dalchian made sure he was alone in the strategium before opening an encrypted hololith connection.

'The device demands we feed it a Navigator,' Dalchian said. 'Yours is only a pet of the Gorelord, is he not? Can we serve him to the machine?'

'*Alas,*' Jathok replied, his projected form crackling, '*Thelissicus, in his wisdom it seems, rigged our Navigator's quarters with plasma charges. Any attempt to remove him will result in his obliteration. Believe me, I've tried.*'

'That is unfortunate.' Dalchian narrowed his eyes.

'*I concur,*' Jathok sighed. '*Besides, the pickled deformity still thinks we're chasing your mutineer. I have been sparing with the details of our accord among my mortal crew, lest word find its way back to the Crimson Slaughter.*' It was a frustratingly plausible excuse. With an effort Dalchian prevented himself from rolling his eyes.

'Perhaps I should be grateful,' he replied. 'The only sabotage my crew seem capable of is extinguishing their own lives. Another gun crew not two hours ago.'

'*Imperial herd-beasts,*' Jathok sneered. '*Dutiful to the last.*'

'Curse them.' His alternative denied him, Dalchian accepted the necessity of sacrificing the *Prideful*'s own warp-guide. 'Osthol it will be, then.'

'*You're sure that is wise?*' Jathok's concern did not reach his eyes.

'It is our only choice. If we succeed, a replacement should be easily sourced.'

'*If we succeed.*'

It took Ibriel and Naritsa two days of relentless toil and the unquestioning assistance of the *Prideful*'s entire cadre of tech-adepts, from the forge specialists of the artisanii technicus, to the ranks of enginseers, to lexmechanics and lowly servitors. The generatorium and lower decks rang with the sounds of novel industry. Many of the adepts met their end in various ways and at various stages of the process, but Dalchian asked no questions. The attrition was within acceptable limits.

The nature of the work was not divulged to Osthol, lest she damage herself to prevent its fruition. When Ibriel contacted Dalchian to say little work remained to be done, the Skin-Taker knew the moment had arrived. He voxed Jathok and told the Abyssal Kindred to prepare.

'*Prepare for what, Skin-Taker?*' Jathok's manner had become less and less confident the longer Ibriel's work had gone on. Dalchian had partly hoped the sorcerer would angrily reject the plan at the last moment, leaving him to pursue it alone, but he knew that a handful of legionaries might not be enough. He needed Jathok's numbers.

'Are your reports from the Warpsmith lacking?'

'*Gyren seems utterly captivated by the work,*' the sorcerer replied, an edge to his tone. '*If you allowed him to adopt your pet tech-priest, then I suspect he would do so without hesitation.*'

'That doesn't answer my question.'

'*No, his reports are not lacking,*' Jathok admitted. '*But even his understanding has its limits. He thinks his contributions to this endeavour are spent, so I am recalling him to the* Ikhtheos.' This surprised Dalchian. Was Naritsa not a spy after all, or had his espionage perhaps yielded unfavourable truths?

Jathok went on. '*I need to hear it from you, Skin-Taker. What awaits us when that device is activated?*'

'Truthfully,' Dalchian replied, 'I'm not sure. But when it happens, we will need to be ready to deploy our warriors immediately.'

'*There are many unknowns to your ploy, Skin-Taker,*' Jathok said, the hostility overt.

'That, I cannot deny.'

'*And there are no guarantees you can make that your pet speaks the truth?*'

'A little late for that, wouldn't you say?' Dalchian shot back. 'Besides, I thought you were the one with faith in the gods' designs?'

'*Beware of mocking me, Night Lord.*'

'Then prepare as I suggest.'

Navigator Osthol was haughty like all Imperial Navigators. The destructive power that could erupt from a Navigator's daemon-eye was considerable, and Dalchian little desired her to stage a last stand, so he brought Dagardis and Ang Heltris with him just in case. Fortunately, Osthol was waiting with her chamber portal open, seated in dignified repose.

'I suspected your coming here, heretic,' she said in bitter tones. She was short and wiry with tightly plaited silver hair and voluminous robes. The mutant third orbit in the middle of her forehead was veiled with an embroidered kerchief. The three Night Lords stood over her throne like cyclopean gargoyles, the only illumination the faint glow of Osthol's rune screens, underlighting the filed-sharp edges of their armour.

'Do you also suspect my purpose?'

'Only that it pertains to my obliteration.'

'Will you walk to your end, or must you be dragged?'

'I will walk, you revolting beast.' She bit the words out, her sharp features crinkled around her nose as if she fought against some hideous stench. 'Dead I'll no longer be a tool of your reaving, so I will gladly go.' She raised herself from the throne, clearly a motion seldom practised, and shuffled her stately way down the corridors and gangways of the vessel she would never guide through the immaterium again.

Not sanely, at least.

When they arrived, the psi-hound bore little resemblance to anything Dalchian had ever seen. In the main it was alike to a hive-spire electrical substation, pylons of welded plasteel spread around a central column of superconductive rings. Thick cables were strung madly between everything, giving the generatorium the aspect of a gigantic arthropod's silk-spun nest, an illusion dispelled none-at-all by Ibriel's skittering arachni-drones. There the Skin-Taker's sphere of comparison ran short. Elaborate towers of crystalline blockwork were adhered together with chemical fixatives, forming geometric stalagmites that bent the light passing through them into exotic new wavelengths. A motorised pulley system kept unbroken rings of chain rotating through collets around the entire structure, with no obvious purpose other than to add a jangling discordancy on top of the already deafening churn of the plasma reactor. Tines of glistening metal stood upright on articulated booms, Ibriel's subordinates making tiny adjustments to the ball joint clamps that kept them oriented. The tech-priest himself hung in a cradle above the whole artifice, a profusion of dataslates, valve dials and numeral displays crowding around his hooded face. He hammered away at rune boards and flicked tiny lever controls with several new manipulator limbs. *More arms, really?* Navigator Osthol's heavily lidded eyes saw only the metal saltire at the dead centre of the machine. Saw only the restraint bands riveted to its four splayed arms and the chain belt around its middle.

'I will not,' she said with a quaver, her poise draining away.

'You will.'

'No.' She took a step back, a tremor stealing over her. 'You cannot activate that… *thing*.'

'I can.'

She took another step back but was barred from retreating further by Dagardis' bulk. Slowly, wrenching her eyes from the diabolical contraption, she turned and looked up at the axeman, who tipped his horned helm towards the restraint bed.

'On you get, mutant,' he said jovially. For a moment she looked utterly helpless, like a toddler banished from her family hab and confronted with the limitless cruelty of the outside world. But then her face twisted and her papery hands clawed at the kerchief that covered her daemon-eye. Dagardis grabbed her hands and arthritic metacarpals within them crumpled like dry kindling. She moaned in pain. With a delicate shove, the Blade sent her reeling back to collide with the plasteel restraint bed. Instantly, tech-savants seized her frail limbs and lifted her bodily onto the cruciform, ratcheting her down tightly. Her thin screams curdled in the hazy air.

'Begin,' Dalchian instructed the tech-priest. Ibriel's lenses turned towards the Skin-Taker for the briefest of moments.

'So I shall,' he said.

Dalchian waited.

'My lord.'

Dalchian's lip curled and he and the two Blades stalked from the generatorium deck. Osthol was still screaming as the reactor's roar began to build.

'All hands.'

Dalchian spoke into the ship-wide vox, his karstic voice tumbling from augmitter horns on every deck of the *Prideful*. Ratings looked up from their labours, their exhaustion vying with their trepidation. What few officers remained stood stoically at their stations, repeating in their minds like a mantra whatever justifications they had made to themselves for submitting to a Heretic Astartes lord. Ground crews on the flight deck attended their charges as they had always done, listening to the broadcast while pretending to ignore it. Qi Umshar tapped a cylinder of intravenous drugs plugged into one of the crusted warriors on his slab, the Skin-Taker's voice echoing from the ivory tiles of his apothecarion.

'Soon we will make an immaterial translation directly into combat. Prepare for the unpreparable, and I'll take the hide of any who fail me.

'To battle stations.'

The hololith jumped and stuttered, Ibriel's distorted form freezing between bouts of motion. From his command throne on the bridge, Dalchian strained to separate the tech-priest's words from the tumult surrounding him in the generatorium.

'Again, priest,' he ordered.

'I said the… sma load is nearing maxi… apacity, but the mechanism has not y… ptimal dilation. Furth… ification will be necess… y lord.' Ibriel was absorbed within the coruscating energies of his project, finally operating before him after all his relentless labour. His aloofness chipped at Dalchian's brittle temper.

'You need more power?'

'Th… s affirmative,' Ibriel replied. 'M… ord.'

'Then obtain it. You are in the generatorium, are you not?' His teeth made high-pitched noises against one another.

'Yes, my l… f course.' Ibriel's image faded away, only for another hail to sound from the panel at Dalchian's left hand. He jabbed the rune key, the scope of all his strategy's various unknowns beginning to expand unnervingly before him.

'Sorcerer,' he said.

'Dalchian,' Jathok greeted him. 'Holding my warp drive at readiness for this long is sapping a great deal of energy, both from my ship and my crew.'

'As it is mine, Jathok. We are in the tech-priest's hands.'

'Are we any closer to establishing translation coordinates?'

'No.' Dalchian felt a serpent whirling in his guts. The psi-hound of Ibriel's conjuring had been his path to redemption all the while it was an abstraction, a mere plausibility. As the machine had grown so too had Dalchian's relish at the thought of winning his enormous victory. He had revelled in Jathok's receding authority, the witch-breed knowing his own liberation relied utterly upon Dalchian and the efforts of his strange Mechanicus pet. With nothing, Dalchian had feared nothing. Choosing between likely oblivion and the guarantee of it had been no choice at all. But he had a ship now. He had a crew that was competent, however lacklustre their devotion might yet be. Now Ibriel's grand artifice was shaking the *Prideful* apart by the sounds of it, and the possibility that he had miscalculated was an unwelcome but unignorable concern.

Jathok was about to say something else, but Ibriel's form erupted in front of the Skin-Taker in frosted projection.

'*My lord,*' Ibriel said, mechadendrites jangling. '*This very moment I have learnt a crucial detail about the operation of the mechanism!*'

Dalchian's brow twitched in concert with Krutaan's claw. Jathok made to interrupt over the second-hand hololith link, but Dalchian muted the sorcerer. Ibriel's feed was now much sharper and the audex clearer than it had been.

'Essential information only,' Dalchian warned him, and the tech-priest checked himself for an instant before speaking.

'*The mechanism makes no distinction between data and context. It describes information and shapes the manifest reality that such information describes simultaneously.*' Ibriel's fascinated wonderment read easily over the hololith. A powerful quake rattled Dalchian in his throne and several of the mortal bridge crew whimpered. They were all untested drafts, filling roles recently vacated. The empty eye sockets of their predecessors stared at them from where Dalchian now sat. There was no room for error. Dalchian had made that clear. But he was presently paying them no heed because every fraction of his being wanted to scream at the tech-priest babbling across the hololith.

'Essential information only, priest.' *By the Eye and the Eight Winds, make that the very last time I must repeat an order.*

'*We are not waiting for coordinates, Lord Skin-Taker,*' Ibriel said, astonishing Dalchian by using his full honorific in earnest. '*The machine awaits our translation. Then it will co-locate the Black Ship and us simultaneously!*'

Dalchian felt the moment unto the very depths of his marrow. If the gods truly cared a jot about him, he knew, then this was their uttermost test. To hurl himself into the warp, the roiling sump of insanity that existed only to render living souls into their basest, most horrifying fragments, without translation coordinates to haul towards was the worst kind of lunacy. A wretched moment of uncertainty stopped his mind dead. The hololith jolted, the muted figure of Sorcerer Lord Leil Jathok gesticulating furiously. Dalchian unmuted him.

'What in the warp's depths is happening, Skin-Taker? Do we have coordinates yet?' The sorcerer's voice reeked of desperation, and a kernel of amusement lodged in Dalchian's mind.

'No, Lord Jathok. We must enter the Great Ocean blind, and trust in the machine.'

'Piss on that, Skin-Taker!' Jathok roared. *'Give me some coordinates or I am finished with this absurdity!'*

And the petulance of the master of the Abyssal Kindred broke through the barrier in Dalchian's mind. As if he had lifted his head up out of smog for the first time in an age, Dalchian saw the situation as it truly was. He still had nothing. His legacy was spent, his glory extinguished, and there was no choice now, as there had been no choice countless times before. And Jathok? The sorcerer's self-serving obsessiveness was pathetic. Dalchian began to laugh as the realisation struck him. Jathok had been partway right, accusing Dalchian of his Imperial-like absolutism. Compromise and vacillation were the purview of almost every Chaos Space Marine lord he had known. Always they trod with one eye over their shoulder, as much slaves to their own conspiracies as those they conspired against, and in every moment beguiled by the temptation to escape a potential defeat before they ever actually bent their full will to achieving victory. Unendingly, they sabotaged themselves and called it canniness.

Dalchian took a chest full of rancid voidship atmosphere, the first breath of a new existence, and the laughter poured from him. Jathok stared across the grainy hololith.

'You are lost, Skin-Taker,' he said bitterly.

'No, witch,' Dalchian grinned, pieces of his face cracking off to reveal the wet flesh that regrew beneath. 'I am found, at last. Attend to whichever fate best pleases you. I tread the only path to greatness that remains to me.' With that he disconnected the hololith feed, Jathok's nonplussed expression dissolving into the air.

'Engage warp translation procedure,' he said. 'Begin countdown on my mark.'

'The Geller field, my lord!' a gunnery lieutenant bawled, tears of horror burning his cheeks.

'Unnecessary for our purposes, so my tech-priest assures me. Mark.' With the faintest breath of hesitation, the new navigation officer authorised the countdown with barely shaking hands.

Perhaps I should give some of them more credit.

Crimson lumens immediately began to pulse throughout the decks of the *Prideful*, accompanied by braying klaxons. Chambers and companionways and gun embrasures and hangar bays filled with the susurrus of prayer; men and women and no few children grasped at aquila fetishes they mistakenly believed unnoticed by their new masters. Keening wails reverberated in the bulkheads and echoed down corridors, sourceless and petrifying. Ibriel's hololithic flickered.

'It is a shame Gyren cannot see this first-hand,' he said, clearly enamoured of the arcane technology at work beneath him.

'You'll have to tell him all about it,' Dalchian laughed as he stood from his throne, filled with a fresh vitality. Ibriel's link terminated and Dalchian favoured Qi Umohar with a serrated grin. 'You have the bridge.'

The surgeon-Apothecary bowed his head. 'Hunt well, my Lord Skin-Taker.'

'I shall,' he said. 'The other two?'

'Their vitals are returning to nominal levels as we speak. I shall send them in with the second wave, as you request, my lord.'

'Hunt well, Qi Umshar,' he said as he strode from the bridge.

His branded voidsmen-at-arms stood in readiness on the flight deck as ground crew made final preparations to the Gnathas assault boats. The troopers wore grey and red, their burnished armour plates glinting in the lumens. They had been ordered to leave their helmets behind so none could mistake them for loyal Imperials. Their shotguns, multi-lasers and breaching charges were armed and ready. At the signal, the troopers moved in good order into assault boat arrestor harnesses and the craft's armoured jaws began to close between the paired melta-projectors that jutted out from either side. Thirty-four assault boats started spooling up their engines, the remaining twelve held back as a reserve to reinforce a breach-head.

Dalchian, Dagardis and Ang Heltris took up an assault boat by themselves, their huge armoured forms barely fitting into the narrow transport bay as the warp translation countdown blared from augmitter horns on the bulkheads.

'This is it then, my lord?' Ang Heltris voxed. Dalchian had replaced his own helm for this action.

'It is. Prepare to slay and excruciate.'

'I am always prepared for those, my lord.'

'Good. How's the arm?' he asked Dagardis.

'Effective, my lord.'

'Good.' Dalchian took a few calming breaths, the combat stimms already circulating around his body as his armour responded to his mental state. The warp translation countdown entered its final stages and the atmosphere within the *Prideful* thickened, frost creeping across plasteel like slime mould. The first-wave assault boats ignited their engines, hydraulic launch clamps holding them secure for now. 'We may be the only remnant Blades of Atrocity, my murder-kin, but our company shall be great once again. I promise you this, in the name of the Eye and the Eight Winds. Win for me today, and I shall give you the galaxy.'

'Our blades yet thirst,' they both intoned, stimms whetting their bloodlust. Dalchian blinked into life the vid-feed from the bridge oculus, needing to see every moment of it.

'Our blades yet thirst.'

A proximity alarm sounded abruptly, and Dalchian blink-clicked access to the ship's augur data. Three rune markers bearing idents relating to Flylords warships were heaving to, rapidly closing on their position. Dalchian registered weapons fire from the vessels, and he cursed the Gorelord again.

But the Flylords were too late.

The countdown reached zero and a thunderous silence washed through the *Prideful*. Unreality blossomed in the space before it, shining hellish hate-light into the black vacuum and yawning to admit the microscopic morsel that was the frigate and its thousands of souls. The vessel's engine stack glowed with heat as mile-long columns of fire sent it lancing into the gluttonous fabric of the immaterium. As the ship submerged beneath the waves of pure emotional energy, Dalchian's lightning claw clamped tight into a fist of its own volition and he heard Krutaan as clear as if he stood next to him.

Close the door, Dalchian.

'Close the door, Dalchian.'

'I did,' Dalchian replied. They stood opposite one another on the bridge of the *Red Galentia*. The ship was desolate, abandoned. 'I closed it here, when I killed you, Krutaan. Surely, you must know that?'

Krutaan shook his head gently, the placed-together stump ends of his neck squelching together at the motion.

'You opened it, Dalchian. You opened it to me.'

'Where are *you*, then?' Dalchian gestured around himself to the empty voidship. 'My mind is my own.'

'I need not seed myself within your mind.' Krutaan lifted his hands in equivocation and they looked odd devoid of his customary lightning claws. 'Souls guide me onto your plane, yes, but my doorways take many forms.'

'What forms?'

'Close the door.'

Static filled Dalchian's hearing and vision for a heartbeat before falling away. He was still in the assault boat aboard the *Prideful* and Krutaan's claw hung relaxed at his side. He flexed the bladed digits experimentally.

'*Brace for impact!*' Qi Umshar's voice caromed across the ship-wide vox, and Dalchian stared at the oculus feed, digesting what he saw there.

A crenellated cliff of ebon armour loomed before them, augur spines jutting from it, gargoyles of black iron in ranks upon its top edge. Curls of darkness more opaque than mere void fluttered from its structure, a spectral cloak of energy that the ship conjured around itself. It had been temporarily blown aside by a frigate with its weapons primed having suddenly exploded from the warp on its starboard bow. Dalchian's ravenous appraisal took in every detail of the huge vessel. *It was all true,* he marvelled, having never really let himself believe it until this very moment.

A Black Ship.

The Astra Telepathica tithe ship was easily eight or nine times the tonnage of the *Prideful,* and a full two miles longer. It bore none of the gilded banding or colourful heraldry of Imperial Naval vessels, though its general shape was clearly of the same family. Every part of it was black iron, and its trunk was swollen with cargo capacity a hundred decks deep. The prow wedge was narrow and bore thinner armour than a warship, but lance turrets still graced its spine. There was no evident bridge structure, so it must have been tucked into the meat of the Black Ship, jealously hidden. The distance between it and the *Prideful* closed to nothing with outrageous speed.

The frigate was designed for making ram attacks during void combat. Its prow comprised of thick, multiple-reinforced armour and was even a shade more acutely angled in comparison to those of similar classes like the Firestorm, lending its chisel edge greater mechanical advantage. The crew stations were equally specialised to keep hold of their human occupants under impact, unlike many other Imperial vessels. The *Prideful* drove at its prey's flank like a harpoon.

The Black Ship heaved to with improbable speed. Knowing they could not avoid the collision, the Black Ship lurched her prow towards the *Prideful* to lessen the penetrating damage of the frigate's ram. The huge vessel turned on a cred-piece and very nearly forced the ram aside completely. But Dalchian's ambush had worked.

The *Prideful* screamed with conflicting forces as its riving tip tore a split down the flank of the Black Ship rather than skewer it dead abeam. The *Prideful*'s sharpened ploughshare burst through the layered plasteel and adamantine of the Astra Telepathica ship's outer hull, splaying a furrow of metal that sparked, edges rearing either side of the frigate's vicious cut. Chunks of debris spun across the oculus' frame as the relative velocity of the two vessels groaningly reduced. Through a glittering cloud of shorn-off hull plating, Dalchian saw the starfield slowly slide as the *Prideful* yawed to starboard. With a lurch, the *Prideful* came free, leaving the terrible incision it had inflicted upon the Black Ship exposed to the void.

'First wave, launch!' Dalchian snarled, and the assault boats blasted into the vacuum.

CHAPTER TWENTY-ONE

Dalchian's assault boat tore through debris-flecked void at hundreds of miles an hour, the other boats stretched out on either flank, but the scale and distances of void combat meant there were still precious minutes before the attack wing reached the target vessel. Spooling through the *Prideful*'s observation data, it became clear that the frigate's suite of augur and auspex systems could determine nothing about the Black Ship. Even the ferocity of the enigmatic vessel's engines, the glow from which Dalchian could see clearly with his own eyes on the vid-capt feed, was somehow nullified to his ship's machine senses. The Black Ship was a slab of nothingness. Clearly the assault boats read the same absence across their systems.

'*I can't lock on to any target coordinates, my lord!*' the attack craft pilot cried through the intervox.

'Use your cursed eyes, wretch,' Dalchian bit back. 'Aim for the rent in its flank.' The voice of Qi Umshar, distorted across the overlapping communication systems, scratched in his ear.

'*The Black Ship's lance turrets appear to be moving, Lord Skin-Taker.* Prideful *manoeuvring to evade.*'

'Acknowledged.'

The wing of assault boats slammed in, banking hard beneath the Black Ship's twisted hull skin at the last moment to wedge their spinning tooth-heads into exposed gangways and stair-wells. Dalchian snarled with anticipation as his harness released.

The mysterious vessel's damage control systems were comprehensive, the unhelmed voidsmen-at-arms disembarking without issue as a flickering energy field held in the ship's atmosphere. The three Night Lords sent the mortals to probe the breach first before following, keeping their huge forms to the guttering shadows. The boarders streamed through tiny corridors, ducking beneath thick plasteel ribworks and edging alongside armoured bulkheads festooned with rivets.

When they had passed several hundred yards in mere minutes, Dalchian began to marvel at the absence of defenders, at the absence even of locked hatches and sealed blast doors. But after several minutes, and under the growing fug of some thought-occluding power, sour realisation seeped into Dalchian's mind. The cavernous gouge in the Black Ship's flank was not the straightforward ingress he had hoped for. Lurching shudders rattled the deck plating intermittently as the vessel duelled with the *Prideful*. He halted the party, and perspiring breachers knelt in the lee of a huge iron stringer, the octal brands across their faces glistening.

'There's no way in,' Ang Heltris said.

'A ship within a ship, it seems.' Dalchian once again felt a twinge of anxiety at the dearth of information they had had with which to plan the assault. Krutaan's claw clacked. 'We must make our own doorway.' He looked at Dagardis, who nodded and began priming the breaching charge at his belt. In a few short seconds the dome of explosives was magnetised to the inner hull and the mortals were retreating to a safe distance.

'Let us examine your innards, then,' Dagardis growled as he flicked the detonator's switch guard open. He thumbed the stud and concussive force slammed into them. Metal vapour flourished in the dimness, the thunderclap ringing along the tight corridor and back. Dalchian leant forward on his feet, ready to pounce through the hole.

But there was no hole.

A bubbled crater of heat-tortured metal had been blown nine inches deep into the inner hull, but there was no trace of a penetration. Dagardis rapped his augmetic knuckles on the centre of the crater, the plasteel still ruddy with raised temperature. The sound was the dead *tack* of still-thick armour.

'Warp's spit,' Dagardis uttered. He had another breaching charge and the voidsmen-at-arms had a few dozen melta bombs, but Dalchian refused to underestimate the severity of the trial they would face once inside.

'Save them. We will find another way in.' As he waved the mortals forward, his vox crackled into life.

'This is Gyren Naritsa, acting shipmaster of the Ikhtheos. *Leil Jathok sends his regards, Lord Skin-Taker, and bids me inform you that he is leading a full assault upon the Imperial Black Ship.'*

Dalchian smirked, his blistered skin rustling beneath his helm.

'Tell him I accept his apology,' he said. The ship heaved and groaned beneath them, and he felt the familiar stomach-pulling sensation as its gravity well generator mitigated for rapid void manoeuvres. 'Is his Thunderhawk's turbo-laser operational?'

'Is…? Yes, it is, Lord Skin-Taker.'

'Good.' Dalchian blink-clicked a databurst across to the *Ikhtheos.* 'Tell him to aim for these coordinates.'

'*I will, Lord Skin-Taker.*'

'And tell him not to miss.'

The eruption of violet laser energy vaporised two of the breachers and blinded several more. Dalchian had neglected to inform the mortals of the imminent reinforcement. The protective atmospheric field snapped into life almost instantly, then only a heartbeat later was made entirely redundant by the enormous armoured beak of the Abyssal Kindred Thunderhawk as it crashed through the hole in the outer hull. As the ramp opened Dalchian closely examined the crater in the inner hull, made twice as deep by the gunship's primary weapon, but still no closer to a breach. His teeth ground in his skull.

Sorcerer Lord Jathok stepped off the ramp and immediately sagged, only just catching himself before falling to one knee. Dalchian looked askance at him.

'Still recovering, witch?'

'No,' Jathok replied thickly. 'This ship is anathema to my kind. Simply standing upon the deck is transcendent agony. My Rubricae would be more burden than asset were I to bring them aboard. I'm unsure if I could direct them at all, or at the very least the effort of trying would injure me severely.' He indicated the gheist-like automatons stood in unmoving ranks at the very deepest point of the Thunderhawk's belly.

'What a shame.' But there was no venom in Dalchian's quip. He was too busy staring at the crater. 'It's healing.' He could hardly believe what he saw. The metal was repairing by itself. Not flowing and reshaping like the hateful fabric of the necron race, but expanding in the gap like synth-skin, so slowly as to be almost imperceptible. Jathok stepped closer and, with obvious discomfort, placed his gauntlet against the gradually swelling plasteel. He snatched back his hand as if burned, the crystalline implants around his crown stuttering with migraine light.

'It's a psy-reactive alloy,' he said. 'I cannot tell which kind.' The sorcerer looked directly into Dalchian's eye-lenses as his Thunderhawk crunched away from the breach to continue its void-borne assault. 'This vessel is far more resilient than it first appears.'

'That is not unexpected. Can you break through?'

At the question, Jathok's eyes widened. 'Can I break…?' He rumbled a magma laugh. 'My gifts are stifled here, Skin-Taker. I can barely think! So no, I cannot *break through*.'

'Then we must find another way.'

Endagur's blackened-armour shape led at the front, toothed blade drawn. Dalchian's three Blades and Jathok followed with twenty of Nallath's Abyssal Kindred behind them, while the mortal breachers sprinted along in the transhumans' wake. The rest of the Kindred, over forty Chaos Space Marines, had deployed via assault pod into the tear in the Black Ship's exterior and none had yet breached the inner hull either, according to the vox reports Jathok was receiving. Dalchian tried to contact Ibriel to see if he had divined any structural data from the Black Ship using the *Prideful*'s augurs, but a tempest of static was his only answer, so he and Jathok had to rely on their own best guesses using data they had previously assembled pertaining to Imperial ships of non-standard construction. They were no better off

As they ascended a narrow companionway that threaded through a knot of girder-work, a litter of small shapes bounced down the steps in front of the vanguard. Endagur's machine vocaliser howled.

'Grenades!'

Acid-bright lightning cut through Dalchian's helm-lens autodampeners, bypassing the protective mechanism and clamping his brain in a vice as the blind grenades detonated. Mortals keened like gutted herd beasts and several of them tumbled back down the steps, crunching as they hit protruding plasteel.

Gunfire slashed down at them, the streaks of high-gain las drifting into grainy focus as Dalchian's blindness subsided. He raised his bolt pistol and the weapon roared in the tight confines.

The other boarders opened fire. Bolters and flamers excoriated the companionway above them. A las bolt burned a hole in a Kindred's greave and made him stagger. The warrior snarled as he pumped mass-reactive rounds upwards into the gloom. The mortals lent their shotgun blasts to the fusillade. The defenders were invisible as far as Dalchian could tell. His helm auto-senses read only empty space before him and the las blasts seemed to emanate from nowhere. But the deluge of Chaos weapons fire silenced them nonetheless.

Dalchian ordered Ang Heltris to scout forwards and the knifeman disappeared into the shadows ahead. The mortals longed to advance with more caution; Dalchian could smell it in their nervous sweat. But the Chaos Space Marines forged ahead, leaving the breachers to scramble in their wake.

Their path emerged into a narrow gallery that forced the transhumans into single file. The gallery was several decks tall and the heights of it were lost in the darkness. It reeked of a trap, but Ang Heltris' voice came through Dalchian's vox.

'*I found them first. You're all clear.*' Dalchian could plainly read the thrill of recent murder in the knifeman's voice.

'I am envious,' Dalchian replied as he waved the party on.

'*Plentiful prey lies ahead, Lord Skin-Taker,*' Ang Heltris said. '*I am certain.*'

'As am I. Continue forward.'

'*Yes, my lord.*'

Dalchian half sensed a shift in the shadows above them, though it passed unnoticed both by the mortals and most of Jathok's warriors. Only Endagur's helm flicked upwards with the briefest of motions before the champion strode on.

Naritsa cursed to himself as the Black Ship rolled out of his firing solution again. The *Ikhtheos* was fast and agile and should have been dancing circles around the lumbering beast, but the Black Ship's manoeuvring capabilities were beyond his wildest consideration. Huge vectored engine stacks were stitched all over the vessel and they abruptly vomited out white fire at intervals, spinning the ship this way then that. Some blackness exuded from its hull, too. The effect was subtle, but in their close passes Naritsa had seen the vaporous wisps boiling from flat armour plating like sublimating mist. The blackness pooled against the Black Ship's hull but the rapid changes in bearing and velocity were not allowing the blackness to congeal across the whole vessel, and every new violent yaw or roll would pluck the strands of cloaking shadow away from the hull to dissolve like fog in a flame. Naritsa was unable to lock his weapons on to the Black Ship using conventional means, but he knew that if he let the vessel go unmolested for even just a few seconds too long, then the cloak would bind and he would lose visual contact with it utterly. Sidestepping his frustration at his quarry's nimbleness, he maintained a madman's stance, running the *Ikhtheos* up suicidally close to keep the big ship flinching away and thus exposed.

'*Prideful*, have you achieved a lock yet?' Naritsa's voice grated through his plasteel throat. The ship-to-ship vox was lousy with all sorts of interference, which, judging by the energy signature, was mostly coming from the *Prideful*'s generatorium. From Ibriel's reality-breaking machine.

'*No, Warpsmith Naritsa,*' came the icily calm voice of Qi Umshar from the *Prideful*'s bridge. '*We are circling with a fourteen-thousand-mile apogee, awaiting Lord Skin-Taker's order to launch our second wave.*'

Naritsa's metal jaw twisted in derision, his hands balled into fists. For a fleeting moment he resented Jathok's decision to follow the Skin-Taker through the split in realspace. Then he remembered that Qi Umshar was a devoted servant of his lord, just as Naritsa was of his own. He unfolded his fists.

There was a thump-snap of disrupted air that felt to Naritsa curiously like a nearby teleportation, which was impossible because the *Ikhtheos'* shields were fully operational. He turned his head and listened. The dry crack of las fire reached him from the portal that led to the strategium, so he turned and started moving. He was halfway down the corridor when the boarding alarm started wailing.

Two mortal soldiers emerged from the strategium portal. They were armoured in satin black, gloves and hoods covering every inch of their skin. Over their hoods they wore silver masks wrought into gargoyle grimaces with sharp brows and cheeks over leering mouths. They wielded ornate hellguns without the heavy back-mounted power pack usually associated with those weapons. They saw Naritsa coming and sent accurate las fire his way. He lifted his combi-melta from its sling and his mechatendrils reared about him, the plasma cutter recalibrating for combat discharge. He stitched the exposed mortals with a burst of mass-reactive rounds, blasting them and their armour to pieces.

'To the strategium,' he roared into the ship-wide vox. 'All hands, repel boarders.' He exploded into the temple fane, dropping another masked human in coal armour with a bolt round to the chest.

A bizarre cage had materialised within the strategium and was canted against the stone altar. It was an oval thing of mesh and plasteel with arrestor harnesses arrayed concentrically within it and flapping gates around its perimeter. For all the galaxy, Naritsa thought it looked like a drop pod without armour or engines.

Six masked soldiers remained, split in pairs, each pair about to venture from the strategium into the rest of the ship when Naritsa made his entrance. There was another figure in the temple, who the warpsmith struggled to see properly. The masked troops dived behind cover, launching smoke and frag grenades his way. He turned away from the shrapnel as the grenades popped, blasting with his bolter at the boarders.

'Ether's depths,' he cursed to himself. 'How in the Eye did you get on board?'

Others of the *Ikhtheos'* crew appeared at the portals and began firing shotguns and autorifles into the smoke. He dropped the combi weapon back into its sling and brandished his tall axe with both hands as he waded into the temple. He perceived a blur of motion to his right and swung his axe up.

Another blade met his like a hammer meets an anvil. The long steel did not belong to a masked soldier. Naritsa forced himself to register details of her appearance, his gaze desperately trying to slide away. He saw her fur-trimmed cloak, which shimmered darkly; a topknot of crimson locks was her only hair, the rest of her cranium smooth; exquisite armour covered her from throat to toe, and a grille of brass covered her mouth and nose. She wrenched her long sword away and embarked on a dizzying assault.

Naritsa blocked, parried, spun in for a high strike, was turned away. His plasma cutter cut a sliver of cloak where it had aimed for her exposed head, the target whirling away preternaturally fast.

'Qi Umshar!' Naritsa bellowed into the vox as he pounded

back against the punishment. 'We are boarded! Keep the Black Ship occupied!'

'*Boarded?*' came the Night Lord's voice. '*I registered no attack craft launched.*'

'Teleport.' His voice was a grunt as he shoulder-barged one of the Imperial agents back to gain some ground. 'They teleported.'

'*Your shields are lowered?*' Qi Umshar sounded incredulous, and Naritsa would have smashed the vox-augmitter with his weapon if he did not need every ounce of concentration.

'Of course they bloody aren't!' he roared as he made a huge upswing, causing the Silent Sister to withdraw for a moment. 'The Black Ship, Night Lord!' The Sister came on again.

'*Very well. Engaging now.*'

Qi Umshar ignored the strobing warning lumens that covered half the consoles on the bridge. Inexperienced crew fought with erratic systems and chaotically perturbed instrumentation read-outs, desperately coercing the *Prideful* to do as they bid.

'Come about to new heading,' Qi Umshar ordered. 'Void shields to full, make ready plasma batteries.'

'Are you insane?' one of the young bridge replacements wailed. 'We can barely read our heading as it is! How are–' The man dropped with a scalpel through his temple. Qi Umshar resealed the medicae pouch at his waist.

'Obey,' he said. The mortals did so, and the *Prideful* raged against them at every moment. Qi Umshar spoke into his mid-range vox. 'Lord Skin-Taker, my apologies, but I have need of a progress report.'

The sorcerer walked with gritted teeth and snatched at his breaths. Dalchian could feel it too. An infuriating sensation like the roaring buzz of a billion insects, but not heard through his ears. In fact, he could not perceive it with any of his senses; it simply existed inside his skull, intrusive and exhausting. It made his throat itch and non-colours dance behind his eyes. It had been growing in intensity as they moved between the skins of the Black Ship, and the attrition was wearing Dalchian thin. But the sorcerer appeared to have the worst of it.

'How do they achieve it?' Dalchian asked, trying to distract himself. Jathok took a few seconds to realise the Skin-Taker was talking to him, and another second seemingly to gather his thoughts. It was obvious to what the question referred.

'In truth,' Jathok replied, the mental intrusion rendering his speech halting, 'I know not. They name it–' The sorcerer flinched at nothing, blinking to clear his vision. One of the Kindred looked at him sidelong. 'They name it an… occluding sphere. Most sentient minds are… diminished by it, but none more so than… a psychically gifted one.' Jathok gasped, and Dalchian's long-held revulsion for psykers bubbled within him.

'It keeps their witch-breed cargo in check,' Dalchian said.

'It does.'

'So, your powers are ineffective here, lord?' Dagardis asked.

'I cannot… focus my thoughts, so I cannot bring them… to bear,' he replied. 'There should be decks free of this… effect, beyond the cargo containment levels.' There was a note of desperation in Jathok's last statement, and Dalchian could not suppress a thin smile, unseen by the sorcerer.

'Just make sure you can still fight,' he said.

'I would not have boarded if… I thought my presence would present… a liability, Skin-Taker.' Jathok raised his drawn bolt pistol to reinforce his point. His hand was steady. 'I will acclimatise.'

'Obstruction ahead.' Ang Heltris' voice came through on vox. *'A corridor or ductway of some kind blocking our path, a handful of decks deep.'*

'That's our way in,' Dalchian said, a surge of adrenaline momentarily overcoming the scratching rush of the occluding sphere. 'Wait there for us.'

Ang Heltris dropped from the girders into their midst as they came to the obstruction. It was a reinforced structure traversing from the exterior hull skin into the ship itself, and conduits and armoured cabling snaked across it. The plasteel was riveted and many layered, but it was just plasteel rather than the uncanny healing metal of the inner hull.

'An air gate?' Ang Heltris offered.

'Or a flight deck,' Jathok said. 'There may be a dozen small flight decks… scattered across the hull. For expedited… loading of cargo.'

'Either way, it's our route in,' Dalchian said.

'Defenders?' Ang Heltris said.

'Without doubt.' Dalchian had thought long and hard about this phase of their hunt. 'I'll wager, though, that these places are built with a keener desire to prevent escape from inside, than breaching from outside.'

'That is most probable,' Jathok said.

'Melta bombs,' Dalchian ordered. 'Now.' His vox crackled with a barely audible signal.

'*Lord Skin-Taker, my apologies, but I have need of a progress report.*'

'We are about to make our ingress, Qi Umshar. Your timing is impeccable.'

'*The credit does not all belong to me, my lord,*' the surgeon-Apothecary said, his voice tinny and distant. '*Warpsmith Naritsa informs me the* Ikhtheos *has been boarded, so I am bringing the* Prideful *in.*'

'Do what you must.' The breachers had affixed a brace of melta bombs to the inside of the plasteel structure and one of the mortals, fingers resting on the priming studs, waited for his lord's command.

'*Shall I order the second-wave launch, my lord?*'

'Absolutely.' Dalchian grinned, tearing the raw flesh of his cheeks.

Screeching rent metal accompanied the crack and flash of fire, and slabs of plasteel whickered through the air, caroming off the latticework of girder supports. The Chaos Space Marines growled their approval as the gaping hole emerged from the settling dust. Dalchian lashed the breachers with his words, cursing and hounding them through the narrow, razor-edged gap. Las fire scorched the air as branded mortals summoned what dysfunctional vigour remained to them and charged into the volleys. The Chaos Space Marines let them soak up the brunt. Mortals scourged by las burns fell smoking onto the deck plates, but more filled the gaps, screaming and weeping and blasting gouts of flechette from their shotguns. Dalchian, Dagardis and Ang Heltris followed them through and Jathok ordered his champion forward next with his coterie of chainsword-revving Abyssal Kindred.

It was a flight deck. Compact, with only space enough for a single suborbital shuttle. Armoured bunkers at each corner provided cover for a score of figures in black armour with beast-masked helms. The black-clad figures would only offer the briefest target as they leant around to unleash unerring bursts of las fire. But a brief target was enough.

Dalchian blew a leering gargoyle to smithereens with a bolt pistol shot before he was among them. His breachers streamed up with him, Dagardis at their fore, huge axe raised high. Dalchian disembowelled another black-armoured soldier with a swipe of his claw, slashing the gun from his arms as he tried to raise it. Dagardis cut a defender clean in two through the midriff and obscene volumes of gore and offal cascaded onto the deck. The branded voidsmen screamed as they swarmed forward, firing incessantly. Ang Heltris' stealth had brought him around the flank of a group of defenders, and as they turned to withdraw they fell with blood fountaining from necks and abdomens as he swept his knives between them.

The boarders cleared the flight deck and regrouped. Dalchian and Jathok had been sure of few factors in advance of their assault, not least the crew complement of the Black Ship. The quality of the defenders was considerable, but the detachment that had met them were not relieved by further reinforcement. He still had no idea what they would face between now and victory.

Victory. It was all he allowed himself to envision.

'Second wave inbound in thirty seconds, my lord,' Qi Umshar told him across an appalling vox-link. Dalchian had the impression that only proximity to their torn ingress wound allowed any such signals to pass at all.

'Good. You track our point of entry?'

'Yes, my lord.'

'Send the second wave in the opposite direction.'

'As you command.' The vox clicked off and Jathok furrowed his brow at Dalchian.

'You do not bring your... reinforcements to our position?'

'No.' *I'm growing tired of our alliance, witch.* 'We remain ignorant of this ship's internal layout. If I send them another way then we double our chances of securing the bridge, strategium or generatorium.' *I have a strategy.*

Jathok seemed genuinely humbled as he accepted the wisdom with a nod, and for a moment Dalchian saw a gulf of exhaustion behind the sorcerer's eyes. *Perhaps this ship tortures him even more than he shows.*

'I just hope Saryuz and Zhikarga are adequately recovered from their injuries.' Dalchian let slip a fraction of unease before clamping it down. 'They suffered as you did,' he said to Jathok's champion. The melted beast helm merely nodded, Endagur staying mute.

Baptised by their first action under new masters, the Branded were flush with novel confidence, the afterglow of adrenaline drawing timorous smiles and breathless coughs of laughter from them.

Jathok had approached a felled defender and seemed captivated by them. The mortal's coal-black armour was smoking where it was broken and their fatigues were sodden with blood. The mortal's silver mask had slipped loose and, while their limbs were inert, their eyes swivelled and their mouth moved silently as their brain died slower than their ruptured body. The sorcerer stared at the fading light in the soldier's eyes, his own mouth making gentle motions in imitation of the dying mortal. Then the light was extinguished and the Black Sentinel sagged to stillness as their final breath rattled from them.

'Do you hear their thoughts?' Dalchian asked, nauseated but curious despite himself.

'Indeed,' Jathok said, his discomfort seeming to have abated slightly. 'A prayer, of course. "Avowed and alight, 'neath holy infernos and by angels watched. Grace deliver me from the clutches of beastly forms, unto His uttermost heights." From the gospels of Orbech, Book Nine, Verse Eighty-three.'

The recitation hung in the air. The Branded looked at Jathok in fascination. Dalchian turned away from the sorcerer, revolted.

'You know Imperial scripture?' Dagardis spat.

'I retain some memories of my distant childhood,' Jathok answered, straightening up to move onwards. 'Someone – I do not know who – once forced me to recite Orbech unendingly.'

'Let us advance,' Dalchian said, keen to put time and distance between him and the noisome Imperial diatribe.

'Indeed,' Jathok agreed.

Fresh magazines were rammed home and slides racked. Ang Heltris flicked vitae from his blades and drew them across his belt a handful of times, the whetstone built into the armour there honing their edges anew. Dagardis nodded his readiness.

Dalchian examined the control niche to one side of the segmented blast door in the interior bulkhead. The panel was sparse and simple. He depressed a rune key and the door grumbled open. Expecting resistance, the boarders tensed, weapons up. When there was none forthcoming, they advanced into the junction of a corridor that ran fore and aft. The corridor was painted brilliant white and constructed of identical, unadorned panels down the entire visible length. Lumen strips ran along the top and bottom corners, bleaching the space with light. The mind-numbing aura of the occluding sphere grew heavier, and Jathok grunted.

'I suspect the bridge and crewed sections are forward rather than aft,' Dalchian said.

'Judging by the external dimensions,' Jathok nodded, 'I concur.'

They moved swiftly down the eye-achingly bright channel, Dalchian's remnant Blades in the lead, Jathok, Endagur and the Abyssal Kindred as rearguard, and the branded mortals running along between them. A shallow stair dropped them half a deck's height, then a sharp right turn. The whole place was blinding and featureless. Combined with the mental occlusion, even the transhumans began to feel disoriented. They came to a cross-junction and paused, any effort at defence still absent.

'Which way now?' Dagardis asked.

Without warning, the deck plating below them slammed open.

The boarders dropped through the trapdoor into empty space.

Mortals and Chaos Space Marines alike grabbed for the sides, but the surface was unnaturally smooth and repelled any grip. They spun as they fell, cracking together and bouncing apart. Dalchian thumped to a stop against a sharp edge, others still falling past him. He had landed on a protrusion of frictionless plasteel that split two curving chutes from one another. He watched Dagardis and Ang Heltris scramble as they swept from view down one way, Jathok and his Kindred snarling as they vanished down another. Breachers yelled as they scattered both ways. One landed as Dalchian had, halfway across the split between channels. They died with a damp crunch and then, dead eyes fluttering, slowly slid after the Abyssal Kindred. Dalchian looked up in time to see the deck above him slam shut, forming a seamless vault. It was not merely the artificial gravity of the ship that pulled at him. He felt a lurching weight superimposed onto his bones that was unrelated to his mass. The dragging force tried to pull him in half over the protrusion. Snorting with strain, he scraped himself over the split until his weight shifted enough and he plummeted down after his Blades.

Warriors in midnight plate and mortal voidsmen-at-arms crashed from an opening onto a new, whitewashed deck. Dalchian, still unable to exert any grip upon the chute's surface and accelerated along it by the unknown force, dropped on top of a breacher. The baseline human was pulped instantly, jetting blood and fluids across the walls. With the faintest *clunk* the embrasure in the ceiling closed. The legionaries regained their feet as the mortals writhed. They had fallen into a small stretch of corridor with a four-way junction at one end and a sealed hatchway at the other.

'That was unexpected,' Dagardis said matter-of-factly.

'Jathok,' Dalchian voxed. 'This is Skin-Taker. What's your status?'

Dead air.

'Vox-net must be dampened in this place too,' Ang Heltris said.

'It seems that way.'

'It's not all bad news, though,' Dagardis put in, gesturing with his power axe to a troop of black-armoured soldiers as they rounded the junction and raised their hellguns.

Qi Umshar pushed the two midnight-clad warriors onto the assault boat himself, both still drifting in and out of consciousness. The stimms would kick in within seconds, he reassured himself.

'Arise, warriors,' he commanded them gently. 'Your lord has need of you this hour.'

He watched the armoured hatch close and the assault boats lance from the flight deck, propelled by tornados of engine flame.

'Second wave will arrive in thirty seconds, my lord,' he voxed.

'*Good. You track our point of entry?*'

'Yes, my lord.'

'*Send the second wave in the opposite direction.*'

'As you command.' Qi Umshar sent the relevant databursts to the assault boat pilots and Saryuz and Zhikarga's armour cogitators, then he opened a vox-link to Naritsa on the *Ikhtheos*.

'Naritsa.' Secondary noise inundated the link from the Abyssal Kindred's end.

'How goes your defence, honoured Warpsmith?'

'*Bloody hard work. Why?*'

'Would an additional warrior be of assistance?'

'*You wouldn't.*'

Qi Umshar was already dropping into the pilot throne of a missile craft. An interceptor would have been faster, but his armoured transhuman bulk would not fit in its tight cockpit.

'Permission to come aboard, honoured Warpsmith?'

After a few moments Naritsa's answer came. The metal-faced

Kindred laughed and laughed and laughed. As Qi Umshar breathed life into the strike craft's engines, he tried Ibriel's vox-link for the umpteenth time.

'Tech-priest, if you read me, I am reinforcing Warpsmith Naritsa aboard the *Ikhtheos*. Lieutenant Nykold has command until you relieve her.' He waited twenty long seconds for a reply, but only static pulsed over the link within his helm. Cogitator banks along the flight deck bulkheads flashed and strobed as the *Prideful*'s systems still reeled. A warning klaxon started then abruptly stopped again, and the deck beneath his craft shuddered. Qi Umshar sighed, dragged his still-crimson helm onto his head, then pushed the thrust lever forward, sending the missile boat lurching through the energy barrier and into the void.

CHAPTER TWENTY-TWO

Three separate detachments of the ship's Black Sentinels had waylaid Dalchian's band since the chutes. The fourth waited for them just beyond a sharp bend in the blinding gangway. Branded breachers stormed around the corner first, screaming and blasting as had become their preferred method. Close behind, the Skin-Taker rounded the corner flanked by his axeman and his knifeman. They were just in time to see a Sentinel over-arm a chrome cylinder into the path of the Branded. The cylinder detonated with a meaningless crump, but a sphere of space ten feet in diameter around the cylinder stopped.

Simply stopped.

Branded mortals stood in tableau, frozen mid-stride or captured grimacing as they squeezed their triggers. The breachers not yet within the sphere skidded to a terrified halt and ran back the way they had come, only stopping when one barrelled into Ang Heltris. The Night Lord lifted the human on his prosthetic blade, the edge slowly tearing its way through the man's sternum.

'There is no retreat,' Ang Heltris whispered. The breachers turned to face the enemy once again, shuddering with petrified anguish.

The silver masks of the Sentinel troops emerged from cover and approached the frozen breachers. Dalchian raised his fist and unloaded a burst of fire from his pistol. The bolts hit the sphere and stopped dead, their tiny exhaust trails equally stilled. The Skin-Taker lowered his weapon and stood watching in rapt fascination. Dagardis spat, succinctly conveying his opinion of such a violation of natural laws. Undeterred, the Black Sentinels took careful aim and shot directly at each individual of the frozen Branded, their las beams likewise halting unnaturally upon entering the sphere. The Sentinel platoon withdrew completely and Dalchian stared as the sphere of un-time blinked away.

Las fire executed each sprinting breacher at the same instant, and Dalchian's own bolts smashed a tight grouping of craters in the far bulkhead. The dead mortals squeaked across the deck as their momentum carried them forwards, their guns dropped and skittering.

'Chrono-bomb,' Ang Heltris said reverentially as he allowed the breacher he had made an example of to slide from his blade. 'I've never seen one with my own eyes.'

'Nor I,' Dalchian replied. Krutaan's claw twitched and the old chasm of doubt threatened to open inside his chest. *Victory,* he thought very deliberately. *Victory.*

As they descended a companionway several minutes later, the shifting labyrinth realigned. The steps beneath their feet slid past each other, transfiguring so they now faced up the stair rather than down. The three Night Lords looked at one another, but there was little to say. The mortals were diverging in humour, some becoming wide-eyed and jittery, but most simply dissociating, their eyes glazing over. At least they obeyed orders without hesitation, detached as they were from the physical reality of their situation. *Hopefully I'll still have some useful thralls after this is done,* Dalchian thought, watching the overwhelmed humans curl up within their own psyches.

'Onward.'

Pulses of azure plasma streaked across the starfield from the *Prideful*'s batteries, splashing against the Black Ship's void shields and making them stutter. The *Ikhtheos* had run itself to long range as it repulsed the Imperials' own offensive, the speck of it almost invisible. Still, the forward lances of the Abyssal Kindred ship reached out to strike against the prey vessel's defences. Continuing to pitch and roll under the sustained aggravation, the Black Ship trailed pennants of veil-smoke that evanesced to nothing in the vacuum.

The assault boats of the second wave banked in tight formation as the Black Ship loomed before them. The pilots of the attack craft chased the flayed stripe of damage across the ship's side, simultaneously dodging columns of defensive turret fire. Several of the Gnathas boats splintered apart under hypervelocity autocannon salvoes, their constituent debris and flailing human cargo immediately lost against the silent backdrop of void war. The rest of the craft stabbed beneath the torn outer hull, slamming with bone-jarring force into the under-structure.

Saryuz's scorched helm was first to emerge from his assault boat's jaws. The warrior shook vestigial disorientation from his skull and dived forwards into the intra-hull lattice of plasteel, meltagun raised, Zhikarga's blasted form following close behind, his heavy bolter dragging at his arms. A cohort of breachers swarmed after them.

It took the Skin-Taker's reinforcements a relatively short time to locate another small flight deck, the data fed to their armour cogitators by Qi Umshar informing them precisely what features to seek. Branded breaching charges and Saryuz's meltagun opened their way, a squad of Black Sentinels waiting to repel yet another boarding party but proving insufficient in the face of overwhelming numbers and the unanswerable violence of Heretic Astartes at close quarters.

It was not long before the labyrinth claimed them, though. Grav-traps tore the mortal breachers away while the VIII Legion's boots mag-locked their occupants to the white deck, only for the transhumans to be encased in a section even Saryuz's meltagun could not pierce and blasted deeper into maddening confines. Deposited at the foot of a tightly spiralling stair, the Chaos Space Marines looked wordlessly at each other before forging ahead. Their long sleep soured their humours, but they had one thought that drove them on.

Their lord needed them.

Jathok let beast-helmed Endagur lead the way, Nallath's squad in tight formation around the sorcerer lord as they sprinted. The Skin-Taker's frail human chaff cried and begged as the Abyssal Kindred outpaced them. They rounded another, identical corner, the flatness of its paint and the actinic gleam of its lumens indistinguishable from the rest of the labyrinth. The featurelessness was infuriating. Jathok avoided ruminating on the wisdom of following the Skin-Taker, whom he was now sure was half mad. He fought to remain present, consoling himself that a great prize could still be won if he just found the right foothold.

They were pounding down another section of bland corridor when Endagur abruptly halted. The champion placed his hand on an invisible energy barrier that bisected the gangway, the silent force field barely flickering at his touch. The sheer refinement of the technology on display within the Black Ship was arresting. *If only I can find the right foothold indeed,* Jathok thought. The Abyssal Kindred turned and moved to retrace their steps, but Nallath at the rear stopped dead, too. He probed a twin energy field with the crossguard of his chainsword.

'We're trapped,' he called. Nigh soundlessly, a portal irised open on the ceiling above them. Jathok looked up and frowned, then a merciless force tore them from the deck and they fell up through the portal.

They hammered into the deck plating of a small round chamber, the Chaos Space Marines mostly managing to keep their feet even as they inverted. Unwelcome nausea pulsed in Jathok's belly, a mightily rare sensation for a genhanced transhuman. He looked up again, straight above him at the deck they had just been stood on. The portal irised shut and instantly was as if it had never been.

The circular chamber had half a dozen tiny mirrors around its circumference, and a single sealed hatchway. The Abyssal Kindred levelled their weapons at the hatch, their attuned combat senses knowing without doubt what was to come.

The hatch flew upwards into its rebate and a cascade of las erupted through. Weathering the storm, the boarders unloaded with bolt pistols and flamers, drenching a handful of Black Sentinels in flame and punching fist-sized holes in many more. A clutch of frag grenades sailed through the hatchway and the hatch drove back down again.

It stopped half an inch short. Endagur levered against the pommel of his serrated sword, the blade wedging the hatch open. The frag grenades exploded around his ankles. Pieces of fire-tortured ceramite shattered under the punishment, but he did not release the blade's handle, instead prying with all his might. Two of Nallath's squad darted forwards and clamped their gauntlets under the hatch, wrenching upwards. The door slid halfway back up and the rest of them ducked through, firing at the retreating backs of Astra Telepathica troopers. They held the hatch for Endagur and his two companions to escape. Once released, the hatch ground slowly down, its mechanism clearly damaged.

'A fine display,' Jathok said, nodding thanks at his champion. Endagur nodded back, saying nothing.

The sorcerer now saw the mirrors were actually windows of one-way glass, and a small ledge at a baseline human's chest height was just deep enough for a dataslate to be set flat upon it. The hatchway only had controls on this side. The round chamber was clearly some sort of observation cell. At least it was something different, he thought, and allowed himself to feel relieved by the variation. The Abyssal Kindred redistributed their ammunition in short order, then followed the way the Sentinels had gone.

His appreciation for the moment of variety soon diminished as the featureless hallways extended before them once again.

Sisters of Silence.

Gyren Naritsa cursed again. The guardian women of the Imperium's psychic orders were more mythical to him than the Black Ship itself. Lord Jathok had known Black Ships existed thanks to his strangely preserved memories, but the sorcerer had never ascertained the existence of the Silent Sisterhood. A caste of warriors so rare, so thinly spread across the galaxy that the highest levels of Imperial bureaucracy might never even learn of their existence, let alone treat with them. True blanks: humans with no immaterial shadow. Impervious to psychic assault, untouchable by Neverborn warp entities. To Naritsa, they had sounded like fictional hyperbole.

And now he was duelling one for his life. Naritsa cursed their luck, that their quarry vessel carried even one such as her. Great Powers preserve them if there were any more.

She had bracketed Naritsa in the strategium and was gradually chipping away at his defence. A handful of mechatendril manipulators were on the deck between pews, shorn from their segmented limbs by elegant sweeps of an execution blade. Naritsa's combi-melta was spent, the secondary weapon charge wasted coring holes in parchment-hung bulkheads as the Sister evaded his every shot. Dead Sentinels and crew serfs littered the deck plates. Robed mortals stood with guns ready, but had no hope of hitting the Sister of Silence, such was her speed, let alone risking Naritsa into the bargain. She lined up an impaling lunge that the Warpsmith knew he could not dodge, and he readied his physiology for sudden, catastrophic damage.

The Silent Sister was jerked aside, a flurry of bolt rounds hammering against her armour and throwing her off balance. Her execution blade dropped a fraction as she flicked a glance to the strategium portal, where Qi Umshar stood holding a boltgun tucked into his shoulder. Naritsa used her moment of distraction and smashed her blade aside. She whirled to recover, but he had closed the gap and drove his axe upwards through the armour at her belly. She shuddered, reversing her grip and trying to bring the point of her blade down into his gorget, but her reach was not enough and the long steel clanged against his armour plate. He ended her with a brutal headbutt and she fell, slithering off his axe's broad blade.

Naritsa turned to the Night Lords surgeon-Apothecary and pointed at him with his gore-slicked axe. The Warpsmith roared a metallic laugh, the sound horrendous.

'You would, it seems!'

'I did, honoured Warpsmith.'

'Ether's depths, legionary. What a fight that was! Our lords are in for a trial if there's more of her on that bastard ship.'

'That is certain.'

The Warpsmith walked towards the curious cage device the Imperials had used to teleport aboard. He lifted a hand to touch it.

'I look forward to examining this in more detail.' As his armoured fingertip ticked against the metal, a bank of coils at the device's heart began to whirr and the air hardened with building power. Naritsa stepped back and the cage vanished with a whip-crack, dust and ozone dryness spiralling in its absence.

'Bad luck,' Qi Umshar said.

'Fascinating,' Naritsa said. Putting aside his thwarted curiosity, he went to a cogitator in a niche and began tapping swiftly on the rune board. He accessed a swathe of tactical data. 'Well, it seems your mortals are obeying you,' the Warpsmith said. 'The *Prideful* is drawing the Black Ship's lance fire. Perhaps the Imperials believed the *Ikhtheos* dealt with?'

'Foolish.'

'Indeed.' A data reading made the cogitator trill urgently beneath his gaze. 'Ah. May have spoken too soon. Looks like your voids just collapsed.'

They returned to the bridge as fast as Naritsa's lumbering armour could manage.

'Oculus,' the Warpsmith ordered. The deck crew had redistributed themselves after the Silent Sister assault, dead serfs heaved aside so fresh mortals could take their place. The wide-arched screen on the forward bulkhead wavered before swiftly tracking the *Prideful*, magnifying the grainy image of the frigate as its plasma broadsides flashed erratically. Even at this distance and at such low resolution Qi Umshar could tell that the Skin-Taker's ship was suffering. Several of the plasma obliterator gunports along its flank were canted at odd angles; haloes of slewing fire clung to patches of its hull, indicating where atmosphere had ignited following a breach; a trail of glittering, spinning fragments winked around the frigate as it heaved.

'Nykold, report!' Qi Umshar voxed. Hiccoughing interference blurted from the augmitters before the lieutenant's voice replied.

'Voids down. Vector control at fifteen per cent efficacy. Port plasma batteries inflicting feedback damage with every volley. Crew at forty per cent mortality. Shall I go on?'

'Have you made contact with Ibriel?'

'The tech-priest? Negative. Magos Loraddan's adepts can't even gain access to the generatorium. The ship has been gutted by that bastard's damned heres… tinkering, my lord.' Qi Umshar ignored the furious indignation bleeding through her words.

'Ikhtheos is closing again,' he replied. 'Disengage, and bend all efforts to securing the tech-priest Ibriel and his works.' There was a long wait before Nykold responded.

'Acknowledged.'

As the terse answer came through, a choir of warning sounds blared to life. On the oculus, as the *Prideful* threw frantic clods of plasma at its target, the aft lance turret of the Black Ship activated, needling twin beams of sun-hot las up into the *Prideful's* keel. An instant passed before the beams exited out of the frigate's gunwales, momentarily spitting the vessel on spears of light. Two caverns of molten plasteel gushed sheets of vapour and flame, and the *Prideful's* own klaxons screeched onto the *Ikhtheos'* bridge second-hand over the vox. Nykold's voice scratched out half-heard orders to her own deck crew before she spoke into her vox directly again.

'Mayday, mayday.' The lieutenant's voice echoed distantly as Qi Umshar watched the *Prideful* twist in pain, engine stacks flaring arrhythmically. *'Ship-wide system failures. Control authority lost. We're rudderless, lord legionary, and plasma reactor containment is in freefall. Requesting permission to abandon ship?'*

'No, Nykold,' Qi Umshar growled. 'Secure the tech-priest, by any means necessary.' The *Ikhtheos* reverberated, spiderwebs of luminance dissipating the Black Ship's lance strike across the ship's void shield bubble, the interference scrambling Nykold's intemperate response.

'Our Mechanicus friend is truly that valuable to you?' Naritsa asked, his grating voice uncharacteristically soft. Qi Umshar leant upon the console, the weight of unavoidable decisions dragging his helmed head down.

'The tech-priest is steward of a trove, both of his tech-lore and our company's irreplaceable legacy.' At the surgeon-Apothecary's words, Naritsa inclined his plasteel brow in comprehension. 'For my lord to win the Black Ship only to lose those would be a bitter victory indeed. He charged me with their safekeeping. And Ibriel's, for that matter.'

The Abyssal Kindred Warpsmith and the Night Lords legionary shared a heartbeat pause in the tumult. The Black Ship swelled in the oculus as the *Ikhtheos* ploughed in afresh, guns thundering. Naritsa abruptly barked into the ship-to-ship vox.

'Nykold, do you still have access to your purge line control systems?'

'I do, but I don't think venting a little plasma is going to improve our situation any. Who is this?'

'Naritsa,' he answered. 'No, it won't, but a whole-core primary expurgation may prevent you from becoming irradiated gas within the next few minutes.'

Qi Umshar slowly raised his gaze to the Warpsmith's and stared. Nykold's stunned silence roared from the augmitters as empty static. After a heartbeat the thought trains of both the Night Lord and the lieutenant arrived at the same inevitable destination.

'Do it,' Qi Umshar commanded.

'*Cycling purgation lines now,*' came Nykold's reply before she cut the connection.

'Will it work?' Qi Umshar asked the Warpsmith.

'It has more chance of working than leaving the ship to tear itself apart. What choice is there?'

Qi Umshar had no answer. The *Ikhtheos* tremored again and warning sirens briefly hooted before a deck crew serf shut them down.

'Void shields nearing overload, my lord,' the mortal said, face illuminated emerald by their viewscreens.

'Keep the Black Ship engaged,' Naritsa ordered. 'Gunnery teams to maintain continuous bombardment.' He turned to the legionary and balled a fist. 'I think we can be of more use elsewhere, eh, Night Lord?'

'A suggestion I was about to make myself.'

Naritsa snorted. 'I must admit, surgeon,' the Warpsmith said as they left the *Ikhtheos*' bridge in the hands of its mortal crew and headed for the embarkation deck, 'I think I underestimated you legionaries of the Eighth.'

'You wouldn't be the only one,' Qi Umshar replied.

'No,' Naritsa agreed, his metal face unreadable. 'No, I certainly wouldn't. You have my thanks,' he added.

'Think nothing of it.'

The spice of his combat stimms burned in Dalchian's blood, but the well of churning despair equally chewed at his guts. Ang Heltris had not said a word in many long minutes and Dagardis bellowed at every new facsimile of the same corridors they passed through. Black Sentinels ambushed them in small numbers here and there, but the legionaries fell upon the faceless Imperial troops with inhuman ferocity. The defenders howled as they were turned inside out and hacked into living pieces, the only outlet for the deranged impotence the Skin-Taker's remnant Blades felt being caged within the labyrinth.

The relentlessness was peeling away Dalchian's fortitude, and with every flush of rage came a faint whisper in his mind.

Close… open… close the door.

'Which is it?' he snarled, not knowing he spoke aloud until he heard the words himself.

'Which is what?' Dagardis bit.

'Nothing. Onwards.'

'To where, Skin-Taker?' There was a loose thread in the axeman's tone that would take little effort to tease asunder. 'It's all the cursed same!'

Clo… open… the door.

'Just onwards,' Dalchian replied. The thought of winning the Black Ship had become a fragile, translucent one. He struggled to envision the victory, the geyser of hopelessness at his core erupting further each time, slowly filling his soul with lukewarm apathy. A scanty few branded mortals limped and staggered along in their shadows, faces puce with ceaseless effort, lachrymal glands wrung dry. A wave of sickening self-awareness crashed over Dalchian as he gazed at the riven humans. *Gods below! If those dregs are still going then I am far from defeated.* He grasped that kernel of granite, unmoving within the swill of his despair.

'Onwards,' he roared, the sudden vigour taking his legionaries by surprise.

The corridor narrowed as they veered around a long curve. The tight path stopped abruptly at a dead end and Dagardis howled like a carnodon, striking the white metal with his axe head. The slice began to heal the moment he pulled his weapon free, and he bawled again.

Flames erupted from the walls, blanketing them. Humans screamed and pressed melting hands into melting faces, collapsing to the deck. The Blades' armour rapidly caked in flesh-soot. Dalchian bellowed.

'Back! Back!'

Open… close… open the door.

They galloped out of the inferno, some of the mortals only caught on the edge of the flames following them, the breachers' skin red and blistered. They ran pell-mell up a ramp Dalchian did not remember descending and the flames finally receded. Clearing bubbling ash from his visor, Dalchian looked up the ramp ahead, which was an even curve that got steeper and steeper until it was out of sight behind an equally formed ceiling. He started moving up the ramp and the others followed.

It was not a ramp. Every step he took felt like stepping uphill, but by the time his weight had shifted and he raised his other foot the sensation below him was of level ground. The ever-increasing ramp went on interminably before him.

Close… open… open the door. Open the door.

'My Lord Skin-Taker,' breathed Ang Heltris from behind. Dalchian turned and looked where the Blade was pointing. Behind them the corridor was an exact mirror of that in front, a curved ramp steepening into obscurity. The despair inside him thrashed, desperate to emerge.

'Go that way,' he ordered in a flat voice, hideous realisation pricking his neck with needles of ice. Ang Heltris turned and jogged up and out of sight. Dalchian watched him go and listened to the steady bootsteps that approached behind him. The bootsteps came to a stop.

'A sealed ring?' Dalchian asked.

'Yes,' Ang Heltris hissed from behind his lord.

Open the door.

Dalchian looked at the deck for a moment as baseline humans of his breacher cohort buckled over, their exhaustion only matched by their logic-defying incarceration. Some began to moan gently, tears they had recently thought themselves empty of now spilling across their burned and branded cheeks.

'Cut holes in the walls,' Dalchian said. Dagardis and Ang Heltris exchanged a look.

'My lord,' Ang Heltris said. Dagardis' fists clenched on his axe haft. 'We have tried that before, the alloy heals before we can–'

'Cut holes!' Dalchian lunged forward and grabbed Ang Heltris by the breastplate. 'In the walls!'

Open the door!

'What warp-forsaken door?' he screamed at nothing. 'Cut holes, curse you!'

Dagardis and Ang Heltris turned away from their lord and drove their weapons into the bulkheads: prized blades, centuries old, that had drunk the blood of countless foes. Sharpened adamantine edges where the gory trade of a warrior was plied. The legionaries hacked and dug, chipping and notching their weapons against the unnatural metal of the Black Ship's labyrinth. Chunks of alabaster alloy shrieked as it came free, the gaps filling with foaming metal as soon as it was exposed. The mortals crept away and hugged their knees, terror at the madness around them subsuming their every thought. The two Night Lords carved faster and faster, grunting and snarling, denying the futility of their effort. Dalchian gazed on, crimson lenses burning as if the furnace of his appraisal could slough away the metal.

No one could ever escape this maze. It was impossible.

Open the door, Dalchian!

Wordlessly, Dalchian Rassaq, Lord Skin-Taker of the Blades of Atrocity, sent coruscating licks of energy down the razors of his lightning claw, Krutaan's voice rattling inside his skull.

He pulled back the claw, digits splayed disgustingly wide, and cannoned it into the bulkhead.

The metal screamed as ribbons of it pared away. He drew back and slammed again, hewing more psy-reactive alloy with each flickering finger blade. Like a frenzied animal he slavered at the wound, tearing and ripping, arcs of lightning dancing across the wall, the deck, his armour.

The other two had stopped and beheld in disbelief the unfettered determination of their liege lord. The mortals rocked and screamed and flattened themselves against the deck plating, arms around their heads.

As Dalchian wrenched and scraped deeper into the wall, a booming laugh began to grate from his helm's augmitters. The fell sound circled the ring-trap room, echoing madly.

For all the insanity, Ang Heltris saw and felt a rush of possibility. He nudged Dagardis and gestured to the edges of the wound Dalchian was still boring into. The metal had blackened and crusted, denying its restorative regrowth. Dagardis' helm drew back in surprise. After a second, they both stepped forward and swung their weapons at the void Dalchian had made. Chipping away chunks of steaming alloy, deepening the hollow as the Skin-Taker slashed and laughed within a storm of forking energy.

With a crump, the last layer of uncanny metal burst beneath his claw blades and he tore the slice free. Darkness and cool air bled through the gap, and Dalchian howled in triumph as he peeled away more material to expose the cavernous inner workings that lay behind the labyrinth's white walls.

'Follow me, my murder-kin,' he hissed. 'For I have opened the door!'

The hatchway rose before Endagur reached it. Nallath's squad lifted their pistols and flamers once more around their lord. The

Black Sentinel who emerged registered an instantaneous flicker of surprise before raising his carbine and unleashing a burst of crackling las fire. One of Nallath's Kindred fell, his neck almost severed by the pinpoint accuracy of the hellgun. A dozen bolts shattered the Sentinel's coal armour in reply, blasting him into slopping pieces.

They careened through the hatch, filling the air with roaring pistols and the buzz of chainswords. The Astra Telepathica foot soldiers inside died in wretched violence as the Chaos Space Marines swamped the chamber. A chamber with a waist-high ledge and a handful of small windows. With the killing done, and as the others wiped gore from their weapons, Jathok brought his face close to a tiny one-way transparency to observe the movement within. He watched for several seconds, an indulgent smile stealing across his bearded face and crinkling his pale eyes.

It was an observation crucible identical to the one where the Black Sentinels had ambushed him and his retinue. The two previously injured Blades from Skin-Taker's second wave were trapped within, along with half a dozen branded mortals. All sound was deleted by the armaglass, and Jathok watched the two flame-desecrated Night Lords, the mortals huddled in fear behind them. One of the Blades' helms was moving in a manner that indicated he was talking or shouting as he rammed the muzzle of his heavy bolter into the hatch repeatedly. The other stood impassive, meltagun slung at his back, forsaken in favour of a long skinning knife for the fight he anticipated.

'Endagur,' Jathok said, 'open the hatch. Let us greet our esteemed allies.' The champion nodded and drew his toothed blade, understanding at once. The Abyssal Kindred formed up at the hatchway and readied their weapons. Endagur held his sword low, hand upon the control panel. He glanced at the sorcerer.

'Now.'

The two Night Lords' heads stared in amazement as the hatch slid up, revealing not a detachment of Black Sentinels but over a dozen Abyssal Kindred and their commanders. The Blade with his skinning knife ready stared at Endagur in stunned silence. Jathok's champion lifted his sword-point and ran him through.

'Lord Jathok!' the other shouted, neglecting to bring his heavy bolter to bear out of abject shock. Bolt rounds riddled him and he toppled backwards, blood bursting from his smashed armour. Endagur lifted the Night Lord he had impaled and stomped into the chamber, the stuck warrior stabbing his knife at his attacker's eye-lenses. Endagur swung his blade and the Night Lord slid off, smashing against the curving bulkhead. The champion raised his sword high and slashed down through the remnant Blade's collar, the toothed edge lodging in the legionary's abdomen. The Night Lord pawed the blade with his hand, then gurgled his death rattle and slumped.

The other of Skin-Taker's legionaries lifted a pistol from where he lay shattered on the deck. He aimed the weapon at Endagur, but a stitching of mass-reactives tore the last shred of life from him, and the pistol fell from his dead grip. Jathok nodded his gratitude at the warrior who had fired the killing shots. His name was Larakh, and he was ensconced in blackened, distorted armour like Endagur, proclaiming him as one of the unfortunates caught in the Sororitas' mad gambit aboard the *Vizier*.

'I've wanted to kill some of Skin-Taker's verminous kin for months,' Jathok confessed, the admission calming him now that he finally aired it aloud.

'As have I, my lord,' Larakh rasped. His vocal cords were still scarred and suppurating from his near incineration, rendering his voice glutinous. The Abyssal Kindred filed out of the chamber, Nallath taking point and Jathok protected among the ranks. Endagur came last as rearguard. His melted beast helm fixed the shivering mortals with a stare, then he resealed the crucible, locking the breachers inside with the two trans-human corpses.

Beyond the observation chamber the grating familiarity of the labyrinth whitewash returned. Executing some of the Skin-Taker's honourless wretches had elevated Jathok's mood somewhat, but that did not alter the fact that he was still directionless in a maze and his Kindred's ammo and tempers alike were beginning to run short. Endagur carved a significant chunk from a corner section with his sword, only for the white alloy to scab over within moments. Even Jathok felt a flutter of discomfort.

After another measureless track through identical gangways, Endagur ascended a tight companionway then stopped dead. Jathok and Nallath drew near him and he indicated around a riveted stanchion at the stairhead. Thirty feet of empty corridor finished at a wide portal of four interlocking leaves guarded by twenty Black Sentinels.

The portal was black iron, not white alloy.

Jathok felt a turbulence of sudden optimism; the potential of escaping the labyrinth. It was a short corridor. His warriors could cover the distance in seconds. He nodded.

They exploded from the stairhead, stampeding towards the Sentinels like pack predators. Bolts flew and mortals fell. Chaos Space Marines roared their fury and hurtled into frigid blackness, their wet boot thuds echoing from distant walls as if they charged through a huge subterranean cavern.

Jathok blinked away the dislocation, trying to take in the pitch-dark environment that suddenly surrounded them. They juddered to a halt, stunned. Inch-deep water covered the floor, which was smooth plasteel free of any weld or seam. The darkness stole details even from their auto-senses, but languid echoes told them the place was wide and high. Above them hung rows and rows of half-seen sarcophagi, chains holding them aloft. There were hundreds of the armoured pods, and a few dozen of them bore a winking light at their edge. The psychic smothering effect was vastly more potent in this place than it had been within the labyrinth, and Jathok could barely look at the sarcophagi.

They were oubliettes. Solitary chambers designed to keep the most powerful psykers suppressed by keeping them frozen within a field of acute mental anguish. They were torturous prison coffins, and they were as effective as they were horrific.

But for the creak of armour seals as the Abyssal Kindred craned their necks, the cavern was silent.

'Ether's depths,' Nallath cursed. 'What was that?' He referred to their sudden, unperceived transportation into this cavernous place. Endagur shook his barely visible helm in ignorance. Jathok's gauntlet creaked as he crushed his hand into a fist, the butt of his staff scraping against the damp deck.

'A chrono-trap,' he said through clenched teeth. Strobing lights fountained behind his eyes and he struggled to keep his feet. 'Find a way out,' he strained.

Great Powers of the Primordial Annihilator, he prayed, *please let there be a way out.*

CHAPTER TWENTY-THREE

The guts of the labyrinth were a harrowing place. Behind the scorching lumens and whitewash lay a nauseating puzzle-box of interlocking hydraulics. Sweeping shafts allowed whole corridor sections to upend, tons of sealed metal pivoting a hundred yards in seconds. Snaking tubes marked pitfalls that disappeared into the darkness, humming grav-impellors girdled around them to accentuate the ship's own. Girder-work gantries and stairwells of plasteel mesh allowed Black Sentinels to move between compartments at will, secret doors permitting them access and escape.

Dalchian, Dagardis, Ang Heltris and the few remaining breachers picked their way across dusty ledges in the darkness, gusting air rank with lubricant and the ozone tang of gravitics. More than once a swivelling or closing piece of machinery had nearly caught them, pistons as thick as Dalchian's thigh pulling slabs of metal on top of them. Each time they had slid through with a hair's breadth to spare. Most of them, at least. A handful of the breachers had been crushed or bisected in the mechanism, one stepping onto the tooth of a yards-wide cog only for the huge wheel to suddenly turn, pulling the gasping human into its gear train.

But his remnant Blades endured, and that was all Dalchian Skin-Taker cared about.

'Let us sabotage this bastard thing,' Dagardis called as a false bulkhead swept past them and disappeared into a slot within the labyrinth proper. The axeman had developed a deeply personal hatred for the maze which had only enlarged since their escape from within it. The pumping, crushing mechanism behind its stark veneer was almost worse.

'No,' Dalchian replied. 'They will know we have slipped its coils. Stealth is our ally, now.'

'In what endeavour, my lord?' Ang Heltris asked. A mortal behind him slipped from the ledge, lost her handhold and plummeted into the shifting darkness, her arms flailing and her mouth agape in a silent scream. If her impact made a sound then it was indistinguishable from the hammering din of the labyrinth, even to transhuman ears. Hardly noticing, Dalchian extended a long finger blade towards a block of shadow in the distance whose edges were half-lit by a diffuse glow emanating from somewhere in the machinery. To the baseline humans it would be invisible in the blackness.

'That looks like a conveyor shaft to me.' As soon as Dalchian said it the other two legionaries saw it too and picked up their pace, the breachers scrambling to keep up. More of the Branded fell away into the shadows, claimed by unseen piston limbs or betrayed by a moving surface beneath their toes, but the rest kept going in spite of themselves.

A maintenance platform protruded from the shaft side and the legionaries dropped onto it with agility belied by their scale. The surviving breachers had only the faintest silhouettes to aim for and, taking leaps of faith, slammed onto the grating on their hands and knees. There were no steps or ladders, and the exterior of the shaft was the same frictionless plasteel as the labyrinth chutes, making climbing it impossible.

'This ship might be the most over-protected piece of Imperial technology not rockcreted to Terra itself,' Dagardis spat.

'It seems we are learning why so few tales tell of one being taken by force, are we not?' Ang Heltris offered.

'If it resists our ingress this effectively,' Dalchian said, 'then it resists egress of those within just as well, which I suspect is the overriding purpose.'

'To confound escape,' Dagardis said.

'Indeed.'

There was a hatch in the curious metal skin, the seam just barely identifiable by touch. Dalchian ignited his claw and icy lightning crackled between the digits. He slid the index finger blade into the seam and dragged the powered edge around the hatch perimeter. The mortals averted their eyes from the sudden glow. Dull *clangs* told of locking bars and hinge assemblies that Dalchian carved through. After a full circumnavigation, the Skin-Taker deactivated the claw and placed its palm in the centre of the hatch.

'Why do I get the impression that my axe wouldn't have done that as easy?' Dagardis asked in a low voice. Dalchian looked at him.

'Our recent trials have taken much from us,' he said. 'But perhaps there are gifts we have received, too. Fate favours us, my Blades. Do not question its purpose.' As an answer it did nothing to reassure the axeman, but it did stop him asking any more questions. *Don't let me down now victory is within our reach, Dagardis.*

Dalchian pushed the hatch and it popped through its embrasure and into the shaft, falling into darkness for a handful of seconds before clattering against some surface. He leapt in after it, Dagardis and Ang Heltris following after an almost imperceptible hesitation. For the second time in as many minutes, the Branded found themselves jumping blindly after the towering, power-armoured monsters.

They landed on a cage floor that had the slightest bounce to it. Rails ran up and down all four faces of the shaft interior. Ang Heltris wrapped his hand around one rail and braced his boot against another, but as soon as he put any weight on it the material brushed him off. Frictionless metal again.

'How in the Eye?' Ang Heltris muttered. They looked up into the murk and saw another cage layer blocking the shaft a few fathoms above. A thicket of long tines hung densely from the cage layer, barely three inches between each frond. Dagardis braced both hands on his axe haft and crouched before springing up with a whine of armour joint servos. He swept the blade up through the tines to break them out of his way. A paralysing arc of energy connected the tines and made his axe glow, engulfing his arm and sending him into paroxysms as he fell back to the cage floor. He crashed onto the sprung surface, his axe landing next to him a moment later. Aftershocks flickered across him, making his unconscious form twitch. After a few seconds he lurched awake, cursing.

'Bleeding Eye and all the Pantheon's hosts.' He stood and took up his axe, fingers still twitching.

'Down it is,' Dalchian sighed.

Beneath the cage floor, they now perceived, was a reef of charged tines exactly alike to the one that hung above them. Dalchian peered through the cage and saw another layer further down. And another. And another, down into infinity it seemed. The cage layers were split in diagonal crosses, and hydraulics recessed into the friction-denying wall of the shaft permitted each quarter to fold down, allowing a conveyor to pass.

Dagardis hewed into the hydraulics with his broad axe-head, splitting the plasteel like timber on a block. In seconds he had laid open the hinge casement and severed two pressure lines, which threw splashing loops of hydraulic fluid over the cage floor. The dripping liquid sparked and fizzed as it dribbled from the energised tines below, filling the shaft with rancid, oily smoke. The floor quarter sagged and began to drop, its mass forcing jets of fluid from the cut hoses. Dalchian took a glance at his branded mortals for the first time in hours. There were eight of them left. They balanced on the inclining mesh until it became too steep, dropping onto knees and thighs and sliding off into the abyss. One whimpered involuntarily as he fell. Seconds later came the bouncing crash of the cage mesh below. The legionaries kept their balance longer, stepping from the sloping mesh with feral poise. Dalchian went for the next hydraulic hinge, carving the waist-thick housing with a single blow of his coruscating claw. The mesh began to droop, and they descended again.

With deliberate monotony they went lower and lower, each cage quarter giving way with an aggrieved sigh and hydraulic tears to the attending of their violence. The quarters dropped low enough that the transhumans would be able to jump onto them and climb back up if needed, but the mortals would be abandoned. *And if we do have to go back?* Dalchian thought. *What then? We can only get as far as where we started. Out into the labyrinth mechanics again?* The question of what lay at the foot of the conveyor shaft was one he had pushed from his mind. None of the others asked him, which at least told him they recognised their dearth of options as well as he did. *Our path leads where it will. I'll cease only when my life is torn from me, and no sooner.* He gritted his teeth. The thought suddenly occurred to him that the Great Powers might truly be testing him, and his voracious contempt of the gods of the immaterium could not entirely quash the profound need to pass such a test that reared its treacherous head within him.

The Great Powers of the cosmos weave mighty threads, Dalchian. He heard the voice that sounded like Krutaan's clear as day. *They watch you, hoping you fail and hoping you triumph in equal measure. Do not doubt that you are tested. What will you show them?*

He spat the bitterness from his mouth.

They had delved some way before he noticed the tiny inspection slits in one side of the shaft. He ignored it once, twice, thrice. But at length, his curiosity steered him to one as Dagardis hewed the next hinge assembly. Leaning against the inch-wide band of armaglass, Dalchian squinted into the darkness. He took a sharp breath.

Row upon row of human beings were crouched within, manacled to the deck. Their heads were down, bodies slouched and listing. Most were in the ragged garments customarily worn in any number of the Imperium's near infinite supply of backwaters, underhives and hab-slums. But there were uniforms, too. Some were obviously military, some ceremonial. Some even wore finery: ball gowns and tailored brocade. There was no delineation. All were bent in on themselves, wretched and weak. About a fifth of those within were also hooded. Not hoods of fabric, but of dull iron with riveted bands and weld lines. These metal hoods were each connected to the ceiling by a bundle of cables and chain. Some of the hooded were clearly unconscious, the cant of their lean pulling the bundle taut against its fixing. Every hundred yards or so, a blocky structure protruded from the ceiling like an inverted ziggurat. Lights winked on its side and Dalchian saw components and arrangements of circuitry on such protrusions. The very faintest touch of amber limned the edges of each incarcerated soul, and Dalchian simply assumed it was some low-level lumens until he saw the graven runes upon the bulkheads. There were thousands of symbols, hundreds of thousands – millions. Archaic devices from languages long forgotten or never even spoken to begin with. Each inscribed character emitted an infinitesimal glow, the multitude casting the cargo hold in smouldering lambency. *Prizes, and the sacrifices of claiming them,* Dalchian thought as he turned his attentions back to the descent.

The *Prideful* juddered with such violence that servitors welded into their niches sheared free, spilling thin blood and lubricant across the deck. The generatorium was a strobing miasma of vapours, noise and lightning. Machinery bent and snapped, crashing down and causing eruptions of sparks and flame. Enginseers and techno-savants screamed, clawing at glowing hot pieces of the ancient, priceless plasma core as it shook apart. Servo-arms lifted detritus and tried vainly to hold them in place.

The saltire restraint where Navigator Osthol had been secured was a column of jade ether-fire, a skeletal silhouette thrashing at its heart. Ibriel's harness heaved and bounced, tearing data-tethers and snapping mechadendrites in the tumult. Lights flickered spasmodically across his machine form and glass powder spilled from the lenses of his face.

Klaxons howled and automated valves ratcheted open. Lumens began dimming and a sucking, whirling uproar sounded, like the void itself tearing in two. Coursing energy in migraine hues thundered from the collapsing plasma core, howling through conduits, between the bulkheads and streaming out into the vacuum.

Desperate, powerless, robed adepts and tech-magi mag-locked themselves into arrestor thrones and began a chanting intonation, beseeching the Machine God, begging the Omnissiah to intervene on behalf of their dying charge. More sirens wailed.

'S-s-s-s-s…' Ibriel gargled from where he dangled amidst the umbilicals and cabling. A vicious charge build-up arced from the deck to his pelvis, making his plasteel endoskeleton glow briefly through his robes, which caught fire.

'S-s-s-s…'

The plasma core boomed with hurricane threat, its fusion heart pumping itself out into the void. The glow began to diminish, more systems winking out, fail-safes aborting them with the last vestiges of power available to them.

'S-s-s…'

Darkness fell abruptly, and the noise brayed, then hissed, then croaked, until the only sound was the ceaseless clatter of debris plummeting to the deck. A four-yard span of transcapacitor relay nodes bounced from the deck and spun in the air, slowly rotating as it drifted. The artificial gravity had perished. The relay nodes just carried on spinning and the chamber filled with drifting wreckage.

'S-s-s…' Ibriel stuttered. 'S-s-s-success…'

The Black Ship's servitor-manned defence turrets were sending streaks of autocannon shells into their path with every bank and roll, but Gyren Naritsa piloted the Serpent strike craft with enviable skill. Qi Umshar could only wait. The missile boat was not given to displays of aerobatics, behemoth that it was, but the Warpsmith somehow coaxed a balletic level of responsiveness from it. A hyper-velocity autocannon round severed a canard, but in the airless void such atmospheric control surfaces were incidental. With a final burst of acceleration, the Serpent lunged forwards to where a shelf of torn hull plating exposed a narrow sliver of deck. Naritsa nosed in and the craft lodged its wide prow between the layers.

Wordlessly, they both popped the harnesses and squeezed down the craft's internal space. Where they had stuck, the canopy would not open, so they had to disembark via the missile bay doors.

Qi Umshar dropped onto the deck, his sparer frame allowing him through first. Naritsa thudded onto the plating beside the surgeon-Apothecary. They both activated their helm lumens and stalked forward into the gantries and galleries of the intra-hull cavity. At length they found Dalchian and Dagardis' ingress, the interior of the Black Ship glowing palely from the other side of the obliterated sarcophagus.

'You first,' Qi Umshar gestured. Grunting, Naritsa placed a riveted boot onto the ruined alloy of the breach.

'*All reinforcements,*' came a rasping, skirling version of the Lord Skin-Taker's voice over the vox-net. '*If you can hear me, make for the dorsal dome, aft of the vox-array. Do not follow our trail into that bastard labyrinth, whatever you do.*'

Naritsa and Qi Umshar looked at each other. The Night Lord shrugged and the Warpsmith cursed, before removing his boot from the rent metal. They turned about and made their way back to the Serpent. Naritsa hesitated a few moments later, cocking his head to a bad vox-line.

'Endagur?' he said, confusion clear in his tone. The vox-set welded to the side of his metal head clicked and whirred for a few moments. 'But, who are–?' He stopped mid-sentence.

'Problem?' Qi Umshar asked, pointing his bolt pistol at the Warpsmith. Naritsa listened to several more moments of vox-transmission before his set fell silent. The Warpsmith looked from Qi Umshar's gun up to the burning eye-lenses of the Night Lord's looted helm.

'It seems,' the Warpsmith grunted, 'that I have a decision to make.'

The first they knew of the shaft base was a yelp one of the humans made as they hit not a mesh platform that absorbed their impact, but cold plasteel instead. The other Branded thudded down, cursing and grunting. The murderers of the VIII Legion made hardly a sound as they dropped, crouching. Dalchian's boots and gauntlet whispered against the metal as he landed, his claw held ready. His red lenses scanned from side to side.

They had dropped an extra few feet into a revetted alcove. Reinforced pillars topped with blocks of rubber showed where the conveyor rested once it reached the bottom, the pillars almost as tall as the branded mortals. A ledge demarcated where the conveyor floor would sit, and Dalchian pulled himself up, balancing deftly on it. Save for the alcove below, this portion of the shaft was the same as any other.

Apart from the sounds.

Like a cathedral bell peal heard from a hundred miles away, arrhythmic booms came to them as ghostly echoes, drifting through the shaft as quiet as breathing. Ang Heltris pressed his helm to the wall. Dalchian edged across the ledge and put his eye to the inspection slit. He saw a broad, toothed blade swing into his face on the other side of the armaglass and his reflexes jolted him back. The blade hit and the half-heard distant bell tolled again. Dalchian smirked.

'Tested, indeed.'

'My lord?' Dagardis asked.

'Nothing.' Dalchian ignited his claw and in the fractured glow he saw a hairline edge around the shaft face that met halfway across in a straight line. Doors. He raked his claw across the metal with a tortured screech, curls of frictionless plasteel twisting away. Dagardis shinned onto the ledge next to Dalchian and swung his power axe in a huge, felling stroke, but the crackling edge simply bounced.

'Looks like it's all you, my lord,' he said.

Dalchian hacked away chunks as he had done in the labyrinth, exposing a score of locking lugs holding the doors fast to each other. He reached to the very top and dragged his claw down, sparks fountaining, to the very bottom. As the last lug gave way a ring of crimson lumens flashed around them, the light pulsing up into the black vault. A deep note blared, then blared again. The alarm did not stop, and the lumens continued to pulse. The gentlest of noises began to shiver down the rails on each wall, betraying movement above. The doors Dalchian had broken slid haltingly aside, revealing Endagur, Jathok, Nallath and a dozen Abyssal Kindred.

'I see you summoned our conveyor,' Jathok said, smiling. Dalchian stepped forth and clasped the sorcerer's wrist.

'At least we've finally made it inside,' he said. Jathok grunted a laugh.

'A triumph in itself.' The sorcerer winced. 'Though I'll admit to having been more comfortable on the outside.'

Dalchian frowned. 'Can you still fight?'

'I said more comfortable, Skin-Taker, not more capable.' The sorcerer indicated two bolt pistols at his hips. He had lashed his staff to his power pack. 'Yes, I can fight.'

'Good.' Dalchian turned to see Ang Heltris step into the conveyor shaft and look up.

'Company in less than a minute,' he said, drawing the knife he had sheathed during their descent.

'Let's give them a suitable welcome, eh, Skin-Taker?' Jathok said.

'You sounded almost as cruel as an Eighth legionary, then,' he grunted. 'This place bringing back fond memories?' A thunderhead of darkness passed over the sorcerer's face.

'You have no idea.'

The conveyor clanged to a stop before the ruined doors. A detachment of Black Sentinels crouched, guns up behind the cage screen. One of them rolled the screen back and they panned rifle-mounted stab-lumens across the mirror deck of the oubliette. The shallow water was flat and still. Exchanging unheard vox commands, the troopers split into two sections and made ready to burst from the conveyor into the crossfire they knew would be waiting for them. Their commander counted them down. The officer snapped his mark, and the Sentinels darted out.

Shotgun sprays cracked armour and shredded fatigues as Dalchian's Branded, admirably motionless until this moment, let loose a full volley. The Astra Telepathica soldiers whipped around and raised their hellguns to counter the threat. One masked helm detonated in a mist of fragments. Another Sentinel's chest erupted apart, two mass-reactive bolts taking him simultaneously. One of the coal-armoured soldiers was spun around by a winging hit before a shotgun blast opened the back of her skull.

Two Branded fell into the water, holed through with burning energy. A dozen Chaos Space Marines rushed the Black Sentinels and the mortals withdrew rapidly into the conveyor, where a masked gunner stood ready with a multi-laser, flanked by two sharpshooters with long-barrelled guns totally different to the las-based weaponry of their comrades. The Abyssal Kindred rounded to face their enemy and multi-laser shots blitzed against their ceramite. Some faltered as their armour was peppered with energy blasts. The sharpshooters tucked the exotic rifles into their shoulders and, with mere feet to spare, sent whickering projectiles with pinpoint accuracy into the neck armour of two Kindred, then four. The Chaos Space Marines dropped instantly, their weapons rolling from lifeless gauntlets.

The floor of the conveyor beneath the Sentinels erupted.

Energised claw blades raked up from below, tearing a gash in the deck with a deluge of sparks, pulverising the multi-laser gunner's legs in the process. The mortal collapsed onto the emerging form of the Skin-Taker as the Night Lord wrenched his way up from the alcove below the conveyor. Another slash with the claw saw the gunner and his weapon bisected. The sharpshooters threw themselves aside, trying to keep their aims true as Nallath's Kindred chewed through the defenders immediately in front of them. Dagardis and Endagur ripped up through the hole Dalchian had made and swept Imperial foot soldiers to pieces with their blades. Jathok fired his pistols into the backs of the Sentinels fighting his Kindred as he stepped up from the cavity below the conveyor. A sharpshooter lined his weapon up on the sorcerer, but Ang Heltris gutted him and took the rifle from him in one easy motion. The melee continued for several more seconds, the Chaos fighters chewing through the defenders despite enviable resistance.

Thirty black-armoured soldiers lay on the deck, their blood fouling the waters. Five Branded and four Abyssal Kindred lay among them. The survivors redistributed the ammunition of the dead, the Branded exchanging their nigh-spent shotguns for the Sentinels' hellguns. One of them took a fallen sharpshooter's rifle.

'Careful with that,' Jathok said to her as he kneeled next to a fallen Kindred. He had pulled the spiked helm from the Chaos Space Marine. Astonishingly the transhuman was still breathing steadily, eyes open, pulse even. Jathok moved the Kindred's face with his gauntleted hand, inspecting. 'A needle rifle?' he asked. The Branded cracked the clip, exposing serried rows of injector rounds with misted liquid swirling within their ampoules.

'Yes, Lord Jathok,' she croaked.

'The round is neurophagic,' he said, abandoning the catatonic warrior. 'A potent sedative delivered by hexagrammically warded ammunition. It temporarily flattens psychic gifts within a target, as well as all their other faculties.' He stared down at the breacher.

'Yes, lord,' she gulped.

They heaved the dead into the darkness and filed onto the conveyor, the three baseline humans fading into one corner. Dagardis cranked the bronze lever control as Endagur slid the cage screen across, blackened armour shedding flakes of soot. The conveyor lurched into upward motion and accelerated rapidly. The thin bands of inspection slits whipped past, alternating with tine mesh lying flat against the shaft wall. The conveyor was still accelerating when Jathok grabbed for the lever and pulled the platform to a stop.

'Jathok?' Dalchian said.

'I have to see,' the sorcerer said, his normally deep voice fragmenting at the edges.

'We have a boarding assault to accomplish, in case you've forgotten.'

'I have to see,' he said again. The sorcerer pulled the screen back and put his eyes to the slit. With the conveyor now in position, unseen registration points had engaged and a locking bar popped from the surface of the doors. Jathok spun the bar and the doors clunked and hissed apart.

A foetid lick of human waste, body odour and terror wiped across their olfactory senses. One of the Branded gagged. Manacled human livestock shuddered and shied away from the portal, pulling against their restraints to try and hide. Moans and sobbing permeated the mass. Their ranks were numberless, rows of chained cargo vanishing into unseen distance. Iron hoods bobbed and swayed. In the far darkness someone screamed from a throat that had screamed too many times to do it properly any more. The papery bark did not sound human.

'Witch,' Dalchian snarled. 'We have no time for your sentimentality.' Jathok did not answer, but rather stepped into the cargo deck and gazed about. Dalchian felt the ship buck as its void battle raged on. He growled. 'Witch!'

Without warning, Leil Jathok leant down and dragged his gauntlet through the manacles of the nearest imprisoned souls, popping the links apart. He strode along the row, snapping restraints as he went. The wretched were too dumbfounded to react, frozen in uncomprehending fear. Jathok went fifty yards then turned back, dragging his hand through the chains of the adjacent row. Broken links scattered and bounced, filling the cavernous deck space with ringing. More of the chained yowled and bleated, thinking some fresh abuse was imminent.

'Remove your hoods,' Jathok commanded them in magma tones. They obeyed. 'Come with us.' He turned and strode back onto the conveyor.

'What does this achieve?' Dalchian snapped.

'As you said,' Jathok said evenly. 'We have a boarding to accomplish.'

Over a hundred waifs shuffled onto the conveyor, dead-eyed and disconsolate. The Chaos Space Marines let the flood of humans break and eddy around them, filling the entire con-veyor save for the gaping hole Dalchian had made in the deck plating. Jathok locked the deck doors and slid the screen back before cranking the lever, setting the platform in motion once again.

The prisoners stank. Someone in the mass was saying 'please please please please please' while others silently wept. Dalchian had to listen to be sure, but yes, one of them was humming a cheerful tune. Dalchian shook his head and ground his teeth.

They all opened their doors, Krutaan's voice said in his ear.

Motionless, Dalchian employed every ounce of his willpower to concentrate on the fight ahead. More fighting to come was a certainty.

It might be the only thing he was certain about.

* * *

The conveyor reached its upper terminus and locked into place with an echoing *boom*. The crammed mob of psykers shifted and held their collective breath. The Chaos Space Marines tightened grips on weapons, their focus tourniquet-tight. Dalchian's own breathing, still gravelly from his injuries, filled his hearing as he tensed. Jathok slid back the screen. There was no locking bar on these doors, but a tiny pin-lumen above the portal went from red to flashing amber.

'I know what they are,' uttered one of the imprisoned mutants, sounding shocked to hear his own voice. 'I know what they are! They're Archenemy!' A frisson of new horror shivered through the gathered wretches. 'They're Archenemy! By the Throne, we're all doomed!'

'You're doomed anyway,' Dalchian said, petrifying the waifs with his mutilated purr.

The pin-lumen turned green and the doors slid open with a *hiss*.

Light and noise filled the space. Bolters, flamers and looted hellguns vomited from the conveyor, scalding las poured back against them. The Night Lords and Abyssal Kindred were out of the portal in a blink. A hundred traumatised souls screamed and tried to claw away from the hurricane of deadly weapons discharge. Some slipped through the gash in the deck plates while others suffocated, crushed against the rear bulkhead of the conveyor. The Chaos Space Marines sowed death and terror beyond the conveyor threshold, reaping from the ranks of ebon-clad troopers with blade, gun, fist and boot. Almost rebounding from the corner in which they were trapped, the prisoners' focus veered without conscious thought, like the direction change of a flock of avians. Their terrified need for escape pushed them out of the conveyor towards the furious battle, into the streaking paths of bolts and las fire. They stampeded with thoughtless determination, flattening the masked Sentinels with their numbers and pummelling them with feet both shod and bare. The Chaos Space Marines were towering islands in the tide of desperate souls as they surged.

Dalchian kneed a Black Sentinel into the path of Ang Heltris' knives. The mortal hung mid fall and twitched, held in place by the legionary's flurry of blows. Dagardis cut the barrel from a hellgun, the finely tuned prismatics inside the rifle detonating with an electric *pop*. The Imperial staggered and Dagardis clove them in twain. Nallath's Abyssal Kindred pushed forth in a disciplined line, flamers washing defenders backwards to where precision bolt pistol rounds blew cavities in them and amputated their limbs, before finally they were chewed to ruin by the Chaos warriors' chainswords.

The Sentinels broke. Dalchian raised his hairless brows in surprise. The troopers had fought to the death in each skirmish of the boarding so far, so the withdrawal created sudden space into which the harvested mortals flailed and crawled. A scattershot rearguard needled them with las fire as the bloodied Sentinels disappeared in short order.

Dalchian saw Jathok, spattered with blood for the first time he could remember, lunge forth to go after the Imperials.

'Hold!' Dalchian snarled, and the boarders held. 'They bait us into a trap. Send forth the herd.' He gestured to the psykers with his claw. Jathok stared at him, then nodded.

'Do it,' the sorcerer said.

The morass of inmates cried and bawled, needing little encouragement to clatter away from the sight of so much murder. 'Archenemy!' one of them yelled again, and Dalchian shot him in the face. They roiled on even faster, leaving a trail of blood and grubby footprints.

The hall was long and wide, with several conveyor doors interspersed between sectioned chambers lining either side. Each of the chamber walls were bedecked with manacles, gurneys and human-shaped cages, and each space possessed a large cogitator unit from which a calipered arm of lenses swayed. Leil Jathok's face was a contorted grimace of rage and disgust as they moved through the hall, its purpose clearly to discriminate between various grades of the human livestock in which the Black Ship dealt. Vid-captors watched their progress from niches within bulkheads, the lenses filigreed into the eye sockets of human skulls.

Tall bronze doors etched with imagery from the Imperium's rotten religion barred their way. The inmates scraped and pounded at the fresco impotently. Dalchian swept through them like an ocean predator through a shoal and drove his thrumming claw into the centre of the doors. Sparks exploded and metal shards bounced across the deck and he shouldered the doors apart. He felt the eyes of the other Chaos Space Marines on him. He felt the heat of their suspicion and basked in it. Another set of doors was set close behind, the gap between the twin pair forming an antechamber to the discrimination hall. Another scrape of flashing finger blades sent them swinging open.

An atrium flagged with marble stretched before them, granite stairs fluting upwards between balustrades of bronze and ivory. A dome of armaglass crowned the space, points of starlight rolling in the firmament beyond. *Gods, it feels good to see the outside again,* Dalchian thought as a blanketing weight lifted from his thoughts. A column of data spines and transceiver masts was visible just beyond the armaglass, and Dalchian suddenly knew exactly where they were on the Black Ship, the location of the antenna array clear in his nigh-perfect recall of the vessel's exterior.

The thought was instantly overridden by other priorities.

The company of Black Sentinels arrayed upon the stair felled half of the psyker cattle in one volley. The Chaos Space Marines were inhumanly resilient and clad in armour unyielding to anything but the heaviest of assaults, but even they dived into cover behind the bronze doorway as las and plasma blasted across their ranks. Shrieking, the psykers turned and fled. Dalchian saw one of them lift from the deck, running through the air as if upon an invisible catwalk.

We're out of the occluding sphere, he realised with a jolt.

A whistling dart flicked from a Sentinel's neurophagic rifle into the levitating psyker's spine. They plummeted to the deck and were swiftly crushed beneath those fleeing in the conventional manner. Snatches of vox-traffic fractured in his helm as he raised his bolt pistol, the signals weak but present now they were away from the hateful labyrinth. He blink-clicked his vox to maximum gain and full-spectrum broadcast.

'This is the Skin-Taker,' he voxed as he leapt forwards, hoping he would be heard. 'All reinforcements, make for the dorsal dome, aft of the vox-array. Do not follow our trail into that bastard labyrinth, whatever you do.'

The Chaos Space Marines sprinted through the screaming psyker masses, raining las fire ionising the air around them and flash-boiling craters in their armour. A bass rumble rolled around the atrium.

'Now you shall feel my wrath!' Jathok bellowed. Dalchian looked at him and the sorcerer's eyes were aglow.

Leil Jathok, sorcerer lord of the Abyssal Kindred, tore the gem-topped staff from his back and whirled it through the air, slamming the butt onto the flags with a gargle of syllables. Turquoise light flashed from the staff, a shockwave of glowing wisps swiping the Black Sentinels to the deck. As they dropped, a lone figure at the stairhead became visible, for she remained standing.

She wore close-fitting armour the colour of oiled copper, and the adamantine rings of a chain mantle pulled a mauve cloak tight across her armoured shoulders. A high grille mask covered the lower half of her face; the cheeks visible above were covered in electoos. One of her eyes was brown and the other grey, and a tall knot of silver-flecked hair stood proud from an otherwise shorn pate. She brought up the long steel of an execution blade, both palms around its handle. Her grip was loose, fluid, assured. From beneath the flared quillons the first two fingers of each hand extended then cut down together in a gesture that, while unfamiliar to Dalchian, made a clear implication. Her sword never wavered.

Dalchian fired his bolt pistol, but she was already moving, slipping like mist through the Sentinels as they lurched upright and brought their weapons to bear. He readied himself to receive her charge, but he was not her target. The Oblivion Knight of the Silent Sisterhood flowed towards Jathok, and the sorcerer raised his staff into a fighting guard. Dalchian moved to intercept her, but the press of screaming human cargo and the ballistic attentions of the Black Sentinels hemmed him in.

The Oblivion Knight was upon the sorcerer uncannily fast, her blade streaking up from a low guard in a wicked slash. Jathok parried with his staff and it flickered, the gems at its top dimming. The Sister spun her blade and jabbed in with a lunge. Jathok dodged, and the execution blade hammered across, chasing him. The sorcerer twisted away with absolutely zero margin for error, the obnoxiously sharp tip of the Sister's sword scoring a hairline incision across his breastplate. He pounded down with his staff, forcing her blade low, and lifted a pistol to her face. She leant back as the weapon fired, the bolt skimming the tresses of her topknot.

Dalchian tore Imperials into pennants of flesh with his claw, kicking legs from under black-armoured troopers and blowing heads into slurry with his bolt pistol. But he could not get close to the duel. Another tidal wave of las fire pummelled him and he snaked away, snarling.

Jathok staggered, the Silent Sister flensing his mind. Her deadening aura muted his psychic powers, but it also made her a smear of barely visible un-sense to him. He felt his eyeballs drying in their sockets with the effort of keeping her position, and the position of her weapon, in his mind. She swung her blade from one side to the other before sweeping it in an arc and carving down. Jathok bellowed with exertion, bringing his staff up to block at the last instant. The Terran steel skidded aside, but the staff exploded into shards, bits bouncing from the deck plates, and Jathok dropped to one knee.

Dalchian was almost there. A bundle of liberated psykers had punched a hole in the Black Sentinels with their bodies, screaming and dragging themselves over the troopers to reach the top of the stairs. Quite what salvation they expected to find there Dalchian could not imagine, but it gave him a momentary reprieve. He gutted a Sentinel who was levelling a volley gun at him, the mortal's vitae fountaining from the grinning mouth of his mask, then barrelled towards the Sister of Silence as she raised her blade for the killing blow.

He was not quick enough.

He felt his ligaments crack as he heaved himself forward, but the execution blade was already falling and Jathok's head was still bowed, defeated. A toothed blade crossed the Sister's sword edge, the two weapons meeting with a *clang* that rose above all other sounds. Endagur's form was interposed above the kneeling sorcerer, the champion's blade notched almost to its fuller by the force of the Sister's strike. She whipped her blade away, weaving to Endagur's off side and slicing upwards before he could turn. Her sword bit into his power pack and the flesh of his back beneath. He lurched, wrenching himself from the blade and swaying around. The Silent Sister made to impale his chest, but Dalchian kicked her aside, his claw falling down onto her. She tucked and spirited herself from beneath the blades, the claw burying itself into the deck.

Dalchian howled like an animal and ripped the claw free. Endagur had recovered and was slicing his sword across from her side. She turned it away almost lazily, their two blades sliding over each other with a *shing*.

Jathok raised his pistol and unleashed a burst of automatic fire. Bolt rounds thundered from his weapon and the Silent Sister moved like water. One of his bolts hit her cloak, a woven thing of billowing lightness, and Dalchian actually saw the round deaden and drop to the deck, inert. The cloak should have had a ragged hole blown through it, but instead it was unmarked. He raked his claw across her again, and again she slithered from its path, her execution blade hacking a gouge from his pauldron. Endagur brought his sword straight down on top of her, making tiny adjustments as the sword fell to account for her dodges. The tip lodged firm into the deck and the champion had to heave the thing free.

Cascades of las fire shredded the human livestock and one of Nallath's squad took a plasma blast to the face plate, his head melting and sloughing off in a white-hot dribble. A frag grenade landed next to Ang Heltris and blew the knifeman from his feet, armour blitzed with streaks of exposed ceramite. Inconsolable psykers trampled him, but he ground their bones with his remaining hand as he dragged himself upright. One of them screamed as he folded her beneath his grip and lightning exploded from her eyes and nose. Mortals nearby died as the etheric energy leapt between them, their organs sizzling.

Ang Heltris ended her suffering with his prosthetic knife and used her severed head as a projectile, smashing a Sentinel's mask with it.

Dalchian and Endagur tried to gain advantage over the Oblivion Knight, but she met every strike and returned it twofold, forcing them to block and parry and give ground. A greyness had suffused Dalchian's vision. The furnace of his rage roiled in his breast, and thoughts of the greater strategy vanished. He screamed with genhanced lungs, the sound appalling. His claw swept and bit, the blade digits drenched in pulsating energy. His pistol ran dry, the last stray shots annihilating wretches but missing his intended target, so he hurled it away and tore a knife from his belt.

The Silent Sister worked like a graceful machine, her every motion perfectly measured and executed with a nightmare precision. Her empty core did nothing to assuage the ghoulishness with which she applied her skill. Her spirit was indomitable, because it was absent. She was simply purpose given form.

Dalchian saw her hollow nature and his claw burned with a need to shatter it. The weapon slashed and raked and grabbed, only needing the vaguest direction from him. He worked his knife hand into the spaces left by the claw, filling the air with razors. She ducked and whirled and sidestepped, her answering blows searing in and forcing his weapons to adjust. Endagur hacked and hacked, nuance surrendered in exchange for power. And still she evaded.

Two more Abyssal Kindred fell, leaving Nallath's retinue at just four. The warriors had surrounded Jathok and he stood with an effort, his champion and the berserk Skin-Taker occupying the null maiden for the moment. As he drew clear of her aura, his powers returned to him. He blasted into the Black Sentinel ranks with sheets of etheric flame. They flailed as the vortices of warp energy tore at their minds and burned their skin, though their armour remained pristine. Desiccated, the Imperials slumped, their charcoal bones crumpling under their own weight.

The Silent Sister's brow knotted in anger at the display. Still keeping pace with Dalchian and Endagur, she detached something from her belt and deftly bowled it through the air towards the sorcerer. It skittered across the deck to a stop at Jathok's feet. It was a brass canister the size of a fist, moulded to resemble a skull with its jaw wide open. The canister popped open and a fine haze of dust filled the atrium. Jathok seemed to deflate and the skirling inferno of his witch-fire abruptly faded to nothing, wisps dissolving into the air. He roared like a carnodon, spittle wafting from his teeth.

Dalchian's claw had snipped in at blistering speed, making use of the distraction. The knight blocked but was forced to step back or lose her balance. Endagur took the chance and stabbed. She swiped his sword aside, but Dalchian's claw was tearing in again. She took another step back. Dalchian felt the hunger in his claw; the yearning it had to delete her abominable soulless-ness from existence. He let the claw chomp at her, rearing and snapping. She took another step back.

A colossal detonation of energy smashed the armaglass dome to atoms, a column of light burning into the bulkhead from outside for the merest instant of time. Then the air whooshed upwards into the vacuum, the pressure dropping like a stone before the ship's field of protective energy blinked across the hole. A black shape loomed beyond the energy field as a handful of silhouettes dropped through the crackling film, the Black Ship's gravity dragging them in. The power-armoured figures clanked down onto the deck plates at the top of the stairs and surveyed the turmoil with impassive, crested helms.

The Rubricae filled the Black Sentinel rear line with warpfire bolts, emerald corposant snuffing out lives as they passed through carapace armour like an arc-welder through vellum. The Astra Tele-pathica soldiers rotated on the spot and drenched the newcomers in las fire.

The Oblivion Knight's eyes snapped away then back, as quick as thought. It was enough.

Dalchian's claw carved the armour at her belly without pause, the long blades of his lightning claw passing into her and straight out the other side. She swung her sword down to cleave the limb from him, but Endagur smashed the blade away. The sword spi-ralled from her grasp as her entrails tumbled. Dalchian slashed again, tearing through the grille and gorget at her neck. The energised talons, usually thirsty for blood to braise upon their edges, rejected the blood of the blank creature, the gore cohering into droplets and running from the blades like oil on water. Her hands dropped and her head slowly tilted forwards until it rolled off and wetly hit the deck. Her body fell a moment later.

The Rubricae filled the Imperials with cursed ammunition, and the surviving Abyssal Kindred warriors tore into their number with chainswords and flamer.

The Imperials all died.

Dalchian saw the final reaping as if from the other end of a long tunnel. With painful slowness he gradually drew closer, his thoughtless abandon cooling and seeping away until he was there again, in full. Endagur stared at him, typically silent. Jathok trudged towards him, purple bags under his eyes.

'I might ask you about your claw later, Skin-Taker,' the sorcerer said, exhaustion undermining his comradely tone. Dalchian stared at the weapon. *It was fighting, not me.*

'Later,' he agreed. They looked up at the Rubricae. The spectral automatons clomped slowly down the stairs, arranged them-selves neatly before their master and bowed in unison. Jathok smiled and inclined his head.

'It's a relief to have you return to me,' he said to the empty suits of armour. Dalchian would have made a face, but he was still churning over the sensation of his weapon fighting of its own accord. Dagardis and Ang Heltris were finishing the wounded with the other Chaos Space Marines. *Do they feign blindness? Do they ignore me?* Dalchian looked at Endagur's half-melted face plate.

'Yours is a murderous blade,' he told the champion. 'I'm glad I do not meet it as an adversary.' Endagur's helm dipped in acknowledgment. A gauntlet appeared at Dalchian's side holding his discarded pistol. Dalchian took it from Larakh, who returned to the remains of his squad.

Eight Rubricae had reinforced them, but that only returned the boarders' number to what it had been when they entered the labyrinth. They reloaded their guns and ascended the stairway, crunching fallen Sentinels beneath their boots.

'My lord,' came a weak, breathless voice. Dalchian turned in astonishment as two of his Branded emerged from the ruin, one bearing a hellgun and one a neurophagic rifle. 'We're still combat effective.'

Before Dalchian could think of anything to say, two more figures dropped from the destroyed dome, their power-armoured forms landing heavily amongst the dead.

Qi Umshar cocked his bolt pistol.

'What have we missed?' Naritsa growled.

CHAPTER TWENTY-FOUR

The corridors beyond the atrium were narrow and dark. Candles of black wax flickered in bulkhead sconces and skull-mounted vid-captors dangled from the cornicework, their machine gazes unblinking as the Chaos Space Marine boarding force rampaged through the decks of the Black Ship. Dalchian and his remnant Blades led the way, the Skin-Taker's claw writhing with power as it carved through armoured hatchways with supernatural ease. The lightning dripping from its talons was turning from its prior blue-white to a rich violet, but glowed no less bright. Behind the midnight-clad reavers marched Jathok's Rubricae automatons, their clockwork fusillades reaching past the Night Lords and excoriating the knots of defenders that lay in wait beyond every portal, glowing shells chattering from gargoyle-mouthed bolters. The Abyssal Kindred followed behind Jathok's Rubricae as they advanced, Endagur performing occasional sorties to cleave defenders asunder with his blade when they came too close. Naritsa stomped along, sending controlled bursts of fire from his combi weapon into the Adeptus Astra Telepathica personnel.

The Imperials were of more diverse stock deeper within the Black Ship. Crew in brocaded fatigues sought to repel them with more traditional shotguns and bludgeons. Adepts in robes or ceremonial breastplates leant out from structural columns to lend their pistol fire to the volleys. A multitude of servitors bore heavy weaponry sutured to their shoulders, the brain-wiped cyborgs striding into the Chaos kill-zone to unleash large-calibre bolt rounds, clots of star-bright plasma, and threads of melta that punched through armour, flesh and bone.

A plasma blast splashed across the armour of a Rubric Marine. The automaton kept firing its weapon as it sagged, molten plate bending and flopping onto the deck. The servitor cycled up its prosthetic plasma cannon again, containment coils keening with barely contained fury, but warpfire bolts shattered the pulsing coils and the servitor vanished in a pillar of incandescence, its blazing demise crisping what flesh remained on other lobotomised slaves nearby.

The Black Ship was singularly capable of subjugating those afflicted with the psyker mutation, its esoteric defences alarming in their subtlety. Leil Jathok sent infrequent bursts of slavering warp energy that pulled down barricades and unravelled human anatomies when a choke-point threatened to slow them down, but every time he did, graven runes across the bulkheads glowed with psy-reactive heat and doused his conjurations within seconds. The effort was dragging at his mind and his muscles. With each passing minute his grey-streaked beard became whiter and the blood vessels in his face thumped with growing pressure.

They came to a concourse that spanned some abyss of darkness between macro-sections of the ship. *A bottleneck worthy of an Iron Warriors fortress,* Dalchian thought as they converged upon it. A phalanx of Black Sentinels knelt across the far end of the walkway, guns up. Two swift volleys of powerful las fire stymied the Chaos advance as the Night Lords and Abyssal Kindred swerved into cover. The Rubricae marched on, undeterred, their bootsteps sounding a gong beat upon the concourse deck plates. Their unearthly weapons gouged into the Sentinel ranks, making skin crackle and flesh run like hot wax under pierced armour.

Four figures lifted from the abyss, vaulting the balustrade and squaring themselves off against the Rubricae. The Silent Sisters' panoply was immaculate, vratine armour layered beneath fur-trimmed cloaks. Above their mouth grilles they wore domed helms, high and arrogant, decorative topknots echoing the flattened hair beneath. One of the women hefted a clutch of psyk-out grenades, the hissing cloud of deadening particles enclosing the whole squad of Rubricae within its billowing circumference. The ghost warriors fought against the effects of the cloud, but it was undeniable. Their guns pitched down towards the deck as the warp magic that motivated them bled away. Crested helms tilted and the suits of ancient armour full of naught but dust were pulled down to the grating, their strength no longer enough to resist even the weak force of simulated gravity.

'Open fire!' Jathok roared, and his Kindred did so. But the Sisters of Silence's slight frames were mostly obscured behind the collapsing mass of Rubric Marines. The sorcerer drew both his pistols and crashed forwards onto the concourse, Endagur, Naritsa and the others following suit.

Foolish, Dalchian chided silently.

Another of the Sisters held a masterfully wrought flamer in her fists that radiated a faint orange glow from its pilot flame. As the Abyssal Kindred thundered towards her, she squeezed the trigger. A cone of raging flame gouted from the weapon and she played it across the falling Rubricae with furious precision. The automatons' power armour began to disintegrate into flakes, and the shapes of the Rubric Marines crumpled like flakboard falling into an inferno. Over the scorching rasp of the fire, Dalchian was sure he could hear the bellows of warriors long since incapable of voicing such a sound, crying out as their last vestiges were scoured away and they succumbed to the true death owed them millennia ago. A heartbeat later, of their baroquely crested armour, only ash remained. The other Sisters of Silence wielded execution blades, and they had scant milliseconds to step forward before the Abyssal Kindred smashed into them.

Endagur and Naritsa brought their blades to bear with trans-human strength. The Silent Sisters and the anointed of the Abyssal Kindred traded a hurricane of blows. The Imperial warriors flitted this way and that, their long swords flashing in lunges and sweeps. The Chaos Space Marines slammed in, sword and axe swinging like forge hammers. The walkway was only wide enough for the two of them to fight, despite the Black Sentinel front rank numbering almost twenty. The coal-armoured foot soldiers opened up again, picking their targets in the wall of ceramite beyond. Nallath staggered, his pauldron holed through. The melee specialist snarled his frustration. Naritsa's mechatendrils formed a writhing briar in front of him as the Warpsmith duelled, blocking Nallath and his squad off from the mortals that were so near.

Loops of gore whipped into the air above the Sentinels. Limbs and extremities spiralled and hellguns fell as hands clasped around slit throats. The front ranks continued to fire, oblivious to the shadows of death slicing their comrades apart behind them. Dalchian pulled himself over the balustrade behind the Sentinels last, Dagardis, Ang Heltris and Qi Umshar butchering the mortals with both skill and joy. Lord Skin-Taker turned his back to the fight and stared with devil-red eyes at the uniformed officer beyond the armaglass.

This end of the concourse terminated in a thick blast door, beyond which a fearful but determined face looked on through a tiny, square window. As Dalchian ignited his claw, the human turned and retreated. Dalchian allowed the eternal gratification of imparting terror kindle within him, and stepped forward to sunder the blast door into ruin.

But the mortal had not run away. He was there, sweat dripping down his brow, at the embrasure of another blast door only eight feet behind the first. As Dalchian watched, a second huge slab of reinforced plasteel shuttered the further opening, hiding the mortal from view and creating an air gate-like compartment. Warning lumens flashed amber either side of the blast door and Dalchian narrowed his eyes.

The small armaglass window flooded with searing brightness, projecting like a stab-lumen onto the fight on the walkway. Dalchian's auto-senses compensated as he stopped before the blast door and examined the window.

Raw plasma rumbled through the compartment between the blast doors.

Dalchian waited a moment for it to pass, but his optimism went unrewarded. The torrent of ship's plasma continued to hurtle through the gap, a stable redirection of the Black Ship's reactor energy glowing blue-green and brilliant white.

Clever bastards.

He turned back to the fight. His remnant Blades had dismembered the Black Sentinels and left them gasping and twitching in their own blood. Devoid of support, the four Silent Sisters had but one destiny, though they rejected it for as long as they could.

Ravaging tongues of orange fire claimed another of Nallath's Kindred, but Endagur had split the skull of one sword Sister, and Dagardis had amputated the legs of the other. She blocked and slashed from her prone position, but the axeman managed to catch her blade beneath his boot and snapped the steel off at the hilt. She pulled a knife from her gore-drenched belt, but Jathok emptied a bolt pistol clip into her grille mask and she stilled. The other Chaos Space Marines sawed their way through the two final Sisters, the flamer rasping into the darkness as its bearer came apart.

The fight done, Dalchian's Blades returned to his side. Endagur went wordlessly to the blast door to inspect it for himself.

Dalchian stepped past and made his way through the charnel mess that had been the Sentinels. The scene would have made him smile, but for the aching hunger in his clawed left hand which soured his joy.

Leil Jathok knelt in the ashes of his Rubricae and slowly dragged the tips of his armoured fingers through the flakes. Dalchian fixed the sorcerer with a look.

'Another obstacle,' he said.

The lord of the Abyssal Kindred raised his gaze then slowly stood. His beard was ice white and tortured exhaustion wafted from him, his cranial implants stuttering and shorting out.

'Nothing your daemon weapon cannot undo, I imagine?' Jathok's deep timbre was leaden as he voiced the one thing Dalchian had been deliberately ignoring for so long. A thrill of rage and disgust shot through the Skin-Taker's nerves, and the claw almost came up to tear Jathok's throat out. Dalchian suppressed it with considerable effort.

'They have a... moat of plasma,' Dalchian said.

'A moat and a bridge,' Dagardis said, gesturing at the concourse deck. 'How quaint.' Dalchian ignored him.

'If I breach the door, then this chamber fills and we are all extinguished.'

Jathok stood next to his champion, whose blasted beast helm was bleached in the plasma glow. Endagur looked at his master and said nothing.

'Gyren,' Jathok called. 'See what you can do.'

The Warpsmith stood upon the balustrade and examined the bulkhead around the blast door, searching for a likely ingress. The segmented tendrils swaying from his power pack snaked over the metal, manipulators tapping, him listening.

'What of your other Blades?' Jathok asked, apropos of nothing. Dalchian's winged helm regarded the sorcerer for a long moment. *What* of *my other Blades?* Dalchian remembered his old warband with a suddenness that unnerved him. Half a company of legionaries lost under his aegis lurked at the edge of his perception, their resentment eating at the corners of his mind. He blinked the judging phantoms away, knowing to which *other* Blades the sorcerer was specifically referring.

'Saryuz and Zhikarga's armour signals have not emerged from the labyrinth,' he said, some of his bereft fury stealing into his voice despite his efforts. 'I am sure those warriors are dead.' Endagur's face plate gazed at him before turning to watch Naritsa's efforts. Jathok looked Dalchian dead in the eye.

'I am truly sorry to hear that, Skin-Taker,' the sorcerer said, laying a gauntlet on Dalchian's battle-grimed shoulder. 'Let us finish this. Let us take this ship.'

'Pray the prize is worth the cost.'

'We'll make sure of it.'

Naritsa cut a narrow slice from the bulkhead using his plasma torch, but the metal swelled to fill the void and the Warpsmith cursed.

'Where?' Dalchian asked, energised claw gleaming. Naritsa described a patch above the middle of the door and Dalchian hopped onto the opposite balustrade, his index blade piercing the alloy and paring it away to leave scabbed edges. Naritsa and Jathok shared a look. The Warpsmith put both hands and several mechatendrils into the gap, working to remove layers of mundane plasteel and insulation before revealing dozens of cables and a command junction. He inserted a mechatendril spike jack into the junction and brought up a baffling screed of runes on his dataslate.

'Ugh,' he grunted. 'I always forget how ugly Imperial rune hymnals are.'

'Is there a way in?' Dalchian asked.

'There's something.' The Warpsmith worked for several minutes, grinding his adamantine jaw as he did. 'I can't bypass it – it needs a ward-signum. We can't halt the flow without the pass phrase, my lord. Eighteen characters, both runic and numeral.'

'How many possible combinations is that?' Dagardis asked, making the Warpsmith think for a moment.

'In excess of one point three octillion.'

A heavy silence followed the proclamation in which Jathok nodded slowly. Dalchian's claw clenched unbidden and he felt bitter frustration lodge in his throat.

'Then we leave the way we came,' Dagardis said. 'Realign our boarding craft to penetrate the forward section, avoiding this obstacle entirely.'

'And risk another labyrinth?' Nallath responded. 'Or the Black Ship suddenly accelerating, leaving us dead in the void?'

'Better than this dead end,' the axeman bit back.

'Eighteen,' mumbled Jathok.

'We stay,' Dalchian ordered. 'There will be a way through.'

'Eighteen,' the sorcerer said again, more stridently. 'Gyren, the passphrase is Orbech, Book Nine, Verse Eighty-three.'

'My lord?'

'Just enter it.'

Naritsa tapped on his dataslate. A second later there was a series of *booms* from within the plasma gate, and the high-energy torrent ceased and faded away, globs of the stuff evaporating into mist as the pressure and temperature dropped.

The blast door unlocked and scraped open.

Immediately, the boarders arrayed themselves for combat. A wave of new hunger washed over the Chaos Space Marines, dissolving the ill humour that had threatened to surface and fan the flames of their battle-lust. Dalchian's winged helm cocked towards the sorcerer, stilled in disbelief.

'Though it pains me to admit it,' he said, 'I'm impressed.'

'It is as I said, Skin-Taker.' Jathok's eyes gleamed where moments ago they had been almost empty. 'Truly, the gods have a sense of humour!'

'So it seems.'

What defence remained was paltry. No Silent Sisters or Black Sentinels confronted their advance, only uniformed crew running and firing blindly behind themselves with shotguns and laspistols. The Chaos Space Marines tore the mortals to shreds. As they moved beyond sight of the plasma gate a new sound began. A shrill tocsin filled the dark companionways and blinking crimson lumens lined the deck. The crew had enacted the Black Ship's self-destruct procedure. Dalchian was fascinated by the idea of the crew abandoning such a vessel, alone deep in the void. But the reality, it turned out, was far more prosaic. The Chaos force found the Black Ship's bridge quickly. The wide doors were open and the deck crew were all at their stations.

They were all dead.

Foaming spittle bulged from mouths where the humans slumped in their thrones, and the air was rank with rapidly oxidising biocide. Even the servitors were deceased. A few tiny coughs made Dalchian look around. One of his Branded still dragged herself along in the wake of the Chaos Space Marines, her breacher armour pocked and rent, fatigues damp with blood. She held her looted neurophagic rifle steady, though. *How extraordinary.*

The bridge itself was buried within the forward section of the Black Ship, swaddled with crew decks, a Sentinel garrison and cloister chambers for the Silent Sisters, rather than standing proud at the vessel's stern as with most warships. Everything about the Black Ship was veiled and hidden away, including its internal structure and the location of its command centre. In spite of that important difference, it still bore all the other recognisable features of a voidship's bridge. Cogitator stations pertaining to multitudinous aspects of the vessel's operation stood in amphitheatric curves, the levels descending towards the nave, where the lecterns of senior officers surrounded the captain's pulpit. The erstwhile master of the Black Ship was slumped over his console, skin turning grey like all the rest.

Dalchian wrenched the captain's frail corpse from his elevated throne and dumped him onto the deck plates. He looked at the sorcerer, red eye-lenses somehow grinning.

'How many of our kin have ever set foot on the bridge of a Black Ship of the Adeptus Astra Telepathica, would you say?' he asked.

Jathok looked from the pulsing oculus to the frothing corpses strewing the nave, a smile on his exhausted face. 'Few indeed, Skin-Taker,' he said. 'Few indeed.'

Gyren Naritsa went from station to station, testing each cogitator for function. His mechatendrils twirled dials and pulled levers, trying anything to coax a response from the ship. Angry crimson warnings flashed from every viewscreen and the oculus was filled by a countdown sequence of glowing red runes. The tocsin wailed on.

'As expected, they've locked all the interfaces,' Naritsa said. Jathok nodded.

'Now we must discuss your claw, Skin-Taker,' the sorcerer said.

'What? Now?' The idea repelled him. His claw's new *functionality* was a boon he was determined to avoid examining too closely. 'Is now really the time?' He gestured at the countdown.

'Your daemon weapon is our way through, Skin-Taker,' Jathok said evenly.

Dalchian growled wordlessly. *It's not a daemon weapon!* he wanted to shout, but he knew doing so would be petulant. Petulant, and incorrect. The frenzy of Krutaan in the days before his death surfaced with aching clarity in Dalchian's mind. The pull of the berserker he himself had felt aboard the *Vizier*. And the hunger within his hand. Even in the throes of his self-deception he had to admit *hands don't feel hunger*. He knew some presence had insinuated itself within Krutaan, just as he knew that same presence had passed from the dead champion into the weapon he had taken from Krutaan. The door in Dalchian's mind creaked, though open or closed he could not say.

Open, Krutaan's voice said, a grin somehow evident. Though it was not Krutaan's voice any more. **Closed open closed open closed open…** it whispered, baiting his temper. A laugh echoed in his skull.

'Explain.'

'I had hoped your virtuoso tech-priest would assist us with this step,' Jathok revealed. 'But the more attention I paid to your lightning claw, the more I realised we had a valid second option, should your tech-priest remove himself from proceedings.'

Dalchian thought about Ibriel for the first time since they had boarded. Qi Umshar had offered no information on the plight of the *Prideful* since his arrival, and Dalchian had not pursued any.

'Ibriel,' Dalchian said.

'Yes, him.' Jathok gestured towards Dalchian's claw and then the column of armoured cables that climbed the captain's pulpit. After a heartbeat, the Skin-Taker lifted the weapon and placed the shimmering blades upon the cables.

'I am uncertain how long the ritual will take,' Naritsa grunted as he stepped down into the nave. 'Pray we have enough time, Lord Skin-Taker.' Jathok gave Naritsa a piercing look, but the Warpsmith was busy. He conjoined the claw to the pulpit's systems with a twisting arrangement of his own mechatendrils and auxiliary uplink leads he conjured from about himself.

'Why this way?' Dalchian asked, though he suspected he knew the answer. Naritsa had unbolted a panel from the wrist-section of the claw and was applying himself to circuitry that looked alarmingly organic to Dalchian's eyes. *Such swift transformation.*

'From my lord's pre-ascendent memories,' Naritsa grated, 'we made several working assumptions on the nature of Black Ship systems. As we suspected, the command architecture behaves in a psy-reactive manner, much like the superstructure. Whatever means I might try to pry it open will only close it further. We had no reliable strategy until your tech-priest coded a synthetic divine animus to override the defences of my Helbrute. Your claw's true possession provided us with an adequate backup, which is fortunate, given our position.'

Dalchian's mouth soured at the word *possession.* 'A synthetic divine animus,' he repeated. 'A synthetic daemon?'

'A simulacrum of a Neverborn soul, yes,' Jathok answered. 'Void of the true divinity associated with the Great Powers' lower orders, but capable of similar metaphysical feats. It's how he mapped the Black Ship's location so superbly. Really, Skin-Taker, you should give the priest more credit.'

'I'm done,' Naritsa said, clapping Dalchian on the pauldron as he stepped away. Dalchian's left arm was bound to the pulpit data-flow with a score of connections. The countdown began to bleat an additional alarm with each second that passed, declaring it to be in its final stages.

'You knew the Black Ship would be here,' Dalchian said, the realisation a cold tendril up his spine. 'You advised the Gorelord to attack this system. You knew it would be here. How long have you been hunting for one?'

Jathok was grinning now, all trace of his exhaustion wiped away by triumphant glee.

'I could not know a Black Ship would arrive here,' the sorcerer admitted. 'But I deduced it to be a possible outcome. The latent psychic reading of the system was considerable, and from the lack of realspace penetration by Neverborn entities I concluded that the mutant stock of this system's civilian colonies would be generally stable. It seemed likely to be a fertile harvesting ground for the Imperials. Naturally, I did not share these details with the Gorelord, but he indulged my suggestion because of the temptation presented by the forge world. It has proven useful that he committed to a full-scale assault.' He took a step back.

Naritsa tapped away on his dataslate, then lifted his metal face to Dalchian, the immobile features somehow conveying an apologetic air.

'This will be painful, Lord Skin-Taker,' the Warpsmith said.

'Do it,' Jathok hissed, eyes narrow. Naritsa pressed a rune.

Power surged through the pulpit network and Dalchian's claw clenched tight. He grunted in pain as the weapon constricted his hand within. Jathok went on.

'I have been searching for a way to seize one of the Corpse-Emperor's tithe ships for nearly two centuries. I thank you, Skin-Taker, for your able assistance.' Naritsa adjusted something and the pulpit throbbed with energy. Dalchian's claw arced and spat ropes of power into the air. Dalchian tensed and snarled.

'My lord?' Dagardis called from the top row of cogitators, anger and unease tightening his voice.

'Worry not,' Dalchian strained. 'Lord Jathok and I are sworn allies.' He fixed his burning crimson eye-lenses on the white-bearded face of the sorcerer. Naritsa glanced at Dalchian, then at the sorcerer. Jathok only laughed.

There was a screeching eruption of energy across the cogitators. Lightning leapt from deck to ceiling. The oculus and all the viewscreens vomited static and distortion. The Black Ship shuddered beneath their feet, low groans echoing from the depths of its structure. Dalchian fell to his knees, left arm held up by its bonds to the pulpit. Sparks drenched him and the mantle of hides across his back began to crisp.

He screamed such as few present had ever heard a living being scream before. His tongue stretched from his gaping mouth, steam erupting from his throat. The agony removed his capacity to think. He knew nothing but pain. His joints crackled as his muscles tensed against the excruciation. He was blind and deaf, and he screamed and screamed. Some utter oblivion yawned within him, a depthless vault of horrifying nothingness. The reptile part of his brain that still functioned clawed towards it in desperate need to be freed of the all-consuming hurt.

Can it be? Krutaan's voice sliced through his paroxysms. *Truly, Dalchian, you honour me with such a gift.*

Abruptly, the furore ceased and the bridge plummeted into blackness.

Dalchian's awareness trickled back to him in slow increments, his vision gradually returning, the bridge coming into focus lumen by lumen. Cogitators, consoles and databanks. Lines of runes scrolled across each viewscreen and the oculus showed an empty starfield within the datascreeds at its edges. Dalchian saw but could not speak; could barely move.

Naritsa was at the generatorium cogitator scrolling through reams of data, then he turned his metal face to Sorcerer Lord Jathok.

'The ship is ours, my lord,' he said, glancing at the Skin-Taker.

Dalchian's head lifted a tiny fraction and his breath hissed through his teeth as he dangled from the pulpit by his arm.

The sorcerer cast his attention back towards him. Jathok opened his fingers and brought his hand up. Dalchian lifted gradually from his knees, then continued to lift completely from the deck, raised by Jathok's warp-given gifts. There was a squealing crunch and Dalchian grunted in pain as his armour broke away from the lightning claw, which was still tightly bound to the pulpit. His bloodied arm hanging limp, Dalchian floated in the air, frozen by the power of the sorcerer.

'The ship is mine, Skin-Taker,' Jathok said quietly. 'And in providing me with victory you, yet again, display that you are incapable of the subtlety demanded by your rank.'

The other Blades launched themselves from the top level, roaring their affront. Dagardis drew his shimmering power axe back above his head as he flew. Ang Heltris sprang like a felid, knives low. Qi Umshar whipped his bolter from its sling.

Jathok reached out his other hand and caught the remnant Blades mid-air. They froze in a haze of power, teeth clenched, limbs heaving ineffectually against the psychic force of the sorcerer. Jathok's power was huge, even in the soul-sapping confines of the Black Ship.

'You disgusting animals have no right to call yourselves servants of the Powers,' he snarled. 'Your indecency in the face of the divine damns you. Your ancient Legion was a wretched caste of woe-begotten creatures long before today.'

Endagur stepped down to stand beside his master. Naritsa's metal face conveyed nothing, but the set of his shoulders did.

'Do not do this, my lord,' the Warpsmith said earnestly.

'Do not abase yourself because of *him*,' Jathok spat. 'You have grown entirely too comfortable in the company of dregs, Naritsa. You will recivilise yourself! As for the Skin-Taker, despite his intimacy with betrayal he still did not foresee this end. He is unworthy of pity.'

The sorcerer sent a pulse of jade fury to the Blades he held fixed above. Dagardis, Ang Heltris and Qi Umshar were cannoned backwards to the top tier of the bridge, etheric witch-fire slamming them into the bulkheads, plasteel distorting with the blow before they collapsed to the deck plates. Jathok's unnatural power robbed the Night Lords of their senses and they writhed, unable to stand. The lone remaining Branded trooper cowered behind a cogitator array, clutching her rifle.

Dalchian watched, trying to bellow but only making voiceless gasps, as the sorcerer levelled both hands at him.

'Such a trial has it been,' Jathok snarled. 'To pretend to be your equal. You served your purpose well, Dalchian, I will acknowledge that, but your utility has run dry.' The sorcerer clawed his fingers and rods of agonising light transfixed Dalchian. Blood and phlegm leaked from his rebreather and his midnight ceramite cracked where the light speared him, the fissures spreading, flakes of armour pinging free. He gurgled and shuddered, the pain like molten iron filling his marrow. Jathok nodded to Endagur, who raised his toothed sword high.

'Your soul goes to eternal agony, Skin-Taker,' Leil Jathok said. 'Goodbye.' With another nod, Endagur's sword hammered down.

The toothed blade severed Jathok's arms at the elbow, causing a psychic blowback that made the sorcerer stagger and released the Skin-Taker from his confinement.

'Endagur!' Jathok bawled in incomprehension. Blood gushed from his stumps for a second before his genhanced biology stemmed the flow. 'What in the Eye's name are you doing?'

The champion raised his blade again and Jathok staggered back. Light crackled from his eyes as he managed to pinion the beast-faced warrior behind a column of force.

A burst of bolter fire stitched across Jathok's plate, breaking his concentration and pushing him back. Endagur stepped forth again, raising his blade against his lord, but Jathok put up another barrier. Larakh had fired the shots, and in answer Nallath smashed him from his feet with a shoulder barge, bellowing.

'What madness is this?' Nallath roared. The last of Nallath's warriors looked on, motionless with indecision. Naritsa's impassive face flicked from Dalchian to Jathok to Endagur, but the Warpsmith did not move. There was a pregnant moment of stillness, events caught perfectly between two paths, balanced on a knife-edge.

At the topmost circle of the bridge, the tiny form of the last Branded trooper stood and pulled her long needle rifle into her shoulder. A whickering dart snicked down and buried itself in Jathok's cheek. The sorcerer's protective power dulled and vanished as the neurophagic did its work. Dalchian raised his helm just in time to see Endagur headbutt Jathok with savage abandon, dropping the maimed sorcerer to the deck.

'What are you doing?' Jathok begged to know as blood bubbled from his crushed nose. 'What are you doing?'

Naritsa looked away from Jathok and locked eyes with Dalchian. Nallath and Larakh wrestled each other as they crashed down the levels towards the nave. Lashes of etheric energy still dancing across his midnight plate, Dalchian dragged himself towards the sorcerer lord of the Abyssal Kindred. The Skin-Taker pulled his helm off with his bare left hand, the neck seals hissing as he did. His shredded, blasted, agonised face looked Jathok up and down as the sorcerer writhed on the deck.

'He does my bidding,' Dalchian rasped. 'What else would you expect from one of my Blades?'

Jathok blinked. 'One of your...?'

Endagur sheathed his sword and disengaged his own helmet,

slowly lifting the misshapen armour from his head. A head that was hale, with a working jaw and sharpened teeth.

'By all the gods,' Saryuz said. 'It stinks of incense in there.'

Everyone present stared at him, including Nallath. Larakh took the chance and slid a thin blade under the Abyssal Kindred's chin, forcing it up through his skull. Nallath twitched and slumped, his moment of distraction costing him his life. Larakh stood and nodded to Dalchian, likewise removing his own helm to reveal the broad face of Zhikarga.

'I'm glad to finally acknowledge your survival,' Dalchian said to the remnant Blade.

'As am I, my lord,' Zhikarga replied, then he tossed away his stolen helmet and leapt up the tiers to where the other Blades were regaining their faculties.

'Who's the mortal?' Saryuz asked.

The Branded wielding the neurophage rifle hesitantly stepped forward, fear draining what little colour remained from her bloodied face.

'Trooper Imal du Golsa,' she said. 'Four Platoon, breacher company of the *Prideful*, my lord.' She held her ground astoundingly well, though her frail human voice was almost lost amongst the hum of the ship's systems and the clanking of power armour as Dagardis and the rest staggered their way down to the nave. She looked like she might be sick.

'Why did you do that?' Dagardis asked the human, suspicious. 'Why shoot the witch?'

'I…' Du Golsa's eyes widened. 'I swore to serve the Skin-Taker, my lord.' She offered the explanation as if it was the most obvious thing in the galaxy. Dagardis, swaying slightly, peered at her, then threw back his head and laughed uproariously.

The Skin-Taker's attention was fixed on the sorcerer prone on the deck.

'It seems,' Dalchian rasped, dragging his body, which was still half-ruined from psychic torture, 'that I have subtlety enough for you, Leil Jathok.'

The sorcerer's mouth opened and closed, strings of blood oozing down to stain his beard. He turned his head to Saryuz in Endagur's armour, refusal and grief contorting his face, then he turned to Naritsa, snarling in rage.

'You betrayed me!'

'No, my lord,' Naritsa sighed.

'In truth,' Dalchian said, 'Warpsmith Naritsa never came to me, nor I to him. Until this moment I had no idea how he would react to my plan. He seems to have reached the correct conclusion.'

'What conclusion?' Jathok croaked, incandescent. He tried to push himself up with his stumps, but Saryuz kicked him back down.

'That you underestimated the Skin-Taker,' Naritsa answered. 'I saw none of the inferiority in him of which you were so certain, my lord.'

'You serve me!' Jathok raged.

'I serve the Great Powers,' Naritsa rejoined. 'And now I serve the Skin-Taker, if he'll have me?' He looked at Dalchian.

'I always have a need of wisdom among my Blades,' Dalchian replied.

Naritsa stomped back up the levels to where the three remaining Abyssal Kindred of Nallath's squad stood. Indecision showed in their stances, but Naritsa was a known figure of proven respect.

'Guard the entrances to the bridge,' he ordered them. 'We don't want any nasty surprises.'

Dalchian continued to stare at the sorcerer, watching the tide of impotent rage break over cliffs of perceived injustice. The desperate indignation made an absorbing play of micromovements across Jathok's facial muscles, gene-wrought vigour draining from him as realisation of the scope of his failure gradually dawned. Dalchian reached out and gently plucked the neurophagic dart from the sorcerer's cheek.

'And as for eternal agony…' he said, grinning from ear to ear.

Leil Jathok screamed like an animal as Naritsa welded him into the sarcophagus. The chamber's former occupant was dolloped on the oubliette deck, throat slit. Jathok's hideous racket was silenced as they sealed the lid, Dalchian turning the wheel himself before it retracted up into the gloom.

'Sweet dreams,' he whispered.

Chapter Twenty-Five

Zorean broadcast his ident phrase to the Flylords picket ship as it challenged the *Red*'s approach. The festering schooner let him pass, lumbering back to its patrol circuit on struggling engines.

'Open a vox-link to the *Torrent*,' Zorean ordered. Those few mortals still alive on his bridge were the ones who had not yet challenged him, or orchestrated their own demise. His crew was pitifully small. The last time the mortals had seen the Chaos fleet it had been during the vicious opening battle between them and the Imperial armada. Zorean sneered at their obvious unease.

'*Lord Zorean,*' came the Gorelord's unctuous voice. '*Can it really be you?*'

'I have returned.'

'*Well done, Night Lord!*' The expansive cheer in Thelissicus' tone was utterly unconvincing. '*In truth I did not expect any of you to survive.*'

'I am glad to subvert your expectations,' Zorean said, teeth grinding.

'Wonderful. I shall send a shuttle, and you can present your warriors to me in my strategium. Wonderful!' The Gorelord cut the link before Zorean could reply.

A dozen of the *Red*'s meagre remaining crew accosted him as he boarded the Crimson Slaughter tender craft. They broke from the shadows behind strewn, empty crates at the fringes of the shuttle bay and sprinted towards the legionary as he approached the ramp. A few autoguns crackled, rounds whining from his armour. Yet more mutineers, he thought, baring his teeth. He shattered many of them with his fists, casting them down, his face twisted in contempt for their pathetic desperation. One got her fingers around his neck and he backhanded her away, sending her skidding across the deck, through the energy field and out into the void. At least one still clung to the shuttle as the ramp closed behind him and the craft launched. As he watched from the porthole a Crimson Slaughter gunship entered the now vacant shuttle bay, and Zorean bid the *Red* an embittered fare-well. The *Torrent* loomed above him, a die-straight scar across its flank testament of the Skin-Taker's animosity.

'You,' the Gorelord said, with no trace of a smile, 'and you alone?' An equally overwrought throne stood in his strategium aboard the *Torrent of Hatred* as the one on its bridge. There were no places for advisors or retainers. How very like the Gorelord. Instead, almost the entire strategium was bedecked in spears of sharp metal, welded to the deck, the bulkheads, even the ceiling. All pointing directly to Thelissicus' throne with a hateful deter-mination, removing any fleeting possibility to mistake who was master of this domain. There was only a small clear space of deck immediately before the throne, where Zorean now stood.

'My erstwhile kindred,' Zorean muttered, 'were unexpectedly intransigent.'

The Gorelord leant forwards in his throne.

'Do you remember your agreement with me?' Thelissicus drawled.

'Yes, my lord.' He unclenched his jaw. 'I command the Blades, in exchange for a place as your vassal.'

The Gorelord spread his arms, brass rings glinting. 'So, what do we do now?' Thelissicus' voice oozed with false humility. 'Help me decide, Zorean. Jathok's Abyssal Kindred have not returned with the Skin-Taker in chains, so I can only surmise the sorcerer has failed in his accord with me, too.'

'As to that,' Zorean said, hoping his information might buy him a grain of favour, 'the sorcerer foolishly allowed Skin-Taker to roam his ship. Whatever has become of Lord Jathok, he will never command his warband again.'

'I see.' The Gorelord nodded, understanding. 'So, not only did you fail to bring the Blades to heel, but you allowed them to rob me of another asset into the bargain?'

Zorean blinked, mouth slightly open. 'Lord, I–'

'I hear you are skilled with a blade?'

The question totally blindsided Zorean. Mind stalling, he simply acknowledged the fact.

'Yes.'

'Good!' The Gorelord's black-toothed grin returned with gusto. 'You may serve in my galley until I compose an adequate answer for your many sorry failures.'

Zorean blinked again as a knot of Crimson Slaughter warriors surrounded him, snapping manacles to his arms, legs and neck before dragging him from the Gorelord's presence.

'No!' Zorean howled as he began to understand. 'No! I did everything I could. The fault is not mine. My lord, please!'

CHAPTER TWENTY-SIX

'Another three, Lord Skin-Taker,' came Saryuz's voice over the vox. Dalchian remained in his new command throne, the timbre of the Black Ship's purring systems still a novelty to be savoured.

'Salvageable?' he asked.

'Yes, my lord.'

'Good hunting. Put them with the others.'

'Aye, lord.'

One of the first things Naritsa had done was access the labyrinth controls and still the infernal environment. Brought to heel, they could scour it for survivors, and had found the remnants of several other Abyssal Kindred boarding parties lost within the bleached halls. Some of the Chaos Space Marines had relinquished their sanity and bleated wordlessly as they levelled chainswords and empty bolters at their rescuers. Zhikarga in particular seemed to take great pleasure in dispatching such lost souls using the Silent Sister's exquisite flame weapon. Apparently, he roared his delight every time the maddened warriors fell apart. The image made

Dalchian smile. Apart from these, there were now eleven competent Abyssal Kindred, who had been found in dribs and drabs. So far, they had been pathetically grateful to be freed from the coils of the labyrinth. Dalchian ordered them escorted to an empty cargo hold to meditate upon their future loyalties.

The wounded Chaos Space Marines Qi Umshar accompanied back to the *Ikhtheos*, as the frigate's apothecarion was better provisioned for such work than the Black Ship's macabre and eerily empty medicae deck.

'*My lord,*' Qi Umshar addressed him over the vox once the worst injuries had been stabilised. '*There is something I believe you should see.*'

Reluctant, but curious, Dalchian left Dagardis in command of the Black Ship and took the Thunderhawk lately belonging to Leil Jathok across to the frigate. The venerable gunship was like a hunting raptor, the controls responsive, the engines powerful. *Gods, how I've missed this,* he thought, banking the deadly craft through the void. A grin split his face and he roared aloud in savage satisfaction.

The *Ikhtheos*' apothecarion was much like the rest of the former Kindred ship. Devotional sigils adorned the bulkheads and grim talismans hung on chains from the ceiling. The armaglass-fronted stasis vaults lining the walls were filled with accoutrements both mundane and esoteric. Phials of counterseptic and plas-wrapped theatre tools shared space with preserved insects and bundles of feathers, tousled with dry gore. Assistance servitors were folded away in niches, and vitacopia apparatus hung like unconscious arachnids from the ceiling above operating slabs daubed in dark, painted wards and charms. The place stank of disinfectant and burned bones. Ang Heltris sat on a slab, finally having his amputated hand prepared for the augmetic he had so long delayed. There were two conscious Abyssal Kindred and two unconscious.

All were devoid of their armour. Those awake bowed deeply as he entered.

'My lord,' they greeted him, the Kindred accepting of their altered destiny.

Dalchian followed Qi Umshar to the far corner of the apothecarion. They descended several levels via spiral stairways, through more storage chambers. There were shelves full of replacement organs stacked in fluid-filled canisters.

'Where is the fleshwright, then?' Dalchian asked.

'He was resistive to my assuming responsibility for his domain.'

The spiral stair descended through a sterile workshop full of chirurgeon components locked securely behind adamantine doors. On the workshop deck was the bloodied corpse of the Abyssal Kindred fleshwright, brutal knife wounds across his neck declaring the source of the huge pool of blood in which he lay.

'I see you addressed his concerns in the proper manner.'

'Of course, my lord.'

Finally, they alighted at the deepest level, stepping off the stairs onto frosted deck plating. Lambent blue permeated the darkness, seeping from pale, translucent columns that marched away into the gloom on either side of them. Qi Umshar found an environment panel and delicately raised the lighting in the frigid chamber. The translucent columns glowed from within, and Dalchian lost count of them as they stretched away into the far depths.

The chamber was a suspension crypt. Each column was a cryo-tube, and in each cryo-tube was a human child. The crypt echoed with slow drips as pre-implantation hormones oozed into their metabolisms, each unconscious subject a potential future Chaos Space Marine. After some time, Dalchian said, 'No wonder the bastard had so many warriors.'

'The Blades may yet have a future, it seems,' Qi Umshar said. Dalchian grinned.

Postponing his return to the *Ikhtheos*, Naritsa himself was leading the recovery operation onto the drifting and inert *Prideful*. Lieutenant Nykold had crammed the entire crew onto the generatorium decks. The plasma core would take days to cool completely, and its residual heat had prolonged the lives of the mortals on board. Many had succumbed to asphyxia or madness during the cataclysmic confrontation, but over a thousand still endured.

Warpsmith Naritsa jury-rigged a winding path through the *Prideful*'s corpse, wiring up temporary heating and oxygen scrubbers so the mortals could float through the gangways without dying and transfer from the wreck into shuttles waiting on its dark flight deck. The Skin-Taker wanted them transferred to the Black Ship, a skeleton crew to replace the suicided Adeptus Astra Telepathica personnel.

Naritsa mag-locked his boots to the generatorium deck plates. Clothes, ration packets, water bladders and human waste floated in drifts through what thin, dioxide-rich atmosphere remained. Frost spread across the vast coils surrounding the core itself, its final measure of warmth siphoning away into the ship's lifeless bones. He came to the vast apparatus with which the tech-priest Ibriel had so precisely pinpointed the Black Ship. Within the nest of cables and screens, at the centre of a web of plasteel struts from which drifted cracked orbs of brass and exploded superconducting coils, Ibriel's form was rimed with ice in its cradle. Naritsa released his mag-locks and used his mechatendrils to pull himself weightlessly to the tech-priest's side.

He began the painstaking task of disconnecting all the linkages and freeing Ibriel's frozen form. The vital monitor on the tech-priest's chest had only one flashing lumen point left, and that was intermittent.

'What have you done to yourself?' the Warpsmith growled, not unkindly.

They released the *Prideful*'s cold carcass onto an eccentric orbital track, and the remnant Blades attended the Skin-Taker aboard the Black Ship to begin a more thorough appraisal of their prize.

Dalchian was surprised to find the human livestock mostly intact within the cargo decks of the Black Ship. He had assumed them to be gassed along with the crew.

'The compound the Astra Telepathica used to self-terminate is called annihilox,' Qi Umshar explained. 'It guarantees death, but is very resource-intensive to refine.'

'A waste to use it on cattle.' Ang Heltris shrugged, flexing the fingers of his new plasteel hand.

'Precisely.'

Dalchian scrolled through the manifest data. Over five thou-sand imprisoned psykers of varying grades, with room enough for twice that number again. Most would be low-level, low-value mutants, but a fair number would be potent enough to have their uses, and a few might very well be prodigious.

The Blades stalked the decks of their prize, fixing its curious shape into their eidetic memories. In the Navigators' sanctum they found five of the mutants reclined in grav-couches, heads sealed within a permanent cloud of ochre fluid beneath a clear dome, tubes feeding them nutrients and oxygen directly into their arteries. A hangar deck held a handful of sleek shuttlecraft and a single Rhino armoured transport vehicle, all of unadorned black metal. A narrow channel led from the hangar to a void door, invisible from without when it was closed.

Even the damage Dalchian's claw had done to the psy-reactive alloy of the ship was not permanent. Eventually the blistered edges cracked apart and the metal swelled to fill the gaps. Naritsa had led a party of servitors seconded from the *Ikhtheos* to realign the gaping rent in the Black Ship's outer hull, and after several hours even that showed signs of unnatural regeneration.

From time to time Dalchian heard faint laughter slither from the bulkheads and words drifted to him on breaths of recycled air.

…open closed open closed open…

He smiled when he heard the words, choosing to interpret them as a reminder of his triumph and a marker of the Black Ship's liberation from the Imperial yoke. Lieutenant Nykold and her scant deck crew were slowly settling into the unfamiliar roles, the Black Ship like a creature out of myth, accepting their ministrations with predatory patience. She had bemoaned a lack of technical staff to fill the void of the dead Adeptus Mechanicus contingent, so Dalchian had ordered her to vet the cargo for voidship experience. Hundreds of low- to mid-level psykers were installed across the ship, their responses varying from thankful enthusiasm to resigned acceptance. The occasional etheric misfire among the mortal crew was an acceptable price to pay. Naritsa had to amend some of the ship's wards to accommodate the new additions, and the character of the vessel began to change. Dalchian had noted that one hatchway adjacent to where a coven of psyker crew now worked had grown teeth at its edge, and shut with noticeable intent too soon after he passed through it.

Prizes, and the sacrifices of claiming them, he thought.

Before taking his rightful place upon the *Ikhtheos'* bridge, Naritsa had made solid work of Dalchian's armour repairs, though Ibriel's efforts would have been more elegant. Dalchian had presumed the tech-priest dead after the silencing of the *Prideful*. Learning that the tech-priest had been installed into his old cargo lifter for life support and was being treated by Qi Umshar, Dalchian felt the tremor of an unfamiliar emotion. He confided in no one, but admitted gladness at Ibriel's survival to himself, at least. Reminded of Ibriel's persistent usefulness, Dalchian blink-clicked access to his armour's mem-coils, bringing up the clandestine recordings of the Blades from aboard the *Torrent of Hatred*, half a lifetime ago, it seemed. He selected Zorean's datalog, which he had neglected to access before. He scrolled through the entries and found a vid-feed from the traitor's helm-lenses. The Gorelord loomed large.

'*I have decided to accept your offer, Lord Zorean,*' the Gorelord was saying. '*If you can indeed achieve what you promise, then I suppose command of the Blades is a worthy exchange.*'

'*My humblest thanks, your excellency.*' Zorean's voice was liquid sycophancy. '*My noble murder-kin have languished under the Skin-Taker's ineptitude for too long.*'

'*I can only agree. Where is he now?*'

'*Hunting wretches in the lower decks, I believe.*'

Dalchian shut the feed, a smile upon his scarred face.

Soon after, clad in his true midnight plate and healing well, Saryuz presented himself to the Skin-Taker carrying a toothed sword.

'The champion's blade,' Saryuz said. 'Used to end the champion himself, and fell his master into the bargain. You have need of a weapon, my lord.' Saryuz held the blade and offered Dalchian the hilt.

'You wielded it far better than I could, Saryuz,' he said. 'Keep it. Make terrible murder with it.' Saryuz smiled as he accepted the compliment, and the sword.

'I will, Lord Skin-Taker.'

'So,' Dalchian said lightly, 'have you found contentment in my service?'

Saryuz smirked mischievously but bowed nonetheless.

'For now, my lord,' he answered. 'For now.'

Krutaan's old claw remained bound into the cables of the pulpit, its edges softening, the delineation between ship and weapon beginning to blur. As he ascended the pulpit steps Dalchian gazed at the weapon and felt conflicting notions of gratitude and scorn.

Why scorn, Skin-Taker? Look at what I helped you achieve!

Krutaan's voice was always at the edge of his perception, now, and never more so than when he occupied the command throne. He took his seat, the ship purring around him.

Lieutenant Nykold, her uniform a patchwork of Battlefleet Odovokan colours and Adeptus Astra Telepathica black, stood at the foot of the pulpit on the port side. The Branded breacher du Golsa stood on the starboard side, her neurophagic rifle cleaned and serviced, a bandolier of phials across her chestplate. Dagardis, Ang Heltris, Saryuz and Zhikarga prowled the upper tiers, waiting for news of a fresh hunt. Qi Umshar's form shimmered into hololithic life from the medicae deck, freshly refitted with *Ikhtheos* hardware. Finally, Naritsa joined them from the bridge of his frigate. The hololith cast him in fluorescent emerald, but Dalchian knew the Warpsmith's armour was now a more befitting midnight.

Dalchian had summoned them.

'Victory is a transient delicacy,' he said. 'Now we have achieved it here, it beckons to us from elsewhere, and we are bound to hunt it down. This vessel can pass where it will, unmolested and unexamined by even the most stalwart of Imperial outposts. Within the guts of the Carrion-Emperor's putrid domain we will terrorise, murder and enslave. We shall rock the foundations of the Golden Liar's edifice. We are the Remnant Blades. We are Night Lords, and fear is our gift.'

The Chaos Space Marines growled their relish, Dagardis lifting his axe at the words.

'Do we set our sights first upon the Gorelord?' Naritsa rumbled, clearly taken with the idea.

'I yearn to flay that maggot Zorean alive,' Dagardis offered.

'Worthy prey,' Dalchian said. 'We do not yet have the strength to challenge Thelissicus openly. But that does not mean we cannot gift him a memento of our alliance.'

The Blades all smirked.

Dalchian dismissed the gathering, the hololiths flickering out and his Blades making for their new practice cages. As he sat back in the throne, cloak of skins rustling between his shoulders, Lieutenant Nykold looked up at him. He could see the torment in her eyes, the disgust she felt at herself for being party to the Skin-Taker's murder and the despair of having no other choice. Her turmoil filled Dalchian with joy. She fell back on the crutch of following orders and doing her job as best she could.

'I have learnt the ship's name, my lord,' Nykold said.

'Go on,' he hissed.

'The *Vitreyu.*' A chorus of whispers bled from the air as she said it, and Dalchian rolled the name around in his mind, luxuriating in the completeness of his achievement. He grinned as he spoke into the ship-wide vox-tube.

'All hands of the Black Ship *Vitreyu*, this is Lord Skin-Taker.

'Our blades yet thirst.'

EPILOGUE

Gorelord Thelissicus watched the last of his alliance's ships fall into formation with a welcome glimmer of satisfaction. They were in a tight orbit around the gas giant, its crazed magnetosphere helping to hide their engine signatures from the roving Imperials. Both fleets had inflicted savage losses on the other in protracted void battle, but the Imperials had got their troop transports past his blockade and begun landing thousands, perhaps tens of thousands, of Imperial soldiers and militia onto the beleaguered surface of Uzurmandius. It was not a force his alliance could easily overcome, so they had withdrawn, holds brimming with valuable spoils from the sack of the forge world. The gas giant would provide enough cover for running repairs to be made, then they could break out and translate into the safety of the warp.

The episode with the Skin-Taker had disrupted his plans. He now recognised that letting the legionaries live when they petitioned him for assistance was an unnecessary indulgence. He had so wanted the vaunted band of Night Lords yoked to his rule, and Zorean had promised just that. Still, whatever that unfaithful cur said, Jathok would have given a good account. And how much damage could a handful of VIII legionaries do against a force as powerful as the Abyssal Kindred, really? No, Jathok would return soon enough, and the Blades of Atrocity would be extinct. Events would revert to his meticulously arranged order, and the next phase could begin.

'Your excellency,' one of his augury serfs rasped. 'A warship has just appeared within augury range, your excellency.'

'Identify it.'

A pause.

'It's the *Ikhtheos*, your excellency.'

Impeccable timing, Thelissicus thought.

'Open a channel.'

The vox-net snarled for a few moments, then stabilised.

'*Hail, Gorelord Thelissicus,*' a gravelly voice said. '*This is Gyren Naritsa, captain of the* Ikhtheos.'

'Ah, Naritsa,' the Gorelord oozed, vaguely remembering the Warpsmith. 'I bid you welcome back to the fold. Lord Jathok is dead, I assume?' Perhaps that wretch Zorean had been partly right.

'*No, your excellency,*' Naritsa answered. '*He lives, though I suspect he wishes otherwise.*'

The Gorelord frowned, but dismissed the strange reply in favour of addressing his true concern.

'And the fate of the Skin-Taker? I desired him taken alive, but I will gladly accept his corpse, if that was the only course available to you.'

'*I deliver him to you alive, your excellency,*' Naritsa said flatly, and Thelissicus' pulse surged. His lips peeled back from his obsidian teeth in glee.

'Then you shall be handsomely rewarded, Warpsmith Naritsa.' The Gorelord interwove his fingers and cracked their joints in anticipation. 'I shall prepare for your arrival.' The ship would take nearly an hour to draw close enough for the transfer.

'Thank you for the invitation, your excellency,' Naritsa said. *'But my company's place in your alliance no longer suits my designs, so I am preparing to translate out-system.'*

The Gorelord was motionless. Some of the older mortals of the bridge crew receded into their pits a fraction.

'Ikhtheos is cycling its warp drive, your excellency,' the augury serf croaked, eyes wide.

'Sadly,' the Gorelord said, veins standing up on his wide neck, 'I doubt your Navigator will permit that, Naritsa.'

'I replaced him,' came the reply matter-of-factly. *'A mind-flattened puppet was no good to me.'*

'Ikhtheos warp translation imminent, your excellency.' The augury serf practically wept as he spoke.

'You… *replaced* him?' The Gorelord's breath was hissing through his teeth.

'Yes.' All deference had gone from the Warpsmith's voice. *'And the Skin-Taker has already reached you. He bears an urgent message.'*

The *Ikhtheos'* rune marker flashed indigo, warning chimes keening on the *Torrent's* bridge. A halo of un-light blinked into existence on the oculus, thousands of miles distant, but the realspace distortion shook the Crimson Slaughter vessel instantaneously. The Gorelord blinked once as the distant frigate disappeared into the immaterium, the flower of unreal energy blossoming for a few moments longer before imploding with a void-bending shockwave. The *Torrent* shuddered again. Strangely, the vox-channel was still open.

'What message?' The Gorelord smouldered, pale skin puce with transcendent rage.

'*That you, Gorelord Thelissicus,*' came a new, cruel voice from the serrated augmitter horns, '*are henceforth marked as prey, to be hunted at will by the Eighth Legion. You are forfeited the mercy of a swift death, and denied the honour of trial by combat for your desecration of Night Lords murder-kin. Fear the darkness, for one night it shall come and claim you.*'

A rending blast cannoned the Gorelord from his throne as the *Torrent of Hatred* quaked beneath him. Klaxons and sirens filled the bridge, the oculus blazing scarlet with damage indicators.

'Multi-deck penetration, your excellency!' a serf shrieked. 'Hull breached, venting atmosphere, fires on decks thirty-one through twenty-six!'

'What was that?' the Gorelord howled as he wrenched himself upright.

'*A lance strike, Thelissicus,*' said the cruel voice. '*Maximal fire, at a range of two thousand feet.*'

Two thousand feet? The Gorelord could not make sense of it. That would be practically in his shuttle bay.

'Auguries!' Thelissicus bawled, his intricate machinations collapsing around him.

'There's nothing out there, your excellency!' the serf cried over the sirens.

'*Just something to remember me by,*' the cruel voice said, audibly enjoying itself. '*Worry not. I've left most of the Imperial Navy unmolested for you. Until we meet again, Thelissicus.*'

'Face me, Skin-Taker!' The Gorelord was apoplectic. 'Reveal yourself and face me like a true warrior!'

'*Oh no, your excellency,*' Dalchian Rassaq said. '*I am wiser than that.*'

ABOUT THE AUTHOR

Mike Vincent fell in love with Warhammer while
peering over his friend's shoulder at a copy of *White
Dwarf* when he was nine years old. When not writing
he spends as much time as possible around a
campfire in the woods, with his wife and his dog.
His work for Black Library includes the Night Lords
novel *The Remnant Blade*, and the short stories 'The
Vengeful Dead', 'Exterminator', 'Blades of Atrocity'
and 'Pursuit of Redemption'.

An extract from 'Shadow Knight'
featured in *Night Lords: The Omnibus*
by Aaron Dembski-Bowden

The sins of the father, they say.

Maybe. Maybe not. But we were always different. My brothers and I, we were never truly kin with the others – the Angels, the Wolves, the Ravens…

Perhaps our difference was our father's sin, and perhaps it was his triumph. I am not empowered by anyone to cast a critical eye over the history of the VIII Legion.

These words stick with me, though. The sins of the father. These words have shaped my life.

The sins of my father echo throughout eternity as heresy. Yet the sins of my father's father are worshipped as the first acts of godhood. I do not ask myself if this is fair. Nothing is fair. The word is a myth. I do not care what is fair, and what is right, and what's unfair and wrong. These concepts do not exist outside the skulls of those who waste their life in contemplation.

I ask myself, night after night, if I deserve vengeance.

I devote each beat of my heart to tearing down everything I once raised. Remember this, remember it always: my blade and bolter helped forge the Imperium. I and those like me – we hold greater rights than any to destroy mankind's sickened empire, for it was our blood, our bones, and our sweat that built it.

Look to your shining champions now. The Adeptus Astartes that scour the dark places of your galaxy. The hordes of fragile mortals enslaved to the Imperial Guard and shackled in service to the Throne of Lies. Not a soul among them was even born when my brothers and I built this empire.

Do I deserve vengeance? Let me tell you something about vengeance, little scion of the Imperium. My brothers and I swore to our dying father that we would atone for the great sins of the past. We would bleed the unworthy empire that we had built, and cleanse the stars of the False Emperor's taint.

This is not mere vengeance. This is redemption. My right to destroy is greater than your right to live.

Remember that, when we come for you.

He is a child standing over a dying man.

The boy is more surprised than scared. His friend, who has not yet taken a life, pulls him away. He will not move. Not yet. He cannot escape the look in the bleeding man's eyes.

The shopkeeper dies.

The boy runs.

He is a child being cut open by machines.

Although he sleeps, his body twitches, betraying painful dreams and sleepless nerves firing as they register pain from the surgery. Two hearts, fleshy and glistening, beat in his cracked-open chest. A second new organ, smaller than the new heart, will alter the growth of his bones, encouraging his skeleton to absorb unnatural minerals over the course of his lifetime.

Untrembling hands, some human, some augmetic, work over the child's body, slicing and sealing, implanting and flesh-bonding. The boy trembles again, his eyes opening for a moment.

A god with a white mask shakes his head at the boy.

'Sleep.'

The boy tries to resist, but slumber grips him with comforting claws. He feels, just for a moment, as though he is sinking into the black seas of his homeworld.

Sleep, the god had said.

He obeys, because the chemicals within his blood force him to obey.

A third organ is placed within his chest, not far from the new heart. As the ossmodula warps his bones to grow on new minerals, the biscopea generates a flood of hormones to feed his muscles.

Surgeons seal the boy's medical wounds.

Already, the child is no longer human. Tonight's work has seen to that. Time will reveal just how different the boy will become.

He is a teenage boy, standing over another dead body.

This corpse is not like the first. This corpse is the same age as the boy, and in its last moments of life it had struggled with all its strength, desperate not to die.

The boy drops his weapon. The serrated knife falls to the ground.

Legion masters come to him. Their eyes are red, their dark armour immense. Skulls hang from their pauldrons and plastrons on chains of blackened bronze.

He draws breath to speak, to tell them it was an accident. They silence him.

'Well done,' they say.

And they call him *brother.*

He is a teenage boy, and the rifle is heavy in his hands.

He watches for a long, long time. He has trained for this. He knows how to slow his hearts, how to regulate his breathing and the biological beats of his body until his entire form remains as still as a statue.

Predator. Prey. His mind goes cold, his focus absolute. The mantra chanted internally becomes the only way to see the world. *Predator. Prey. Hunter. Hunted.* Nothing else matters.

He squeezes the trigger. One thousand metres away, a man dies.

'Target eliminated,' he says.

He is a young man, sleeping on the same surgery table as before.

In a slumber demanded by the chemicals flowing through his veins, he dreams once again of his first murder. In the waking world, needles and medical probes bore into the flesh of his back, injecting fluids directly into his spinal column.

His slumbering body reacts to the invasion, coughing once. Acidic spit leaves his lips, hissing on the ground where it lands, eating into the tiled floor.

When he wakes, hours later, he feels the sockets running down his spine. The scars, the metallic nodules…

In a universe where no gods exist, he knows this is the closest mortality can come to divinity.

He is a young man, staring into his own eyes.

He stands naked in a dark chamber, in a lined rank with a dozen other souls. Other initiates standing with him, also stripped of clothing, the marks of their surgeries fresh upon their pale skin. He barely notices them. Sexuality is a forgotten concept, alien to his mind, merely one of ten thousand human-ities his consciousness has discarded. He no longer recalls the face of his mother and father. He only recalls his own name because his Legion masters never changed it.

He looks into the eyes that are now his. They stare back, slanted and murder-red, set in a helmet with its facial plate painted white. The bloodeyed, bone-pale skull watches him as he watches it.

This is his face now. Through these eyes, he will see the galaxy. Through this skulled helm he will cry his wrath at those who dare defy the Emperor's vision for mankind.

'You are Talos,' a Legion master says, 'of First Claw, Tenth Company.'

He is a young man, utterly inhuman, immortal and undying.

He sees the surface of this world through crimson vision, with data streaming in sharp, clear white runic language across his retinas. He sees the life forces of his brothers in the numbers displayed. He feels the temperature outside his sealed war armour. He sees targeting sights flicker as they follow the movements of his eyes, and feels his hand, the hand clutching his bolter, tense as it tries to follow each target lock. Ammunition counters display how many have died this day.

Around him, aliens die. Ten, a hundred, a thousand. His brothers butcher their way through a city of violet crystal, bolters roaring and chainswords howling. Here and there in the opera of battle-noise, a brother screams his rage through helm-amplifiers.

The sound is always the same. Bolters always roar. Chainblades always howl. Adeptus Astartes always cry their fury. When the VIII Legion wages war, the sound is that of lions and wolves slaying each other while vultures shriek above.

He cries words that he will one day never shout again – words that will soon become ash on his tongue. Already he cries the words without thinking about them, without *feeling* them.

For the Emperor.

He is a young man, awash in the blood of humans.

He shouts words without the heart to feel them, declaring concepts of Imperial justice and deserved vengeance. A man claws at his armour, begging and pleading.

'We are loyal! We have surrendered!'

The young man breaks the human's face with the butt of his

bolter. Surrendering so late was a meaningless gesture. Their blood must run as an example, and the rest of the system's worlds would fall into line.

Around him, the riot continues unabated. Soon, his bolter is silenced, voiceless with no shells to fire. Soon after that, his chainsword dies, clogged with meat.

The Night Lords resort to killing the humans with their bare hands, dark gauntlets punching and strangling and crushing.

At a timeless point in the melee, the voice of an ally comes over the vox. It is an Imperial Fist. Their Legion watches from the bored security of their landing site.

'What are you doing?' the Imperial Fist demands. 'Brothers, are you insane?'

Talos does not answer. They do not deserve an answer. If the Fists had brought this world into compliance themselves, the Night Lords would never have needed to come here.

He is a young man, watching his homeworld burn.

He is a young man, mourning a father soon to die.

He is a traitor to everything he once held sacred.

Stabbing lights lanced through the gloom.

The salvage team moved slowly, neither patient nor impatient, but with the confident care of men with an arduous job to do and no deadline to meet. The team spread out across the chamber, overturning debris, examining the markings of weapons fire on the walls, their internal vox clicking as they spoke to one another.

With the ship open to the void, each of the salvage team wore atmosphere suits against the airless cold. They communicated as often by sign language as they did by words.

This interested the hunter that watched them, because he too was fluent in Astartes battle sign. Curious, to see his enemies betray themselves so easily.

The hunter watched in silence as the spears of illumination cut this way and that, revealing the wreckage of the battles that had taken place on this deck of the abandoned vessel. The salvage team – who were clearly genhanced, but too small and unarmoured to be full Astartes – were crippled by the atmosphere suits they wore. Such confinement limited their senses, while the hunter's ancient Mark IV war-plate only enhanced his. They could not hear as he heard, nor see as he saw. That reduced their chances of survival from incredibly unlikely to absolutely none.

Smiling at the thought, the hunter whispered to the machine-spirit of his armour, a single word that enticed the war-plate's soul with the knowledge that the hunt was beginning in earnest.

'Preysight.'

His vision blurred to the blue of the deepest oceans, decorated by supernova heat smears of moving, living beings. The hunter watched the team move on, separating into two teams, each of two men.

This was going to be entertaining.

Talos followed the first team, shadowing them through the corridors, knowing the grating purr of his power armour and the snarling of its servo-joints were unheard by the sense-dimmed salvagers.

Salvagers was perhaps the wrong word, of course. Disrespectful to the foe.

While they were not full Adeptus Astartes, their gene-enhancement was obvious in the bulk of their bodies and the lethal grace of their motions. They, too, were hunters – just weaker examples of the breed.

Initiates.

Their icon, mounted on each shoulder plate, displayed a drop of ruby blood framed by proud angelic wings.

The hunter's pale lips curled into another crooked smile. This was unexpected. The Blood Angels had sent in a team of Scouts...

The Night Lord had little time for notions of coincidence. If the Angels were here, then they were here on the hunt. Perhaps the *Covenant of Blood* had been detected on the long-range sensors of a Blood Angel battlefleet. Such a discovery would certainly have been enough to bring them here.

Hunting for their precious sword, no doubt. And not for the first time.

Perhaps this was their initiation ceremony? A test of prowess? Bring back the blade and earn passage into the Chapter...

Oh, how unfortunate.